Acclaim for David Gates's
PRESTON FALLS

'David Gates has a superb reporter's precision, an analyst's ear, a teenager's glee in exposing deception and a moralist's eye that is as unforgiving as Evelyn Waugh's' *New York Times Book Review*

'David Gates has produced the funniest, sharpest, most strangely exciting novel about men and women in a long time' *Maxim*

'Gates is a masterful chronicler of the dynamics of a family melt-down' *Publishers Weekly*

'*Preston Falls* is incontestable evidence that Gates is indeed a brilliant, if caustic, analyst of marital rancour. And in Doug Willis he has fashioned a memorable protagonist . . . a deeply, darkly funny novel . . . this is a marvellous book, an unsparing study of how life can run away from us and how we may never truly know what, and who, will make us happy' *The Times*

'Breathtaking stuff . . . Gates renders the bitchiness of a bad marriage in deft dialogue' *Time Out*

'*Preston Falls* is mesmerizing, disturbing, a brilliantly overheard monologue – the nada of a man who has been there, done that, and is out of places to go' *Boston Globe*

'If you've been to see *American Beauty* and liked it, then you'll also enjoy David Gates' *Preston Falls* . . . Where did Doug go? The rest of this slow burning, superb novel, crawls bleakly to the despairing answer. Powerful, dark stuff' *Uncut*

'This sharply adept novel works with scathing precision as a rancorously funny commentary on the bizarre geography of life within the parameters of turn-of-the-millennium North American suburbia . . . an exactingly crystallised novel of judi-ciously scathing observation, one that is consistently propelled by exceptionally proficient and authentic dialogue, and that never loses touch with its quiet, intelligently felt humanity' *Sunday Tribune*

David Gates writes about books and music for *Newsweek*. He lives in New York City and in a small town in upstate New York.

PRESTON FALLS

Preston Falls
A Novel

DAVID GATES

PHŒNIX

A PHOENIX PAPERBACK

First published in Great Britain in 2000
by Victor Gollancz
This paperback edition published in 2001 by Phoenix,
an imprint of Orion Books Ltd,
Orion House, 5 Upper St Martin's Lane,
London WC2H 9EA

First published in the USA in 1998
by Alfred A. Knopf Inc, New York

A CIP catalogue record for this book
is available from the British Library.

ISBN 0 57540 317 9

Printed and bound in Great Britain by
Clays Ltd, St Ives plc

Thanks to Jeff Giles, who read it first, for his advice and encouragement, for ridiculing several bum titles, and for not campaigning longer than six months for *his* bum title.

To Susan Szeliga, for letting loose with telepathically apt suggestions.

To David Spry, for reassurance early on.

To Marjorie Horvitz, for vigilant copyediting and embarrassingly good catches.

To Gary Fisketjon, for the kind of editing that supposedly doesn't get done anymore, for a green-penciled *duh* where *duh* was the mot juste, and for taking this on in the first place.

To Amanda Urban, for state-of-the-art advocacy and cut-to-the-chase commentary.

To Cathleen McGuigan and my other editors at *Newsweek*, for the leaves of absence that helped me get this done.

And to Susan and Kate, for just about everything.

This book is for my father, Gene Gates.

So I saw in my dream that the man began to run. Now, he had not run far from his own door, but his wife and children perceiving it, began to cry after him to return; but the man put his fingers in his ears, and ran on, crying, "Life! life! eternal life!"

John Bunyan, *The Pilgrim's Progress*

ONE

1

Late Friday afternoon they start for Preston Falls: Jean and the kids in the Cherokee, Willis in his truck with Rathbone the dog riding shotgun. When Willis proposed that Roger ride with them and make it an all-male expedition, Roger said, "I don't want to." The one boy in America ashamed to be seen in a pickup truck. Or was that not the problem?

Among his *colleagues* (a word he precedes with a half-beat's hesitation, to suggest quotation marks) Willis keeps dropping the odd allusion to his truck, lest they forget he's a badass outlaw. And five mornings a week it's his fuck-you to the Volvos in the commuter lot at the Chesterton station. A '77 Dodge V-8, with mustard-yellow paint flaking off to show the original dark green, patches of gray Bondo on fenders and rocker panels, and—this is the best thing—a black driver's-side door that must've come off a whole different model, because the chrome doesn't line up. He spotted it one weekend in *Want Ad Digest*: "4WD, some rust, runs good." Guy wanted eight, Willis beat him down to seven, then put another seven fifty into it, not counting five for a pullout tape deck and decent speakers; so for fifteen hundred smackers he's got himself the hillbilly shitheap par excellence, complete with old-truck smell, but actually semireliable. Willis is Director of Public Affairs for Dandineau Beverages, bottlers of Sportif: the original caffeine-laced Gatorade knockoff, plus the line of flavored iced teas without all the minerals and shit.

Jean backs the Cherokee out of the driveway, then sets the hand brake and walks back to the truck. "You want to lead the way?" she says. Otherwise she's going to have his headlights in her mirror the whole trip.

"Ah," he says. "The alpha dog and his dog." One of his jokes or whatever they are. He salutes, touching the visor of his Raiders cap; she looks up at the embroidered pirate, complete with cutlasses and eye patch. This is going to be a long weekend. In both senses. Tomorrow

Willis's brother is coming up, probably bringing the girlfriend, and the Champ-and-Willis show can be wearing.

Waiting behind him for the light at the corner of Route 9, she sees him reach across and stroke Rathbone's head and say something. Probably *That's my boy.* Melanie, who won the coin toss for front seat, complains that taking two vehicles is wasteful. Jean walks her through it: Daddy's staying in Preston Falls and they have to come back to Chesterton Monday night, because Tuesday's the first day of school *and* a workday, *and* because Aunt Carol's coming Tuesday night. Mel says, "Right, I *know* all that. I'm not *stupid*, Mother." Roger's by himself in the back, going *Poom, poom.* He's found his old Shredder action figure in the little storage thing, and he's working its bendable arms to make it punch itself in the face.

She follows Willis's truck to the McDonald's just before the Tappan Zee, their traditional Friday night stop back when they first bought the place in Preston Falls. When he pulls up to the squawk box, Jean watches him talk down from his window, then ceremoniously touch his cap again; the truck lurches forward to the pickup window. She can hear that he's got music going, but she can't make out what. She orders a chicken fajita, the only thing even vaguely healthy. Roger orders all the stuff in a Happy Meal but won't *call* it a Happy Meal, and she thinks, Well, good for you, you're not buying into *that* at least. (Putting the most hopeful interpretation.) Melanie won't eat anything from McDonald's. She's brought along rice cakes in a plastic bag and insists on eating them dry.

Willis has finished his Big Mac and fries before they even get onto the Tappan Zee, and Rathbone guzzled down his plain burger in three jerks of his head. The Friday of Labor Day weekend at six o'clock: could they possibly have timed it any worse? Traffic on the bridge creeping and stopping, creeping and stopping, Willis sweating like a bastard in the heat and golden glare, trying not to look at his temperature gauge too often, worrying about his clutch. He snaps the tape deck off; at zero miles an hour, Steve Earle is just another fucking irritant. Poor Rathbone has his head out the window, panting, sides heaving, tongue dripping drool. Willis unsnaps his seat belt and takes his eyes off the road long enough to lean down and swish a finger around in the weighted dog dish on the floor, hoping the sound will remind Rathbone. Rathbone looks over, and Willis says, "Yes, water. You know, *water*? Lap lap lap?" He turns back to the traffic just in time to see a Lexus cut in front of him.

He yells that the Lexus is a cocksucking son of a *bitch*, but its tinted windows are up.

Back in the Cherokee, Jean's running the air conditioner, but if this traffic doesn't start moving, she's going to have to turn it off and open the windows, because the needle's creeping up toward the red. There's probably some music all three of them could agree on, but she doesn't have the energy for negotiations. Maybe Mel and Roger will be on better behavior when her sister gets here. Carol said she'll stay in Chesterton for September, and perhaps into October. Because she misses fall in the Northeast. Jean supposes anything's possible.

"How come Daddy gets so much vacation and you don't?" says Mel.

"It's not actually vacation," Jean says. "It's a leave of absence."

"Oh. Well, excuse *me*." Mel opens the glove compartment, takes out a tape—Jean can't see what—then tosses it back in, making the plastic clatter.

"In answer to your question," Jean says, "I haven't been at my job as long as Daddy's been at his. And anyway I can't afford to just take two months off." Jean is the in-house design person for The Paley Group, a firm of investment consultants. After she took the job, Willis started doing a little faux man-of-the-people riff, where he'd go on about how the whole stock market was a conspiracy to bleed the working stiff.

"Can Daddy afford it?" says Mel.

"So he says. He worked the numbers on the computer, and he thinks we might actually make out a little better because of taxes."

Willis is far up ahead; she's let three cars bully their way in front of her. She sees his palm banging on the roof of the truck.

"I don't get it," says Mel.

"I'm still hungry," Roger says.

"You just ate," says Jean. Then, to Mel: "If you make less money, your taxes are lower."

"I know," Roger says, "but I still *am*."

"You'll just have to hang on," says Jean. "There should be food up at the house."

"But I might be asleep then."

"Why don't you just go to sleep *now*, Roger?" says Mel. "So Mom? He's just going to stay up there and work on the house the whole time?"

"I don't know how much he'll actually get done. I think he really just needs to get away."

"Yeah, right," says Mel. "Away from *us*."

"That's not so," Jean says. "Everybody needs to recharge sometimes."

"Yeah, right," says Mel.

"Are you disappointed that he's not coming back down for the first day of school?"

"Why would I be?" says Mel. "I mean, I've already *had* like how many first days of school in my life."

"What about you, Rog?" says Jean. "Do you feel disappointed that Daddy won't be there?" This is dancing on the line between encouraging them to voice their feelings and egging them on against their father.

"I don't care," Roger says. "*Mom*. I'm really hungry, I'm not kidding. How much longer is it going to *be*?"

"Quite a while," says Jean. "Especially with this traffic."

"But like how long?"

"I don't know. Maybe another four hours?" This sounds terrible. "Three and a half?"

Roger throws Shredder to the floor and says, "Shit."

"You have a time-out," says Jean. When they're in the car, this means nine minutes without speaking. One minute per year. In the mirror she sees Roger shrug and mouth *Shit shit shit*.

After Newburgh the traffic finally gets up to speed, and Willis ejects the Steve Earle and feels around in the bag of tapes for something else. With no kids and no Jean, he can play whatever he wants as loud as he wants. Rathbone never seems to mind, maybe because riding with Willis for years has made him deaf. Willis sticks in *Straight Outta Compton*, gives the volume a good crank, and on comes the Nigga With Attitude, saying *You are now about to witness the strenth of street knowledge*, and then that boomy drum machine, and he wishes he had a pair of those huge fur-covered speaker boxes to do the son of a bitch justice. Crazy motherfucker named Willis.

He's done this drive pretty much every Friday night for the past five years, more and more often by himself. Mel's gotten to the age where she'd rather do stuff with her friends; since it's her life too—Willis and Jean agree on that—somebody has to stay in Chesterton, and there's no point in them both. And Jean says the drive wears her out. They've talked about how some weekends maybe it should be the boys hitting the road and the girls hanging out at home. But the one time they tried it, Roger spent the weekend whining. At one point he wantonly stomped a Raffi tape, and Willis (though he knew how satisfying it must have felt, plastic smashing underfoot) had to give him a time-out. Finally, in desperation, he drove Roger all the way to The Great Escape in Lake George. But Roger slept for most of the trip, woke up cranky, and refused to go on any of the shit, so they turned around and drove back to Preston Falls, with Willis thinking *This is my life ticking away.*

Jean was never gung-ho about Preston Falls in the first place, and he can sort of sympathize. In cold weather (meaning half the year) she can't use her workroom up there, which he pissily calls her atelier, because it's unheated and uninsulated and those oil-filled electric radiators they bought at Ames do fuck-all. So she'd end up playing Monopoly with the kids at the kitchen table, while he tried to get work done on the house. And maybe steal half an hour to play guitar, Preston Falls being the one place he can crank his Fender Twin. Mel likes dropping remarks to her friends about their "country house," but the one time she actually dragged What's-her-name—the fat one—along for a weekend, Pudgette complained that there was nothing to do and that the house smelled. And so it does: of good old woodsmoke. On winter weekends when the family's not there, Willis sometimes takes the batteries out of the smoke detectors and opens the doors of both woodstoves just to keep that smell intense, which he knows is like Marie Antoinette dressing up as a shepherdess. But hey. And now winter's rolling around again. Already the days are depressingly shorter: a month ago it was still light at eight-thirty.

John Coltrane is squealing and honking and Elvin Jones is crashing and bashing as Willis turns off of 22A onto Quaker Bridge Road. Quakers because they quaked before God, supposedly. This is the home stretch: Quaker Bridge Road to County Road 39 to Goodwin Hill Road to Ragged Hill Road, and bingo. Uphill all the way and scary as shit in winter; still, it beats going straight into the center of Preston Falls and then over, which they did the first two years, until Willis bought a county map. He shifts down—it's pure bullshit, but he likes to think even the clutch works better up here—and starts to climb. He feels the air turn chilly on his arm, rolls his window partway up and turns the music partway down, so as not to jolt awake the sleeping farmers and their farmwives.

They come bumping into the dooryard sometime after one. When his headlights hit the woodshed, Willis sees that Calvin Castleman finally got around to delivering the two cords of wood he'd promised a month ago—and he's dumped the whole fucking pile against the door that connects the woodshed and the kitchen. Willis gets out of the truck and Rathbone scrambles past him, runs over and lifts his leg against the corner of the shed. Limping a little—his limp is always more noticeable at night—Willis walks back to the Cherokee, making circles with his fist to tell Jean to roll her window down.

"You're not going to fucking believe this," he says. Using clenched-teeth intensity rather than volume to show he's good and pissed. Jean shoots him a remember-the-children look regardless.

"Yeah, okay. Fine," he says. "But check it out." He twirls his hand three times and then—*ta da!*—stretches forth his palm to indicate the pile of wood. "So what do *you* think is an appropriate reaction? Stupid son of a *bitch*."

"Will you please watch yourself?" she says.

"Yeah, sorry, but this is completely unbelievable. I mean, the guy hasn't seen a *door* before? That goes into a *house*? Jesus." Mel, in the passenger seat, is rubbing her eyes; Roger, in back, is yawning and peering out his window into blackness. "This is called class hostility in action."

"Let's just get in the house," she says. "It's late, the drive was *exhausting*—we just need to get to bed."

"Right, so we can be rested for a wonderful day of moving two cords of wood."

"Well, what time is your brother supposed to get here? Can't he give you a hand?"

"Yeah, just what *he* wants to spend his weekend doing."

Jean closes her eyes and says, "Can we please go in if we're going in?"

Willis carries in the stuff while Jean gets the kids to bed. He brings their black canvas duffel bags and Jean's yellow nylon one upstairs, then starts loading his own shit in. He keeps clothes up here, so his shoulder bag has only books, tapes and CDs. And he's brought along the guitars that weren't here already: the Rick, the J-200 and the D-18, which he brings in last and leaves in the kitchen. He goes into the pantry and gets the boombox out of its hiding place behind the canning jars they'd bought the first year and never used. He takes CDs out of kitchen drawers and puts them back in the wooden Coca-Cola crates on the counter. He's sitting on a kitchen chair playing along with Merle Haggard singing "Wake Up," when Jean comes down in her long cotton nightgown.

> *Wake up, don't just lay there*
> *Like cold granite stone.*

This is so hit-you-over-the-head applicable that what can he do but pretend it's not.

"The upstairs windows were open," she says.

"Yes. I *left* them open," he says, turning the guitar strings-down and laying it across his thighs. "Otherwise it gets too stuffy to sleep. As you know." He leans forward and hits Stop.

"What if it rains?" she says. "You don't have to stop, by the way. I'm just going to bed."

"If it rains," he says, "the windowsills get wet. I think that's preferable to rolling in here and having it be *baking* upstairs. Or don't you agree?"

"I just worry that it might do damage."

"Then I suggest you raise the point with Mrs. Danvers," he says. "Have her come in and air our rooms an hour before we arrive."

"I'm sorry I said anything," she says. "Do whatever you want." She walks over to the sink.

"What a concept," he says.

She takes the thing of Advil off the windowsill over the sink and a box of Tampax from her purse and goes into the bathroom. Okay, okay, he gets the picture. When she comes out she gets down the bottle of Dewar's. He plays a D scale with no open strings, then works his way up. An E-flat scale. An E scale. An F scale. All with the same fingering, so what's he proving?

"I'm sorry, did you want some?"

He looks up: she's already put the cap on the bottle, and she's clutching her glass with her palm over the opening. Now, what would all this be telling him if Freud hadn't been debunked?

"What's funny?" she says. He sees she's poured herself one whole whopping finger of whiskey, good girl that she is, even when trying to be a bad girl.

He shakes his head. "I get punchy after putting in a day of work and driving till one in the morning." He stands up and puts the guitar in the case. "It's something you can remember about me." He lets that hang there while he closes the lid and snaps the snaps, then adds, "In case I have a heart attack moving two cords of wood."

"You were planning to stack it anyway, weren't you?"

"Ah," he says. "Then I guess you've found the silver lining."

"I'm going up to bed," she says.

"I'll be up in a while," he says, but she's already brushed past him. He watches her walk barefoot through the doorway into the dining room. The fabric of her nightgown clings to her buttocks, of which her bare, rounded heels seem a mocking analogue. Once, when they were first married, he had let loose all over the soles of those feet. "O my," she had said. "Dr. Scholl would not approve." True, it had been his idea. But she had been keenly interested.

2

Jean wakes up at the first faint gray light before dawn and can't get to sleep again. Willis is lying there on his back, no covers over him, growling in rhythm, jaw slack, a white slice of eyeball showing, a long bulge in his jockey shorts. One time, years ago, such a sight had so tempted her that she'd slyly sucked him in his sleep, though finally she didn't dare, like, *finish*. He never woke up, and she never told.

She slips out of bed, pulls the sheet over him, silently unzips her bag and finds clean underwear, socks, t-shirt, jeans and her book; still in her nightgown, she creeps out into the hall. She stops outside Mel's door, then Roger's, to listen for their breathing, then tries to steal down the stairs without making them creak (good luck), to change in the bathroom. But Rathbone has heard her: he waits at the foot of the stairs, tail wagging.

She opens the kitchen door to let him out and stands barefoot on the cold stepstone. Beyond the unmowed meadow, it's still dark under the trees. So empty of sound this morning; depressing up here when the birds have gone. This has been the worst summer she can remember: too hot, too tropical. Probably because of what's being done to the planet. In Chesterton, weeds crowded out the basil and fennel and dill she'd planted in the backyard, even though she tried to get out there for at least a couple of minutes every day. (One more thing that was her fault yet not her fault.) Plus the rabies epidemic, mostly in raccoons but also in bats and foxes and skunks. She'd even been afraid to let Mel and Roger pet Rathbone: though he'd had his shots, what if he tangled with some rabid animal whose saliva . . . and so forth and so on.

Though she hates to admit it, Preston Falls was probably no worse than Westchester County. Right in Ossining, a woman was bitten by a fox while working in her garden. Another woman, in Larchmont, was attacked by a raccoon while putting out the garbage. Jean warned Mel

and Roger: *You never, ever, approach a strange animal.* And guess how
the epidemic started. She found this out from the vet where they took
Rathbone. A bunch of coon hunters in North Carolina ran out of local
raccoons to kill, so they trucked in new raccoons from Florida and a
third of them turned out to be rabid, and the rabies has just crept north
and north and north. Completely and absolutely a male thing.

But her own truly scary moment came in Preston Falls. On Fourth
of July weekend, a raccoon tottered into the dooryard in broad daylight,
eleven o'clock in the morning. Rathbone—who, thank God, was in the
house—started barking his head off and the raccoon didn't even react.
Willis ran upstairs and came back down with this *gun*, for God's sake,
that Jean had no idea he even *had*. This *rifle*, with a *telescope*. A real Lee
Harvey Oswald special. In their *house*. He slid aside an inch of the
screen they'd put in the kitchen window, dropped to one knee, and
rested the gun on the windowsill. The *crack* of it echoed off the house,
then off the hills, but Jean could swear she also heard just the little
thoonk that was the bullet hitting. The raccoon stood still a second, shiv-
ered, then tipped over, his legs started clawing, and Willis shot him again
as Mel came running in, shrieking, "What is going *on*?" Jean said, "My
God, where's Roger?" and Roger said, "I'm right here, *Mom*," giving the
Mom that extra little edge of contempt. He was standing in the doorway
to the dining room, taking in the whole scene. Willis shot the animal a
third time, and Jean said, "Isn't that *enough*?"

He turned and looked up at her. "*You* want to do this?"

Gun in hand, he walked out into the yard as Jean and Mel and Roger
crowded at the screen door. Like the young'uns and womenfolk watching Pa, in some movie. Willis approached the animal slowly, keeping
the gun pointed. It didn't move. He stood right over it and shot down,
twice more.

He came back into the kitchen and asked if there were rubber
gloves.

"What are you going to do?" said Jean.

"Dig a hole, stick him in, torch him, cover him up," said Willis.
"Thing was obviously rabid."

"I want to watch," said Roger.

"Shouldn't you call the health department or something?" said Jean.

"I doubt they care," said Willis. "Rabid raccoon number ten thousand eight hundred and fifty-seven. We have those gloves or not?"

"Let me look," she said. "What about—did he bleed out there?"

"No. He was one of those new-model raccoons that's all solid-state."
Then he quickly said, "Actually, he bled less than you'd think."

"But it could spread from just blood, couldn't it?" she said. "Like
what if some animal got into it? Or if Rathbone—you know."

"Fine," he said. "You're worried about it, pour gas over it and we'll
torch that too. That can be *your* contribution to public health."

Willis went for the gas can and the shovel, and she found a pair of
yellow rubber gloves under the sink; he leaned the shovel against his
shoulder to put them on. Then he walked over to pick up the raccoon,
Roger a step behind. (Mel had gone back upstairs in tears.) Jean sloshed
gasoline over where she saw blood on the grass—Willis was right; she'd
expected more—then carried the gas can way far away. She wadded a
page of the *Times* business section into a ball, touched a match to it,
tossed it at the spot, and a wall of flame whooshed up. When the fire
died down, she rubbed the sole of her shoe across the burned earth, and
tiny pale flames sprouted up again.

Finally she went inside. From the window she could see Willis out
in the meadow, standing watch over his own fire, shovel braced in his
armpit, baseball cap on his head, looking, at that distance, just like a
local. His big dream.

At least none of them got rabies, that was one good thing you could
point to. Except for Memorial Day and the Fourth, she and the kids
ended up not spending much time in Preston Falls. She'd already used
up most of her vacation on days Mel and Roger had off during the
school year. And after working all week and taking the train home, she'd
be too bushed to face that four-hour drive on Friday night. And then the
four hours back on Sunday afternoon. So on Friday evenings Willis
would stay long enough to have dinner and help put the kids to bed,
then stick some things in his truck and off he'd go. *We can deal*, he'd
said, way back when she told him she was pregnant the first time, and
admitted the timing wasn't terrific. This was the answer she'd wanted.
(The tone was just Willis being Willis.) And that, Jean thought then, was
their true wedding day. Though of course she never said so, for fear of
putting him off. *We can deal.* So of course who's dealing now?

She definitely had the right to say something about this *gun* suddenly appearing out of nowhere, no matter *how* seldom she came up
here. But even by the Fourth of July, with two months of summer still to
get through, she was weary. So she simply said, "I trust you keep that
thing locked up."

He sighed his martyr sigh. "I'm not a complete asshole," he said. "Whatever opinions there are to the contrary."

But the next day, after he came back from doing errands in town, she was rooting around in his truck, looking for his county map, and found a True Value bag behind the seat, with a bicycle lock in it. All the bicycles were down in Chesterton. And they already *had* locks.

The stepstone's too cold to stand on any longer with bare feet. She comes back inside, leaving Rathbone to run; Willis claims he knows to stay out of the road. She takes her clothes into the bathroom, lifts off her nightgown, pees, puts in a new tampon, washes her hands and face, brushes her teeth. Toilet needs a good scrubbing, especially with people coming today—one of those things it's easier just to do yourself than to nag Willis about fifty times. Though it does seem excessive to be up scrubbing toilets at five-thirty in the morning. She gets the can of Vanish out from under the sink, pours some in and closes the lid on the frothing and hissing.

She makes a pot of coffee, takes down the white mug that says JOE, puts it back and takes the black mug with the picture of Alan Jackson—a gift from Carol, who calls him a "babe." The JOE mug had been a gift to Jean's father for his seventy-sixth, and last, birthday. Mel had picked it out, from a revolving rack at Kmart; she was five then, and so proud of being able to read. He thanked her and patted her head, but he was second only to Willis in seeing what crap everything was. When he gave Mel that little mocking smile Jean had seen a million times, she could've hit him: her own father, who she knew was dying. The mug turned up in a box of stuff Carol had packed for Jean when she went through the house in Sarasota after Mom died. Jean, in turn, stuck it in a box of stuff for Preston Falls, where Willis took to using it. Figure *that* one out. Because Willis hadn't liked her father (who had?), and it was like drinking out of a dead enemy's skull. Or because of the expression *cup of Joe*. Or because he thought Joe was a joke name. Willis always has about five reasons for everything.

It's still only quarter to six. She takes her coffee into the living room (Alan Jackson really *is* a babe) and settles in on the sofa with *Sense and Sensibility*. It's the part where Willoughby publicly humiliates Marianne, and Jean's secretly cheering him on. Which worries her. You're supposed to identify with Elinor and feel bemusement at Marianne, but Jean absolutely *loathes* Marianne and wants to see her get her stupid face rubbed in it. So she must be bringing her own whatever to this.

3

There's a tv in his dream, the old cabinet kind where the screen's behind doors, and he opens it to a movie where a whore is taking off her blouse, then her actual brassiere; you see the man's hard-on beneath his jockey shorts. Unbelievable: this is on television, where children might be watching? Willis resists getting involved with the whore himself, aware that he's in bed dreaming and there's the problem of cleanup. Instead he goes out to the sidewalk, realizes he's got no clothes on and wakes up. He's alone in bed in daylight in Preston Falls. The Unnamable is arching and aching: he reaches into his jockey shorts and grabs the shaft so the head's sticking out of his fist. Just a boy and his dick. No. Better just get up, go downstairs and piss.

Through the open window, a phoebe's two notes, like someone softly beckoning. Otherwise, silence. He pulls on yesterday's jeans (the Unnamable already subsiding) and yesterday's t-shirt. Rathbone hears him from down in the living room; his nails come clicking up the stairs and here he is, panting and wagging. Willis strokes his head and sings, *Oh doggie, doggie, it's a wild world—doody-doody-doody-doody-dump,* then goes downstairs with Rathbone pushing past him, trotting to the kitchen door, looking back, wagging harder. Willis lets him out, then sees, sticking out of the refrigerator door, an envelope with a note written on the back:

> *Took kids to town to get chicken etc.*
> *Coffee is on the stove.*
>
> *J*

He gets the JOE mug down, pours in milk, then fills it with cold coffee. He splits a fork-split Thomas' English muffin with a paring knife— hey, fuck *them*—sticks the ragged, cratered halves in the toaster and gets out the butter. Be a kick to do that thing where you make the Indian maiden's tawny knees into her breasts, which is still about the most hilarious fucking thing in the world. Except Jean will see the creases in the cardboard. Unless you stick the box in the garbage. No. Insanity. It's also insane to start off your day—your two months—with a bunch of butter when the idea is to be light and free. *Dear God, help me,* he prays, and is amazed to find himself actually putting the butter back, as if a higher power were guiding his hand. Woo, scary shit.

He eats the English muffin dry, washing it down with seltzer *à même la bouteille*. With the kids gone, this would be a good time to wrap those condoms, if he can remember where he put them. They're a gag present for Champ and Tina, the comic prologue to their real present: a weekend at Mohonk Mountain House, where they'd once spent a night after Tina won five hundred dollars in the lottery. Oh right: they're still out in the truck, behind the seat. And there used to be wrapping paper on the top shelf in the pantry, left over from when they spent Christmas here three years ago. (They kept it out of sight because it was the paper Santa's gifts had been wrapped in; three years ago Roger still believed.) Willis drags a chair into the pantry and finds the dusty rolls still up there: snowflakes, holly and shit, Christmas balls, Falstaffian Santas, one roll just with SEASON'S GREETINGS over and over and over. Hey, in for a dime: let's go with the balls. He cuts off what looks about right with a carving knife—thinking *Did you ever see such a sight in your life?*—and then it takes him ten minutes of yanking drawers and banging cupboard doors before he finds where the fucking Scotch tape got put.

He steps outside, still barefoot, onto the sun-warmed stepstone, and smells the air. Loamy, grassy, little hit of pine—Jesus, you could bottle this shit. At the top of the maple tree, a few leaves have turned red. Rathbone, who must have heard the screen door slap, comes tear-assing around the side of the woodshed with a stick in his mouth. So Willis walks a few steps out into the wet grass, soaking his feet and the cuffs of his jeans. This gets old in a hurry. He makes a token lunge for the stick while Rathbone dances away, then he goes back inside, thinking *Du wuschest mir die Füsse.* At one point in his life (when Jean was pregnant with Mel, in fact) he went to see Hans Jürgen Syberberg's *Parsifal* film twelve times in twelve days.

Time *is* it, anyway? Ten o'clock? Better go pay off Calvin Castleman before he comes pulling into the dooryard honking his horn. One morning last fall, Willis came back upstairs (still half asleep) after paying

Calvin for a load of wood, took his pants off again, got back in bed and explained to Jean that this was a country thing, the noninvasive alternative to coming right up and banging on your door. "Oh please," she said. "People with manners *call*, on the *telephone*, at a civilized *hour*, to ask if it's *convenient*."

Willis puts on his green Dickies work shirt, mostly so he'll have a pocket to stick his checkbook in—certainly not to make Calvin Castleman think he's anything but a weekend pussy from Westchester. The thing is, what could you wear in Preston Falls that *wouldn't* be a costume? This morning it no longer seems worth getting into a big thing about where Calvin dumped the wood. Shit, it's got to be stacked anyway.

He takes the truck over, though really he should walk the three-tenths of a mile, whatever, if he's so serious about getting healthy. But that would be a gaffe in Preston Falls. By his driveway, Calvin has a sign saying GUN SHOP SAWS SHARPENED FIRE WOOD, and what could pass for a piece of metal sculpture: an oil drum sliced lengthwise with a cutting torch to make a trough, welded to an angle-iron stand. HOG ROSTER FOR HIRE. Calvin also wheels and deals used cars, sells vodka and Canadian whiskey on Sundays for a five-dollar markup and works on slate roofs. He once offered to install a new metal roof for free in return for Willis's roofing slates. Willis turned him down, then worried that a real country person would have jumped at the deal. You also used to see BMWs and Lincoln Town Cars jouncing in and out of Calvin's driveway late at night, but he seems to have cooled that after he was busted last year and his lawyer got him off on some bullshit technicality. Ever since Willis started coming over, the gun cabinet in the shop part of the trailer has had the same three guns, with manila tags hanging from their trigger guards: a single-shot 20-gauge ("Asking $55"); a double-barrel 12-gauge ("$175 firm") and a 12-gauge pump ("$125"). This was where Willis bought his .22, a Marlin with a scope and a composite varmint—head of woodchuck, tail of rat—carved into the stock. Calvin hides his real guns in the living quarters of his trailer, in a compartment behind a curio cabinet with blown-glass elephants and little china Dutch girls.

Calvin Castleman's out front, leaning into the engine of a rotting Cadillac with a peeling vinyl roof; over the fender he's draped a greasy red plastic thing with indecipherable traces of white lettering.

"Ho," says Willis. Preston Falls-speak for *Hello*. "This your rig, Calvin?"

Calvin straightens up, wiping blackened hands on blackened work pants. "Is now," he says. His pubic-looking beard has an inch-wide white streak down one side, whatever that's about. Deep, grimy lines in the red face, though he can't be forty.

"Where'd you find 'er?" says Willis. Probably pushing it, though Calvin's asked *him* shit that's way more personal. When Calvin first came by and introduced himself—Willis had been unloading a U-Haul with stuff from Chesterton—he asked straight out what they'd paid for the place. Willis thought it was stupidly coy not to tell him; he was also proud of getting it for his lowball offer. Calvin pressed his lips together as if with sudden heartburn, turned away and shook his head; then he turned back and said he'd had his eye on the place for the woodlot but didn't have any use for another house. Willis assumes Calvin hasn't forgotten getting boned—or giving himself away for that little moment. He also assumes that Calvin assumes *he* hasn't forgotten.

"Took it in trade," says Calvin.

"So what's she need?"

"Oh, this and that. Leastways the engine's free and the fuckin' block ain't cracked."

"You keep it or fix up to sell?" Willis talks the talk better and better.

"Somebody come by and twist my arm they probably could have it. Hell, fresh coat of paint? Little bodywork? Set of wire wheels instead of them fuckin' piece of shits they got on there?"

Willis nods to show he can envision it. "Listen, let me write you a check for that load of wood."

"Tell you the truth, I just as soon wait till you got the cash on you. More I can keep my business the hell out of everybody's fuckin' computers, happier I fuckin' am."

"I hear you," says Willis. "Sure. I can go down to the cash machine."

" 'Cause it's all the one computer, you know? That's where we're gettin' to. After that bullshit here last year, I had 'em come and take out their fuckin' telephone. I told 'em, I said, I don't even want your fuckin' cable goin' in my house. They were listenin' in on the fuckin' telephone. My lawyer found that out."

"Yeah, I remember you telling me," says Willis.

"Good job I had *him*, or I'd been in jail right now with all the niggers. And this is what your God damn taxes go for."

"Hey, that and Bill Clinton's salary." Contempt for Bill Clinton is their common ground politically. True, Willis comes at it from the left and Calvin from the right, but still. Willis sometimes thinks Calvin's shit about niggers and liberals might just be a sort of ritual ordeal he puts you through to test your worthiness. "So listen, I better get a move on if I want to hit that cash machine. I got my brother coming up later on."

"Hell, you got company this weekend I ain't in no hurry," Calvin says. "Next time you come up be good enough."

"I *am* up," says Willis. "I'm here the next two months."

"The hell happen, lose your job down there?"

"No such luck." Which is a shit thing to say to somebody up here scrabbling to get by. Or is Calvin simply a free man doing exactly what he wants? "Just took some unpaid leave." Willis wants to make sure to get that *unpaid* in there. "See if I can get some work done on the house."

"Hell, then," says Calvin. "I'll catch up with you. I know where you live." Structurally this is a joke, though only Willis smiles.

4

He's just hit the part of *Dombey and Son* where Mrs. Skewton has her first stroke, when Rathbone starts barking outside. Willis gets up and goes to the kitchen door, and into the yard rolls this big-ass convertible, a Monte Carlo or something, rocker panels rusted to shit. It's Champ and Tina, both in sunglasses and white t-shirts. Rathbone's up on his hind legs, paws against the driver's-side door. Champ gets out, tousles Rathbone's ears, then stretches, his t-shirt pulling up. He's starting to get a belly too, Willis is glad to see. Tina jackknifes herself over into the back seat, biker-shorted ass in the air.

"Some wagon," Willis calls. Not a Monte Carlo but an LTD. "Rathbone, enough. Sit." He has to not look at Tina's ass. "So whatta we got here, about a seventy-seven?" Shooting for the most ironic year possible.

"Hey, seventy-fuckin'-*two*, bro," says Champ. "Last year they made the ragtop. Hundred and sixty-eight thousand miles, and that son of a bitch *purrs*."

"She's a honey." Willis wishes Tina would hurry up and get whatever she's getting.

Champ switches to radio baritone. "Madge and I appreciate the built-in safety that only an American car can offer."

"So hey, welcome," says Willis. "You guys made good time. You must have been up with the fuckin' lark."

"You know me, early to bed," Champ says. "Fuckin' *Tina*, had to haul *her* out by the fuckin' hair and pour coffee into her."

"He lies," says Tina.

"So how was the trip up?"

"Well, *I* loved the shit out of it. I think the Jesus stations started to get to old Tina."

"Oh, you noticed that," she says.

"You got the best fuckin' Jesus stations up here, man. Except for maybe Ala*bam*a. This guy was like interpreting and everything? All this completely addled shit. Six sixty-six? *All* that stuff. He was gettin' *into* it."

"I would even listen to Howard *Stern*," she says.

"Hey, that your rig?" Nodding at Willis's truck. "*I'm* fuckin' impressed."

"You've seen that," says Willis.

"No way. Last time, you still had that Honda piece of shit."

Tina extricates herself, slams her door (big American ka-thunk) and comes around the front with a purse-sized Bert-and-Ernie bag slung over her shoulder.

"I help you guys carry anything?" says Willis.

"Carry your hostess present if you want." Champ walks around and twists a key in the trunk lock. "Here, back here." But Tina's hugging Willis (he feels liquidy breasts, smells dirty hair) and saying, "Ooh, it's nice to *see* you."

"Here." Champ's holding up two six-packs of Budweiser tallboys by the plastic. "Replace those essential minerals." He always gives Willis shit about Sportif; the good way to read this is that Champ agrees flacking for Dandineau Beverages is beneath him. Champ, meanwhile, is clerking at the Counter Spy Shop.

"Hey, replace *this*," says Willis, giving him the finger.

But Champ isn't looking. "So, Teen," he says, setting the six-packs on the ground, "should I give him the test?"

Tina cocks her head.

"*You* know. The—c'mere." Tina goes over, he whispers, she shrugs. "My animal companion here," he says to Willis, "blew the test big time."

"You're a *man*, for God's sake," Tina says. "If you were wearing a skirt or something—"

"He'sh going to guessh," says Champ through bared teeth, "ish you don't shut ut."

Tina turns to Willis. "He did this at the service area. I was mortified. All these like families and everything?"

Champ climbs over the closed door into the back seat, sits down and calls, "Okay, you ready? Now watch, and tell me who this is." He gets to his feet, turns and crawls over the seat and across the trunk on his hands and knees.

"Rats leaving a sinking ship," says Willis.

"Whoa, getting warm."

"Let's see—me taking a leave of absence."

"You dick," Champ says. "Everything's not about *you*."

"Hey, so they tell me," says Willis. "Okay, I don't know. Good money going after bad? Pride going before a fall?"

"Cold, very cold. Shit, I got to take a piss something wicked."

"Why don't you make him happy," Tina says, "and say you give up."

"That would make me happy? To know my brother is an ignorant slut?"

"Okay," Willis says. "I give up."

"Jackie Kennedy!"

Willis whams his forehead with the heel of his hand.

"Unreal." Champ dusts the knees of his black jeans, then wipes his palms on the thighs. "I thought at least somebody *your* age would get it. Isn't that what fucked all you guys up?" He holds up a hand for silence and says, "Okay: Jackie, for three hundred. How did Jackie dislocate her back? Or, like, sprain her back?"

Tina fetches a loud sigh. "Didn't you have to go pee-pee, honey buns?"

"Give up? She was reaching around, or kind of bending over backwards, trying to touch her Onassis. Get it? Reach her Onassis? I didn't tell that very well."

"No kidding," says Tina.

"Christ, I gotta piss." Champ trots around the corner of the woodshed.

"I think it's this country air," says Tina. "So where's the family?"

"Jean went to hustle some provisions," says Willis. *"À la recherche de Frank Perdue."* He'd thought of this on the way back from Calvin's; Tina's the lucky one who gets to hear it. "And I guess the kids went along to get their little hit of civilization. Store in town has video games."

"Wow, you'd think they'd be running around in all this woods."

"You'd think," he says, as Champ comes out from behind the shed, fiddling with his fly.

Tina claps her hands over her eyes: see no evil. "Jesus, Champ. Why don't you just shake off in front of us too?"

"Hey, it's my bro," says Champ. "So listen, where's the family?"

Jean takes Mel and Roger to breakfast at Winner's and stays at the counter drinking coffee and reading the *Times* while they play the video games. She leaves them there while she runs stupid errands: to the post office, to the cash machine, to the Grand Union, to Rite Aid for Off and Caladryl, to the new little hippie place for decent bread. But she can't stay in town forever.

When she pulls into the driveway, she has to go up onto the grass to get around this huge, sagging hulk of a convertible—the sort of car locals drive, except they don't know any locals besides that creature Willis buys wood from. Mr. Hog Roster. (It took her the longest time to realize this was a misspelling and not some kind of registry, or an obscure farm tool.) So this must belong to Willis's brother—who of course would also drive some V-8 rustbucket. The father really did a job on those two. She gets out of the Cherokee and sees the three of them—Willis, his brother and the girlfriend—sitting out on the plastic-resin Adirondack chairs Willis bought at Ames for $6.99, each with one of those tall cans of beer. Champ and the girlfriend look like a Gap ad with their matching white t-shirts and sunglasses. Do they plan their outfits? She wouldn't put it past them. Willis has his boombox outside, plugged into the long orange cord. Champ stands up and raises his beer can at her when she gets out to unload the shopping bags. (Mel and Roger are still in the car, arguing.) Finally the girlfriend bestirs herself to pick her way across the grass in fetching bare feet and give a cheek-to-cheek air kiss. Tina: that's the name. This apparently shames Willis into getting up and coming over too. Jean can hear some sort of depressing fifties country music going—not Hank Williams, she doesn't think. Him she can usually tell.

"Hi," she says to Tina. "You must have made good time." She looks at Willis, who's just *standing* there. "Could you help with the bags, please?"

"Melanie, that is one of the *great* t-shirts," says Tina, touching a finger to Courtney Love's fat red lip. Mel shrugs.

Champ has finally roused himself and come over. "Cool," he says to Mel. "And you, Killer," he says to Roger. "You're getting huge. You play middle linebacker? Here, what can I carry?"

"Sit, both of you," says Willis. "I got 'em."

"This is *Roger*?" says Tina in fake disbelief. "Roger, I wouldn't have even recognized you." Of course not, Jean feels like saying; she's met him, what, once before? *My guit-tar stays a little better in tune,* the singer sings. *The sun shines bright and there's honey on the moon.*

Roger says to Willis, "She said we can't go swimming."

"Roger," says Willis. "When we have guests, it's nice to greet them? You too, Mel." He grabs up two plastic bags by the handles with his right hand and takes a third in his left.

"But how come we *can't*?" says Roger. Willis looks at Jean and raises his eyebrows: take a stand here, or let it go?

"We ran into Arthur Bjork and the kids coming out of Winner's," Jean tells Willis. "They invited Mel and Roger over to swim in their pond, but I said we had company."

"I'm sure they'll give you guys a rain check," Willis says. "Speaking of *which*, it looks like it's clouding over anyway. Tell you what. While I'm helping Mommy with the stuff, why don't you show your uncle and his friend where they're going to sleep." I.e., Roger's room, which he agreed to give up if he could sleep in his pup tent.

"Why don't *you*?" says Roger.

"Hmm," says Willis, setting the bags back on the ground. Heavy sons of bitches. "This is not going to end pleasantly."

"Roger," Jean says, "you were warned earlier about talking back."

"You're wrecking everything, Roger," says Mel.

"Melanie," Willis says. "Let your mother handle this?"

"Fine," says Jean. "Yes, let *me* handle it. Roger, you have a time-out. You can take it in your sister's room." She picks up a bag of groceries in each hand and starts for the house.

Willis picks up his bags again. "Wait, let me get the door."

Jean keeps walking.

"Mom?" Mel calls. "Can I take a shower?"

"Fine," Jean says. She sets down a bag, opens the screen door and lets it slap behind her.

Willis sets the bags on the kitchen table and goes upstairs to make sure Roger's doing his time-out. When he comes back down, Jean's standing at the counter, chopping an onion and stinking up the place like a fucking tenement. "Now, where to *stow* all this shit," he says.

She turns around, tears all down her cheeks. "I can deal with that." Her voice is okay, therefore it's the onion. "I'd rather you got the fire started."

He salutes and says, "Your wish." To add *is my command*, he decides, would be too pissy. "You did remember charcoal, right?"

"Yes," she says.

He finds it in one of the bags, under some celery and shit. "Ah, Kingsford: what ho. Now, I *think* we've got some lighter fluid left."

"I bought a new thing of it," she says. "It should be there somewhere."

He brings the charcoal and fluid out to where they've got the hibachi set up on a flat rock. He takes off the black-crusted grills and dumps the old ashes into the high grass and weeds on the other side of the stone wall. He pours in a pile of charcoal and squirts on probably way too much stuff. Looking up from the tall, smelly flames, he sees a dark cloudbank in the east. He sucks his index finger and sticks it in the air, but his finger feels equally cool on all sides, so who the fuck knows. He brings the grills into the kitchen.

"When you're finished cleaning those," Jean says, "could you put some olive oil or something on them? Maybe that'll keep stuff from sticking this time."

"Yeah, when I'm *finished*."

He stands at the sink scraping burned-on grease from the grills with a putty knife, deftly dodging when Jean ducks in from time to time to wash a vegetable under the running water. He sprinkles Comet onto a piece of steel wool, scours and rinses, then saturates a corner of paper towel with olive oil and rubs it over the grills. To absolutely no purpose, it seems to him. Won't it just burn off?

He takes the grills outside and puts them on the fire; sure enough, the olive oil starts hissing. Shit, that sky looks evil. He washes his hands at the kitchen sink with Lemon Joy and goes into the living room. Roger's back down from his time-out and he's got his sneakers up on the couch: a no-no in Chesterton, but this couch is coated with hair and stinks of dog. Tina and wet-haired Mel sit cross-legged on the floor, Mel talking, Tina nodding.

Champ's perched like an ape on a pressback chair, sitting on his heels. "Say there, *Dad*," he says. "These kids say they never been in a ragtop. We got time for a little spin before we chow, right?"

"Can we?" says Roger.

"Yeah, short one, I guess," Willis says. "Ten, fifteen minutes? I just started the fire. Aren't you sick of driving, though?"

"Hey, not with the mighty turnpike cruiser." Champ climbs down off the chair, stands and stretches. "Got to pick the music, though. What are you guys into—Metallica?"

"Yess!" says Roger.

"Oh *God*," says Mel.

"Uh-oh, gender gap," Champ says. "*Some* kind of gap. Okay, you can look through, we got Alanis What's-her-ass, we got Green Day, Green Bay, whatever the hell. My animal companion keeps me up on all this crap."

"Yeah, guess what *he*'d be listening to if I let him." Tina, holding an imaginary mike, sings, *"Sometoms it's hord, tuh be a wum-mun."*

"She lies," says Champ.

"Could we have Alanis?" says Mel.

Roger pretends to vomit. And they all troop through the dining room, into the kitchen and out the door, like a happy family.

Willis goes back into the kitchen, and Jean looks up from chopping. "I take it you think he's all right to drive."

"What, because someone's in a decent mood they're not fit to be behind the wheel?"

"He's been drinking," she says. "On top of whatever else he does." She cuts the stem out of a green pepper. The horn honks.

"He's had a can of beer, for Christ's sake." Willis looks out the window and waves. "Now. What can I do?"

"It would help if you put the chicken and the vegetables on the skewers." With the knife, she pushes chunks of the pepper into the pile of other vegetables on the cutting board.

"Ah. So I take it we're shishking."

"The chicken's in a bowl in the refrigerator," she says. "Don't throw out the marinade, please?"

"Using it to baste?" See? *He* knows.

"Yes," she says.

He takes out the earthenware bowl with the blue rings. She's been marinating the chicken in her usual pink goop: raspberry Dannon Light plus whatever else. "Hey, the old Lost Frank," he says. "So. Where did the skewers get to?"

"They're on the counter," she says.

"Ah," he says. "What do you know. If they'd been a snake, dot dot dot."

He gets down the oblong white platter, then washes his hands at the sink again (more Lemon Joy) to show he's oh so careful about contamination. Under cover of the running water he chants, in Nigga With Attitude voice, *"Mah ahdentity bah itself causes vahlence."* Then glances over his shoulder. She couldn't have heard him anyway; she's in the dining room, folding paper napkins into triangles.

He takes a skewer in his right hand and with his left thumb and forefinger picks the first chunk of translucent chicken out of the goop. Meat that light shines through: does that fucking nail it or what? Fit emblem for Man! For are we not all of us meat that light shines through? And is it not meet that we should be meat? He holds it up and runs the skewer right through the son of a bitch—zow! Take that, you fuck.

He turns around and there's Jean, pinching three water glasses in each hand. She takes them into the dining room; he skewers a square of green pepper, then a piece of whatever this other thing is.

A peal of thunder: a sharp crack widening and deepening into a kaboom that rattles the windows.

Rathbone comes scuttling into the kitchen, tail between his legs, and Willis strokes his head; poor bastard's trembling. Then in comes Jean. "Oh my God," she says. "They're out in that car with the top down."

"I assume Curtis has the sense to put his top up in a thunderstorm," he says. "Anyhow, a car's supposedly the safest place to be."

"Yes. Thank you. I'm aware of that."

"Okay, fine," he says. "I'm going to go try to get the fucking grill under cover."

He opens the screen door and stares at the sky: dark now all the way down to the horizon. There's this weird hush, then another rolling thunderclap. He goes out to the hibachi—the flames have died and the briquets are white at the edges—picks it up by the wooden handles and starts for the open doorway of the woodshed. A breeze comes up, leaves rustle overhead, and a raindrop hits the charcoal with a hiss and a wisp of smoke. He makes it underneath the woodshed roof just as the heavens open and the rain comes roaring down. Faster than he would've thought possible, a plinky tune starts up where something's wrong with the gutter.

Thunderclap.

He looks out at the rain, coming down so hard it raises a mist above the ground, and spots the boombox sitting out by the plastic chairs. He should at least unplug the orange cord in the kitchen before lightning strikes the boombox, races along the cord and nukes out everything in the house. Or is that idiotic? He turns and looks at the fucking hill of firewood blocking the door into the house. He's nerving himself up to make a run for it, when here comes the convertible—with the top down—pulling up to the kitchen door, lights on, wipers going madly. Mel and Roger scramble over the sides of the car as Tina opens her door; the three of them dash for the house, but Champ just sits there behind the wheel. He looks in the rearview mirror, slicks back his sopping hair with both hands, then opens the door and walks through the rain over to the woodshed. "Fifty fuckin' times I had that son of a bitch top up and down," he says. "Switch must've got wet or something."

"It won't go up?" says Willis.

Champ puts index finger to temple and speed-talks: *"The sum of the square root of an isosceles triangle is equal to the hypotenuse of the other two sides."* He slicks back his hair again. "Listen, how about we move some of this shit to one side so I can get the thing under cover?"

"Try it, I guess," says Willis. "It's pretty big. Might get it part-way in."

"Hey, just what the little woman says, nurk nurk nurk."

When they come into the kitchen, Jean's just mopping the muddy floor where Tina and the kids came through. "That's awful about your top," she says to Champ. "You're welcome to take a warm shower when Tina gets out. You just have to wait a few minutes for the hot water to build up again. It's a little primitive up here."

Champ goes stiff and raises a palm. "Me *like* primitive. You not worry. *Hey*-ya hey-ya *hey*-ya hey-ya."

Jean turns to Willis. "Did you get the grill under cover?"

He snaps her a salute.

Champ points to the platter stacked with shish kebabs. "Us heap good plenty eat." Rubs his stomach. "Me checkum squaw."

"How are the coals?" Jean says.

"Getting there," says Willis.

She fetches a sigh. "How long until it's ready to cook?"

"Probably by the time everything's together it should be ready."

"Everything *is* together," she says.

Well, who could resist? "Isn't it pretty to think so," he says. Then he adds, "I guess we could start bringing shit out."

He gallantly holds a garbage bag over her as she bears the platter to the woodshed, then drags over a cinderblock. She sets the platter on it; he takes a skewer and lays it on the grill.

"Why don't I do that?" she says. "You could take the platter in and wash it."

"How're you going to get all this shit back to the house?"

She looks at him. "You are going to bring the platter back *here*," she says. "After you have *washed* it."

"Ah," he says. "Silly me." Then he stands there.

"You *have* heard of salmonella? Or is this all beneath your notice?"

"Got it." He salutes again. "I had not been clear as to why it was that the platter had to be washed. I now understand." He takes up the platter and stalks out into the rain.

In the kitchen, he cracks another tallboy, takes three monster gulps and waits for the rush. The rush: dream on. But he thinks he maybe feels just the slightest little added distance from things. When he's got the platter washed—not just rinsed, as he could've done with no one the wiser, but *washed*, with Lemon Joy—he can't find the fucking dish towels. He flumps into the dining room like the prince of all put-upons to see if they're in *here* for some reason, then glances into the living room: Champ and Tina are sprawled on the couch, her bare foot at the crotch of his jeans, his leg up to the knee under her sleeveless sundress.

Champ looks up and sees Willis looking. "Hey," he says. "So when's din-din?" He looks out the window—to misdirect Willis's gaze?—and eases his bare foot from between Tina's thighs.

Willis consults an imaginary wristwatch, scowls and barks, "Ten minutes, Mr. Whiteside."

"Can we do anything?" says Tina. She's rubbing the sole of her foot along Champ's fly: couple inches up, couple inches down.

"Just make sure your hands are clean when you come to the table," Willis says. "We like to keep it sterile around here."

"Sounds hot," she says.

Willis polishes off the rest of the tallboy, cracks another one and gulps down about half of that. And as he's bringing the platter back out to the woodshed, son of a bitch if he doesn't feel like he's getting a little buzz on. This fleeting moment—a late-summer rainstorm slowly letting up, a bird's sad little rain song, the muskiness of the country air—will never come again. So fuck it.

Squatting on the dirt floor of the woodshed, Jean lifts a skewer and tilts her head to peek at the underside. She always worries that the vegetables will burn before the chicken's cooked, but it always turns out okay. Except the vegetables always get a little burned. Well, fine; she's not Martha Stewart. And nobody else, frankly, is lifting a finger. Though in fairness, Willis has been helping—here he is with the platter. Still, she's seen about enough of that salute.

When she finally sets the shish kebabs on the dining room table, she sees Champ and Tina on the couch in the living room. "Hey hey hey," he says.

"Lunch is ready," she says. Absolutely classic: this man going *Hey hey hey* while she runs herself ragged. And the girlfriend, what's her problem? Recuperating from her shower? Jean could've used a shower too. She steps into the hall and hears herself yell the kids' names like a fishwife.

Willis pokes his head in from the kitchen. "So we need two more chairs, right?"

"If everybody intends to sit, yes."

"We got 'em, we got 'em," Champ says, pulling Tina to her feet and leading her by the hand toward the kitchen.

Willis goes to the sink and washes his hands with Lemon Joy one *more* time, just to be pissy, then wipes them on his jeans and brings what's left of his beer into the dining room. He hears the kids trudging down the stairs and Mel saying, "Cut it *out*, Roger."

Champ and Tina, each carrying a chair, squeeze through the doorway. "Now the motorcade is making a sharp left on Elm," Champ says. "We can see the President waving—"

"Will you *stop*?" says Tina.

"You can't say Texas doesn't love you, Mr. President."

"Why can't he be into the Civil War?" says Tina.

"Anywhere anybody likes," says Jean. They all sit. Roger pointedly next to Champ, Mel pointedly not next to Roger. Rathbone lies down on his side in the corner, looking lonesome and defeated.

"Good dog," says Willis. One thing they've done right, at least: not feeding the dog at the table.

"Does anybody care for lemonade?" Jean says. Willis wonders when she found time to make lemonade.

"I'm set," says Champ.

"I'm fine, thanks," says Tina. They're both working on tallboys.

Willis says nothing. Seems better than heaping it on.

"Me," says Roger.

"Is that a yes-please?" says Jean.

"Yeah," says Roger.

"Yes please," says Mel.

"Yes please," says Roger in a pinchy voice.

"Hey hey hey, and what have we here?" says Champ, rubbing his hands.

"Roger?" says Jean. "Once more and you have a time-out."

"Chicken *droit du seigneur*," says Willis. This jeu d'esprit just came to him.

"Ooh la la," says Champ.

"Well, you *told* me to say yes please," says Roger.

"You have a time-out," says Jean. "Go. Up to your sister's room."

Roger shrugs and gets up. Mel stares down at her plate.

When he's trudged into the living room, heading for the stairs, Jean aims a finger-and-thumb pistol at the doorway and goes *Pyew*. "I'm sorry about his behavior today," she says. Willis waits to hear her add that Roger's not always like this, so he can say something cutting. But she leaves it at that.

"Don't even think about it," says Tina. "*I* was a bratty kid at that age. Jean, this looks so *excellent*."

Champ looks at Tina and does zip-your-lip. Tina frowns in puzzlement.

"Ahem," Willis says to Champ. "You were supposed to say, 'Why do you call it chicken *droit du seigneur*?' "

"Anything for a giggle," says Champ. "Okay, why?"

"Because I get the first piece." Willis grabs a skewer, puts it on his own plate and passes the platter to Tina.

Champ just looks at him. "That was the punch line?"

"Please help yourselves," Jean says. So at least *somebody* got it. Then she looks over at Mel, which really pisses Willis the fuck off. It was *deliberately* over the kids' heads, for Christ's sake. And Mel's not paying attention anyway. She's looking over at Roger, who's peeking around the doorway, giving her the finger.

"Mo-*ther*?" Mel says.

The way Willis feels—he's buzzed, no question—they can all take a flying fuck. This will never be over.

5

When it clears up, late in the afternoon, Willis takes Champ and Tina for a walk to the top of the hill. Jean claims she's got stuff in the house to take care of; Mel, friend of the rain forest, stays inside cultivating her boredom; Roger's having yet another time-out, this time for calling Mel a cunt.

On the path, sunbeams slant with false cheer through the dripping trees. At last, breathing hard, they stand in wet grass on the hilltop and look across at other hilltops. "Shit, it's already fall up here," Champ says.

"Hey, this is the North Country, bro," Willis says, meaning he's man enough to take it. In fact, he's been trying not to notice the few red leaves.

Back at the house, Champ and Tina go upstairs and Willis gets a start on stacking that wood. When they come down, an hour later, Champ tries to tinker with his top, gives up and insists on taking them out to dinner, to celebrate Willis's quote liberation.

Jean's not thrilled, but she's also not thrilled at the prospect of getting a dinner together for these people she just got a big lunch together for. She calls the Bjorks to ask if that invitation to swim still holds and if it could possibly be stretched so the kids could stay for dinner. Jean is *never* this pushy, but the Bjorks owe them one: last summer the Willises took the Bjork kids overnight so Arthur and Katherine could go to a resort on Lake Champlain for a twenty-four-hour Marriage Intensive.

The Bjorks live on 82nd between Central Park and Columbus; God knows why they chose Preston Falls for a weekend place. Though their house *is* great: a big old two-and-a-half-story Federal on Watson Road. White clapboards, dark-green shutters, red barn, pond with a dock and a sandy beach—your basic $750,000 country retreat, which they probably got for like one seventy-five because it's in Preston Falls. He's a something at ABC and Jean's forgotten what *she* does. Lawyer? They put up with the Willises because otherwise it's down to the locals, whom Katherine calls "a bit rough-hewn." Jean knows what she means. Once, at an auction, Mel befriended a pretty, grubby little girl who called her father "fart-face" and got smacked across the mouth by her three-hundred-pound mother, whose sloppy arms were as big around as the child's waist. Sorry, but Jean has zero regard for these people.

Willis herds everybody into the Cherokee: Jean shotgun, Mel in back between Champ and Tina. Roger refuses to sit on his mother's lap and share her seat belt but climbs over everybody into the wayback, where of course he starts whining about getting carsick. (The dirt roads are in washboard mode, because the town can't afford to grade.) At the Bjorks', the kids disappear and the adults do their dance. Stay for a drink? Gee, wish we could. Willis notices that Arthur Bjork's got this fucking cap on: *P* inside a star, from some old Negro League team. (He recognizes it because he once priced these caps himself.) Watching him and Champ together might be fun, but only in retrospect.

"Why don't I go in back with Tina," Jean tells Champ. "Be a little more room for your legs."

"*No*-no-no-no-no," says Champ. "*Plenty* of room. Fuckin' Taj Mahal back here."

"Taj Ma*hal*?" says Tina.

"Really, do take the front," Jean says. "I never get to ride in back."

"Well, if that's your dream."

"Yes, that's my dream," she says.

For the next two hours they drive around Vermont and New York State, looking for a place Champ thinks has the right vibe: nothing log, nothing steakhousey, nothing too seventies (by which he seems to mean big windows with plants) and nothing that calls itself an "inn." And no Mexican. He tells Willis about a document that says a George Bush of the CIA briefed the FBI about something the day after Kennedy was shot; the CIA claims this was a different George Bush, but researchers managed to track down *that* George Bush and he says it wasn't him. Willis catches bits of what Jean's talking about back there with Tina: shit about kids and school, how lucky she is that her sister will be around while Willis is away. But he knows she must be ready to jump out of her fucking skin; Jean hates just aimlessly driving.

At last Willis remembers this place called the Old Tuscany, on the access road to one of the big ski areas on the other side of Manchester. He and Jean ate there once and it was okay. Pretentious enough to be

camp: maybe *that*'s the vibe. He pulls over onto a sandy shoulder—
"What are we doing?" Jean says—and makes a U-turn. Champ tries to
find a Christian station, but Willis heads that off and gets Hot Country,
which Jean dislikes but will usually sit still for.

"Isn't that a new awning?" says Willis, when they finally get to the
entrance. White canvas with gold trim and a lion rampant.

"I wouldn't know," says Jean.

Champ breaks into song: *It's a neeeew awning. Doodle-a-doodle-a.
Neeeew awning . . .*

"Champ missed his calling," says Tina. She doesn't go on to say what
his calling might have been.

Champ and Tina, goosing each other, follow Jean up the flagstone
walk while Willis gives the keys to a shaven-headed kid with white shirt,
black bow tie, knife-creased black slacks and running shoes you're not
supposed to notice. A red-faced alcoholic in Swiss Guard's uniform (the
idea seems to be Tuscany = Italy = the Vatican) pulls back the heavy,
studded door, thick as the Manhattan phone book, and in the dark foyer
the greeter lady waits at a rostrum whose bronze lamp lights her book.
Do they have reservations? "Who wouldn't?" says Willis, affecting to
quail before a suit of armor in the entryway. She gives him the smile he's
extorted.

Some guy in black takes them to a table and hands around upholstered menus, and somebody else comes to turn the water glasses right
side up and pour ice water from a sweating metal pitcher. Then yet
another guy arrives and asks if they'd care for drinks. "Definitely," says
Willis. "I'm a very caring person."

When the drinks arrive—martini, martini, martini, Pellegrino—
Willis says, "Now that I have you here." He feels in his pocket. "It's not
much, but hey—what is?"

"Now what the fuck is this about?" says Champ.

Willis shrugs. "I don't know. Anniversary? Labor Day two years ago,
I remember you were up here and you said you'd just met this amazing
person. Little did I know you wouldn't screw it up—I mean, so *far*."

"You dick," Champ says. "What are you, trying to guilt me?"

"So who does the honors?" says Willis.

"Shit, now I *will* have to pick up the fucking check." Champ pokes
a thumb at Tina. "Better let my animal companion open it. Everything I
am today, I owe to her."

"Sure, blame *me*," says Tina.

It's not until Tina's actually got a fingernail under the wrapping paper that it hits Willis what an incredibly bad idea this was.

"Now what have we here?" says Champ when Tina holds up the box of Touch Thins. Willis doesn't dare look at Jean but hears her take a breath.

"Well, you know," Willis says. "I just figured the madness has to stop at some point, right?" He's alluding to overpopulation; even Champ looks puzzled.

"Would you excuse me, please?" says Jean. She gets up and goes off toward the rest rooms.

Willis figures his best stance at this point is unremitting joviality. "There, ah, should be something else in there?" he says. "An envelope, perchance?"

"Is Jean all right?" says Tina.

"Hey," he says. "When you gotta go, you gotta go."

"Now what have we here?" says Champ. Which he's said already. He picks up his butter knife and slits the envelope.

Willis waits, then says, "That confirms you guys for the second weekend in October, which should be pretty near peak foliage. If you had plans for then, better start weaseling out of them."

Looking at Willis, Champ passes the printout to Tina. "Are you shitting me?"

"*Oh* my God," says Tina. "We *loved* this place—it is *the* most fabulous. Champ actually *relaxed*."

"Me? Bull*shit*." The chatter and the silverware noises around them suddenly hush. "Oopsy," Champ says.

"Besides, they make you dress for dinner?" says Tina. "That's like a thing there? And he looked so cute in his jacket and tie."

"I looked like a fucking anchorman," says Champ.

"I'm going to go in and just make sure Jean's all right." Tina gets up, comes around and kisses Willis on the cheekbone. "You are so sweet," she says. "I can't believe you."

"Hold that thought," Willis says, and commands himself not to watch her ass as she walks away.

"Listen, bro," says Champ. "Can you really swing this?"

"Hey," says Willis. "If MasterCard says I can, who am I to argue?"

"*There* you go," says Champ. "So Jean doesn't like it when the jizzbags arrive before the soup?"

Willis shrugs. "Fuck 'em if they can't take a joke, right?"

"What *I* always say."

"Dames. Can't live *with* 'em, dot dot dot."

"I hear you," says Champ. "So listen, this might be the moment for us *boys* to powder our noses." He pats his shirt pocket. "Little cut in your strut? Glide in your stride?"

"What is this, the eighties?" says Willis. "I'm just *about* keeping it together as it is."

"That's why you need to lively up," says Champ. *"Lively up your-self,"* he sings, *"don't be no dra-hag."*

Willis shakes his head. "Bad idea."

"Well, shit if *I'm* not going to go get festive."

"God help us." Willis picks up his martini. "Listen, be discreet, will you?"

"Yeah, right. I'm going to stand at the fucking urinal wagging my wang with one hand and—"

"You're being very loud," Willis says.

"Oopsy." Champ raises his hand and whispers, "May I be excused?"

Willis sits there alone at the table. So *now* what the fuck. He takes a sip of martini. Fair. Except too much of whatever shit vermouth they pour here. He should've gone in with Champ; Jean never saw him in his druggy days and wouldn't have a clue. Hell, he could go in *now*. But. He takes two more gulps and beckons the waiter while emptying the glass. And bingo: when Jean comes back to the table he's got another, drier one in front of him that anybody would think was still the first.

"Mel and Roger are fine," she says, sitting down. "If you're interested."

Already he's mellow enough to let that one roll. "Oh, you called up?" he says, a blithe and blasé martini-drinker like Mr. Postmodern Collage Man on the Tanqueray posters. Mr. Something.

"Yes. I called up."

He'll ignore her tone too. Superciliously, he sips again.

"They want to stay overnight."

"And you told them?" he says.

"I told them fine. I thought under the circumstances it was just as well."

"The circumstances?" Dear me, whatever can the woman mean?

"Oh, stop," she says. "Just stop. Tell me something, have you lost your mind? It was just so *loutish*. A box of *rubbers*, for God's sake."

"Hey, I *am* a lout. That's my big aspiration anymore. To be a fucking lout."

"Well, you're succeeding," she says.

"Well, good, great," he says. "You know who I want to be? Fucking John Madden." It's the example that leaps to mind.

"I'm sorry, this is all too deep for me," she says. "I'd appreciate it if after we get our food we could get out of here as quickly as possible."

"We haven't even *ordered*, for Christ's sake."

"Yes, I know that, thank you." Then she looks up and says, without moving her lips, "Oh, great."

Tina sits down. "Oh, I feel so much *better*. What happened to my one and only?"

"Went to the men's," Willis says.

"This place is so happening." Tina's looking at another suit of armor, in a wall niche. "Do you think these are actually real?"

"Not unless they were for midgets," says Willis.

Jean has gone behind her menu.

"But weren't people smaller in the old days?" Tina says.

"*I* was," says Willis. "You should've seen me in 1954."

Tina does a batting-at-him gesture. "No, I mean—like wasn't Napoleon five two or something?"

"Hey," says Champ, sitting down and rubbing his nose. "*Heya* heya *heya* heya."

"Champ?" says Tina. "Wasn't Napoleon like five two?"

"Could be," says Champ. "Napoleon? Could very very well be. I do know they pickled his dick and put it in the Smithsonian."

"Oh-oh," says Tina. "What's this vibe I'm getting? You weren't being a bad boy in there?"

"Unbelievable," says Champ. "Guy takes an innocent whiz. You want to pat me down?"

"Could be hot." Tina narrows her eyes. "Hmm. I don't know about you."

"I think we should order," Jean says.

"Ah yes, I'll have the, ah, pickled *dick*?" says Champ. "Served with a light cream sauce?"

"Sweetheart," says Tina.

"Oopsy."

"Honey lamb," says Tina.

"Ah yes, I'll have the, ah, honey *lamb*?"

As the rest of them eat, Champ combs his pasta into patterns with his fork and explains that "Maurice Bishop" had been seen with Oswald before the assassination, and that if you looked at the sketch of "Maurice Bishop" and then at the photograph of David Attlee Phillips, it's just unmistakable, even though the guy who saw them together backed off from explicitly making the identification because he was scared shitless of the CIA.

"So the whole thing came out of Langley," says Willis. "What else is new."

"*Langley?*" says Champ. "You don't seriously believe headquarters is at fucking *Langley*, do you? Langley is the fucking *cover*."

"Okay, so where's the real place?"

"Orlando. They got this whole like underground city underneath Disney World, right? Fifty thousand million people with their kids and shit walking around overhead, fat, dumb and happy." He teases out a strand of pasta, regards it, then drapes it over a piece of broccoli. "Nah, shit, how would *I* know? I don't *want* to fucking know. That kind of information could be very very dangerous to have." He whistles the little four-note *Twilight Zone* thing.

"You live with him," Willis says to Tina. "Does he really believe this stuff?"

"Hey, talk about me like I'm not here," says Champ.

"He gets off on it, I know *that*," she says.

Willis is pretty well hammered after his three martinis (officially two) plus wine with dinner, so he lets Jean drive them back to Preston Falls while he rides shotgun and plays deejay. Hot Country really *is* unlistenable, so he settles on a classical station—it's that Hovhaness piece of garbage that everybody likes because they're getting old and right wing. The Magic Mountain or whatever. Willis is smashed enough to where he finds himself enjoying the hell out of it. As they pull into the dooryard, he sees stars in the black sky above his own hilltop, and that is just about fucking *perfect*. He gets out of the Cherokee and stands there staring in shit-faced reverence.

Champ and Tina call good night. Yeah, yeah, good night.

Jean touches his arm. She came right out of nowhere. "I'm going up to bed."

"Good," he says. "That's good." And now Rathbone is here too, tail wagging. Rathbone! Forgot he even existed! Rathbone races off and lifts his leg against the spooky white birch tree.

"This probably isn't the best time," Jean says. "But do you think you could give me a clue as to what's going on?"

"In what sense?" he says.

She goes *Oh* as if somebody knocked the wind out of her.

This tells Willis he'd better try and be lucid for a second.

"Look," he says. "We've been *over* this. It's like I've been in the wrong life."

"Well, do you have any conception of what your life properly *is*? I mean, is it really up *here*, driving a *truck*?"

"That's what I hope to figure out," he says. "In my big two months." But hey, Rathbone's back! Willis gets to his knees, roughs up Rathbone's neck and tells him *That's my boy*.

"Something else you might want to figure out," says Jean. "What role, if any, do your children have in this real life of yours? Not to mention your wife. Have you given thought to any of that?"

"To my shame, no," he says.

"I'm not that interested in your shame," she says. "I know *you* find it fascinating."

"Hey, give the little lady a brass ring," he says. "The low blow award." He strokes Rathbone's silky side and stands up again. Reelin' and a-rockin', but basically okay.

"Oh, I'm sure you took it to heart," she says. "You've fixed it so nobody's even in the same *universe* with you. I don't know, I just truly *worry* about you. As someone who knows you."

"You know me very well."

"Oh, please," she says. And goes inside.

He sits down on the stepstone; Rathbone comes over, circles, then lies at Willis's feet sniffing the night air. There's the good old Big Dipper up there, the only constellation Willis knows. *Or* gives a rat's ass about. Light from the upstairs window makes a night-baseball-green parallelogram on the wet grass. Lawn needs mowing. Tomorrow, without fail.

Jean gets her nightgown from the closet, shoving aside old shirts of Willis's that he's put on hangers even though they're dirty. He'll wear them when he's working, sweat them through, then hang them back up.

Unbelievable. No wonder it smells in here. She makes space on both sides of her cotton dress with the cerise flowers, the one halfway decent thing she keeps in Preston Falls. Willis bought it for her three birthdays ago at—where else?—Laura Ashley, and it's actually not that dreadful, though she had to exchange the six he'd gotten for an eight. So obviously he should have married Laura Ashley, some willowy honey-haired size-eight hippie princess with a fetching little English accent and Pre-Raphaelite pallor and breasts that get magically gigundo once she takes off her chaste Laura Ashley dress. Jean puts her underwear in the laundry bag, gets the nightgown on and goes downstairs to the bathroom. Through the screen door she sees Willis sitting out on the stepstone with his back to her. Feeling lonely and misunderstood. Or sensing his own insignificance in the vastness of the universe. Or planning how he's going to dump her. Or wondering whether to buy a motorcycle or another guitar. Really, at this point, how would anybody know?

She pees, puts in a new Tampax, washes, brushes her teeth and pops two Advils. The cramps have pretty much passed, but Advil might help her sleep. In addition to everything else, she's worried about the kids. Though it's crazy to suspect Arthur Bjork is a pedophile just because he's overweight and because he and Katherine have marriage trouble. After all, don't she and Willis have marriage trouble? Isn't that what this is?

When the upstairs light goes out, Willis gets to his feet and goes inside, holding the door for Rathbone, who comes clicking in, leaving wet footprints on the kitchen floor. The footprints make Willis think the seat of his pants must be wet too, but damned if he can feel it. He reaches around: yep. He gets down that bottle of Dewar's and pours himself some. Pours himself really quite a bit, actually. He brings his glass into the living room, stretches out on the couch—Rathbone lies down on the floor by his side—and starts looking through *Dombey and Son* for just any scene with Old Joe Bagstock, old Joseph, Joey B., Sir. Funny as shit. When he's polished off the whole glass he rests the open book on his chest and closes his eyes. Then the room starts to spin. Oh shit. Shit shit shit. He tries to pretend this is actually desirable and he can just merrily spin away into dreamy dreamland. No good. He opens his eyes, sits up a little and tries to read, but now *that's* no good. He eases back down and the room goes so crazy he wonders if he's having a stroke on top of being drunk. He gets to his feet and moonwalks into the bathroom, closes the door behind him, drops to his knees and flips up the toilet seat. The sight of a pubic hair on the rim does the trick: he sticks out his tongue and out it pours, vanity after vanity, this whole evening's stupid history. He wipes his mouth with toilet paper and lies sweating on the floor, thinking *At least that's over with*. Knowing God damn well it's not.

6

He wakes up on the sofa, mouth nasty, head throbbing. Still in his clothes. Turns his head, and the son of a bitch throbs worse. Yellowish daylight in the living room. Rathbone rises from the floor, stretches and sniffs Willis's face. Willis pats his head and tells him *Good dog*, then gets up to piss and take Advil. The house is silent. Before going into the bathroom he gives Rathbone fresh water and makes sure he's got food, hoping to placate whoever might be watching and judging all this shit from on high.

He's putting on water for coffee when he hears somebody coming downstairs. Jean? Please, no. Rathbone's tail gets going. But it's Champ, thank God.

"Hey, the hostess with the mostest," says Champ. "Didn't expect *you* to be up." He squats and tousles Rathbone's ears. "Yes, you're a good guy."

Willis spoons coffee into the filter paper. Then he turns and sees Champ's t-shirt and says, "Jesus H. Christ."

"What—*this*?" Champ tugs out a little tent of fabric with thumb and forefinger. "Had a guy silk-screen it. He's got the image on file, if you want one."

"I'll pass," says Willis. "Listen. You just put this on to model it for me, right?"

"No, not—oh. I see what you're saying. Too punk for Preston Falls."

"Well, not just that."

"*Oh.* Gotcha. Okay, that's cool. I got another thing I can put on."

"That's a real autopsy photo?" says Willis.

"Yep. Well, actually sort of yes and no. It's like it's really him dead, but the CIA dicked around with the photo. *Or* they dicked around with the body. Like right here, see?" He cranes his neck to look down at his chest, then puts a finger just above and behind JFK's ear. "When you look at the Z film, right? This area here should be completely blown to fuck. So *something's* fuckin' weird. I don't know. Shit, I like wearing it, you know? Tina has the same reaction you do, by the way."

"I'm past the point of having reactions," says Willis. "All I want now is an easy life." Champ plays an invisible violin at him as he gets down the JOE mug and the mug with the green band around the rim. "What got you started on *this* shit? You were like three years old."

"I don't know. I saw the movie and then I just started reading up on it."

"Yeah, but I mean why *this?*"

Champ puts palm to elbow and fist to forehead. "The Thinker is thinking," he says. He puts index finger to temple. *"The sum of the hypotenuse is equal in angle to the square root of the sum of the remaining three sides."*

"I should know better by now," says Willis.

"You're afraid I'm going to wind up like the old man. And lose my mi-yi-yind." Champ sticks his tongue out and twirls index fingers at his ears. "Speaking of which, you been in touch with the mom?"

"Talked to her a couple weeks ago. I probably should go visit sometime while I'm on leave."

"You're a hero," says Champ.

The water's boiling; Willis goes over to turn the burner off. "You *are* going to change out of that, right?" Jean could come down any minute.

"No worries, mite." A couple of years ago, Champ would keep up the Aussie-talk for a whole conversation. "Listen, you remember that time you drove me up to see the old man? I think I was like ten? You had this thing back then about him and me spending time together and shit?"

"Yeah, I remember I was on spring break. I had that black Ford Fairlane."

"Right," says Champ. "I *remember* that."

"I guess we picked a bad day."

"What you mean, *we*, Kemosabe? I remember he spent the whole time playing this, like, Dave Brubeck record—"

"Time Further Out," says Willis.

"Right, and we were supposed to count the number of measures in a beat or some shit? Which was this secret code that hooked up with people's Social Security numbers?"

"Something like that."

"You know, thinking back," Champ says, "it's bizarre that the mom let you take me."

"Yeah, well, it was all bizarre."

"Ah, but look at us now. Okay, listen, I'll be right back down." Willis hears him go clomping up the stairs. He doesn't return.

When Jean comes downstairs, Willis is lying on the sofa drinking coffee and looking through *Dombey and Son* for more Joe Bagstock shit.

"Morning," he says.

"Good morning."

"Coffee's all ready," he says, swinging his feet off the sofa and getting up. Makes his head throb, but he deliberately keeps his eyes open to make the wince less obvious. "I get you some?"

"No, thank you." She goes into the kitchen.

He salutes her backside and sits down again. Then lies down. He hears her go into the bathroom. Sometime later the toilet flushes. Then drawers opening and shutting in the kitchen, utensils chinging. He closes his eyes.

The next thing he's aware of is Champ saying "Hey, bro," and the smell of bacon. "You missed a happening breakfast, man. Jean said let you sleep."

Willis sits up. Classical music coming from the kitchen, Mozart-sounding shit that might even *be* Mozart. So some kind soul brought the boombox inside, and the rain didn't fuck it up—at least not the radio part. "Time is it?" he says.

"I don't know, ten-thirty?" says Champ. "Listen, man, we're going to head out."

"Wait. What? This is Sunday, right? I thought you were going back tomorrow." Willis sees Tina, sleepy-eyed, fucked-looking, sitting in the armchair, one leg draped over the arm. Back in her same biker shorts.

"Well, see, we were sort of talking it over upstairs," Champ says, "and we were feeling like—I don't know if I told you, but we've been doing this thing Sunday nights where we watch Tina's sister's kid? You know, so she can go to her meeting."

"She's been doing really really well," says Tina.

"She's a puker," Champ says. "It's like AA, what she goes to, except it's all pukers and fatties."

"Sweetie pie."

"Yes, dear."

"It's really helped her incredibly," says Tina.

"Hell, I'd be a puker too if I had *that* little shit to deal with."

"Father material." Tina flips a thumb at Champ.

"Anyhow, we were thinking maybe we better get down there. Like what if the Higher Power blew off the weekend? She's sitting there stuffing down chocolate cream doughnuts and the finger's getting closer! Closer!" He moves a trembling index finger toward his mouth.

"Stop," says Tina. "That is *really cruel.*"

"The other thing, I got to get the mighty turnpike cruiser in to like Rayco or someplace, see what the fuck's the matter with that top."

"On Labor Day weekend?" Willis says.

"Well, you know, plus Tina has shit she's got to do. And we just thought, you know, with the top and everything, better get in before it starts to cool off, 'cause we didn't bring any jackets or shit."

"We've got jackets," says Willis.

"Plus if we wait till tomorrow we're not going to find a place to park. Shit, we been thinking of moving out to New Jersey just to have a fuckin' driveway."

"We have *not*," Tina says.

"She doesn't want to."

"I'm too young to die," Tina says.

"Hey, Jersey is happening," says Champ. "They got towns with all these big-ass houses, the white people are moving out, and stuff's going for nothing. What the fuck, so you get a gun and a fuckin' security system. We got shit at the store—you know, put fuckin' *razor* wire. I want to have a big fuckin' sleaze palace, about ten bedrooms, you know? Mattresses on the floor? Great big speakers?"

"What Champ wants in his heart of hearts," says Tina, "is a free-sex commune."

"Yeah, well? That can still work too. You know, you test everybody once a week."

"He is so dear," says Tina.

"Tina has no ideals. So listen, bro, we better do it. Now where'd Jean get to?"

They find her out behind the house where the stream cuts through in springtime. Rathbone's strutting back and forth with a stick in his mouth. She gets up, knees of her jeans muddy, and brings Tina a plastic bag with green stuff in it.

"This is that mint," she says. Champ claps his hands and Rathbone trots over with the stick.

"Oh. *Thank* you." Tina clearly has forgotten whatever conversation they apparently had about mint.

Champ grabs for the stick and Rathbone dodges away.

"Hey, bro?" says Willis. "Show you something for a second?" He leads Champ over toward the woodshed. That God damn gutter's just hanging off the eaves; everywhere on this whole fucking place something needs to be done, urgently. "Listen, I'm sorry about how tense things are here."

"Ah, this shit happens. I just thought it might be easier with us out from underfoot."

"Well," says Willis, "easier on *you*, for sure."

"Doesn't bother *me*. I think Tina's sort of bummed that you guys—but shit, she's young, you know? Hasn't quite achieved that Zen-like detachment. She likes you."

"Well, I like *her*," Willis says. "I think you really scored."

"Of course I *scored*. Nurk nurk nurk."

"You dick. Listen, we'll be okay."

"Right, I know that," says Champ. "And you know you can call me anytime."

"Now there's a vote of confidence."

"So," Champ says. "I guess we better do it."

Willis puts Rathbone in the house—the boombox is still playing the same diddle diddle, or similar diddle diddle—and he and Jean walk out to the road to watch them off. When the convertible disappears around the corner, Jean says, "I think I'm going to go too."

"Say again?"

"If you'd like to have a little time with Mel and Roger," she says, "you could go pick them up while I get their stuff together."

"What do you mean—you're leaving *today*?" Willis tries to put the right English on this to make it sound like disappointment.

"I just don't see what's in this for either of us. You might as well have the place to yourself, which is obviously what you want."

"But this is your time off too."

"That's right. And I've worked really hard for it, and I really need for it to be restful. Or dare I say *fun*? If that's even a possibility anymore?"

"But what about the kids and *their* weekend?" Willis says. Telling himself *Shut up shut up shut up*.

"Oh, well I'm glad you're so con*cerned*," she says. "I think I'm going to take them camping overnight. To the place we went that time. That you hated. The state park? And I would really appreciate it if you could be too busy to come along."

"Camping for one day? *Half* a day?"

"That's the time we have."

"What do you plan to do with them once you get them there?"

"Swim," she says. "Throw a ball. Cook hot dogs. You know, normal things. I know you have nothing but contempt for all that, so you can do what *you* want for a change and not be bothered with *us*. I'm hoping it'll cool me out enough to maybe be able to deal with the trip back. *And* getting them ready for school on Tuesday. *And*—you know."

"Sleeping in a fucking *tent* with two kids is going to cool you out?"

"Right. But see," she says, "I *like* being with them."

7

While Willis is picking up the kids, Jean searches the bedroom closet for the down-filled sleeping bags Carol gave them when they got married. Now they seem like a bad fairy's wedding curse: *May you always sleep apart.* The kids' sleeping bags are in Chesterton; she'll let them have these and make do herself with a couple of blankets.

She stows bags, blankets and three pillows in the back of the Cherokee, then goes into the woodshed for the tent—just in case all the lean-tos are taken—and the cooler, a red-and-white Igloo, which smells like something *died.* Or so she'd say if she were telling somebody; all it really smells like is a cooler that hasn't used all summer. She brings it into the kitchen and cleans it out with Pine Sol. She wishes she could stop saying things she doesn't absolutely mean.

Actually, taking the kids camping is about the last thing she wants to do. But hanging on here—well, it's not that she couldn't do it, because what else is her life about? Yet if only they could have just one moment, one image to take away of summer and family, one smell of campfires and pine trees . . . Pathetic. And her little speech about hot dogs: what was that supposed to do—bring Willis to his knees? Well, they *will* cook hot dogs—she'll pick up some vegetables to grill for Mel—and there must be a ball someplace that Rathbone hasn't ruined.

So stupid. She should have seen all this coming. Like his Prince Hamlet period when she was pregnant with Mel—no, even before that. Right from the first. But: towels. She has to remember towels. And something to sit on at the beach—another blanket? And her bathing suit, which is where? (*Their* suits they took with them to the Bjorks'.) Flashlight. Bug stuff. Sunscreen. She could kill him for making her do this. Except it's her idea. Camera: to carry out the pretense that this will be something they'll want to look back on. Still, it should be fine, right?

Cook hot dogs and go swimming? They'd probably think it was weird if
their father *was* there.

Willis finds everybody down at the pond. The Bjork kids—Nelson,
Frida and little Amina, the adopted one—are out in the inflatable boat,
yelling. Mel's sunning on the dock, bikini top unfastened. Roger's at the
far side of the pond, stalking frogs on the bank the Bjorks left muddy
on the advice of a pond consultant. It's that summer's-over-but-we're-
pretending-it's-not vibe. He calls out a hearty good morning to whom it
may concern. The Bjork kids stare, then go back to yelling; Mel lifts and
lowers a limp hand, a gesture he's supposed to take for a wave; Roger
doesn't even look up. Willis guesses from the look of things that his kids
have outstayed what welcome there was.

Arthur and Katherine Bjork are sitting at the edge of their trucked-
in sand in honest-to-God wooden Adirondack chairs, each with a piece
of the Sunday *Times*; the sections they're not reading are weighted down
by an antique brick with an embossed star. On the broad, flat arm of
Arthur's chair, a cloth napkin and both halves of a plump bagel mounded
high with scallion cream cheese. Arthur Bjork is one of those fat, red-
faced walrus-men, with blond hair and gold-rimmed glasses; scrawny,
overtanned Katherine must have to get on top if they bother anymore,
though Willis is a great one to talk.

"So how has it been?" he says.

"Oh, fine." Katherine Bjork always sounds borderline exasperated,
with good reason for all Willis knows. *Or* fucking cares.

"No problems?"

"Well, none to speak of," says Arthur. Poor son of a bitch looks like
he's hanging on by his fingernails until he can get back to the office Tuesday morning.

"Good, good," says Willis. Hear no evil. "Yo, Melanie and *Roger!*"
he calls. "Time to hit it, guys."

"Darn," says Mel. Roger just goes on doing what he's doing.

"Your mother has a surprise for you," says Willis.

"What kind of surprise?" says Mel.

"Hold *still*, you cocksucker!" Roger yells.

"Roger! *Get* the hell over here!" Willis shouts. "I apologize for my
son," he says to the space between the Bjorks.

Roger comes trudging over. "I wasn't gonna *hurt* him," he says.

"You don't use language like that," says Willis, fixing him with a pointed finger. "Go get in the truck. *Now.*"

"I have to get my stuff."

"I said: in the *truck*, mister." Ooh, the heavy father. *Mister*, yet. Roger, head down, starts making his way toward the driveway. "Melanie," Willis says. She's guiltily hooking the top of her suit behind her back, skinny elbows out like chicken wings. "Get your clothes on, collect your brother's gear, and get in the truck."

"Can't I just put a shirt over my suit?" she says.

"I don't care what you *wear*. I want you in that truck in two minutes."

Since the Bjorks are right there, she risks an eye roll as she turns and heads for the house.

"Rog-*er?*" Willis calls. Roger's not exactly hauling ass, and stops dead when he hears his name. "*Move* it." He resumes ambling up the path.

"We seem to be having one of those days," Willis says to the Bjorks.

"Well, I guess we all have them." Arthur doesn't even deign to put down the Travel section.

"Except you, right?" says Willis. "You fat fuck."

That gets the son of a bitch focused: down goes the paper, covering his sausage thighs like a skirt, as Katherine's mouth opens to an O. (Billie Burke couldn't have done it better.) Mel stops but doesn't turn around.

"I think you'd better go," Arthur says, though he doesn't stand up.

"Hey, don't worry about it." Crazy motherfucker named Willis. The Bjorks just look at each other. Willis can imagine: Arthur's thinking his wife expects him to deck this guy, and she's thinking if her old man gets in a fistfight he'll finally have that heart attack. Out on the pond, the Bjork kids have the rubber boat spinning as if in a whirlpool, slashing away with the paddles, whooping and shrieking. Willis turns to follow his children up the path, and only now does his chest start pounding. Christ, *he's* the one who's going to have the fucking heart attack. He hauls off and kicks over the milk can the Bjorks have put at the head of the path to amp up the country charm, then looks back toward the pond. Resolutely, the Bjorks face the water.

As the truck goes rumbling and crunching down the white-graveled drive, Mel stares at her feet. "Daddy, I can't believe you *said* that to him."

"What'd he say?" says Roger.

"Nothing, Roger," says Mel.

"You can tell him," Willis says. "Long as it's a direct quote, you're off the hook."

Mel, still looking at her feet, turns red.

"*What?*" yells Roger.

"Well, for reasons I don't fully understand myself," Willis says, "I called Mr. Bjork a fat pig."

"That's not exactly what you said, Daddy," Mel says.

"What did he *say?*" says Roger.

Mel takes a breath and looks out the window. "He called Mr. Bjork a fat f-u-c-k."

"All *right*," says Willis. "Melanie has spelled *fuck* for us. We've all heard the word, yes?"

Mel and Roger say nothing. He grinds gears as he shifts down to make the turn onto County Road 39; can't decide if the clutch is really going or if he's babying it and not pushing the pedal down far enough because he *thinks* the clutch is going.

"So," he says. "Isn't anybody curious about this surprise?"

"*What* surprise?" says Roger.

"Should I just tell you?" Willis says.

"*Yes,*" says Roger.

Mel says nothing.

"Okay, what it is, you guys are going camping with your mom this afternoon."

"Do we have to?" says Roger.

"I knew you'd be thrilled to the—"

"Daddy, watch where you're *going*," says Mel. Willis swerves back over to his side to miss a tractor, cutter bar down, mowing brush on the other side of the road. "Are you coming too?" she says.

"No. I'm going to stay and see if I can't get some work done. Rathbone'll keep me company."

"I don't want to," says Roger.

"*You,*" says Willis. "We haven't gotten around to you yet, mister. What's gotten into you, using that kind of language around people?"

"So? Look what *you* said."

"True," says Willis. "But the difference is—" Right. What *is* the difference? "Look. This is the kind of thing where, you know, fairly or *un*fairly, if you're a kid, it sounds worse to people than it does if you're

a grownup." Great: he's just told Roger how he can get a rise out of people. "When they hear you using bad language, they're going to think,
Well, that's a bad person, and I don't want to be that person's friend." '

"So? If they don't want to be my friend they don't have to be."

"What?" Willis has blanked out for a second. What the fuck are
they talking about?

"I don't care if they don't want to be my friend," Roger says.
"They're probably a feeb like *her* that has to spell everything."

"Watch out, Roger," says Mel.

"Watch out, Roger," says Roger.

"I'm not kidding," says Mel.

"I'm not kidding," says Roger.

"Enough," Willis says.

"Yeah, well, she started it."

"I did *not.*"

"God help you both," Willis says.

He shifts down again, double-clutching but still grinding gears, and
turns onto Goodwin Hill Road. Setting one more piss-poor example by
cruising through the stop sign.

"So," he says. He keeps the truck in second to get up this first steep
stretch; it feels as if he's fucking up the engine by revving it to a roar
while the thing's just crawling, but in third it'll clunk and lurch. "I imagine your mother's just about packed."

Not a word from either of them. But what are they supposed to say?
There's truly something wrong with him; you don't act this way with
your children. The thing to do is to pull over, fall on them with slobbery
kisses, clutch at their bare knees, bathe their bare feet with your tears
and dry them with your hair. At least he's sane enough just to keep
driving.

8

Willis stands in the middle of the road, holding Rathbone by the collar with one hand and waving the Cherokee out of sight with the other. As they turn the corner, Jean's arm comes out the window: the hand flutters and they're gone. Willis lets go of Rathbone, who looks down the road, then up at him. Summer's over. It's one o'clock in the afternoon.

Okay. To work, to work.

Okay, first thing he's going to do, he's going to tear out the living room ceiling, where some asshole smeared joint compound over the sheetrock in modernistic swirls. Probably the same asshole who nailed particleboard over the foot-wide floorboards upstairs, for carpeting he never put down. *Asshole*, though: that's a little harsh. Really just somebody doing his best to make an old house less depressing by his lights. So Willis is going to expose the beams, which he hopes are hand-hewn, then frame around them with two-by-fours and cut sheetrock to fit in between. True, this chichi severity is basically bullshit. But if not that, then what? He's asked Jean, who went to fucking *Pratt*, for Christ's sake, and now spends her days advising those sharks she works for on exactly this kind of shit. What color to paint the walls in the fucking shark tank. She told him, "Do what you want."

He brings the stepladder and his toolbelt in from the woodshed, then starts moving shit out of the living room. He carries the armchair into the dining room, along with the oak end table he doesn't like but belonged to Grandma Willis, and the lamp that goes on it. The books, Jesus. He ends up just putting them out in the hall, in tall, tottering Dr. Seuss piles, and stacks the bricks and boards out there too. The boards he'll recycle when he gets around to doing built-in bookcases. And the blanket chest they use as a coffee table? Well, how about up in the bedroom, at the foot of the bed. Like the fucking blanket chest it is.

Which leaves the sofa. Maybe just throw some plastic over it and work *around* the fucker. But when you get a room this close to empty you want it fucking *empty*, so he decides to wrestle the cocksucker out into the hall. It's so wide he has to slip the pins and take off the door between the hall and the living room, and as it is the son of a bitch makes it with about that much to spare. He wedges it catty-corner, which blocks the front door, but at least you can squeeze past to get upstairs. Good. He brings the floor lamp in and lifts it over into the triangular space behind the sofa. Makes a cozy little nook.

"So what do you think, bro?" he says to Rathbone. "C'mere." Rathbone pads over, toenails clicking on the bare floorboards. "Our new headquarters—okay, bud?" He pats a sofa cushion; Rathbone climbs up, settles and sighs, chin on the cushion but eyes open. Willis goes back into the living room: dead empty. Okay. Ready to rock and roll.

He buckles on his toolbelt, picks up the decking hammer and, standing in the middle of the empty room, takes a two-handed swing at the ceiling like fucking Thor, the heavy head plowing claws-first into sheetrock.

Except it doesn't feel satisfying. And there's just a pissy little foot-long gash the width of the hammerhead.

He pokes the claws into the gash and rips, which is supposed to make a heroic expanse of ceiling buckle and come thundering down; it only busts out a little piece the size of a saucer. This is *not fucking working*. He grabs the stepladder and climbs up to tear at the gash with his hands: just a few more dipshit pieces. He gets down off the stepladder and tries the hammer again. Maybe if he can smash across in a straight line, *perforate* the son of a bitch, he can pull down a huge fucking section. What it is, he really doesn't know how to do this. And meanwhile all the dirt and mouseshit from up under the ceiling is falling into his face and he's coughing like a fucking miner—and can't you *die* of some virus that's carried in dried mouseshit?

So he goes looking for the fucking dust masks he bought last year and used *one* of and put the rest someplace, but he can't *find* the cock-suckers. He thrusts the hammer back into the loop of his toolbelt, stomps upstairs, paws through the laundry bag to find a dirty t-shirt, and brings it back down to the living room. He drapes it over his nose and mouth so he looks like a fucking harem girl, ties the son of a bitch around back of his neck by the fucking sleeves—which of course fogs his fucking glasses because he's sweating like a pig because he's fucking out of shape.

He rips the t-shirt off his face, yanks the hammer out of his toolbelt, and throws it overhand at the window, which knocks the window screen out onto the grass which brings the sash crashing down.

Then he picks up the stepladder and heaves *that* at the fucking window: top end first, shattering glass, splintering sash. It smashes through in slow detail, like a Japanese wave.

The noise brings Rathbone into the living room, wagging his tail to placate Willis, who races into the kitchen and out the screen door, afraid that next he'll damage his dog. He throws himself down and starts tearing up grass and earth with his fists—hoping to God Rathbone won't jump through the smashed window thinking it's a game—jamming his face into the ground, biting at grass and earth. The feel of grainy dirt in his mouth makes him stop, finally; either that or something has simply run its course. He lies there on his stomach, spent, panting, his heart feeling like something in there's hitting him.

When he gets to his feet again, his lower lip is smarting and he's got a headache above his right eye, drilling into a single spot the size of a .22 hole—the classic warning sign of a stroke, isn't it? This could be the ballgame right here. He stumbles back inside, kneels on the kitchen floor and calls Rathbone, who cowers away, though still wagging his tail. This starts Willis weeping, and he lets himself collapse onto his side. Which seems to reassure Rathbone, who comes clicking over, sniffs, and lets Willis reach up and pat his head. Willis tries to get him in a bear hug, but the dog struggles and slithers away, and Willis starts blubbering all this shit, how sorry he is, how he'd never hurt him, so forth and so on. Thinking *Hey, this time you really* have *fucking snapped. Congratulations.*

He gets up and goes to look in the bathroom mirror. Yeah, nice job. Scraped the shit out of his chin and lower lip, dirt in between his teeth. Lucky he didn't *break* a fucking tooth. He washes his face gingerly and presses a towel on to dry it. Brushes his teeth and goes back into the living room. Nice, really nice. What's truly sickening, that was the original sash, nine-over-six, old glass with flaws that looked like floaters in your eyes. Absolutely smashed to shit. He thinks back to the moment he did this, and wonders if, contrary to the usual rule, there isn't a way you could go back and change it. This isn't one of those events in time where endless chains of other shit depend on it; it was just minutes ago, and nobody even saw it happen. Truly there's no reason this couldn't be wound back and then allowed to go forward again.

Outside, he finds the hammer in the grass, sticks it back in his toolbelt, and carries the stepladder (undamaged) back to the woodshed. The hammer he's going to need. Out by the barn he's got a pile of scrap lumber he tore out of the house; one of those old pieces of particleboard should do the trick. Except just now he doesn't trust himself with the circular saw. So what the fuck: why not just put plastic? The true North Country look. He lays out two black garbage bags, joins them with duct tape, gets his staple gun—one thing, he's fucking equipped—and staples the plastic to the outside of the window frame. Then he nails scrap one-by-twos over where he's stapled so the shit won't rip away in the first stiff wind. He steps back: pretty decent-looking job.

He wrenches apart the pieces of wrecked window sash and busts them up for kindling. He puts what broken glass he can find inside folded newspaper inside more folded newspaper and dumps it in the garbage, along with the few fragments of sheetrock he clawed down; then he sweeps up the dirt and mouseshit. Rathbone's lying on the kitchen floor watching him. He must like that cool linoleum on his belly. Willis whistles, and he raises his head.

"C'mon, Big. Go for a walk?"

They take the path that leads down into the woods. A road to the lower pastures when this used to be a farm. Rathbone finds a stick, head-fakes Willis with it, jumps back. Willis lunges a couple of times. If his heart's not even in *this*, what's he doing with a family? Rathbone fakes with his stick again. "Sorry, Big," Willis says. "I just feel so shitty."

In addition to whatever else, he's starting to worry about what could happen at that campground. First he can't wait to get rid of them, now he's imagining serial killers and buggering, throat-slitting prison escapees. (Yes yes yes, he knows fears are secret wishes. What *doesn't* he fucking know.) And he let them go—no, he didn't *let them go*, he fucking *drove them out*. Well, not exactly. But. What he'd better do, he'd better put Rathbone in the truck and get the hell down there before dark. Which is insane. But what if you ignored this premonition and something happened to them? Oh, so now he's elevated this bullshit to a premonition.

Back at the house, he hides his guitars: the Rick and the Tele behind shit in the woodshed, the J-200 under the bed, the D-18 in the cellar. CDs into drawers, boombox back behind the canning jars. Rathbone, thinking they're going back to Chesterton, where he gets cooped up all day, cringes away when Willis comes for him.

He's pouring some Eukanuba into a plastic shopping bag when it hits him that maybe he should bring the .22 just in case. That shit about serial killers *is* a little over-the-top, but don't campgrounds breed raccoons? He goes upstairs, gets down on his back and springs the bicycle lock that holds the rifle up under the bed. From the sock drawer, he takes the rolled pair of socks with the clip inside.

The gun just fits into the long duffel bag, which is excellent because he can sleep with it right by his side and Jean and the kids won't know shit; he sticks it behind the seat of the truck. So. All squared away. But wouldn't you know: just as he's pulling out of the driveway, some asshole cruises by and gives the swivel-head stare. Might as well have a fucking loudspeaker announcing that Willis of Westchester and his faithful watchdog are now vacating their weekend home and that every teenage doper in the county is now invited to come on in and rip off all his expensive shit. Though he's probably overreacting. It's a Lumina van, which always makes Willis think of Sendero Luminoso, but which is in fact a car for decent people.

9

By the time they get to Lake Edwards, Jean actually wishes the trip could have taken longer. It felt so good getting farther and farther from Preston Falls; couldn't they just go and go, the three of them, forever? The kids were a joy. They stopped at Grand Union for picnic stuff and Roger didn't whine when she told him he couldn't have some Schwarzenegger video he picked up and brought to the cart. (She did let him get a bottle of Sportif; the caffeine wouldn't kill him this once.) They stopped at a Stewart's for ice cream, and Mel took Jean's word for it that Stewart's stuff didn't have bovine growth hormone (in fact Jean has no idea) and ate a small dish of peach frozen yogurt.

And her luck's holding: they score the last available lean-to. The ranger points out the location on the big map and gives her a small map, on which he traces the route in yellow highlight pen, marking their lean-to, Aspen, with a star. The afternoon has stayed hot and the kids are eager to get in the water, so they'll probably eat well, then sleep well. And it's supposed to stay sunny, so they can hang here till late tomorrow afternoon and get their fill of swimming; she'll worry about fighting the holiday traffic when it's time to worry about it. (The Tappan Zee will be a nightmare.) Maybe she can even get them to go on a hike. And if she can keep them from napping on the drive home—car games? loud rock and roll?—they'll be ready to pop into bed right after supper and be well rested for the first day of school. Which she truly can't believe Willis wouldn't want to be home for. But let's not get into that.

She parks in the space by their lean-to and just leaves all their things locked in the Cherokee; great as it would be to come back and have their camp all set up, stuff gets stolen even in places like this. She hands Roger the map and has him find the path to the lake; really, it takes so little to make him feel proud. As he leads them down sandy switchbacks through the pine trees, she considers telling him he's the man of the family today, but that's laying it on too thick. Just let him feel good about himself, without getting him thinking about *why* he's feeling what he's feeling and so on and so on—what Willis used to call Willis's Disease. And maybe still does, to somebody.

Roger spreads their blanket on the hot white sand, and Jean waits until his back is turned to smooth out the folds and creases. Mel says she's going to go change: the first word out of her, now that Jean thinks of it, since they were at Stewart's. So something's up with her. It's all fine and good to tell yourself they're hardened to their father not being around, but the fact is.

"How come you have to go change?" Roger pulls at the neck of Mel's t-shirt; she yanks his hand off and twists away. "You have it on under there, stupid," he says. "Why don't you just take your pants off? That is so stupid."

"Roger," says Jean.

"It's not any of your *business*, Roger," says Mel, turning red. *"It's not any of your—"*

"Stop," Jean says. "Your sister's entitled to change where she wants to change, with no input from—"

"But she's *not* changing," says Roger. "She's just—"

"One more word," says Jean. "Got it? Let's *please* not have anything ruin this beautiful day, all right? All we have is today and tomorrow, and that's it for the summer. You guys are back in *school*, I'm back at *work*. . . ." Admitting, in effect, that despite all the propaganda she feeds them, school and work are a drag and a burden.

"But Mom?" Roger says. "Isn't it summer until September twenty-second?" Borderline backtalk, which he thinks he's craftily disguised as a point of information.

"So they say. See how you feel about it Tuesday morning."

Jean watches Mel walk toward the bathhouse; she's gotten so lanky you can see space between the thighs of even those loose cotton pants. Mel's being silly, but Jean goes through the same thing: once you're on the beach in a bathing suit you're on the beach in a bathing suit, but taking down your pants in public to *reveal* the bathing suit feels immodest. Well, better to have Mel be this way than the other. Roger, meanwhile, has pulled off his t-shirt and is working on his shoes and socks.

"You know, I forgot to ask," she says. "What was it like staying at the Bjorks'?" With Roger you have to make questions open-ended; if she asks *Did you have a good time?* he'll just say yes.

"Okay," he says.

God give her patience. "What did you do?"

"I don't know. Watched this video *Raiders of the Lost Ark*."

"Oh really?" Hmm. Well, probably not so bad. From what she can remember. Some little girl in Roger's class had a slumber party where they watched *The Silence of the Lambs*; even in Chesterton this was considered a bit much. "And how was that?"

Roger shrugs. "It was okay. It had Nazis."

"That's right, I forgot that part," she says. "They were after the Ark too, weren't they?" Nazis: just lovely. "I mostly remember the snakes," she says. "And the big rock. You know, that's chasing them?"

"Can I go in now?"

"Sure," she says. "Just don't get wet."

"*Ma*-om." He sounds genuinely irritated, and she guesses she can't blame him.

He walks to where the sand is hard at the water's edge, then gets down and starts doing push-ups; a woman next to him, holding her little daughter's hand, stares and steps back. Aha. Jean *thought* his arms and shoulders were getting big; how long has this been going on? He probably started at day camp, maybe something he picked up from the older boys. This must be his way of announcing it to her. So should she mention it or not? He gets up, wipes his palms on his swimming trunks and strides into the water.

Really, he's such a little striver. It's just that he's wound so terribly tight. Which is right at the top of the list of things she can never forgive Willis for. Once, when Roger was six, his friend Adam came over for a play date and she and Willis took them to Waldbaum's to pick out stuff for lunch. When they got to the chips-and-soda aisle, Roger went running to the bottles of Sportif, yelling "My dad *makes* this!" And Willis said, "I don't *make* it. I work for the *company* that makes it. As I've told you several times." You could see Roger just shrivel; little Adam (a cool customer) looked up at Willis as if he were some strange specimen of something. When the boys moved on, Jean said, "You're the one who's being a *child*." And Willis said, "Fine. In that case you can be the grownup." He took out his car keys and dangled them at her until she felt she *had* to stick out her hand. Then he walked all the way to the station, took a train into the city, spent the afternoon in his office—he *said*—and didn't call until about seven o'clock: he was shocked at himself, he must be more stressed out than he realized, would she forgive him. And she did. At the time.

She waits until Mel gets back to watch Roger, then goes in to change into her suit. Not exactly your luxo bathhouse. But places like this are part of what a child's summer ought to be: cement floor, gray-painted wood benches, cubicles with canvas curtains down to knee level. And even that smell, of other people's excrement. She's glad to be able to give them this at least. Though God knows if it leaves them with anything, really. Like no kid ever got into drugs after smelling pine trees and human shit in the summertime. She finds a vacant cubicle, draws the curtain (which leaves an inch at each side) and gets out of her clothes. Her poor legs are so white. And that line down the inside of her thigh where the seam of her jeans presses in: *that's* attractive. And of course she's forgotten to shave up top, and she hates those little curls peeking out. Oh well. Actually, this is not the world's absolute worst body. For someone who's forty and has had two kids? Except she might as well weigh three hundred pounds. In fact that might make things better: maybe Willis would think it was camp to make love to her.

The sun sparkling off the water hurts her eyes when she comes back outside. Where's Roger? Okay: Mel's out there with him, knee-deep; they're splashing each other as if the thing about Mel's bathing suit had never happened. Carol would say there was something healing about water; Jean guesses they're playing together because they don't know any other kids here.

Should she go in? The sun's getting low, and that blue, glinting water looks so cold. But Mel and Roger seem to be having a ball, and she did go through the whole thing of getting her suit on. And who knows what the weather will be tomorrow, really. She takes her clothes over to the blanket, makes sure the car keys are safe in the pocket of her jeans and that the jeans are covering up the camera. Then she walks across the hot sand to the water's edge; a cool breeze comes in off the lake and she hugs herself. Hmm, let's think about this a second. It's so typical of her: imagining she's deciding something that she's already decided.

Willis pulls into the entrance with "Fuck tha Police" blasting; not until he sees the booth up ahead does it hit him that this isn't quite the Lake

Edwards vibe. Yet to turn it off would be craven. He edges way over to the right, then cuts the wheel hard left to pull a U-ey. Poor old truck has trouble making even this wide a turn, and the passenger-side wheels crunch gravel on the other shoulder. He gets back on the state highway and goes another mile before "Fuck tha Police" is over and he can eject *Straight Outta Compton* and stick in *Back to the Barrooms*; he pulls over to the side, waits for traffic to get past, then makes another U-turn and heads back for the park. But then it strikes him that while either Merle Haggard *or* a pickup truck might be plausible, both are too much. So he pulls over yet again, takes out Merle and sticks in *Who's Gonna Fill Their Shoes*, although isn't George Jones even more of a cliché? All this bullshit so that whoever's at the booth won't think he's what he fucking *is*. And now watch: it'll end up being the one black park ranger in all of Vermont.

At the booth—hey, it *is* an old white guy—he lets 'em have maybe three seconds of George, then turns the music down and leans out his window. "Hi, how you doin'? My wife and kids should've got here, I don't know, like an hour ago? Came in a Jeep Cherokee?"

The ranger looks up at him. He's a fat old geezer with hair coming out of his ears. "You know how many cars come through here today?" Then he looks at Rathbone.

"Don't people have to register when they come here to camp?" says Willis.

"Oh, so they come to *camp*," the ranger says. "You didn't tell me that."

"Name would be Willis." Guy wants to be a prick? Fine.

"You better pull it over there." The ranger points, then goes into his hut. Booth. Whatever. Being told *you better* this or that isn't Willis's favorite thing, but he parks over on the grass, rolls his window two-thirds of the way up so Rathbone can't jump out and walks back to the booth. On the far side of the parking lot he sees blue water through the pine trees; a motorcycle-looking guy in a sleeveless denim jacket is lugging a cooler on the path to the beach.

"They're in Aspen," the ranger says. Willis thinks for half a second that this is some bizarro put-down, something to the effect that people from Westchester should be off skiing with Jack Nicholson. "That's this lean-to right here." The ranger's pointing to a plexiglassed map on the side of the booth. "You go up that road. All the way up the top of the hill. And you stay to your left where it forks."

"Aspen," says Willis.

"They go Aspen Birch Cherry Dogwood," says the ranger. "Now, your dog there stays in the campground. You come down to the lake, you leave your dog, you understand?"

"What's *your* problem?" says Willis.

"Say what?" The ranger puts a hand to his ear.

"I said what's the problem," Willis says. Pissed at himself for backing down even that much.

"*I* don't have a problem, mister. Unless you give me one."

"Fine," says Willis. "So what do I owe you?"

"Your wife paid," says the ranger. Little note of contempt here for a man who would allow his *wife* to pay? Never mind the fact that his *wife* got here an *hour* ago and therefore *had* to pay. "I'm charging you the day rate for your second vehicle there," says the ranger. "Be three dollars."

Willis gets three limp singles from his wallet and holds them out just far enough so the fat son of a bitch has to reach for them. Willis flatters himself that he's done it so subtly the poor stupid bastard doesn't even understand *why* he's now angrier than ever. This is about class, really: Willis of Westchester gets to loll, while this sad old fuck has to spend the last glorious weekend of summer in a hot uniform. But hey, who is Willis to fly in the face of Providence?

The ranger produces a card with a hole in the top the size of a quarter and a mingy little white plastic bag with a stylized green pine tree. By this time, four cars are lined up at the booth, engines running.

"You hang this on your rearview mirror." He hands Willis the card. "This here is for your garbage." The bag. "Anything you carry into the park, you carry it out again, you understand? You're not out of the campsite by eleven a.m., you pay another day irregardless."

"Noted." Willis snottily enunciates the *t* and the *d*. *Irregardless:* love it.

"You're to drive directly to the campsite."

One of the lined-up cars honks.

The ranger looks over his shoulder and gives them what he must imagine is a Clint Eastwood stony stare—poor bastard has a stomach on him that comes out to here—and while his head's turned, Willis flips him the bird, pumping once, twice, three times.

"Are we finished, then?" Willis says.

The ranger turns the stare on him. "Don't forget it, your dog stays in camp at all times."

"Yeah, I think we've covered that," says Willis. But the ranger's already motioning to the first car in line.

The campground is half a mile up a winding blacktop road; Willis spots the Cherokee parked by the last lean-to, which looks just like all the others, Birch and Cherry and Dogwood and whatever the fuck E would be. Eucalyptus? Depressing beyond belief: plywood walls painted forest green because this is a fucking forest, *that* whole trip. The lean-tos are strung along this ridge above the lake. You'd have a better view looking off if they'd thin out some of these pine trees or whatever they technically are—F must be Fir—but God forbid. He pulls in beside the Cherokee; Rathbone's already dancing back and forth on the seat. "Who's here, boy? Go *get* 'em." By loosing Rathbone first he's preparing them for who's bringing up the rear. *Rathbone! What the*—and then it dawns on them. And the little faces light up.

He opens the door and Rathbone scrambles over his legs and begins madly sniffing the ground. "Where's your friends?" says Willis, getting out of the truck. "Go get your friends." The lean-to is empty except for a Sportif bottle the ecopolice must have missed. Weird to see that logo. Okay, so what must've happened, they must've walked down to the lake and left their shit locked in the car. About the millionth reason not to go camping: having to worry all the time about your shit getting ripped off. As he's sure he'll find occasion to point out, since he doesn't seem able to keep his fucking mouth shut.

"Bone-face," says Willis. "Which way did they go?" Rathbone wags his tail harder. "Lassie! Go find Timmy!" Ridiculing his dog for being a dog.

Between Aspen and Beech, a rocky, dusty path leads steeply down. Canny woodsman that he is, Willis reasons that if you keep going down-hill you'll eventually hit the lake, and after a couple of switchbacks he spots blue water below, sparkling through the trees. And then he re-members: no dogs. Shit. He stops, whistles again, turns around and starts back up the path. Rathbone looks at him and cocks his head. "Yeah?" says Willis. "Well, fuck you too." Then he says, "Sorry, buddy. C'm'ere." He squats, and Rathbone approaches; Willis roughs up his ears with both hands and rubs his chin across the top of the dog's head. As they near the lean-to again, Rathbone in his whatever-is-is-right mode, capering and sniffing among the pine needles, it occurs to Willis that E must be Elm. Not fucking Eucalyptus. This is why all the George Jones tapes in the world just aren't going to do it.

So he's got a problem. He can either (*a*) sit here with his thumb up his ass and wait God knows *how* long for them to come back; or (*b*) walk down to the beach and leave Rathbone tied up here, where he'll bark and yap and yowl the whole time and probably get them kicked out of this shithole. So he'll have to put Rathbone in the fucking truck, drive back down to the parking lot by the beach, leave the dog in the truck while he tries to find Jean, then beat it back up here before anybody can bust his chops.

He gets Rathbone's leash back on him with a low-down trick—offers a stick, then grabs his collar—drags him into the truck and sets off down the road the way he came. When he gets in sight of the booth again, he peels off into the parking lot and takes a space as close to the beach as he can find. He rolls the windows up, leaving the usual gap, and says, "Stay. I'll be right back, okay?" Rathbone yips and whines as Willis walks away.

Before he reaches the head of the path he hears someone yelling "Hey, you!" Which he ignores because it can't be happening.

"You! Hey! You get back over here!"

Now what the *fuck*? Willis turns and glares. Sure enough, it's that same asshole ranger, bearing down on him in this fucked-up gimpy gait that's partly a jog-trot and partly a stride, belly swaying from side to side. Willis waits for him to get closer—not deigning to raise *his* voice—so he can say *Are you talking to me?* Not De Niro style; more your frightfully-sorry-old-man-but-do-we-know-one-another tone. Except isn't that going to sound rehearsed, given that the son of a bitch is yelling right *at* him?

"You were told not to bring that dog to the lake area!" The ranger's sweating and panting. A mouth-breather, literally.

"The dog," says Willis, "is in the truck. The dog," he says, "cannot get *out* of the truck."

"Now, what did I say? I said you were to proceed with your dog to the campsite. Isn't that what I told you? You read that sign there?" The ranger jabs a finger at a NO PETS sign by the head of the path. This character must have been in the military. Fucking Korean War.

"Yes, I can read, thank you. I am now going down to the beach," he says, "to let my family know that I am here. I will be back. Good? Good." He turns and starts along the path.

"You get back here, mister. You hear me talking to you?"

Willis stops, turns again and stares at this cartoon man with vast sweat stains darkening the underarms of his uniform. Some flunky who takes tickets. Is Willis not a patron, whose three-dollar admission pays this fellow's salary? And is not the spirit of the NO PETS rule—i.e., that grass and sand not be shat upon—being complied with? And in fact, since the dog is in the truck, is not the fucking *letter* of the NO PETS rule being complied with?

"You know what?" says Willis. "Why don't you go fuck yourself, okay?"

"You're out of here, my friend." The ranger's face has gone aneurysm red. "You're to leave the park immediately. And you don't come back, you understand? You *don't* leave the park immediately, I call the sheriff's deputy and he'll *see* to it you leave. You think I'm foolin' now?"

"Yeah, why don't you call him, man? I'd like to see you fucking explain to a fucking deputy sheriff why it is I can't keep a fucking *dog* in a fucking *truck* while I walk a hundred fucking *yards* to the fucking *beach*."

"You got it, mister," says the ranger. "*I'm* done foolin' with you. You'll move when *he* says to. He don't fool around." And the son of a bitch starts gimping back to his booth. Willis turns and starts along the white-graveled path, bordered by these stupid foot-high logs painted a redundant brown. Hopes the son of a bitch *does* call a cop: somebody needs to set this motherfucker straight.

He passes grills and picnic tables, fat laughing fathers in baseball caps and dumpy teenage girls groping empty air for badly thrown Frisbees. A spastic in a motorized wheelchair, putting Willis to shame. Smells of woodsmoke, pine trees, hot dogs roasting. A radio somewhere (which shouldn't be allowed) playing "Jimmy Mack" by Martha and the Vandellas. A "mack," we now know, is a pimp. In the maple trees, more hints of cautionary red. Bathers crowding the sand: a scrawny old bozo with a white goatee, a teenage thug with shaved head and iridescent sunglasses, a mom with a wide ass and oatmeal thighs holding her little girl by the hand—and there's Jean, her back to him, toweling herself off, wet hair hanging. She's looking out at the glinting water, and he sees how the insides of her thighs do that nice thing at the top where they bulge out a little and then go back in. Still so slender after two children. *His* children. There's something wrong with him.

Now, what the fuck is that—a lucid moment?

He calls her name. Willis hates yoohooing, but to sneak up close and then suddenly start talking normally will scare the shit out of her, which'll piss her off good. Not that she won't be pissed anyway. After he yells it out enough times for the whole fucking beach to know *Jee-yeen's* husband is here, she turns around. He could swear he sees a flicker of glad smile before she remembers what the deal is.

"What are you *doing* here?" she says. Then she clamps a hand to her mouth. "Oh my God." She takes the hand away. "Did something happen?"

"No. No-no-no, nothing. I just sort of had a change of heart."

"Oh," she says. "Well, good for you. I guess." She drapes the towel around her shoulders.

"I missed you guys." Not precisely true, but it would be insulting on feminist grounds to say he suddenly got afraid for them. Or maybe it *is* true, and he's such a head case that his missing them can only take the form of imagining them buggered and murdered. Just a boy and his mind.

"You missed us," she says, "so you followed us here. And what's your plan now?"

"Well, I guess I'd hoped to stay and camp out with you guys." A little hat-in-hand shit seems called for just here. "I sort of thought we should try to leave things on a better note, you know? Where are the kids?"

"Over there," she says, not pointing. "What about the dog? You just left him at the house?"

"Of course not," he says. "He's out in the truck—in fact, I should get back to him. I just wanted to let you know I was here."

"And what did you plan to sleep in? Did you bring blankets for yourself?"

"Shit," he says. "I knew there was *some*thing."

Silence.

"Well," she says. "I suppose you could use this." She nods toward the old blanket spread out on the sand. "Did you remember to bring any *food* for the dog?" Translation: *My darling, I'm so glad you've come.* Though he guesses he should admire her for not snapping to it. They've *done* reconciliation-and-relapse.

Mel comes stalking over, in what he could swear is a different bathing suit from the one this morning. Right, because wasn't she sunning with the top off? This is a metallic-blue one-piece with a gold boomerang. So he is *not* a totally head-up-his-ass father.

"Mother, I *told* Roger, and he *still* won't come. Hi, Daddy. I knew you'd be here."

"You *did*?" he says. "That's more than *I* knew."

She shrugs. This is her more-mystic-than-thou mode.

"I'll go deal," Jean says to Mel. "I want you to get dried off and changed, okay?" Mel picks up a towel and starts scrubbing it at her hair; Willis notices what might be the beginnings of breasts trembling in rhythm. He looks away, and sees a man in gray uniform and Smokey hat heading their way through the bathing suits. Gun in a holster.

"Jesus, *he* got here in a hurry," he says. "Good, I'm glad."

"Who?" Jean turns around, sees the cop, looks at Willis. "What's *this* about?"

"Actually nothing, really," he says. "Guy at the gate was being an asshole. I guess he's here to adjudicate."

"Would you watch your language, please?" Jean says, and looks at Mel, who's making a turban of her towel.

"Right," says Willis. "She's never heard the word *adjudicate* before."

Melanie blushes down to her collarbone.

Jean says, "Sometimes your humor—"

"Excuse me, folks," says the cop. Sheriff, deputy, whatever he is. Marine-looking guy about Willis's age, one of your not-an-ounce-of-fat-on-him cops. "Are you the gentleman owns the dog?"

"Yep," says Willis. "I sure am." He says to Jean, "I better get going. You guys want to meet me back at camp? Or I could drive us all up in a few minutes."

"I'm sorry, sir," the cop says. Embroidered patch on his sleeve says SHERIFFS DEPT: no apostrophe, no period. "I've been requested to escort you out of the park."

Jean and Mel both look at Willis.

"Whoa, wait a minute. Let me explain what happened." He pauses before launching in.

"You can explain on the way to your vehicle, sir. Your family can join you outside the main gate. But you need to leave right now, sir." He comes a step closer to Willis and nods toward the path.

"This is unreal," says Willis. "You're kicking *them* out too? For what? They weren't even *there*."

"What is going on, please?" Jean says.

"I'm sorry, ma'am." The cop gives her a glance, then turns his eyes back on Willis. "There was an altercation with a park personnel which led to abusive language being used by this gentleman."

"*You're* a smooth son of a bitch," says Willis.

The cop doesn't move, but he's clearly gone to a higher state of alert: his eyes move from side to side, in case this character has buddies. "It's necessary for him to leave the park immediately."

"Unbe*liev*able," says Willis. "I don't have the right to explain what the hell this so-called altercation was even *about*? I left my dog in the—"

"You need to leave, sir." The cop moves half a step closer. "We don't want any trouble."

"Hey, this guy is definitely a pro," Willis says to Jean. "See how he keeps dialing it up? We're now into the veiled threats."

"Sweetheart," Jean says to Mel, "go in and change into your clothes right now, please?" When Mel bends to get her clothes from the blanket, the cop's eyes go to her, then quick back to Willis.

"As of right now, sir," says the cop, "you are not under arrest."

"Doug," Jean says. "Please don't push this."

God, and there's Roger, staring at the cop's gun. God knows how long *he's* been drinking in the scene.

"Look," Willis says to the cop. "She and the kids have nothing to do with this, okay? They're all set up at their campsite and everything. I mean, fine, if you're going to kick *me* out of here, you know, *fine*. But would you let them have their thing?"

"That would be up to them. You can talk it over outside the gate, sir. Now let's move it."

It strikes Willis that either he has to let himself be marched out of here in disgrace, which is the sensible thing, or he can cross over into who the fuck knows what. He looks around. Everybody on the beach is watching; balls and Frisbees have stopped sailing, and the sun is glinting absolute white off the blue water. In the silence that's fallen, a blue jay screams. Willis looks back at the cop, who's moved in close enough to put hands on him.

"Tell you *one* thing," Willis says. "I don't like your fucking tone."

Jean says, "Oh my God."

The cop nods. "I'm placing you under arrest, sir. Charge is disorderly conduct. You have the right to remain silent, right to be represented by an attorney, and anything be used in evidence against you. Now. You don't come along quietly at this point, it's going to be necessary to place you in handcuffs. Which you'll also be charged with resisting arrest."

Willis feels suddenly weary. "Shit, do what you have to do," he says. "This is getting away from me."

He sees the cop's eyes narrow. A crazy man, about to go for my gun? Willis could almost smile at him in pity. This is that feeling you always hear about: the clarity you attain by submission. He's been fighting it all this long day, and it's the very thing he needed.

"Sir? I'm asking you very politely to come along. Now, are we doing this the easy way or not?" The cop hasn't understood; he's still stuck back in the thing they were playing out before. "I don't think you want to do anything foolish with your family here," he says. "And we sure don't want anybody getting hurt."

Willis sees the creases around the man's eyes, and the places he missed shaving: this sheriff's deputy, too, is a weary soul.

Jean says, "Officer, is there any way you could—not do this?"

"Not at this point, ma'am. I'm sorry."

"Oh *God*," she says. "We don't even know a lawyer up here. Where are you taking him?"

"County lockup. Basement of the courthouse."

"Listen, Calvin Castleman knows a lawyer," Willis says to Jean. "If you could get hold of Calvin."

"Great. *He* must be a—"

"But wait. The thing is, Calvin had his phone taken out."

"Well, then I can't call him, can I?"

"Let's get moving," says the sheriff's guy. "You're allowed a phone call at the lockup. You can work it all out then."

"Can I just give her the keys?" says Willis. "My dog is—"

"Don't go in your pocket, sir," says the cop. "Keep your hands where I can see them." And, at last, he touches the back of Willis's arm.

"Oh fuck," says Willis. "Listen, where will you be later?"

"Taking care of my children," she says.

"Right," he says. "Okay. Got it." He wrenches his arm free of the cop's hand. "Come on, come on. If we're really doing this, let's do the whole fucking thing." He turns around, slowly, and slowly walks toward the lifeguard chair. He counts: eleven steps. If he gets shot in the back before he makes it there, fine. He puts his hands on a chalky white two-by-four. Spreads his legs, bows his head.

10

How could he have asked her to do this? Drive all the way back to
Preston Falls, deal with the wood man, whom she's never spoken two
words to, and then turn around and make the endless drive down to
Chesterton? But what was she supposed to do? Just let him sit in jail?
Which she actually should have done. *Would* have done, if the kids
weren't with her. Or likes to think she would have done. So as Mel and
Roger wait with Rathbone in the Cherokee, she finds herself knocking
on the door of this trailer and asking this filthy man for the name and
number of the lawyer who'd kept him out of prison.

The tv's blaring behind him in the dark, and he doesn't even ask her
to come in. Not that she'd dream of it. She stands there on the cinderblock doorstep while he goes looking. Finally he comes back with a surprisingly white business card she's loath to take from his grimy hand.
Philip Reed, Attorney at Law. She can just imagine.

Well, since they're here, why not go on to the house to make the call.
And while she's doing that, might as well let Rathbone out to stretch his
legs and pee; should give him some water too. When they pull in, Roger
says he has to go to the bathroom, and then Mel gets out too and sits on
the hood of the Cherokee, legs in full lotus. Jean goes into the kitchen
(Willis left the door unlocked), calls the number, gets a machine and
babbles a message, leaving the number in Chesterton and then the one
here as well—just on the off chance he should call back in the next
minute or two. Though actually, since they *are* here, doesn't it make
sense to feed the kids now rather than stop at some awful place on the
road? There's food in the cooler that's just going to go to waste, plus left-
overs from yesterday in the fridge. (*Yesterday?* Amazing.) They could be
on their way in an hour. Which would still get them home, what, probably midnight, a little after.

She goes out to the Cherokee, tells Mel the plan (zero response) and brings the cooler inside. She hears Roger flush, but no faucet running afterwards. When he opens the bathroom door, she asks if he washed his hands. "Yes," he says.

She starts taking stuff out of the cooler. Roger wanders into the dining room, probably headed upstairs, then she hears him yell, "Hey, Mom? What happened in here?"

"What?" she calls. He doesn't answer.

She goes in and finds the dining room crammed with furniture from the living room and the living room completely bare. There's plastic over one of the living room windows and a ragged hole in one part of the ugly old ceiling. He's taking out the windows? To paint them? The door to the front hall is leaning against the wall, the sofa's wedged in there diagonally and books are piled everywhere. "I guess your father started work," she says.

"Can you break handcuffs if you're strong enough?" says Roger.

"You'd have to be pretty strong. If you were Superman, I guess."

"I mean *real*."

"No," she says. "Somebody has to unlock them."

"Do they hurt?"

"I wouldn't know. I don't imagine they're too comfortable. Did it bother you, seeing that happen to Daddy?"

"No," he says.

"Well, it bothered me. And it made me angry."

Roger says nothing.

"I was angry at the policeman for not listening to Daddy," she says. "*And* I was angry at Daddy, for not staying out of trouble."

No go. Nothing.

"What are you thinking?" she says.

"About a frog."

"What? *What* about a frog?"

"They make you mad when you can't catch them," he says.

Jean tries to think how this connects up. The idea of getting mad, maybe. "*God* you're impervious," she says. Should she be *saying* that? Well, most likely he doesn't know what it means. "But sometimes, when something upsetting happens, it's best to *let* yourself get upset, you know?"

"Can I turn on Daddy's computer?" he says.

"To do what?"

"Play Mortal Kombat," he says.

Well, maybe he'll process what she said on his own. "Sure, go ahead," she says. "We'll be eating in about ten minutes."

Jean goes back into the kitchen and looks out the window: the first stars have appeared. She finds herself saying *Star light, star bright* (she *must* be desperate) but can't honestly decide which one is the actual first star she sees tonight. Mel's still sitting out there on the Cherokee. Must be getting chilly. But maybe the engine's warm under her. Mel's already talked about what she's feeling: she's feeling that the cop was a pig. And she's furious at Jean for suggesting that Willis might also have been at fault. Jean gets out two skillets—one for the hot dogs, one for Mel's vegetables—and the double boiler for the leftover chicken and stuff. Mel will ask why she has to eat couscous that was in with chicken. Easy one: she *doesn't* have to.

The phone rings just as the hot dogs' skins are starting to split; Jean rolls them over with the fork, turns off the burner and gets the phone in the middle of the third ring, before the machine can pick up. It's the lawyer, Philip Reed, who actually sounds civilized. He's calling from California and will be flying in to Burlington late tomorrow night. He'll be glad to help out—based on what she's telling him, it's completely outrageous—and he'll see Willis first thing Tuesday morning. No, unfortunately, because of the holiday, that's the soonest anything could be done anyway. But what he *will* do, as soon as. he gets off the phone, is send Willis a fax introducing himself and letting him know help is on the way. Sure, they've got a fax in the hoosegow—all the modern conveniences. Would she like the fax number? Got a pen handy? And how is *she* bearing up? Not to worry, this is all going to work out.

And again the kids surprise her. Roger comes downstairs the first time she calls him; Mel says the sautéed vegetables are yummy—they're not, so she must be trying to make up for sulking—and eats the couscous without remark. *And* thanks Jean for making dinner. Roger says, "Yeah, thanks, Mom," and pretends to vomit. These are good kids. You just have to know how to read Roger.

She feels like leaving the dishes for Willis—he'll get back here sooner or later—but she doesn't want to see herself as being that small a person. Though she does decide to let them dry by themselves in the dish drainer, just so he'll see them and know she washed up. She takes Philip Reed's card, on which she's jotted the fax number, and goes up to

Willis's study, which used to be the walk-in hall closet. She sits at his computer (Roger neglected to turn it off), clicks out of Mortal Kombat and into Word:

> *Willis,*
>
> *Your friend's lawyer says he will be there on Tuesday morning to handle things. (He says he's faxing you, so maybe you've already heard from him. Anyway his name is Philip Reed.) Apparently nothing can be done until Tuesday (bail, etc.) because of the holiday. The children and I, and the dog, are driving back to Chesterton tonight (Sunday). I really don't know what to say, except that I would have never imagined you allowing a thing like this to happen. Whenever this is over, I would appreciate you not suddenly showing up in Chesterton, if that was your plan. As of now I really don't want any communication with you, though we will have to talk.*
>
> *Jean*

She prints the thing and feeds the printout into his fax machine. It's already creeping through when she realizes this last part is a fairly personal thing to be sending for everybody at the jail to read. But guess what: too bad. Now *he* can be humiliated, though it's not her actual intention.

At least when Carol gets here Jean won't have to try to hold all this together by herself. Not that she couldn't. Not that she *doesn't*. Let's see: it's Sunday. Carol was planning to arrive Tuesday, so she must be somewhere in the Midwest. Iowa, maybe. Nebraska. Jean pictures her coming to the rescue in her sporty little red truck, shooting along down a two-lane blacktop alley between green rows of tall corn. Though around Preston Falls the corn's already being harvested. And put away in silos. With tractors. Jean is so sick of country this and country that.

When she comes downstairs, Rathbone's lying on the couch in the hall. Mel's sitting, full lotus, in the middle of the empty living room. Roger's at the kitchen table, looking at the old *Weekly World News* Willis thought was so hilarious, with this badly faked picture of Hitler with lots of wrinkles; at age one hundred and something, he'd come out of hiding in Argentina to help Saddam Hussein. Willis's riff about this is that it's great because the story's written absolutely straightforwardly, like a piece in the *Times*. God, a respite from Willis's riffs about things: there's that to be thankful for. Up and at 'em, she tells the kids, then whistles for Rathbone and puts his leash on him. She turns off the lights, clicks the lock on the kitchen door and closes it behind them.

As they go jouncing down Ragged Hill Road, she thinks, *What if this is the last time?* Which it could very possibly be, considering. Okay, well, what if. Before she even gets to the stop sign, she's gone through the whole thing: the divorce; the settlement leaving her the kids and the house in Chesterton and him the place in Preston Falls; Willis quitting work and moving up here and falling apart like his father and not being able to make his support payments; her and the kids ending up in an apartment, though maybe still in Chesterton so at least they won't have to change schools. Above one of the vacant stores on Main Street, maybe. Would that be depressing enough?

TWO

1

In his dream, they've widened the Tappan Zee—a dozen westbound lanes—but Willis still can't move for all the traffic. Then he finds a special exit ramp no one else seems to know about, and he's suddenly on a dirt road, passing weathered gray farmhouses with dingy white chickens pecking in the dooryards. This place, he understands, is Rockland. But now he's clipping by so fast he doesn't dare look away from the road, which begins climbing steeply uphill; off in the distance he sees higher hills and a gaudy blue-gold-orangey Maxfield Parrish sky. As the truck melts away beneath him he shouts, "Oh *yes*, God!" and tries to soar, but it must be too soon and he wakes up.

He's in jail. Lying on a bench welded together out of steel laths, bolted to a cinderblock wall. His feet are cold because he's taken off his boots to use as a pillow. At the rear of the cell, a seatless toilet bowl and a sink, with a piece of polished metal screwed into the wall for a mirror; the front of the cell is bars. He looks up at the caged lightbulb they never turn off; it could be any time, any day. He closes his eyes and regards a throbbing black spot burned into the general redness. But let's not go back to sleep again. He's been here overnight and then all of Monday. He knows this because he's had three meals: an Egg McMuffin and coffee (breakfast), a McDonald's hamburger, small fries and coffee (lunch), and a drumstick, mashed potatoes and coffee from Kentucky Fried (dinner). So it must be either Monday night or early Tuesday morning. He's been handed two faxes: one from a lawyer, saying he'd be here Tuesday morning, the other from Jean, telling him the lawyer would be in touch. And not to come to Chesterton. Weird that a prisoner could receive a fax. And a cop came in with the news that a gun had been found in his truck and a weapons charge would be filed. Is it actually against the law to have a gun in your truck? Shit, you always see these people with gun racks. Maybe it's against the law only if you're not really that kind of person.

So far he's done a good job of keeping himself together. He's tried remembering famous poems: "Stopping by Woods" was too easy and "Prufrock" too hard; he couldn't get past the patient etherized upon the table. The half-something retreats of oyster shells. He's figured out the changes to "Gee, Baby, Ain't I Good to You" if you're in G, though he can't be dead certain until he gets an actual guitar in his hands. He's named all forty-eight real states, picturing a map in his head and counting on his fingers. He got down and did push-ups. Three, actually, which left him sweating and gasping, his chest pounding. Still, this could be a beginning.

Movies have turned out to be the best thing. Better than books, he's ashamed to say; *Dombey*, at least, should be fresh, but he can't remember the sequence after the mother dies and they get the wet nurse—which is what, the first chapter? He's able to keep *The Godfather* going for a good long time. First the guy saying "I believe in America" and you find out he wants these guys murdered that raped his daughter and Brando does that thing where he brushes up at his jawline with the backs of his fingers and says, "That I cannot do." He's also holding a cat. Then something like "But let's be frank. You never wanted my friendship. And you were afraid to be in my debt."

He tries *The Wizard of Oz*, but it gets vague in the middle. *The Man Who Came to Dinner,* same problem. Ten minutes, Mr. Whiteside!

But good old *North by Northwest*: he can keep that one together, sort of. Someplace around where Cary Grant rear-ends the car and the cop car rear-ends Cary Grant's car or however it goes and the black Cadillac with the bad guys makes a U-turn and vanishes, he falls asleep again.

Somebody says "Hey" and he wakes up. Another of these cops or guards or sheriffs. "Your lawyer's here."

Willis gets his feet onto the floor and sits up, his forearms on his thighs. His head hurts and wants to loll.

Somebody else says, "Doug Willis? Philip Reed," and sticks a hand through the bars. Willis should get up and shake his hand, but first he's got to close his eyes again. "Benny?" says the lawyer. "I need some privacy to confer with my client. You want to check up my ass for contraband?"

"You want to bite this?" Willis hears footsteps going away.

"So what happened to *you*, man? Let me guess—you fell down."

Willis opens his eyes. Philip Reed has this long gray hair pulled back in a ponytail. Corduroy jacket, blue oxford shirt bulging out above his belt, top button undone, yellow striped tie loosened. Sharp nose coming at you out of a puffy red face with bushy white sideburns. Foxy, the whole effect of him.

"What time is it?" says Willis.

"Eight o'clock. Five of. I thought we better schmooze a little before they want you upstairs. Here." He opens a Dunkin' Donuts bag Willis hadn't noticed and hands a coffee cup through the bars. "Cream and sugar?"

"Just cream." Willis gets up and takes the cup, still hot, and two little cream things. "Thank you. This is very civilized."

"Don't worry, you'll get the bill. I also brought you a razor, which you have to promise not to cut your throat with." He opens his briefcase and hands Willis a blue plastic razor, a can of Colgate regular and two paper towels patterned with geese.

"You came prepared," says Willis. "He said inanely."

"This actually is more for you than for the judge," says Reed. "He's got to cut you loose no matter what the fuck you look like. This totally bullshit gun charge, which he'll throw out immediately, and all he's got left is just some little Mickey Mouse situation where you had words with somebody. The reason I want you shaved, you're going to walk in there feeling like you're a little more glued together, which in turn is going to give a boost to your demeanor, *which* in turn could save you a couple of bucks on your fine."

"Right," says Willis.

"Okay, now the other thing—and you're going to think this is weird, but trust me. After you get shaved we're going to fix your face a little. Anytime there's a question of resisting arrest, I bring along a thing of Cover Girl. The lip I don't know, but the chin definitely."

"What are you talking about?" says Willis.

"You look at yourself?" Willis brings the razor and stuff over to the sink and looks in the metal mirror: a strawberry on his chin and jaw, scabby scrapes on his swollen lower lip and at the corner of his mouth. "Now, the reason we're doing this—okay?—is we don't want you looking like some hardened criminal who had to be clubbed into submission.

Your goal is to get out of here with like a fifty-dollar fine for disturbing the peace or some bullshit and just put the whole episode behind you, am I right? Sad to say, but the attitude upstairs is going to be that if the boys beat the shit out of you, you probably—"

"No no no, this happened before."

"Before what?"

"Before I even went down there. I was, you know, up on a stepladder, working around the house, and I just sort of lost my balance." Willis turns on the faucet; there's only cold.

"You fell off a stepladder and landed on your face," says Reed.

"Yeah, okay. Hey, anything's possible."

"What can I tell you?" Willis lathers his face. What *can* he tell him? He makes the first swath, a boulevard down the right cheek.

"*Ho* boy. Well, whatever, we still cover up the damage as best we can. Otherwise it just becomes confusing. I *am* correct in assuming that you want to do this the easy way and get on with your life?"

"What are my options?" He's working on the patch between the sideburn and the corner of the jaw.

"What are your options," says Reed. "Okay. Option one: total war. You did nothing *wrong*, you're a family man on your little family *outing*, solid *citizen*, no criminal *record*—right? Any record at all?"

"Nope."

"No criminal *record*, you're harassed for no *reason*, first by an asshole park ranger and then by an asshole sheriff's *deputy*, who refused to listen to your side of the *story*—and so forth and so on."

"Which is what happened," says Willis. He's on the tricky shit now, throat and under the chin.

"Okay, whatever. Anyhow. You know that saying *Pay the two dollars*? Now, if you strongly feel you want to pursue this, we'll go upstairs, enter a plea of not guilty, we'll get a date, and we'll make the best case we can. *With* the stipulation that I don't think it's probably the wisest use of your time and money."

Willis goes lightly around the chin, trying not to slice scabs. "No, fuck it. Forget it. I just want it over."

"Good man," says Reed. "We'll make a lawyer out of you yet. Okay, dry off and come over here."

Willis goes over to him and stands at the bars, gripping them the way they do in old movies, or old editorial cartoons about Nixon and shit. He's wanted to do this the whole time he's been here, but didn't want to be seen doing it: it's such a *jail* thing, like putting X's on the calendar. Sure enough, the sons of bitches are cold. Philip Reed takes a compact out of his briefcase, flips up the lid, and tells Willis to turn his head. Willis closes his eyes and feels a finger smoothing creamy stuff on his chin, around his lips. First time his face has been touched in however long.

The courtroom upstairs has rows of slatted wood folding chairs facing a gray metal desk on a plywood podium. A limp, gold-fringed American flag on a pole at one side and what must be the state flag at the other. Behind the desk, a portly old character actor in a black robe: white hair, bald dome, and those black-rimmed glasses that made people look intelligent back about the time Willis's mother used to get the *Saturday Review*. He could be the park ranger's brother who went to college. Willis follows Philip Reed to the front row of chairs. Over to their left sit the deputy who arrested him and a pudgy young guy in a too-tight suit who turns out to be some assistant under-assistant prosecutor.

The judge looks at Reed, then at Willis, then turns to the state man. "Okay, so what have we got here?"

The prosecutor stands up. "This is Douglas Willis, Your Honor. His driver's license says Preston Falls, but his vehicle has a commuter parking sticker from the Town of Chesterton, New York, and on his own information he works in New York City. He's charged with disorderly conduct, resisting arrest and criminal possession of a firearm."

The judge is looking at a sheet of paper. "Douglas Willis," he says, then looks up. "That's you?"

Willis nods.

"How do you plead?" So this is officially going on? Like, court is in session?

Philip Reed says, "If I may?"

"Yeah, go ahead," says the judge.

"Mr. Willis is willing to save the court time by pleading guilty to the charge of disorderly conduct."

"Isn't that nice of him," says the judge.

"Mr. Willis lost his temper—with some provocation, I have to say—

while he was camping at Lake Edwards with his family. As I understand it, a park ranger refused to allow Mr. Willis to leave his dog in his vehicle very briefly while he went to inform his family he had arrived. They ended up having words, and the ranger took it upon himself to call the sheriff's office. At no time whatsoever did Mr. Willis resist arrest. He was simply trying to explain—"

"Oh, balls," says the sheriff's deputy, who's been sitting there shaking his head. "I gave this guy every—"

"*May* I?" says Reed.

"Let the distinguished counsel say his piece, Don," says the judge.

"At any rate, Mr. Willis now regrets having allowed himself to be provoked. Due to the holiday, he's already spent two days in jail. He has no criminal record, he holds an extremely responsible position with his firm in New York City, and right now he's anxious more than anything to get back to his family, who I have to say are a little shocked that this thing was allowed to go so far. Oh yes, I almost forgot: this weapons charge, so called. Now, this, I have to say, with all due respect, is *really* throwing in the kitchen sink. The *weapon* in question is a .22 rifle belonging to Mr. Willis, which was kept behind the seat of his truck. Correct me if I'm wrong, Your Honor, but I believe in this state a man is still allowed to own a .22? Or have the liberals managed to get the Second Amendment to the Constitution repealed over the weekend without—"

"You can spare us the sarcasm, Mr. Reed."

"I'm just pointing out that I don't understand exactly what law Mr. Willis is supposed to have violated here. I might add that this .22 stayed behind the seat of the truck during this whole episode, that Mr. Willis never mentioned or in any way so much as *alluded* to this .22, much less *produced* it or *threatened* anybody with it. It simply happened to be in his vehicle, hundreds of feet away, at the time of this very silly, very unnecessary dispute."

The judge looks over at the sheriff's deputy. "What about it, Don?"

"Your Honor," says the prosecutor, "the weapon was found in a routine search of the defendant's vehicle incident to the arrest. It's not clear what he was planning to do with it."

"What's *clear*, Your Honor," says Reed, "is the fact that he didn't do *anything* with it. What's the implication here? That Mr. Willis was planning to stick up the concession stand? Mr. Willis"—glancing at his yellow pad—"is the Director of Public Affairs for Dandineau Beverages. I don't know what his salary is—I didn't ask—but I assume he's got the price of a hot dog."

The judge looks at Reed over the top of his glasses. "You must be coming up in the world, Mr. Reed. That or Mr. Willis is coming down." He looks at the prosecutor. "Well?" he says.

The prosecutor looks at the sheriff's deputy, who shakes his head and waves a hand as if batting away a mosquito. "In the interest of saving time," the prosecutor says, "we're willing to be satisfied with the defendant's guilty plea to the charge of disorderly conduct."

"I should think *so*," the judge says. "But I'm surprised at *you*, Don. He must've annoyed you considerably." He looks at Willis. "You. I'm fining you fifty dollars. You pay the clerk, down the hall there. Your distinguished counsel will show you."

"But Your Honor—" says the prosecutor.

"Bang bang," the judge says, pumping his fist to suggest an imaginary gavel. "Court's in recess."

"He's a beauty," says Reed, leading Willis to the door. "Roy," he says to the prosecutor, "how's everything? Don?" Neither the prosecutor nor the deputy says anything back. "Hey, we put the hurt on 'em," he says in Willis's ear. The deputy meets Willis's eyes. Willis considers snapping the son of a bitch a salute. But no.

Reed gives the clerk two twenties and a ten, brings Willis back downstairs to claim his wallet and duffel bag, and they walk out the basement door into a sunny morning. Grass still wet with dew. Couple of leaves falling.

"Well, listen, thanks," says Willis. "This turned out to be pretty painless. And I appreciate the little touches, by the way. Coffee and everything."

"Like I say, you'll get the bill," says Reed. "So listen, you have time to grab some breakfast? Bet you a hundred dollars they didn't bring you breakfast this morning, am I right?"

"God, did they? No. Yesterday they did."

"Shitheels. See, they knew you'd be out. And that way Benny gets his breakfast this morning on the taxpayers' dime. This is the level they think at. Anyhow, we'll make it quick. I know you got a long drive ahead of you."

"Just back to Preston Falls," says Willis.

"Oh well. Hell, then. I thought you were driving all the way down to Westchester."

"No, actually I'm up here for a couple of months. Hell of a way to start it off."

"Nowhere to go but up," says Reed. "So listen, there's a little hole-in-the-wall place that makes decent omelettes, there's Denny's and *that* whole spectrum, and then there's a couple places with scones and latte and all that bullshit."

"Anything," says Willis. Actually, the scones-and-latte thing sounds best; he's just been in jail, for Christ's sake, with a toilet on the wall.

"Then Dudley's it is. Here, let's take my wheels and I'll drop you back here after, so you can get your vehicle out of hock."

Willis follows him over to a sharky black sports car, a Z-something, parked cheekily next to a police cruiser. Its roof comes up to Willis's waist. He opens the unlocked passenger door, sits way down and opens his window so he won't stink up the cockpit. He still has on the jeans and t-shirt he pulled out of the dirty clothes whatever day it was he tried to rip down the ceiling. And he hasn't had a shower since—well, not in jail, that's for sure.

Reed climbs in and twists the key, and the sound system blasts so loud Willis flinches. After a little he recognizes it: "Smells like Teen Spirit," which he understands can only be coincidence. Reed turns it down to reasonable. "This gets on your nerves, say so."

"No, I'm into it," says Willis.

"Well, it's funny." Reed noses out of the parking lot, waits for a Saab to go by. "For the longest time I thought either I was getting old or this shit was the emperor's new clothes, you know? But then when he killed himself I started picking up on it." The Saab passes by, and they're off.

"That's amazing," Willis says. "I went through that same exact thing. But the guy could *play*, no question. I mean, he couldn't *really* play, but *within* that, you know?"

Reed looks over. "You play music?"

"Yeah, in a half-assed way."

"Weird. You know, I *thought* so. I don't know, there's a look or something. Fuckin' Calvin, man. He never told me he had a musician next door. I got to take this up with him. So what do you play?"

"Guitar, like everybody else in the world."

They stop at a stoplight behind the Saab, which has one of those ANOTHER SHITTY DAY IN PARADISE bumper stickers. Willis keeps

being surprised that there's nothing unique about his sensibility. The
song's going *Oh we oh we oh we oh* or whatever it really is in that part.

"Electric?" says Reed.

"Mostly." Which Willis isn't sure is true, but to play acoustic is to be
a sensitive plant. "So, you too? What do *you* play?"

"Like you say. What does anybody. You play in a band?" The light
turns green. Reed honks and the Saab moves.

"Used to," says Willis. "Couple years ago. Now I just haul the
thing out once in a while and play along with stuff. Try not to lose my
calluses."

"Well, hey, you're welcome to come jam with *my* sick crew," says
Reed. "What kind of guitar you have?"

"Tele."

"Cool. So who are you into?"

"Whoever. You know, lot of people. I guess if it came right down,
Keith more than anybody."

"Cool."

"Speaking of people who can't play but can *play*," says Willis. "But
if I'm jamming along with something, it'll be anywhere from, I don't
know, country shit—"

"Cool."

"—to James Brown to—"

"Cool. Listen," says Philip Reed, "you got to come jam with *us*, man.
We finally, after three *years*, found a kick-ass drummer."

"Hardest thing," says Willis.

"Yeah, see, *you* know. I've been trying to get this *across* to these ass-
holes. All the guy asks is that we let him sing 'Get Out of My Life,
Woman'—you know, that's his little number that he likes to do—and
these guys are like 'He's em*bar*rassing us.' Unbelievable. This is a guy
who used to tour with Anne Murray, man. You know, he *says*. Course
he's also a major fuckup, but come *on*. Here, this is the place right here."

A plastic Diet Pepsi sign hangs over the sidewalk from a two-story
brick box with fresh white paint and red geraniums in the window.
Willis holds open the screen door, not out of courtliness but because he
doesn't want Philip Reed behind him, where his most shameful stink
must be.

"So does your band play out?" Willis picks up the menu, a Xeroxed
page in a clear plastic sheath with metal corners.

"Once a month, that's it. The Log Cabin, over in Brandon? Shit, we're all busy. I mean, *Sparky's* not busy—the drummer I was telling you? But everybody else, you know, between jobs and families. We do get together once a week and just kick shit around. Guy who plays bass lives down in Sandgate—*way* out in the fuckin' boonies—and he fixed up a spot in his barn where we can make some serious noise." Willis notices for the first time Philip Reed's wedding band. "In fact, what are you doing tomorrow night? We're supposed to get together about nine o'clock, and we usually go to one, two in the morning."

"Shit, I don't know," says Willis. "What kind of stuff you do?"

"Ah, you know, just whatever anybody feels like. And knows some words to. All covers, that's the one stipulation. Anybody writes an original song, they're out of the band. So it's like anything from 'Call Me the Breeze' to—I don't know—'Gloria'? 'Sweet Home Alabama'? Shit like that."

" 'Farmer John'?" says Willis.

"*There* you go."

A plump, pimply young waitress comes and asks for their order. She pronounces it like Nabokov's *Ada*. Cheese omelettes: cheddar for Willis, American for Reed. "I think I'm in love," Reed says when she's gone. "See, she's the real thing. Fucking eugenics is going to come in and you're going to have a world of Sharon Stones drinking fucking latte."

"I could get into that," says Willis, who in fact has never seen a Sharon Stone movie.

"So could I, actually."

"What's this place like, where you play?" says Willis.

"The Cabin? Your basic dive. I like to say it's the *other* B and B crowd—bikers and burnouts? Some real *down* hillbillies. Old Calvin used to come by once in a while—speaking of down hillbillies. Fuckin' Calvin." Reed shakes his head, and the ponytail wags. "Calvin's a piece of work. But hey, he's mah bud. Anyhow. Basically they keep having us back because we suck and we *know* we suck and we just sort of get up there, you know? Like we make up a different stupid name every time, that they can put in the paper. You know, *Saturday night: Cowflop.* Whatever it is. Like, Okay, we're hacks and that's the deal—you know what I'm saying? Or you could also just look at it as an excuse to do drugs and get away from the wives, which it also is."

So this means they do drugs?

The waitress sets down coffees and little things of half-and-half.

When she turns away, Reed kisses bunched fingertips. "So what do you say? You want to come over tomorrow? Kick some shit around?"

"I don't know," says Willis. "If I wouldn't be fucking up your practice."

"Our *what*?" says Reed. "Hey, practice is for lawyers."

Willis doubts it's the first time he's said this.

2

Since he doesn't have to be anywhere anytime for anything, he takes his
sweet time getting back to Preston Falls. He stops at the junk shop in
East Wakefield that always has the same shit, hoping, as always, to find
like a Danelectro guitar—something they don't know is anything. As if
people who make their living buying and selling shit don't know what
shit's worth. No instruments at all; just an empty wooden violin case. But
he finds a copy of *Fear Strikes Out*, which he's always meant to read.
Fifty cents? Can't go wrong.

When he opens the kitchen door, the place already has that empty-
house smell. He gets one of Champ's tallboys out of the refrigerator and
brings it into the front hall. Everything else can fucking wait until he settles in and zones out for a while. He sits down on the sofa and takes off
his boots: a connoisseur's stink, like a fine old cheese. He brings his feet
up and lies back, head elevated to optimum angle by the sofa arm and
one throw pillow. He pulls the comforter over him, then reaches up and
switches on the floor lamp, though it's the middle of a sunny afternoon.
Now he's safe. He picks up *Dombey and Son*, waiting faithfully where he
left it. The lamp turns the white page a warm yellowish—unless this
cheap fucking paper is already rotting because it's not acid-free—and he
imagines the warmth reflecting back and soaking into his face.

He wakes up blank, as if after a shock treatment: he's someplace
with a light on. Then all the old shit coalesces.

The sun's gone down: it's dark outside those oh-so-New-Englandy
panes of glass on either side of the front door. He reaches for the tallboy
he remembers must be there on the floor. Warm and raspy going down:
dry, like light, powdery sand in his throat, as if it weren't seeping into the
tissues. He climbs over the back of the couch, opens the front door, and
goes out onto the doorstep. The sky is a dark slate blue with a salmon
tinge at the horizon, which fades even as he's looking. Chilly out here in

just t-shirt and stocking feet. He pisses down into the grass. A bat flitters by. He hears an owl, and a faraway car melodiously going through its gears. He grips his goosefleshed upper arms. Shit, let's get back in.

What he'd better do, he'd better call and let Jean know he's out and this thing is over, and thank her for doing the thing with the lawyer. True, she said no communication, but this would simply be observing the ordinary decencies, no?

The phone rings five times, then the machine comes on and he gets to hear his own voice saying leave a message. It beeps, and the silence starts unrolling. "Yeah, hi," he says. "Just calling to say I got back, ah, to the house okay"—almost said got *home*, a faux pas for sure—"and, ah, the whole thing was over really quickly and it just turned out not to be that big a deal. So. I hope your trip back went okay, and that, you know, all is well? It's Tuesday night—Tuesday evening, actually. I'll talk to you later. Hello, Mel, if you get this. Hello, Rog. Hope school went well. And, I don't know, talk to you later."

He opens the refrigerator. Two tallboys left. Plus the usual shit that accumulates. Bowl of fruit salad that might still be okay, with a drumhead of plastic wrap. Eggs. Half a package of cheese with a rubber band around it, which Jean must have put away; Willis always just folds the excess plastic under and lets the cheese itself weight it down. Thing of bacon with a couple of strips left. Polaner All Fruit: raspberry, strawberry, apricot. Stick and a half of butter. Paul Newman salad dressing with the once-amusing garlanded *N*. So he can eat through all this shit before he gets back to the subsistence food he eats when he's here alone in a stupid attempt to lose weight, which he undermines with shit like beer. Oatmeal when he wakes up; the rest of the oatmeal, cold, for lunch. For dinner, brown rice, with garlic browned separately in olive oil.

"Tell you what let's have," he says aloud. But he can't think what. He stands there staring into the open refrigerator until the thermostat kicks the motor on, and his body twitches at the sudden noise. Fucking *silent* in here. Well, that was the idea, no?

He ends up eating Cheerios and working away on another tallboy while lying on the sofa reading Sherlock Holmes as a warmup for *Dombey and Son*. He reads the one about the guy who murders his sister and drives his brothers insane by burning some kind of hallucinogenic poison in their room, and then the one about the guy who builds the fake partition he hides behind so they think he's dead and his body's been burned in the woodpile. He never does get back to *Dombey and Son*, but that's cool too. Eventually this should make him sleepy, because what he *doesn't* want is to be up until five in the morning and then wake up at like three in the afternoon.

But around midnight, still wide awake, he figures he might as well play some guitar, and starts a thing of coffee. Crazy motherfucker named Willis. He goes out to the woodshed for the Twin and the Tele—got to finish stacking that wood tomorrow—and lugs them into the kitchen. He wedges *The Woman's Home Companion Cookbook* under the front of the Twin to angle the son of a bitch so it's rearing back and blasting in his face. He sets the boombox on the kitchen counter, on the theory that the whole cabinet underneath acts as a resonating chamber. Then he picks out CDs to play along with: *Guitar Town, Serving 190 Proof, Talk Is Cheap, Ragged Glory, Slow Train Coming*. And then feels guilty that it's all white music, so he puts *The Best of Buddy Guy* on the stack, even though he won't actually play along with it, because Buddy Guy is too discouraging. Coffee's ready.

He starts out with the Neil Young, that song about how Neil Young is thankful for his country home. Slow tempo, three chords, nothing too fucking subtle. Willis isn't your world's best guitar player, but neither is Neil Young, so he can more or less keep up—which is why he's into Neil Young. That and because he's smarter than Neil Young, or at least more cynical. Although maybe Neil Young is in fact smarter than Willis and has managed to get his head so Zen simple that he can go to his country home and get peace of mind the way the song says. All of which is probably making too much of what's basically a trite piece of shit. Unless it's actually a sendup, but Willis doesn't think so. Though later on Neil Young does send up "Farmer John," unless that's not a sendup either. Willis worries about this exact same shit every time he plays along with *Ragged Glory*. Because he's a fucking *machine*.

After he's done with the Neil Young, he puts on the Dylan and cracks the last of the tallboys to help him start thinking about starting to think about going to sleep. Except one poor tallboy can't do much against all that coffee, so he washes down a Comtrex to level the playing field. He gets sick of the Dylan—all that medium-tempo shit in A minor—and pops another Comtrex, then puts on the Keith. At last, partway through that, he starts to feel he's losing track of things. By now trees and shit are starting to emerge in the brightening grayness outside the windows. He hits Stop and switches off the hissing amplifier. In the sudden silence, amid residual buzz in his ringing ears, he hears a blue jay scream, then a crow cawing as if in response. Day birds.

He sets the Tele on the guitar stand and goes upstairs, taking along *Dombey and Son* just in case he's not as far gone as he estimates. In the bedroom, it's gray enough to make out all the pieces of furniture but not to read print. So fuck it. He pulls off his jeans, which it occurs to him he hasn't had off for however many days, and gets under the covers. Slipping his hand under the waistband of his underpants, he grasps the Unnamable; to warm his hand as much as anything. Son of a bitch swells, though you wouldn't call it hard. Now his eyes are adjusting, and it's not dark in here at all. But that's cool. Better, actually. A whole waking world standing guard while he sleeps.

3

The plan they used to have went like this: Willis would stick it out at Dandineau and support them while Jean was finishing Pratt, then she would turn around and support them with some incredibly satisfying job and Willis would figure out something. "You could just do your music," Jean used to say. Yeah, well, his music. With like eight hours a day to practice, maybe he could cut it with some hundred-dollar-a-night bar band. *Maybe.* Time has marched since Willis learned Mick Taylor's break on "Can't You Hear Me Knockin'?" note for note.

What Willis knows about himself is that deep down he's a word man. Which is contemptible. He got his first promotion for the press release he wrote when Dandineau shut down the plant in Meridian, Mississippi. (Hey, the hometown of Jimmie Rodgers.) On the first draft, Marty Katz underlined a throwaway reference to "counseling" for employees left high and dry, and wrote in the margin, "Pls amp up." There was nothing to amp up: a ten-minute presentation in the lunchroom by some woman from the Mississippi state employment service. In his rewrite, Willis called this "an intensive counseling program with a range of placement services" and made up a quote from James Buckridge, chairman and president, about Dandineau's commitment to its people. Marty wrote "Kudos! (Singular!)" in the margin, and changed "commitment" to "loyalty." Which amped up Willis's respect for Marty Katz.

Willis pissed and moaned to Jean that what little integrity he'd ever had was down the toilet, but he secretly trusted he'd be okay as long as his cynicism held out. He was making money, however worldly that was, and winning praise from father figures, however pathetic *that* was. So: in for a dime. After the first couple of years at Dandineau he let his hair grow back and started wearing black t-shirts under Armani-knockoff suits, keeping an emergency dress shirt and tie on a hanger behind his door.

He bought his first good acoustic guitar: a '59 J-200, because Martins were a cliché. And then a John Lennon–type Rickenbacker— for a while, Willis loved that clangy shit—and then a '39 D-18 because he'd always wanted a Martin. All this, of course, was when they still lived in their rent-controlled shithole on West 108th Street, before the kids and the house in Chesterton. He got his old Telecaster worked on by the guy who did Danny Gatton's guitars, and he had the blackface Twin he'd owned since high school completely gone over: even a new cord with a three-prong plug. For a while he was getting together on Wednesday nights with a hip dentist, an assistant dean at City College and an abstract painter who actually played decent guitar. They chipped in on a rehearsal studio in the West Thirties and worked away for months on the same ten or fifteen songs: "Jolly Green Giant," "Charley's Girl," "I Fought the Law," a Sex Pistols–sounding version of "White Lightning."

Then, with a year to go at Pratt, Jean got pregnant: an inadvertency with the diaphragm, supposedly.

"But what do you expect me to do with *her*?" Jean said, when Willis reminded her of their old plan. They were cleaning up from Mel's second birthday party. "Just stick her in day care?"

"It's not exactly unprecedented," he said.

"Oh, but I'm so into her now," she said, scraping ice-cream-sodden cake into the garbage. "I just want to *drink* her. This time with her is so short."

"Short for you," he said. "I'm going right out of my fucking *mind*."

"Do you realize in three years she'll be starting kindergarten? And after that she'll just be gone."

"Three *years*? I don't know if I can do another three *months* in that place." He popped a balloon. "This is *not* what I signed on for."

"You have such a memorable way of putting things," she said.

"I'm asking you to honor an agreement we had."

"Yes, when things were totally different." She turned to scrape another plate, and he drank the red wine from some parent's plastic glass.

"Besides," he said, "she needs to be interacting more with other kids. You saw what she was like today."

"She's only *two*."

"Still," he said. "And you need to start working back into *your* life."
He tossed the glass into the garbage.

"How dare you tell me what I need?"

So they were into the how-dare-yous. He held up a hand. "Fine. Just
wanted to know what I could count on. Now I know."

But apparently the shit about interacting with other kids did its
work. It might even have been true. Once they were speaking again, they
renegotiated the plan: Jean was to go back for one course that fall, then
two in the spring; Melanie was to be put in day care for the afternoons;
Willis was to pick her up after work and cook dinner while Jean did her
school shit. Since Willis had just been kicked up another ten thousand,
he thought they could swing the day care, though after taxes ten thousand dollars worked out to about nothing per paycheck. And now there
was Jean's tuition. Plus payments on the year-old Honda he'd bought
with the excuse that Melanie should be exposed to trees and grass and
fresh air. Another thing that might have been true.

After Jean's fall semester Willis was made head of Public Affairs and
got kicked up another twenty. This was when his eleven- and twelve-
hour days began, and he started putting on weight and getting short of
breath. Yet even with just the early afternoons and late nights to herself, Jean thought she could still have her degree in another two years,
three max. By which time Mel would be in school. Jean could take a
full-time job and Willis could start thinking what he might want to do
with his life.

Then, right before Jean's last semester, another inadvertency. She
obviously had it in for him, as well as for herself. Now he got it: he
would work at Dandineau Beverages until he died of a heart attack, and
that would be his fucking life.

On the other hand, he had a son. To his shame, he had been secretly
put off by Mel's babyhood, but with Roger he was able to feel, mostly,
the way a father should feel. Including the feeling that time was short.
First the tiny scrunched face that seemed to mutate more each day into
the face Roger would someday have. Then holding him up by his arms
as he skimmed along making walking motions with his legs, forced wide
apart by the bulky diaper. Roger talking, then talking in sentences.
When neither Jean nor Mel could hear, Willis used to sing to him: *Love
is lovelier the second time around.* And Roger would sing, in that fluting
voice, hoarse around the edges: *Twinkle twinkle yittle star.* When Mel

corrected him, he'd say, "That's what I *said*, twinkle twinkle yittle star."
He was scared of Dr. Seuss books—and there *was* something sinister
about how things popped into existence only because the words for
them rhymed with the words for other things Dr. Seuss had just thrown
out there. He liked "Ain't Got No Home," by Clarence "Frogman"
Henry.

Okay, let's not beat this shit to death.

When Roger turned nine this past January, he announced he was too
old to be read to anymore. And since, in the oh-so-white public schools
they moved to Chesterton for, the kids seem to spend half the day watching supposedly educational videos and the other half playing with computers, Willis fears for his future. As if *he* were a walking advertisement
for the life of the mind: whoring himself and buying toys as compensa-
tion. The guitars, the truck, the good sound system, the sagging shelves
of books and CDs. Hey, Preston Falls itself.

He found the farmhouse five summers ago, while they were tourist-
ing around that weird New York–Vermont border country. Heading for
Fort Ticonderoga, more to have something to head for than as a history
lesson: Roger was only four, and Mel's first-grade teacher had pissed
away the whole year on the fucking Indians. Willis bought the Preston
Falls *Argus* to check out the—whatever the word was—the spatial analogue to *zeitgeist*—and there was the ad: *"Owner Says Sell! Country
Setting, 20 ac+–. Needs TLC."* And a picture of the house with bare
trees around it. It had those eyebrow windows. Like the house Willis
grew up in, until he was twelve, in Etna, New Hampshire. He pointed
out the bare trees to Jean: since this was July, the place had obviously
been on the market awhile. "Fifty-five thousand?" she said. "It must be
a mess inside."

The old Somebody place—Willis has heard the name fifty fucking
times—had once been a five-hundred-acre farm: from the top of this hill
to the top of that hill, way up the road, way down the road, on both *sides*
of the road, including the land where Calvin Castleman's trailer now sits.
The owner saying "Sell!" turned out to be the National Bank of Preston
Falls; they'd foreclosed after the poor son of a bitch who'd bought the
house and the last twenty acres got laid off at the woodworking plant. A
real estate lady with glasses like the wife who gets strangled in *Strangers
on a Train* showed them through. Her big selling point was that the
house was post and beam. Right. Didn't all houses have fucking beams?
And since the beams weren't hanging in space, what was holding them

up but fucking posts? Upstairs in what he imagined as Roger's room, Willis sat cross-legged on the particleboard floor, looked out the eyebrow window and pictured his son on a summer morning, sitting on wide, sun-warmed floorboards, lacing up his sneakers and peering out at the day being offered to him. Willis's old bedroom—before his mother took him and Champ to live in Cambridge—had the same shin-level windows. He used to sit cross-legged and look down at his tire swing hanging from the big maple tree, though he never actually swung in it much. Willis was never a jock, even before he broke his leg playing baseball and spent three months in a cast. Well, enough. He took the real estate lady down into the cellar, jabbed a jackknife into a post or a beam or whatever the fuck, which had the consistency of angel food cake, and offered her forty.

The owner said "Sell!"

Jean said, "It's your money."

Willis was flush that year. His father had died and his mother had moved back up to Etna, into their old house with the eyebrow windows; the old man had never taken her name off the deed. She sold her apartment in Brookline and split the proceeds three ways with Willis and Champ, actually using the word *reparations*. Willis did some rough figuring. If he put twenty thousand down, it would mean making payments on a twenty-thousand-dollar loan, plus property taxes. What, three hundred and change a month? It was nothing. It was like an extra-bad phone bill. He could actually do this. And once he'd exposed the beams and the wide floorboards, built bookcases and brought in Oriental rugs and blue-painted pie safes, Jean might be less freaked out by the whole Preston Falls gestalt—*that* was the word, gestalt. The trailers. The ratty chalets and A-frames. The Bondo'd-and-primered cars up on cinderblocks. The wandering chickens. The dead raccoons and the roadside litter. The snarling dogs coming at you until their chains stopped them short.

This was before he saw that these were his secret allies.

4

When Willis wakes up it feels like late afternoon, and the Unnamable's rigid. Sort of tries to polish himself off but can't think what to think of. The temptation: Tina bent over in biker shorts. Some taboo there he can't articulate.

He goes downstairs, pisses, starts coffee. Clock says 3:27. Only *mid*-afternoon. Wednesday? So it's tonight he's supposed to go jam with What's-his-name. An hour to get there, probably, and an hour back. Which is crazy. But to play with actual people again? And if he stayed here he'd do what—lie on the couch reading books where the men say *Damme, Sir!* and the women are named shit like Louisa. Peter some-body—no, Philip. Philip Reed. He'd have to leave around eight. So four and a half hours to kill? Well, cook some oatmeal and take a shower and you're down to four. Play guitar a little to get the feel, maybe take another crack at that ceiling? He ends up reading more of *Dombey and Son.*

It's dark again when he loads the Twin and the Tele into the back of the truck. He sticks the guitar stand behind the seat, then decides he'll look like a dilettante and takes it back to the house. Then he wastes more time dithering over tapes; he ends up with Buddy Guy for the drive there, to make his playing subliminally blues-drenched, and Public Enemy to keep him awake on the way back.

He stops at the cash machine in Preston Falls and gets FAST CASH $40. Pitiful: in Chesterton it's FAST CASH $100. But he's only got about a thousand to last him these two months, and nothing coming in. Then over to Stewart's, where he pours a cup of coffee and pisses away a dol-lar and a quarter of his forty on a *Want Ad Digest*. Showing up early would be pushy, so he sits in a booth and looks through Musical Instruments, Motorcycles, Personals and Farm Equipment. He'd like to find an affordable 8N with a brush hog, not that he could afford it. The coffee gets him queasy, so he goes back up to the counter and buys a kaiser roll with butter *and* peanut butter, on the theory that it's porous. Then he feels as if something big is swelling inside him, pushing up on his heart. Willis and his body, those ancient enemies.

Halfway to Sandgate, he remembers he forgot Calvin Castleman's fucking hundred and fifty dollars.

Philip Reed's directions turn out to be good. The house either is or is not lime green (too dark to tell), but it sure does have a plastic gila monster on the porch roof. Fucker's the size of a German shepherd and glowing, lit from within; you can see the cord going into its mouth. Party boys. Willis comes jolting up the two-rut driveway past the house, as instructed, to a barn where he recognizes Reed's Z-whatever between a rusted-out Econoline van and an old bulbous Volvo from the days before they made them boxy. When he cuts the engine he can hear electric guitars tuning.

He hauls his guitar and amp through the tall barn door, held open by a cinderblock, and follows the sound up steep, trembling stairs to a hayloft, resting that fucking Fender Twin on every other step. When his head clears the floor of the loft, he can see a few sagging brown haybales and, in the far corner, a giant cube of cloudy plastic sheeting over a frame of two-by-fours, and the blurred, faceless forms of people inside. What might be a billed cap. A red shirt. A guitar neck, probably. Willis lugs his stuff over to where two sheets of plastic overlap, parts them with his guitar case and gets a skunky noseful of reefer.

Reed's kneeling on the shag carpeting that covers the hilly floorboards, plugging cords into a couple of stomp boxes, a black Les Paul slung over his shoulder on a tooled-leather strap. He looks up and says, "Hey, *here's* the man."

"I think I found the right place," Willis says, and sportively sniffs the air. There's a drum set (a fat longhair is tightening a snare), a mixing board set up on a card table, two old-time capsule-shaped mikes on mike stands, two speaker horns on sturdy tripods, two scuffed-up floor monitors. For decor, campy LP covers pushpinned to a beam: Lawrence Welk with lifted baton, Sgt. Barry Sadler, Jim Nabors, some goony-looking country singer even Willis doesn't recognize: *This Is Tommy Collins*. A rusty oil-drum stove resting on cinderblocks, with a salvaged piece of corrugated aluminum roofing underneath: the stovepipe sticks right out through a circular hole in the wood siding, without a baffle, or flange, whatever you call it.

"Gentlemen?" says Reed. "Doug Willis."

"Hey."

"Hey."

"Okay, we got Sparky"—leveling a finger at the fat-boy drummer—"and Dan"—finger moving to a tall, lanky guy in a plaid hunting cap with the earflaps down—"and Mitch"—to a short guy with bug-eye sunglasses and a red shirt, wearing a low-slung Strat that looks too big on him.

The little Strat guy nods at Willis's case. "So what have we here?"

"Tele," says Willis. "Nothing special. Early seventies."

"Cool," the little guy says. "Come on, early seventies? They hadn't gone to shit *then*. By *any* means."

"Yeah, me either," says Willis.

"You got *that* right," says the drummer. He cocks his head and hits the snare once with a drumstick. Shakes his head.

"So whip it out," says Reed.

"Yeah yeah, whip it out," says the little guy.

"You fuckin' guitar sharks," the drummer says. "Man just *got* here. Here, man—I forgot your name." He offers Willis a stubby brass pipe from an ashtray sitting on his floor tom.

"Oh right," says the one with the earflaps. "Get the fuckin' guy dusted, good idea. Everybody ain't a fuckin' animal like you, man, that they can play behind *that* shit." He picks up a Fender P-bass with most of the finish worn off.

"Fuck you, man," says the drummer. "Try to hoover up enough of that shit of yours to get off, man, I fuckin' choke to death."

"Gentlemen, gentlemen," says Reed.

"Why don't you plug in over there?" says the bass player. He points to a power strip that's plugged, in turn, into an orange cord snaking outdoors through a knothole.

"Here, I got some weed here that's just weed." Reed takes a half-smoked joint out of his shirt pocket.

Willis holds up a hand. "No, I'm good. I just had a bunch of coffee." He stopped smoking dope years ago: officially because it made it harder to stay off cigarettes, actually because it made people around him seem evil. These people *already* seem evil.

"Well, listen," says the bass player, taking his bass off again. "I'm a do a couple lines here and like whoever wants to join me."

"Ah hell," Reed says.

"*Ho*-yeah," says the little Strat guy. "Yeh-yeh-yeh." He puts his tongue out and pants like a dog, which is all Willis needs to cross *him* off.

"Twist my arm," says the drummer.

"Hey, twist my *dick*," says the bass player. "I thought you said you choke to death."

"Hey, I *like* to choke, man." General laughter. "Like those dudes that hang theirself to get a boner, you know?"

"Hmm," Willis says. "I guess a little of *that* never hurt anybody." Suddenly he feels like he has to shit: the excitement of being bad.

The bass player has taken the pushpins out of *This Is Tommy Collins* and set it on top of his amp. He pours white powder from a Band-Aid box onto Tommy Collins's sincere face, and hands the little guitar guy a box of plastic straws and a pair of orange-handled scissors. "Hey, anybody got anything with some kinda edge?" he says. "Never mind, fuck it." He grabs a cassette, dumps out the tape and the paper insert—Stevie Ray Vaughn and Double Trouble—and uses the plastic box to chop and scrape and push the shit into a pair of parallel lines. The little guitar guy hands him a two-inch length of straw, and he bends down and hoovers them up. Then sinks to sit on the floor, snuffling and flogging his nose with his index finger, saying "Wowser."

Willis scrapes together a pair of lines half as long and half as wide, out of both good manners and caution. He snorts a line into each nostril; it stings his sinuses and begins dripping and burning down the back of his throat. Except that his heart's racing just a teeny bit—which is probably just psychological because he's all of, what, five seconds into this—he actually feels surprisingly great, though he does hope his heart won't start going any faster.

He watches the little Strat guy take his turn. Shit, these aren't bad people. He'd actually really like to get to *know* them. "So," he says, "you guys are all married?"

This gets a big laugh. Willis didn't realize what a really funny thing it was to say at this juncture, but he now feels privileged to have the secret key to cocaine humor: to be completely out there, yet at the same time right *in* there.

"Hey, Counselor," the little guy says, "you better step up to the plate. This shit is so fucking excellent, man. It's definitely Howdy Doody Time."

"You're dating yourself," says Reed, straw poised above two ridges of powder.

"Fuck it," says the drummer. "I'm a fuckin' get ripped." He picks up his pipe and starts slapping at his shirt pockets with his other hand, right side, left side, right side.

"Like you ain't fuckin' ripped already." The bass player's back on his feet. "Here, this what you're after?" He hands the drummer a pink butane lighter.

"So we in tune here approximately?" says Reed. "Whew. Holy shit."

"Yeh-yeh-yeh, let's do it," says the little guy. "Break out that bad-ass Telecaster, man."

"Absolutely," says Willis. He opens his case, *snap snap*, and slings his guitar on. "Anybody got a tuner?"

Reed hisses and makes a vampire-repelling cross with his index fingers. "We're strictly organic here. Fuckin' goat cheese, whatever. Mitch, you're in with yourself, right? Whatta you got for an E?"

So they all stand there stoned as pigs, tuning for about eight hours. Twang twang. De de de de de. With the tuner this would take two seconds. But on the other hand it's great, like lights going down at the movies.

"Dan, you somewhere close?" Reed says.

"Fuck if *I* know." The bass player flips his amp off standby, twaddles strings with the first two fingers of his right hand, and big notes come hooming out. "Somebody give me a fuckin' G?"

They all stroke G chords at him.

"Yeah, how about just one a you?" he says. The little guy plays a G chord and the bass player starts hitting harmonics and cranking at his tuning pegs, trying to get one howl up level with another howl. "Golden," he says, though it doesn't sound like he's improved things any. "So what are we doing?"

"Can you play 'Far, Far Away'?" says Reed. "Rimshot—where's the rimshot?" He turns around to the drummer. "Ah fuck." The drummer's lying on the floor; he's taken the round seat cushion off its chrome-plated tripod to pillow his head.

"Hey, what about 'Walk This Way'?" says the little guy. "You do 'Walk This Way,' right?" He plays the riff at Willis.

"You know I actually never have?" says Willis. Aerosmith was always too thug for him. "I mean, I *know* the tune."

"You'll pick it right up. Starts off in E, man, then the verse goes to C, like *yah dah DAHT!* up from B flat, like." He plays it to demonstrate, yelling *yah dah DAHT!* as he moves the bar chord up the three frets.

"Right," says Willis. *Normally* this would be within his scope. "Play the hook again? The E part?"

He plays it at Willis again and, amazingly, Willis plays it back at him. Either cocaine is a miracle drug or this hook is something a retard could play. "Yup," says the little guitar guy. "That'll work. Okay? 'Walk This Way'? Starts with the drum thing?"

"Let me get my shit together just a minute here," the drummer says from down on the floor.

"Oh fuck," says the little guy. "Fuckin' Sparky, man."

"Hmm," says Reed. "Looks like time to bring in Iron Mike."

The little guy winces. "Oh *man*? I *hate* fuckin' playing with a fuckin' drum machine. I mean, what do we have a fuckin' real drummer for?"

"Makes a great conversation piece," Reed says. "You got to give him that."

"No problem, man." The drummer's eyes are closed. "Use the thing for a couple songs, man. I'm gonna be right with you."

"Unbelievable," says the little guy. "*Sparky*, man."

"Fuck him. Forget it," Reed says. "So what are we doing, again?"

" 'Walk This Way,' " says the little guy.

"Okay, cool. You got the tune programmed in there, right?"

"That's not the point, man. You know what I'm saying? Last time we played the Cabin we played half the fuckin' night with the fuckin' *drum machine.*"

"I don't know, I sort of dug it," says Reed. "Like with his head inside the bass drum? *Crowd* was into it."

"Hey," the bass player says. "The thing keeps better time than him."

"Hey, fuck you," says the drummer.

"Okay, so 'Walk This Way,' right?" Reed says. "Does it start in E?"

"*Jesus*," says the little guy. "No, it starts in fuckin' W."

"And it goes to what, again?" says the bass player. "In that other part?"

"Come on, man. We *played* the fuckin' song last *week*. Through B flat to C. Right?"

"Right right right. Yeah, no, okay, man, I remember it. It's just weird to me. Comin' off a E to a B flat. It's like out of nowhere."

"Yeah, but then you're in C," says the little guy.

"Yeah, I *know* you're in C, but what I'm sayin', Mitch, that little thing is still weird to me."

"Well, that's how the fuckin' song *goes*, man."

"But it seems like it would make more sense if you went A, B, C."

"Are we gonna play this fuckin' thing or what?" Reed says.

"No, let's fuckin' *talk* about it for another fuckin' hour," Mitch says. He takes off his Strat, goes back to the board, does something, and the drum machine starts up: *Boom boom ba-doom-doom-DOOM. Boom boom ba-doom-doom-DOOM. Boom boom ba-doom—*

"Too slow, too slow," the bass player yells.

"That's exactly where we had it last week," says Mitch.

"Bull*shit*."

"Okay, fine, man. You know so fuckin' much about this tune, man, you fix it how *you* want, okay?"

"Well, it's gotta go faster than *that*, man," says the bass player.

"Okay, so put it up where you *want* it. Put it up your ass, all I care. Can we just play the fuckin' song?"

"I *hate* this fuckin' song, you want to know the truth," the bass player says. "Why don't we just play a blues?"

"I suggest we play *something*," says Reed. "Not a blues, necessarily."

"Okay," says Mitch. "You fuckin' masterminds work it out and you let me know, okay?"

Willis wants to think this is still banter. But he doesn't know these people, and it's too much to process when you're having such a great time being high, which he really is.

"Okay, okay, fine," says Reed. "Mitch, why don't you just put the thing on sort of a shuffle, you know, doot ta-doot ta-doot ta-doot-ta, doot ta-doot ta-doot ta-doot-ta." He sings in embarrassing fake Negro: "Checkin' up own mah *bay-bay*, doot ta-doot ta-doot ta-doot, find out what she been puttin' *daown*, ta-doot ta-doot ta-doot ta-doot." The drum machine is still going *boom boom ba-doom-doom-DOOM*.

"So that's what you want to play now?" Mitch says.

"Well, not *that*, necessarily," says Reed.

"So you want like a medium shuffle."

"Well, yeah. *Sort* of medium."

"Five fuckin' hours later . . . ," says the bass player.

"Well? So what do *you* have in mind?" Reed says.

"I don't *give* a shit. Why'n't we just play the fuckin' song, man? That way we'll have it the fuck over with."

"Come on, it's a killer *song*, man," Mitch says. "It sounded fucked-up last week because nobody knew it."

"Like we really know it now," says the bass player.

"Hey, the new guy," calls the drummer, still on the floor. "I forgot your name, man. You do any Stones?"

"We're doing this now," Mitch says.

"I'm just askin' him, man," says the drummer.

The drum machine keeps going *boom boom ba-doom-doom-DOOM.*

"Shit, man," Mitch says. "I feel like I'm starting to crash already."

Boom boom ba-doom-doom-DOOM. Boom boom ba-doom-doom-DOOM.

"Hey, can't have that," says Reed. "You mind turning that thing off? Drive me fuckin' bananas."

"I'm just gonna be a second." Mitch takes his Strat off and sets it on the floor with that ugly clang of an electric guitar in standard tuning.

"Fuck *this.*" The bass player takes off his bass and goes over and shuts off the drum machine.

"Sweet relief," says Reed.

The bass player looks over at Mitch, who's already snuffling and pawing at his face. "Shit. Is this going to be one of *those* fuckin' nights?"

"Here, while we're at it." Reed gets the joint out of his shirt pocket, lights it, takes a hit and passes it to the bass player, who takes a hit and holds it out to Willis.

He puts up a hand. "Some reason, I can't play behind that. I might go for a tad more of the other."

"Uh-oh," says the bass player. "I think we got another Spark-man on our hands. Hey, can you play drums?"

The drummer has rolled onto his side to light his pipe, his sloppy stomach bulging out his t-shirt. He sticks up the middle finger of the hand holding the lighter.

"I like to give him shit," the bass player says.

Willis snorts up a pair of inch-long lines. He wants more, but he can take a hint, if that was a hint.

Reed takes another hit off the joint, holds the smoke in, finally lets it out. "By the way. Since we're taking a break. Griff's got to have a name by tomorrow latest so he can put it in the paper."

"Great. We worry about *this* shit and meanwhile we're not even in *tune*," says the little Strat guy.

"You see?" Reed says to Willis. "Mitch's problem is that he still thinks this is about competence. But in a way that's cool too. Sort of that little edge of desperation. It's like, for him, he's been busted back down to a garage band. Whole different energy from just *being* in a garage band, you know what I'm saying?"

"Bullshit," says the drummer from down on the floor. "It ain't even *that*. Where's the fuckin' garage?"

"Figure of speech," says Reed.

"Fuckin' *cows* used to live here, man," says the drummer. "We're playing for like the ghosts of cows, man. Dig on it."

Reed looks at Willis. "This is what I'm up against. So, names. Who's got one?"

"Hey, what about the Grateful something?" says the bass player. "The Grateful Cowfuckers, man."

"Well, on some level that's perfect," Reed says. "But I don't think that's a level we can realistically be on."

"You should call yourselves the Robert Blys," says Willis.

"Love it," says Reed. "But—ah—" He goes *Ssshewww!* and zips his hand past his eyes. "See, he's too much the one thing and you're too, you know, the *other*. Anybody go for Confucius Say?"

"We already been that," says the bass player.

"We *talked* about it. We never actually used it."

"Neon Madmen," says Mitch.

"Too college," says Reed.

"Fuck it," the bass player says. "You want to call it that Jap thing, I don't give a fuck."

Mitch has put his Strat back on. "What about just Jap Thing?"

"I *don't* think so," says Reed.

"Jap thang," Mitch sings, and strikes some totally other chord. "You make mah heart sing."

"Hey, you want to do that?" Reed says. "We should be doing that— that's a fucking fabulous song."

"What about Air Bag?" the drummer calls.

"What the fuck does *that* mean?" says the bass player. "*Air* Bag? I mean, what is that *about*?"

"I was just thinking, you know, about these cars with air bags," the drummer says.

"Air Bag," says Reed. "Done deal. Objections?" The bass player only shrugs.

"Hey, the new guy," calls the drummer. "What Stones shit you do?"

"You fuckin' burnout," says the bass player. "You can do *my* stones."

"So are we going to play this thing or what?" Mitch says. He checks his low E. "Fuck, I'm out."

"What? What are we doing?" says Reed.

"Well, I can see where *this* shit is heading," the bass player says. "Sparky, man, will you fuckin' get up off the fuckin' floor?"

"Fuck him," says Mitch. He turns on the drum machine. *Boom boom ba-doom-doom-DOOM.*

"I thought we were doing 'Wild Thing,' " Reed says.

"Well, could we fuckin' do *something*?" says the bass player.

"Hey, I know. What about we do a line?" says the drummer, still down on the floor. "Shit, that could be like a saying: 'You want to do something, do a line.' I feel like if I did a couple lines I could really get into some playing."

"So get up off your ass," says the bass player.

"That's the problem, man," the drummer says. "I think I might be too fuckin' ripped."

"Shit," says the bass player, taking off his instrument. "What am I, your fuckin' servant?" He brings the stuff over, and the drummer rolls back onto his side while the rest of them circle around.

After these next two lines, Willis finds he's gotten up to a place where it seems a long way back down. He sits on the carpeting and tries to work out a theory about how the mountain landscape could be encoded in microminiature into the molecules of the coca plant, which would account for this steep lofty feeling. Like what is that thing—ontogeny recapitulating phylogeny? Maybe this is a little specious; he's sure it is. Still, it's cool to have come up with the word *specious*.

"Fuckin' Charlie Watts," the drummer's saying. "I love that motherfucker. Hey, the new guy. You do any Stones?"

"You know something? We should be doing some real biker shit," says Reed. " 'Born to Be Wild,' shit like that."

"What's your point, man?" says the drummer. "Fuckin' Stones ain't *biker* shit? Man, a biker *stabbed* some son of a bitch to that shit, so you don't know what the fuck you're talkin' about. I seen the movie of it, man, several fuckin' times."

"What are we, onto the sixties now?" says Reed.

"That wasn't the sixties, you dick," the bass player says.

"Altamont," says Reed. "Nineteen sixty-nine."

"Well, that's a fuck of a lot different from the *sixties*," says the bass player.

"Oh really?" Reed says. "That's an interesting remark. How is it that 1969 isn't the sixties?"

"Shit," says the bass player. "Will somebody tell fuckin' Perry Mason here what the fuck I'm tryin' to get across?"

"Danny," Reed says, "you're stretching my sense of camp to the breaking point."

"Yeah, whatever the fuck *that* means," says Dan.

"Hey, are we gonna play or what?" Mitch says. "I'm really pumped to play, you know?"

"I've been *trying* to mobilize you people to play for two *hours* now," says Reed.

"Hey, I don't think I can make it, man," the drummer says. "I feel like I might be too wasted to play."

"Well, if we ain't gonna play," says the bass player, "let's fuckin' get ripped."

"Listen, speaking of ripped," says Willis. "I'd be glad—I don't know if this is tacky, but if people are like chipping in or something."

"Yeah, I don't think you have to sweat it," Mitch says. "Old Calvin just—"

"Hey, Mitch?" says the bass player. "Why'n't you shut your ass?" To Willis he says, "Don't worry about it, man."

"What the fuck?" Mitch says. "I thought this guy—"

"Mitchell," says Reed. "C'm'ere. Talk to you for a second?" He takes off his Les Paul, walks over and parts the plastic sheeting, holding it open; Mitch takes off his Strat and follows him out. The bass player puts his bass back on and flips his amp off standby.

"They're bringin' in a new drummer, man," the drummer says from down on the floor. "I'm not fuckin' *stupid*. See, I get too fucked up to play."

"That ain't what they're talkin' about," says the bass player.

"Yeah, sure. Then it must be the latest stock quotations, man."

Willis can make out the two blurry forms on the other side of the cloudy plastic. The bass player begins to play what sounds like the hook to "Start Me Up." Willis guesses it would be politic to make some noise too. "Cool, you want to do that?" he says. "What Keith does, he takes off the bottom string and tunes to G. That's how he plays *all* that stuff."

"No shit," says the bass player. Willis absolutely can't tell if he's genuinely surprised, or putting him down for saying something everybody already knows, or just doesn't give a fuck.

"Are we in tune, gentlemen?" Reed's back; he and Mitch are slipping guitar straps over their heads. Willis knows Reed's looking at him. But when he finally can't stand it and looks back, Reed's checking his watch. "Night's still young," he says. "So. Enough of this shit."

5

Drops of rain on the windshield. Then more drops. Willis turns the wipers on, and the rubber blades fart against the glass. You need either a higher intensity of rain or a lower frequency on the wipers; as it is, it's just a fucking disaster. Chuck D is rapping about how they *Got got got got got me in a cell*, some infantile fantasy about a jailbreak, and the wipers are going this way and that way and this way and that way, supremely out of sync with the drumbeats.

Willis is headed home, crashing like a motherfucker. Gray daylight now, but he keeps the headlights on because the speedometer and all the dashboard shit look cozier lighted up, like having a fire going. But this music's irritating the fuck out of him. Even the name, Public Enemy: like it's some big irony. He flips up the little handle on the tape deck and yanks it out of the dash, and *that* by Jesus shuts the son of a bitch up. He rolls down the window, heaves the thing backhanded right across the road and into the brush, then the bag of tapes after it, plastic cassette boxes flying open in the wind, clattering on pavement. In the mirror he catches them scattering in an instant of red taillight.

This road *should* be familiar; it's just that the rain and fog are fucking everything up. And it really pisses him off, because he is *not lost*. He thinks about stopping the truck and getting out and chucking the God damn guitar and amp over the side too. But he's sort of out of that mood now and on to money worries. Up ahead he sees a billboard with the Marlboro Man slinging what looks like a pair of leg braces over his shoulder. Shit, so he's somehow crossed over into New York State? Vermont has that billboard law. Actually, they must be branding irons. Leg braces, Jesus. Willis himself used to be a Marlboro Man, in the sense that he used to smoke Marlboros. Oh, years ago. He could do with a fucking Marlboro right now. Maybe he'd better pull over somewhere, put the guitar and amp in the cab out of the wet and see if he can't nap a little.

Sometime after the billboard he passes a picnic area: green-painted tables, green-painted trash barrel with a crow perched on the rim. He finds a driveway to turn around in and doubles back; the crow flies away when he pulls in. He shuts the engine off, his ears still roaring, gets out, smells the good piney smell and lets rain soak his hot head. He starts to shiver. He wrestles the amp out of the back and sticks it on the floor of the cab on the passenger side, then tilts the seat-back forward to put the guitar case in the space behind. And there's the duffel bag he never remembered to bring into the house, with the .22 inside.

Now the rain's pinging on the metal and bouncing off the windshield. So it's hail, actually; can that be possible? He locks the doors and lies down on the seat, knees bent, face jammed into the woven seat-back, heavy feet hanging off into space. He closes his eyes: white sparks seething.

When he finally makes it back to the house, he just leaves all his shit right in the truck and slinks inside like an evil thing exposed in daylight. The rest of this day is nuked out for sure. Though he's proud to have a day nuked out by drugs again after all this time. He reads *Dombey and Son* until he falls asleep on the couch, then wakes up with his head hurting. Takes Advil, makes coffee, finishes *Dombey*. Starts *Our Mutual Friend*. In the chapter about the R. Wilfer family he falls asleep again, then wakes up from a nightmare he can't remember. It's dark outside.

He steps into the bathroom to piss in the toilet like a civilized man, and down goes his left foot through the fucking floor and up goes the other end of the board like a seesaw. It's just crawl space under there; his bare foot touches wet, cold earth. Great: so now we've got a hole in the fucking floor. Plus he's scraped the living shit out of his calf and shin, right through his jeans. He works his leg free, goes outside onto the step-stone and pisses into the grass, which is what he should have done in the first place. Big skyful of stars. He feels guilty for not having spent more time looking up at them during his life. Christ, the fucking *stars* and you're not impressed?

Okay, better get back in there and start dealing. He yanks that floorboard out, kneels and shines the halogen flashlight in underneath: sure enough, got two floor joists rotted through. And *why* have two floor joists rotted through? Because there's a pipe down there and the son of a bitch is leaking. And what does *this* mean? This means ripping up enough floor to get down in there to patch the fucking pipe, and then doing something about those joists. Maybe cut away what's rotten—looks like a foot or two of each joist—and piece them back together with pressure-treated two-by-six.

He gets the pinch bar and wrenches up a couple more floorboards to make room to work, then plugs in a droplight so he can see what the fuck he's doing. Yep, there's your problem right there: little bulge in the copper pipe, with water pissing out of a quarter-inch slit. Son of a bitch froze and split down in there, maybe last winter, maybe the winter before. Or the winter of '72—who the fuck knows? Okay, so the next step is to shut off the water to the bathroom and hunt around for the plumbing shit.

He gets that section of pipe cut out, cuts a piece to patch in there and steel-wools the ends. Only then does he discover that he doesn't have any straight fittings. Son of a *bitch*. So this means he's got to go into town. For two fucking thirty-five-cent pipe fittings. Except everything's probably closed anyway at this hour. Okay, fine: tomorrow. He can make it one night without a bathroom.

So back to *Our Mutual Friend*. When he comes to where Silas Wegg tries to buy the bones of his amputated leg, he gets up and starts more coffee. And of course forty-five minutes later has to shit. He takes the roll of toilet paper and the flashlight, gets the shovel out of the wood-shed and heads out behind the house. In a stand of sumac he's been meaning to cut down he sets the flashlight on the ground; by its light he digs a hole, takes down his pants and squats over it like a fucking aborigine. The Robert Blys *was* a good name and *not* too obscure.

He takes three fingers of Dewar's up to bed. This puts him under, but an hour later he wakes up quaking from some dream about the devil. He turns on the light and reads awhile. Goes downstairs for more Dewar's. Sleeps again, sort of. Eventually it's gray outside the window, then blue. He goes down and starts coffee.

He makes it into town in time to have the morning bowel movement in the rest room at Stewart's. Front page of the *Rutland Herald* says it's Friday; so a week ago he was in his office in New York? Not possible. He remembers to get Calvin Castleman's $150, then hits the post office for the first time since he's been up here. Bunch of junk mail, and bills for fucking *everything*. Then to True Value, where he picks up four fittings—couple extra just in case.

In Calvin's dooryard, he pulls up behind that big-ass Ford F-250, with the homemade stake body and the deck of rough-sawed lumber where Calvin's piled his woodcutting shit: two chainsaws, peavey, gas can, jug of bar-and-chain oil. He finds Calvin out by the Cadillac; the engine's suspended above the gaping hood by block and tackle rigged up to a branch of a maple tree, and yellow leaves are plastered on the windshield.

"Look like you're raising holy hell," says Willis.

"Yah, had to pull the fuckin' engine." Calvin sets an extra-long wrench down on the fender.

"Thought I better come pay you for that wood." Willis gets out his wallet. "I'd have come by sooner, but I guess you heard about my little— adventure." He was about to say *contretemps*. No response. "Hundred and fifty?"

"Yup." Not quite an *ayup*. Calvin wipes hands on pants and works his bulging wallet out of his hip pocket.

Willis counts out the bills. "By the way. I also wanted to thank you for putting me onto your lawyer."

Calvin nods. "He *will* get the job done." He takes a pack of Luckies out of his shirt pocket. "So you and him hit it off, did you?" He lights the cigarette with a pink plastic lighter.

"Yeah. He seems to be an okay guy." It feels like a bad idea to tell Calvin about going over to jam. Though why, exactly?

"I had an idea you and him probably hit it off," says Calvin. "Him playing in a band, and I know you play some. Once in a while I'll hear you if the air's just right."

"You're kidding. Shit, you have to let me know if it bothers you." He sees the pure white paper of the cigarette is grimy where Calvin's fingers touched it. Jesus, every once in a while the smell of a fucking cigarette.

"Nah, don't bother *me*. See, I had an idea you probably hit it off."

It's like every other conversation with Calvin Castleman: the subtext is that Willis doesn't know what the subtext is.

———

Crouched in that hole in the bathroom floor, Willis smears on the soldering paste and pushes pipe and fittings together; he fires up the BernzOmatic, touches the solder wire to the hot copper and sees it melt away into quicksilvery liquid racing in to seal the joint. He gives it a minute to cool, then goes and turns on the water. The pipe shudders and goes still again. He comes back and looks the joints over. Good. But shit—there's a drop of water gathering. Then another. Then a tiny spout whizzing up out of a fucking pinhole. God damn it to shit.

He goes and cuts off the water again and tries to sweat the son of a bitch apart, but of course now that there's water in the pipe, you can't get it hot enough. So he ends up cutting the son of a bitch. And now he has to go through all this shit again? No fucking way. Out in the shed he's got some radiator hose that should be about the right size and if he's lucky some hose clamps. He cuts off six inches of hose with the hacksaw, works soldering paste into each end with his pinkie, then twists and forces the ends onto the cut-off pipes. He tightens the hose clamps to the point where he's afraid he'll crimp the pipe, turns the water back on, and bingo. After all that fucking BernzOmatic *Sturm und Drang*. Hillbilly plumbing: why the fuck not?

The thing with his greased pinkie working in that tight hose inspires him to lie on the couch and haul out the Unnamable just on the off chance. But he can't get it happening. Which is cool. Okay, so now the next thing is, patch those joists and put the floorboards back. Though of course he forgot to stop at the lumberyard for two-by-sixes. Fine. Tomorrow. Today he'll stack that wood, maybe hit that lawn too. He zips up and reads *Our Mutual Friend* until he starts to doze, then has to wake himself from another devil dream, which he can't remember except that the devil really does have horns.

Eventually he notices the sky out the window is reddish. If you don't even go out and look at the sunset, then what the fuck is the point? So he goes out and looks at the sunset and what the fuck *is* the point? Orange cloudbanks, pulsing gold at the edges, and Willis standing there regarding them, with all his bullshit that he can't drop for a second. He goes back inside, the sky still blazing away. It occurs to him that he hasn't checked the answering machine for God knows *how* long. Shit: the son of a bitch is blinking. One blink. He just knows.

He hits Play, and Jean's voice says, *"I need to talk with you."* So he *did* know. Which is scary just by itself. It's too late for her to be in her office; she must be home. He goes into the kitchen and dials. She picks up on the first ring.

"Hi, it's me," he says. "I just got your message. When did you—"

"I can't talk now."

"Sorry," he says. "When would be—"

"I'll call you later." Dial tone.

Fine. Fuck you too, lady. May he remind her that *she* asked *him* to call? Though on the other hand, she's obviously in the middle of putting together a dinner, vetoing unsuitable tv shows, listening to Roger piss and moan about how Net Nanny blocks him off too many Web sites, starting subtly to steer the evening toward a quiet bedtime. All the shit he should be there to help with. It's the end of their first week of school, and he hasn't so much as spoken to his children. Though wasn't he forbidden to? Okay, what you *don't* want right now is to start thinking about when you used to read to them, Mel always on your left and Roger on your right, both in flannel pj's, a child's head resting against each shoulder. But hey: there *they* are and here *you* are. And isn't this the way you wanted it?

He puts on VPR and starts fixing oatmeal. They're playing some generic nineteenth-century piano shit. Schumann? He stirs in raisins, and it turns out the old ear's still good: the piano goes into fucking *Träumerei*, so this must be *Kinderscenen*. And that's enough of *that*. He kills the boombox and eats his oatmeal while reading the part of *Our Mutual Friend* where Noddy Boffin starts pretending to be obsessed with misers; then he takes his bowl and spoon out to the kitchen and steps outside into the warm, breezy dark. Stars and a half-moon. He just can't get his head around it that each of these things is like the sun and that some could be whole fucking galaxies. Well, not really at the top of his list.

By eleven o'clock Jean still hasn't called back, and he starts coffee. (What would be great is some cocaine.) He's halfway through his first cup when the phone rings.

"I was starting to wonder if you'd gone to bed," he says.

"No. I've been busy. What happened at your thing?"

"What, the court thing?"

Jean says nothing, which he takes to mean yes.

"It went okay," he says. "Fifty-dollar fine."

"Well. Good for you."

He says nothing.

"So now what happens?" she says.

"In what sense?" he says.

She says nothing.

"Listen," he says. "I agree that things haven't been going well."

"Oh, so you agree with that."

"That's not helpful, Jean."

"Well, what do *you* think would be helpful?"

"I don't know," he says. "Maybe having this time apart?"

"Oh," she says. "So you come back at the end of October and everything will be fine."

"Why are you—"

"We could go somewhere as a family again and not have it end up you being taken away in *handcuffs*?"

"That wasn't completely my fault," he says. "As you know. But I understand that I should have controlled myself. And I'm incredibly humiliated that you had to see it—and especially that the kids saw it."

"*You* were humiliated? Tell me something. Have you thought about trying to get some *help* in controlling yourself? Or with any of your other problems?"

"Like what other problems?"

"I don't even really know anymore," she says. "Whatever it is that's making you so dissatisfied."

"Well, I'm hoping that I can use this time away to get a handle on some of that."

"But since you already spend as much time away from us as possible, I don't quite see how this is supposed to help."

He says nothing.

"You're due back at work when?" she says.

"October thirty-first. Halloween. Appropriate, wouldn't you say?" Whatever this means: probably something as witless as *Witches are bad and so is going back to work.*

She says nothing.

"That's a Monday," he says.

"Then I guess we'll see you that Sunday night."

"This feels so terrible." He takes a sip of coffee, which has gotten cold.

"Listen," she says. "It's eleven o'clock, I'm exhausted, I've just gotten the kids to bed, and now I have approximately half an hour to myself. In which I can either wash my hair and clean the downstairs bathroom or I can do what I *feel* like doing, which is have some scotch and feel sorry for myself. What I *don't* feel like doing is trying to think of something to say that will make you feel better about yourself. Because I don't actually think you should."

"Isn't Carol there?" he says. Damned if he's going to let her bait him.

"No."

"But I thought she—"

"She'll be here sometime next week. She stopped off for a couple of days in Taos."

"I think I'd better come down there," he says.

"As someone who wishes you well, I wouldn't."

"Would *not*?" he says.

"You'd be coming back to someone who would not be fun to be with. And who would probably not snap out of it at the first kind word."

"Well," he says, "maybe you need this time too."

Silence.

"I have to go now," she says.

"Wait."

"For what? For me to break down weeping? Or for *you* to? So you can get your little jolt of feeling for the night?"

"Jean, you're not actually telling me anything about myself I don't know."

"Good night," she says.

Dial tone.

Well. Okay, so whatever that was about, he guesses it wasn't a summons to Chesterton. Unless it's up to him to figure out that it *was*. Willis unplugs the phone to prevent a hysterical callback: he didn't like the sound of that thing about the scotch. The coffee's starting to brighten him up, though, so maybe he'll play some guitar. But maybe instead of punishing his ears with the electric tonight, he should get out the J-200, which he feels sorry for because it never gets played anymore. He fetches it in from the woodshed and opens the case: the strings are rough with rust. There should be steel wool under the sink; he looks, then remembers it's still in the bathroom with the plumbing shit. He loosens each string in turn, pinches and rubs the steel wool along it until it squeaks, then tunes it back up. Shit, great-sounding guitar. A crime that it never gets used.

———

By Saturday night, Wrayburn has married Lizzie and Rokesmith is still dodging Lightwood, who could finger him as Julius Handford. Willis sets the alarm so he can go to church in the morning—not because of this devil shit, especially, though it *is* weird to have so many dreams about the devil. Though you could dismiss that as a father thing, probably. It's because he just feels sort of out there. But won't it make him feel even more out there to watch himself going to church for the first time in however many fucking years? Since he was thirteen, probably, during his mother's Unitarian phase. Still: if shit like the Lord's Prayer makes AAs feel better—look at Marty Katz—then dot dot dot. It's like he doesn't want to get into magical thinking but he's almost at the point where it's sort of that or get somebody to put him on Prozac. What he wants, really, is more cocaine, which is probably the worst thing for this, whatever *this* is. Tonight it takes two three-finger jolts of Dewar's to put him under, and he dreams that the devil is sitting on a tall throne that's also sort of the electric chair, except the devil's own energy is powering it.

When the alarm goes off, he starts coffee and puts on his man-of-the-people Sunday best—brown Dickies work pants, khaki work shirt, with a brown knit tie. Kind of a Nazi vibe, actually. Hey, the old man would be proud. So balmy this morning he doesn't need a jacket. Can it be Indian summer already?

Inside the First Congregational Church of Preston Falls, the organ is wheedling away to a quarter-churchful of mostly white-haired people. Willis scuttles sideways into an empty pew in the back; he's the only one here alone, which makes him look as if he's even deeper in spiritual crisis than he is. Fuck, if only it would *be* a crisis. Though isn't this a good way to bring it on, coming here and screwing around with the irrational?

Nice old church. All white inside, bare wood floor, tall windows, and up behind the pulpit a plain, squared-off gold cross—no faux tree bark, no writhing Saviour—against a hanging of burgundy-colored velvet. Either laudably severe or contemptibly bland.

He's deciding this when the organ cranks up and they all rise for the opening hymn—which sounds like "Morning Is Broken." By Cat Stevens. And it is. Too bizarre: he can't do this. He scissors-steps out of the pew and heads for the exit, doubled over with his hands across his belly, miming a sudden attack of stomach flu. Back in the truck, he loosens his tie. Well, at least he's found out that he's not far enough down yet to start begging help from "Jesus."

He stops at Stewart's for milk; the old farmer type in front of him asks for a pack of what he calls Pell Mells and takes for-fucking-ever picking out three different kinds of lottery tickets. When Willis sets his half gallon and his Milk Club card on the counter, he surprises the shit out of himself (though not really) by saying, "And a pack of Marlboros."

"Hard or soft?" says the girl. Pretty girl, a little beaten down.

"Make it hard, please?" he says. Willis, you dog.

He waits until he gets home to try the first cigarette; it's been ten years—no, more; he quit before Mel was born—and he's afraid if he lights up while driving it will hit him so hard he'll have to pull over. He finds a book of matches and a saucer, and settles on the couch. He zips the cellophane off, lifts the lid, slips out the square of dull silver paper to expose the caramel-brown filter ends. Sniffs them. Extracts one with a pinch and a tug of thumb and forefinger, then slips it between forefinger and middle finger. Which is just the way they found his father: smiling in his La-Z-Boy, his last Chesterfield burned all the way down, the skin fried in the crotch of his fingers. Harmlessly. Willis scratches a match, lights the cigarette, inhales, and *whump*. Yep, good thing he's sitting down.

When Willis got the call about his father, the doctor simply said it was a "sudden, massive" heart attack; he heard about the cigarette later, from Kenny Bishop, his best friend in sixth grade, who'd stayed in Etna all these years and who happened to be on rescue-squad duty that day. Willis had always expected something more operatic. If not a shootout with ATF agents, at least a Hemingway: both barrels in the mouth, brains on the wall. Shit, this was a guy who'd named his sons after Douglas MacArthur and Curtis LeMay—and that was *before* things got heavy. (In Cambridge, Willis's mother used to tell her new friends he'd been named for William O. Douglas, which they must have thought was an odd thing to volunteer.) Willis had learned to avoid visiting him during manic episodes, but the old man could still fool you. One time, just after Mel was born, his father had sounded fine on the phone, and six hours later, when Willis walked across the porch to knock on the door, he heard the tv going, looked through the window and saw him in his recliner scribbling on a legal pad. He was writing down the words of the newscast that coincided with Dan Rather's eye blinks.

Champ blew off the funeral and Jean stayed in Chesterton with the kids, then six and three. (Mel had seen Grandpa Willis once and didn't remember him; Roger had never seen him at all.) Afterwards Willis drove his mother on up to the house. While she prowled around in the attic—a bunch of her books and her old term papers from Smith were still up there—he sat in the La-Z-Boy and looked at a composition book he'd picked up off the floor. On the cover, his father had written "2/8/89–." A journal, the last entry dated April 22, the day he died: "Colder, mostly sunny this morning. Trees getting red with buds, grass getting green." Most of the entries simply recorded the time he'd gotten up (always between 6:30 and 7:00), the weather and his daily errands: "To P.O., paid light bill, bought bread and tuna fish." Had he found these simple things numinous? Or was he just completely shot to shit? On the back page, he'd been listing the small animals killed by his cat, Geoffrey: "3/12/89, 1 mouse. 3/17/89, 1 mouse. 4/3/89, 1 blue jay (feathers only found)." Willis and his mother split a Harry and David pear from a box he and Jean had sent the old man, then captured Geoffrey, put him in his Kennel Cab and drove back down to his mother's one-bedroom condo in Brookline. Next thing Willis heard, she was putting it on the market and moving up to Etna. Less because she'd gotten sentimental (though who the fuck knows) than because it was her one shot at ending up in a nice old farmhouse somewhere reading M. F. K. Fisher and shit. Or is that unkind?

When the cigarette's half gone, Willis stubs it out in the saucer, light-headed and about to vomit. He closes his eyes: worse. Well, he won't be getting hooked on *these* sons of bitches again. Throw 'em out. Put 'em under the faucet and *then* throw 'em out. So maybe what he'll do is, he'll go and see his mother.

6

Etna looks close enough on the map—Route 4 all the way to White River Junction, across the river into Hanover—but it's all mountains and fucking little towns, so by the time Willis gets there it's dark and he's got a headache from squinting against sun in the rearview mirror. And probably from *thinking* the whole way, because he was asshole enough to throw his tape deck out the fucking window.

The porch light's on and all four eyebrow windows are lit up; since she doesn't use the upstairs much, this must be to welcome him. *The house I grew up in,* he calls this, for simplicity's sake. He sometimes soothes himself with this absolutely bullshit idea that his mother's actually been here the whole time, keeping safe his childhood things: the Thornton W. Burgess books, the yellow seven-inch Burl Ives records, the Nichols Stallion cap pistol. In fact, she never set foot in the house from 1963—the year she split for Cambridge with Champ and Willis—until his father died.

His mother comes out onto the porch. As always, she looks an increment older than he expected; as soon as he's adjusted to the last incarnation, she's on to the next. But she looks good: suntan, silver-and-turquoise necklace with earrings to match, white hair in a single long braid. That and the hurt smile make her look like Willie Nelson.

"Come in, weary traveler," she says. "I was just starting to get anxious."

He gives her a one-arm hug. "I didn't know what to bring you, so I didn't bring you anything. You've got all the same crap here we've got in Preston Falls."

"Oh, I know; isn't it *terrible*?" she says. "If I *never* again taste maple syrup, do you know? Come in, come in."

His mother got rid of the really butch accoutrements—deer head, gun rack—when she first moved in. And of course the La-Z-Boy. Where he used to have a gray metal file cabinet, she's put a dry sink with worn blue paint the color of a robin's egg. But she's kept some of the Ayn Rand touches: Willis follows her into the kitchen, and through her copper cookware hanging from the beams he sees the old IBM wall clock. She's got the radio on—huh, she's bought herself one of those glorified boomboxes made to look like a stack of components. An Optimus: Radio Shack's house brand. Successor to Realistic. It's depressing to picture his mother walking into Radio Shack. He's looking through her meager stack of CDs on the kitchen counter when that fucking jiggety theme music starts up: *BUM BUM BUM BUM, BUM BUM BUM BUM, dump tadumpta dump tadumpta.* "I'm Noah Adams," says the voice.

"I know this program annoys you," his mother says, reaching for the Power button.

"And I'm—" Silence.

"Thanks," says Willis.

"But really, they *are* a lifeline up here. Especially living alone. I always send them money. Now, what can I get you? I have some lovely single-malt scotch. With just a little water? That's how the real Scots drink it." So apparently she's been reading the John McPhee collection he sent for her birthday.

"And how is *Jean*," she says. "And my *grand*children, who I never get to see. Let's sit out on the porch, do you mind? We won't be getting many more evenings like this."

They sit in a pair of bent-willow chairs, angled toward each other. Willis's tire swing used to hang from that branch of that maple tree.

"You won't believe what I found the other day," she says. "The first letter your father ever wrote me."

"In secret code?" he says. Right out of the gate, boy. What a shit he is.

His mother squinches her eyes shut, then opens them and takes a sip of her scotch. "Oh dear. Well, what did I know at twenty-two? A stupid little Smithie." She pronounces it *styewpid.* "But really, how was I to know? He was very normal, *I* thought. From my vast experience." Sip. "Well, it was such a long time ago. But it *has* been a strange life." Sip. "So are you off now?"

"Am I *off*?" he says.

"From your work? Aren't you on sabbatical?"

"Oh right. Two months."

"And you'll be at your farm?"

"Yeah, the endless project. I just patched a pipe in the bathroom that's probably been leaking since I got the place."

"But it's splendid that you can do that work," she says. "You do take after your father in that respect." Sip. "It *has* been a strange life. Do you ever hear from Cynthia, by the way?"

"Not since the last time you asked." Cynthia was Willis's girlfriend before he met Jean.

"I always liked her. And she's gone where, again?"

"Madison, Wisconsin, the last I heard."

"Oh yes," she says. "It's supposed to be very civilized." Sip. "How's yours holding out? Dinner's going to be another half hour."

"In that case," he says. Something rubs against his leg: Geoffrey, come to greet him.

"We're having *pollo coi funghi secchi*."

"Mam-ma mia," he says, bouncing the heel of his hand off his forehead. "I trust we aren't going to be having visions of the Absolute after the *funghi secchi*."

"Dear God, don't even joke about such a thing." Willis's mother had once been talked into eating psilocybin mushrooms during those first years in Cambridge.

"Oh come on," he says. "I was proud of you. I always remember that thing about how you were listening to Beethoven and—"

"Stop."

"—and seeing purple penises wiggling in sync like the—"

"*Stop.*" Hands over her ears.

"—Rockettes. I was hugely impressed." He strokes Geoffrey's head, and the cat arches his back.

"Dear God, *imagine* telling that to your *child*. What were you, fifteen? *Fourteen?* Well, it gives you some idea of the state I was in. *Horrible.*"

"Hey," says Willis. "Sounded great to me."

"Yes, I know." She gets up and takes their glasses into the house.

Willis stares out at the maple tree. Scotch must be kicking in; his legs feel heavy. The light from upstairs catches that tree branch: the rope that held the tire swing is long gone, and even the scar has healed. After it rained, you used to have to lift the tire exactly right to dump the water out, or it would just race around inside.

"Are you in touch with your brother these days?" He didn't hear his mother come back out. "He's not still at that dreadful store?" She hands Willis his glass.

"He's making the best of it," says Willis. Better not to tell her Champ was just in Preston Falls. "I admire him for hanging in." He takes a sip; she's put more water in this one.

"Apparently he's still punishing me."

"You could call *him*, you know."

His mother raises her glass. "Cheers." She sips, then sighs. "I understand his new friend is very nice. I hope she's not on the stuff."

"*On the stuff?*" Willis says. "I love it. What are you, keeping low company in your old age?"

"Well, whatever the expression is nowadays."

"She seems fine to me," he says. "Of course, she *does* wear long sleeves and she always seems to have a cold."

"Now *you're* punishing me." Sip. "What else shall we talk about?"

"Hmm," he says. "Okay, what did Jeffrey Dahmer say to Lorena Bobbitt?"

"Dear God."

"Nope," he says.

After dinner, Willis pours himself more Macallan, and his mother puts *Charade* in her VCR. When they get to where Audrey Hepburn says, "You know what's wrong with you? Nothing," Willis gives his mother an appreciative smile, sees she's fallen asleep and touches her arm. She tugs down her skirt, gets up and says good night. Willis watches *Charade* to the end, with Geoffrey purring on the arm of his chair, then pours more scotch. He stupidly forgot to bring *Our Mutual Friend*, but he does find the fat old Washington Square Press *Pickwick Papers* he had in high school. So he reads the trial scene, then some of the shit where Mr. Pickwick gets drunk with Ben Allen and Bob Sawyer. He pours more Macallan, which he brings upstairs along with *Pickwick* to his old bedroom with the eyebrow window. Sleeping here after all these years is less weird than it used to be, he'll give it that.

And he *does* sleep. Not even a dream, that he remembers.

When he comes downstairs, she's just putting water in her little Braun espresso maker; stiff strips of bacon are already stacked on a paper towel. She's listening to *Morning Edition*.

"Good morning," she says. "Scrambled, yes?"

"Is that some kind of innuendo?" He sits down at the table, ungrateful dog for thinking she might have made some fucking coffee before she started dicking around with bacon and shit. She pours the grease from the skillet into a Medaglia d'Oro can, then cracks four eggs into an earthenware bowl. He can't watch the rest. Eventually he hears the skillet sizzling.

"You don't have to go right back, do you?" She takes two plates down from the cabinet and sets them on the counter, then turns again to the skillet.

"Not *right* away," he says. "I should start back this afternoon, though, so I can get up early tomorrow and get some work done."

"Oh, fooey," she says.

"Why?"

"Well, I have tickets to the chamber series in Hanover. Elaine Cooper usually goes with me, but they've got Bartók on the program tonight and she can't stand anything at all screechy. What *she* calls screechy. She's a bit of a wuss—is that the word?"

"She's probably on the stuff," he says. Elaine Cooper is the widow of a Dartmouth history professor whose specialty was Froissart.

"Stop," she says. "I don't suppose I could tempt you."

Fuck, why not. Follow her to the concert in the truck and just leave right from there. A good old late-night drive. "Boy, Bartók—woo, I don't know." He flutters his fingers. "Pretty scary. I guess I better come along in case you need to be talked down."

"Oh, goody," she says, and brings the plates to the table. She's given him four pieces of bacon and most of the eggs. So much for eating better. Well, so he should've said something. "Voilà." She sits down, then bounces up again. She's forgotten forks.

His dream comes back up to him out of the dark, like prophecy in a Magic 8 Ball. He and Philip Reed are onstage, singing that Louvin Brothers song: *Satan is real, working in spirit.*

"Enjoy it," says his mother.

He picks up the stiffest strip of bacon and bites, then has to bring his palm up under his chin to catch a splinter. He pushes down the thought that he could be satanically possessed.

Morning Edition has a report on what happens to computers when the year 2000 hits. The gist is that somebody will think of something.

He's taken the plates to the sink and begun running water, when his mother says, "Oh, leave those and come for a walk. I have something to show you."

"And what might that be?"

"You'll see."

He opens his eyes wide and flutters his fingers again. She smiles.

They walk up the old overgrown road that goes behind the house and through the gap in the stone wall. Geoffrey follows this far, then turns back, meowing piteously. Past here you have to push through the saplings that have grown up in the track. A bright-blue sky, but it's turned chilly overnight; Willis left Preston Falls without a jacket, so he's put on a flannel shirt that belonged to his father. They step over the brook where it cuts across the trail and continue uphill. The old spring-house was over to the left: now it's just a glimpse of gray, mossy boards lying among the raspberry bushes. They follow the stone wall and the line of thick old maple trees, regularly spaced. Once, this was a real road, leading to a long-gone farm.

They pass the cellar hole his father called the Griffin place and keep walking uphill. In what used to be an orchard, his mother stops and touches a rotten old apple tree. "This is it," she says. "No, wait. I think I'm turned around. *That* one." She points to a different tree, similarly ancient and deformed, nearer to the stone wall. "That's where you were conceived."

"Out here?" he says. "Al fresco? My God, you *were* a couple of bohemians."

"It was just about this time of year—well, obviously, since you were born in July. It wasn't quite so cool, but of course it was later in the day. Dear God, it does come back. We made a little nest of all our clothes. Right there, in that patch of sunshine."

"What do you know," he says. He walks over to the spot. Tufts of grass, ferns, old rotted leaves. A flat rock, flush with the ground. With clothes under them, they wouldn't have felt it. He gets down on one knee, digs his fingers under the edge of the rock and lifts it: ants. He lets the rock back down, stands up and brushes off the knee of his jeans. "And you're sure that time was the one."

"Oh, no question," she says. "This wasn't one of our . . . better periods, shall we say. Though of course not as bad as—you know—it got."

"Right." He looks at the flat rock.

"I never told this to anyone," she says. "But it's so odd: when I woke up this morning I just had the strongest feeling about it. And I remem-

bered it so clearly. It frightened me all of a sudden—do you know?—
to be the only person alive who knew about it. Because for that just to
be gone, for it never to have even *happened*, in a way . . . I think if you
hadn't been here I would've called poor Elaine Cooper and burdened
her with it."

"Well," he says. "I mean, I'm glad you told me. . . ."

"I thought you ought to know. Because it was—it's *your* story, really,
more than mine."

"Right," he says.

"Well, so now you know." She shakes her head. "It kills me that it's
not precious to you." She begins to weep, then quickly stops herself.
"But I suppose it's one more chicken come home to roost, isn't it?"

He puts an arm around her; she seems to shrink and harden. "I'm
sorry," he says. "It means a *lot* to me, that you, you know, brought me
here and everything."

"Stop it," she says.

"I'm sorry," he says.

Silence. Then a crow starts cawing.

"I thought someday," she says, "you might want to bring *your* children here, because . . . This is all crazy, isn't it?"

"Of course not."

"Would you know your way back here?" she says. "If you wanted to
come sometime?"

"Sure. I actually know this spot. He and I used to come through
here hunting."

"Oh dear," she says. "Yes, and I used to worry so about you."

"And all for naught," he says, bright and breezy.

Another move or two and she'll say *Shall we?* and they'll start back
for the house and that'll be that.

"You won't come back here," she says. "You'll forget I ever told you
this." She looks back down the hill, toward the old cellar hole. "Well.
Shall we?"

7

He rolls into the dooryard at three in the morning, still buzzed from the coffee he got at the Dunkin' Donuts in Rutland. He lies down on the couch, pulls the comforter over him and picks up *Our Mutual Friend*. No point in trying to go to sleep until he's cooled out a little. By daylight he's polished it off. Piece of shit, basically.

He gets up, finds *The Mystery of Edwin Drood* and settles back in, but drifts off into a thing where Jasper in the opium den gets confused with Hildegard Behrens trying to take his pants down, except Willis doesn't know what Hildegard Behrens looks like, so he's using his mother's friend Elaine Cooper for her. It's probably a pun, and he's telling himself he's lost his bearings—that would be about his speed. But at least it's not another thing about the fucking devil.

He wakes to the phone ringing, jumps up and goes running.

"Hey, man," the voice says. "It's Reed."

"Uh-huh? Yeah?"

"What did I, wake you up? Listen, man, you going to come rock and roll tonight?"

"Shit."

"I think I woke you up," says Reed. "You get my messages?"

"I was in New Hampshire. Shit, what time is it?"

"Noon? Something like that. So you remember how to get there, right?"

"I don't know, man. I'm fuckin' beat."

"Yeah yeah. So go back to sleep and we'll see you over there like nine o'clock, right?"

"I don't know," says Willis. "Maybe."

"Hey,. we got to have our swingin' *guit*-tar man. Plus we, ah, have mucho business to discuss, you and me. I got your statement here, which we need to go over together."

"Shit," says Willis. "Yeah, okay. I may not stay all that late."

"Cool. We'll talk about that too."

Willis pisses away what's left of the day reading *Drood* and falling asleep and reading more *Drood*. For what it's worth, he figures out that Datchery, the guy who shows up out of nowhere, has to be Bazzard, Mr. Grewgious's clerk. Who the fuck else can it be? He wakes up from another nap, and it's dark outside. Time to make some coffee and hit the trail. Feels like he's coming down with something. Well, if the coffee wakes him up enough to get there, the drugs will keep him going. Though coming home last week was a little hairy. Still, it's great doing cocaine and playing rock and roll, or even just standing around being high with guitars and shit. No wonder it's such a *thing*. Bending over to put his boots on, he thinks he should at least change these socks. But.

He stops for gas in Preston Falls, and it's so chilly he pulls the hood of his sweatshirt over his Raiders cap and sticks his left hand in his pocket while he pumps. And this is only what, the middle of September. Still summer, technically.

When he gets to the farm, the gila monster's glowing on the porch roof and everybody's parked up by the barn. He opens his door to a blast of cold air and the smell of woodsmoke. You can hear them playing what turns out to be "Get Out of My Life, Woman," with real drums. Willis exhales and sees his breath. He's lugged his guitar and amp into the barn as far as the bottom of the stairs, when they finish with a ragged collective whomp.

"Soundin' good!" he calls.

A hand parts the plastic sheeting, and Philip Reed's foxy face appears. "My man. Give me *one second*."

Through the plastic Willis sees a blurry form lift a blurry guitar shape over its head. Then out comes Reed and down the stairs; he bats Willis's hand away from the handle of the Twin and carries it up himself. Willis can hear his ragged breathing. "Hell to get old," Reed says. "Here." He parts the plastic for Willis. Inside, the stove has made it stuffy, and everybody's down to t-shirts.

"Hey, how's it going," says the Strat guy.

"Hey," the bass player says.

"Hey, what's happenin'," says the drummer.

"Hey, sounds great," says Willis. "What *I* heard."

"Missed our swingin' *guit*-tar man, though," Reed says. "Here, why don't you get set up. I'll dig out that statement, we'll get *that* shit squared away and then—rock and *roll*. Don't forget, you got to do our gig with us. Saturday night." He opens his guitar case. Willis plugs the Twin into the power strip.

"Ah. Here's that rascal." Reed sticks something in his shirt pocket. "Listen, what about some vodka and grapefruit juice? My man Sparky here just did up the last of the pixie dust."

"Fuck you, man," says the drummer. "Like *you* didn't do none of it."

Reed holds up a plastic jug of Popov. "You want a lot or a little?"

"Sort of medium." Willis kneels on the shag carpeting and snaps his guitar case open. Damned if he's going to show how bummed he is. He slings the Telecaster over his shoulder, plugs into his analog delay—purist that he is, he won't use digital—then into the Twin, flips off the standby switch and plays an E-seventh: how'd he get so out of tune?

"Beautiful." Reed hands him a trembling Dixie cup, full to an eighth of an inch below the brim.

"Jesus," says Willis. He has to take a good sip just to get it under control.

"Hey, it's that little bit extra I always give my clients."

The Strat guy sticks his upper teeth over his lower lip and makes a fart noise.

"Let's go where we can have a civilized discussion," Reed says, nodding toward where the sheets of plastic overlap.

Willis follows him out into the cold dark of the barn and down the stairs, dangling the Dixie cup from his right hand.

"What a night, huh?" says Reed when they get outside. Willis looks up and sure enough: stars and a crescent moon. Bigger or smaller than the last time he saw it? "Here, why don't we sit in the car."

He opens his passenger door for Willis, who reaches across and gets the driver's side for him. Cold in here too. Reed squeezes in behind the wheel and turns on the dome light.

"So." Reed touches the limp rim of his Dixie cup to the limp rim of Willis's. "Better days."

"Cheers." The vodka reeks, like rubbing alcohol.

"*That'll* put hair on your chest," says Reed. "Okay, so here's the thing." He takes a piece of paper out of his shirt pocket and hands it to Willis.

Willis looks at it, then looks back at Reed. "Two *thousand dollars*?"

"What can I tell you," says Reed. "My expenses on this thing—well, you can see." He leans over to Willis and points to a line that says *Out of pocket expenditures: $1,050.* "The fifty's your fine," he says. "The thousand is what it took to grease His Honor. And the fee, the nine fifty, has to take into account my specialized knowledge of the legal system around here." He turns off the dome light.

"I don't believe this," says Willis. "You're telling me you bribed the judge?"

Reed takes another sip from his Dixie cup. "You were looking at some very serious criminal charges, my friend. And you waltzed out with a fifty-dollar fine. These things take a little doing."

"But you told me they were *bullshit* charges."

"Bullshit is as bullshit does." Reed laughs. "Christ, whatever that means." Sips again. "Listen, you're a good guy, a horseshit guitar player—almost as bad as *I* am—and I like having you around, you know? So let's just get this done, go back upstairs and rock out, what do you say?" He takes a good big gulp, ending with the rim of his cup on the bridge of his nose.

"I don't have it," Willis says.

"Come again?"

"I *literally* don't have it. I've got like a thousand dollars to live on until the first of November."

"Excuse me?" says Reed. "Am I missing something? You're the head gazakis there with Sportif, whatever the fuck you are, chief bottle washer. Your wife, I understand, works full time, you own a house in Westchester, another house up here . . ." He shakes his head. "Does not compute."

"And you know what it takes to keep all that shit together?" says Willis. "*Plus* car payments, *plus* bills, *plus* insurance, *plus* all the other shit? Two kids in school? Commuting? We're right up to the fucking edge every fucking month. To take this time off—okay?—I had to put a thousand dollars on fucking MasterCard."

"Hey, so there's your answer." Reed raises a finger and says, "Don't leave home without it."

Willis shakes his head. "That thousand brought me up to the limit. I'm paying *those* bastards like three hundred a month."

"Then I guess you have a problem." Reed takes a long swallow and looks into his empty Dixie cup. "But shit, you know? Maybe it's not as bleak as you think, man. There's that Telecaster, you know what I'm saying? Nice old Fender Twin to go with it? The classic setup. That's got to be worth a few thousand dollars to the right person. And I remember you saying you had a prewar D-18? See, you're in a lot better shape than you think." He crumples his Dixie cup, opens his hand and lets it fall.

"So in other words," says Willis, "you want to take the guitar and amp."

"Tell you the honest truth," Reed says, "I don't *like* fuckin' Fenders. I don't like the way they *sound*, and I don't like the way they fuckin' *look*." He takes a pack of Kools out of his shirt pocket, lights up and blows out a cloud of smoke, then cracks his window and flicks the match outside. Willis sees a wave of smoke flow over the edge of the window glass; he breathes in. "Hell, there's got to be another answer to this thing. I mean, I don't want you to have to give up your instruments, man. Like giving up a *child*."

Willis says nothing.

"Okay, maybe this is stupid, trying to tiptoe up to this. I'm used to dealing with—" Reed tosses his head in the direction of the barn. He takes another drag, blows smoke out. "Okay, what would you say if I were willing to give you a very substantial knockoff on your legal fees? In return for doing me a favor."

"Shit," says Willis, shaking his head. "Okay, let's hear it."

"See, I knew it. Here, let me have that fucking thing." Reed takes the bill out of Willis's hand, puts it on the dashboard and takes another piece of paper out of his pocket. "This look any better to you?" He turns the dome light on again.

Willis takes the paper. Like the other bill, it's typed on Reed's letterhead: *Legal fees and expenses, $250.* He looks at Reed, who turns up a palm and cocks his head. "I see," says Willis. "Nice. So what's this favor?"

"Oh, pretty straightforward. On your way home tonight, you stop by our friend Mr. Castleman's place and you hand him a manila envelope. Like a—what do you call 'em—padded envelope. Here, I'll show you." He bends forward, grunts, reaches under his seat and comes up with a mailing envelope taped shut with glossy tan tape. He sets it on the console between the seats. "You drop this by Calvin's on your way home, then Saturday night, on your way to our little gig, you stop by again and he gives you a package. He'll help you find a good safe place to put it. And then you just drive on over to the Log Cabin, obeying the speed limits and traffic signs as I know you *always* do, and at the end of the evening, I give you another envelope, which you again bring to Mr. Castleman on your way home. Simple."

"Fuck." Willis looks at the envelope, then takes a too-big gulp from his Dixie cup and gags on it.

"Hey, you okay, tiger?" says Reed. "Let me open a window here." He rolls his window halfway down, crushes out the cigarette on the outside of the glass and tosses it. "Too much excitement," he says. "So what do you think? Not so terrible."

Willis says nothing.

"See, on Calvin's end you're just a neighbor dropping by. And on this end you're a guy showing up to play his gig. Shit, not that anybody's probably keeping tabs. But Calvin did have his little trouble, so the cops are on *his* case, and of course they'd love to put *me* away because I'm old-fashioned enough to believe that under our system every person has the right to an attorney."

"Fuck," says Willis.

"But you, see, you're just a regular citizen to them, so *your* only risk is not showing up with what you're supposed to show up with. Which ain't gonna happen, right? Plus of course you get to share in the bounty, and I *know* you like the bounty."

He sniffs and flicks at his nose, and Willis feels a jolt of what, in another context, he'd swear was sexual envy. Champ's foot between Tina's thighs.

"Here," says Reed, reaching in his other shirt pocket. "I saved you a little taste."

8

Willis wakes up with his right cheek in shag carpeting. Head hurts. He looks up at a woodstove resting on cinderblocks. The carpet, he can feel, is made up of many, many little hard artificial fibers. He's got all his clothes on—his boots, even—and somebody's put a stiff blue plastic tarp over him, with metal-rimmed holes along the edges. The tip of his nose is cold, but his clothes and the tarp hold in his body heat. Sick to his stomach, though not to the point of having to vomit. Got to stop doing this shit eventually.

He props up on his elbow, which makes his head hurt so much his eyes water. These headaches must be a brain tumor; they really are *not normal*. He looks over and sees the drummer lying there. Right, now he remembers: Sparky passed out before he did, not that Willis passed out, strictly speaking.

He has to piss, and his head hurts so much that it doesn't make a shit's worth of difference if he stands up or not. He steals over to the drum set, footfalls noiseless in the carpeting, and looks down. Willis guesses the guy's okay: shoulders seem to be rising and falling. Booze fumes coming up—unless they're coming off *him*. Willis packs up his guitar and shit, lets the lid of the case down quietly and holds each button thing to the side with his thumb so you don't hear the snap. Pats pockets for his keys.

Shit—the envelope. Now he really *does* remember.

He parts the plastic sheeting and these cheesy-religious shafts of morning light are pouring through gaps in the barn siding. The good old truck's where he left it, next to the Econoline; the other cars are gone. There's a note or something on his windshield. He sets the guitar and amplifier down in the wet grass and takes a piece of yellow legal paper out from under the wiper: *Drive safely.* He unlocks the truck and feels behind the seat: envelope's still there.

He goes around behind the barn to piss, out of sight of the house. Just the tiniest steam rises where it hits the ground, so he huffs out his breath to see if it smokes and of course, of *course*, manages to piss on his fucking boot. To punish himself, he bites into his lower lip with his left-side canines: hurts like shit, which serves him right. He sucks the lip, tastes salty metal and spits blood on the boot he pissed. Fucking teach *you*, you fuck.

The sun's just above the treetops. As he goes bumping down the driveway, he looks over at the house: a light on in the low-roofed part and wavy clear air above the cinderblock chimney. Probably the bass player's wife is getting ready for work, if she works. A woman's disapproval: you can feel it radiating.

All along the two-lane road, Willis sees little girls and little boys waiting for the bus, wearing blue denim jackets, or red-and-black-checkered wool jackets, or puffy nylon jackets in combinations of turquoise, red and yellow. Some peer from shacks their parents built to shelter them, others bounce up and down on their toes in the cold. One little boy sits reading inside a sentry box with a Union Jack painted on it. At the corner of a dirt road, near a bunch of mailboxes, a mom in sweatpants stands talking with a mom in jeans as five or six kids play tag, getting their shoes wet in the long grass. He's tempted to yank the wheel and plow through the bunch of them. Well, not tempted, exactly: alive to the possibility. He squeezes the wheel tighter and passes by.

The temperature gauge is up a hair now, so he tries the heater; sure enough, warm air blowing on his shins. A chill goes through him, the body giving up the tension it maintained against the cold; at least that's Willis's little theory. His head's starting to feel better, so maybe he'll stop off in Preston Falls for some coffee and pick up a paper. Jesus, reading the paper. But when he gets to where you can either turn off into Preston Falls or keep going straight until you hit Brown Road, he figures why push it. With this envelope behind the fucking seat, all you'd have to do is have a brake light or a turn signal out.

Willis turns into Calvin Castleman's drive; Calvin's truck, heaped high with split cordwood, almost blocks the way. When he shifts down to creep around it, the clutch feels funky again. Could be the cold, maybe: isn't there grease inside a clutch? That hardens and softens? He taps his horn and climbs out; in a window of the trailer he sees a corner of curtain pull to the side, then drop. The door opens and Calvin comes out in his shirtsleeves, unlaced work boots flopping.

"Hey," Willis calls.

Calvin stares at him. "You were supposed to been here last night."

"Well, we sort of ran late," says Willis, "so I ended up sleeping there. We were over—"

"Yah, I *know* where the fuck you were. Reed know you stayed there instead of coming here? Look at me when I talk to you."

Willis meets his eyes. They're set so close together that he can't stop the thought: *genetic inferiority.* If Calvin can somehow read minds, he's fucked. Willis blinks. Blinks again. Calvin's not blinking. Willis sucks his lip where he bit it. Which must look submissive.

"Look," he says. "If there's a problem about this, you need to take it up with Reed. All he told me was—"

"Yah, there's a problem. There's a *big* fuckin' problem. These guys I deal with, these are fuckin' serious guys, you know what I'm talkin' about? I was supposed to left here last night."

"Look," says Willis, putting up both hands, "I don't know anything about it."

"Well, that's nice for *you*, ain't it?" He shakes his head. "Son of a bitch mother*fucker*. You got it, right?"

Willis points a thumb at his truck and Calvin follows him over; when Willis reaches behind the seat, Calvin grabs the envelope. "Let's go in the house."

"What for?" says Willis.

"Fuck are *you* worried about? All here, ain't it?"

"Whatever was in it is in it."

"Then you ain't got a thing to worry about." Calvin starts for the trailer. "Long's he ain't out to fuck *you*."

"How would he fuck *me*?" says Willis, catching up to walk beside him.

Calvin looks at him. "How would he fuck you? All right, let me ask you something. I bet you ten dollars he didn't tell you how much is in here. Right or wrong?"

"Okay," says Willis.

"Let's say we go in here and I open it up." He steps onto his cinderblock doorstep and turns to face Willis. "And you're short a thousand—whatever it is. So all's he's got to do is turn around and go, Well, it was all there when I give it to him. You with me here?"

Willis says nothing.

Calvin nods. "All new to you, ain't it?"

"I see what you're saying," says Willis.

"Anyways," says Calvin Castleman, "I doubt he try to dick around on this end of the deal, see, because he knows nothing's about to go down till I get *that* straightened out. And he's got people waiting on *him*. Me, though, I'd watch my ass on the back end." He opens the door to the trailer, and Willis follows him into the smell of stale woodsmoke.

Willis sits on the old car seat facing the display case with boxes of shells and bottles of Hoppe's No. 9. Calvin rests a buttock on his gray metal stool, lays the envelope on his workbench, picks up a box-cutter and slashes through the tape. He sticks a hand inside, looks at Willis, stands up and turns his back. Willis looks around the room. The skin of some animal, tail hanging down, pushpinned to the paneling. A yellowing *Far Side* cartoon he can't quite make out from here, taped up with yellowing tape.

"Yah, okay." Calvin opens the top drawer of a metal file cabinet and sticks the envelope inside. "So you come by here Saturday. What time you come by?"

"We're supposed to start around nine. He wants us there eight, eight-thirty to set up. So—seven o'clock?"

"Best make it quarter to. Bring all the shit you're going to bring, and you go straight there from here."

"Right."

"And you tell Reed he can go fuck himself. The last fuckin' time, tell him. I like to know what the fuck I'm dealin' with. And I ain't so fuckin' stupid I don't know you get more than a taste."

"Then you know more than I do."

"Yah, so what is this, fun for you? Your fuckin' weekends up from New York? You ought to stuck to auctions. Church suppers, that shit."

"Tell me about it," Willis says. "This is *not* my idea of fun. Yours either, I guess."

"Yah, I give up on *that* shit a long time ago." Calvin spits on his floor, rubs it with his boot. "So I guess you got the bill."

Back at the house, Willis starts coffee and checks the machine. Four blinks. He hits Play.

"*Hey, man, it's Reed. Listen, you got to come rock and roll to-morrow night. Give me a jingle, right? It's real real important we get together.*" Beeeep. "*Hey. Reed again. You there? Shit.*" Beeeep. Long nagging buzz. *Beeeep. "Willis. It's Marty. Listen, bud, I hate like hell to bother you up there, but we've got a mini-situation on our hands, and I was sort of figuring, Well, by now he's probably bored out of his mind up there staring at the trees, so, ah, if you get a chance. It's Wednesday morning? Eight-fifteen? Actually, tell you what. You have a fax up there, why don't I just fax the thing to you. At the very least you'll be amused." Beeeep.*

So Marty Katz is still on the planet. Dandineau Beverages. All very strange.

Up in his study he finds the fax curling out of the machine: a page of *Time* magazine with the Sportif ad where the sweaty blonde's tipping one back and it's, like, do you *really* see her nips or is it just a trick of the light. So? He wrote a form letter to cover this six months ago. Willis tears it off the roll and takes it over to his worktable. Oh. Next to the ad there's a photo of a syringe poking into a forearm (inset, head shot of teenage boy) to go with a story about high school jocks and steroids, plus some thought-provoking shit about values. Who among us is not implicated when some high school jock someplace shoots steroids? Willis picks up the phone.

"Steroids," he says when Marty answers. "Make-a you strong like bool."

"Hey," says Marty. "Mighty white of you to call, old man."

"So do we really care?"

"*You* don't care. What do *you* care? You got trees to stare at. Bucky, however, cares deeply. And through Bucky *I'm* learning to care."

"Well, so that's good, isn't it?" says Willis. "There's too little caring in this world. That's why our young people are turning to steroids."

"So you have any thoughts?" Marty says. "He wants a statement."

"Aw*right*, good *idea*. That way we can point out the irony, just in case anybody missed it. Somebody should tell Bucky it's now okay to bottle up your rage. I read somewhere that it doesn't give you cancer after all."

"Why don't *you* tell him? Here, I'll transfer you."

"Okay, okay. Uncle," says Willis. "I take it you already tried talking him out of it?"

"We don't all have your raw courage. I got Carey Wyman started on the thing."

"Oh, well, hell. Then you don't need *my* help."

"Very funny," says Marty. "Any chance you could look over his efforts?"

"Sure, no problem. With or without him knowing?"

"Oh, he knows. Probably easiest to talk with him online. You're wired there, right?"

"If you only knew," says Willis.

"I appreciate this. It shouldn't take up too much of your morning. What exactly *are* you doing up there?"

"Oh, you know. Drinking heavily. Doing drug deals with the locals. Got thrown in the slammer the other day."

"What did you, rape a cow?" Poor Marty thinks this is still heartless businessman badinage. "So you're getting stuff done on your dacha?"

"Little bit," says Willis. "Mostly sitting on my ass."

"What the good Lord made asses for. Something to sit on while you're watching football. Except you don't *watch* football, right?"

"No, I'm an intellectual. Don't you read my stuff?"

"I swear to God, if you're writing a fucking *novel* up there . . . Anyway, look. I told Carey you might be in touch. And I'll make sure Bucky knows you were pulling an oar on your time off. Might help you out of the doghouse. I told you what he said, right? When I told him we were having a pour for you? He said, 'I think I'll be busy.' "

"So he was probably busy."

"You know, you worry me, little guy," says Marty. "You're kidding, yes? When you come back, you're going to have to be a very good boy. You let it be known that you have a life. That's the mother of all no-nos."

"Call this a life?" says Willis.

"Bite your tongue. Somebody's apt to hear you." Marty's big on counting your blessings.

Willis hangs up, turns the computer on and types an E-mail message to cwyman.dandi@aol.com: *just spoke to marty. you have my sympathy. how far along are you?*

He goes downstairs and gets another cup of coffee. When he comes up again, he's got a thing back: *hopefully i'll be finished by noon. do you think this works as a through-line? we start out deploring any form of drug use (flick at our say no msgs on labels for last five years), then transition (still need to work this out) to idea of sportif as healthful alternative to empty-calorie soft drinks. minerals etc. etc. cheers, carey.*

Ah, youth. But that's unfair to youth. What explains Carey Wyman is that Buckridge has a soft spot for job candidates from the shit-ass college he went to in Indiana. Willis hits Reply to Sender and types: *starting off with antidrug shit seems fine. the lie du jour, right? but think we*

*need a whole other level of bogosity slash deviosity here. since we've
already got the name out there for free (which is the object of the game),
why not bag the ad copy (bound to look self-serving) and just say we vig-
orously applaud time's reporting, over and out. or what the fuck, maybe
we're even proud to be associated with. the high road. valderi, valdera.*

A message comes back: *thanks, i'll try that. do you think b will go for
it, though? cheers, carey.*

Willis hits Reply and types: *marty can probably sell it to him. (if you
want, i'll sell marty.) one thing in its favor, from b's pee oh vee: it'll come
from you, not me. i predict a happy honeymoon.*

Message back: *thanks, but hopefully i can sell m. don't want to take
up your time. cheers, carey.* The one endearing thing about Carey Wyman
is how right out there he is about wanting Willis's job. Willis hits Reply
and types: *go for it, with an old man's blessing.*

He's still logged on, to see if Carey Wyman is going to try a snappy
comeback, when the phone rings. So he was smart to get separate lines;
Jean said it was a waste since he was only there weekends.

And in fact it's Jean.

"Am I interrupting you?" she says.

"Nope," he says. "Just—you know. What's up?"

"The school just called. Apparently Roger hit a little boy this
morning."

"Is he okay?"

"Roger? Yes, he's okay in that he didn't get hurt. I wasn't going to
call you, but then I thought you should know."

"Right," he says. "What about the other kid?"

"He's fine, apparently. They took him in to see the nurse, but she
sent him back to class."

"So I guess we'll have a codefendant when the parents sue. Was this
self-defense?"

"Apparently not," she says.

"Hmm. Well, *that's* not so good. So how's the school playing it?"

"Mr. Giles sent him to the Quiet Room for the day." This is the
school's euphemism for detention; Roger's done time there before,
though never a whole day. "He'll have to make up the work, and—okay,
I'll be right there."

"You're in the office?" says Willis.

"Yes. Where else would I be? Ms. Schoemer's going to see him this
afternoon." School psychologist. They've dealt with her too.

"Then I guess justice has been served," says Willis.

"Listen, I have a meeting. I just thought you should know. Are *you* all right?"

"Never better," he says.

"Okay, I have to go," she says.

"So I guess I should come down."

"What for?"

"You know, to help deal with this. Did Carol get there?"

"Not yet," she says. "There's no need for you to interrupt what you're doing. I'm taking off early so I can pick him up, and I thought we'd go someplace, just the two of us, and try to talk."

"Hey, good luck."

"Well, what would *you* suggest? *Not* talking?"

"No, you're right," he says. "What else can you do? It's just, you know, first the *shrink* talks his ear off and—"

"That's not what she does," Jean says. "Listen, I have to get going."

"I'll be down sometime this afternoon."

"Please don't. I don't want you to."

"Jean, this is my responsibility too."

"Is that supposed to be funny?" she says. "I have to go."

Willis goes down, gets more coffee, eats some Cheerios. When he comes back upstairs there's E-mail from Carey Wyman: *here's a draft. would welcome your input. cheers, carey.* And then the spiel. Willis dumps it without reading, hits Reply and types: *suits me if it suits you.* In case that sounds hostile, he adds: *break a leg.*

And a message comes back: *thanks. it's with marty now, so i'm keeping my fingers crossed. cheers, carey.* Meaning he'd already sent it on. So much for Willis's input.

The phone rings again.

"So what do you think?" says Marty. "He sent it to you, right?"

"Yeah. I told him it seemed fine."

"Including the 'hopefully'? You've heard Bucky on the subject of 'hopefully.'"

"Oh," says Willis. "Oopsy."

"I guess you've got other things on your mind."

"I do, actually," says Willis. "Jean just called and told me that Roger got in a fight with some kid at school."

"Yeah? Clean his clock for him?"

"Sounds like it. The other kid was the one they had to take to the nurse's office."

"Hey. Way to go."

"Well, opinions vary," says Willis. "At any rate, I've got to go down there this afternoon, so give a shout if you need me to come in tomorrow."

"For *this*? Nah, I can clean it up from here. But listen, while we're on the subject. You *are* coming back, right? Reason I ask, if anybody let *me* out of the cage for two solid months . . . you know. Be like putting the toothpaste back in the tube."

"But you'd *go*," Willis says. "I mean, you'd have to."

"*Have* to, what's that?" Marty says. "You know? You *have* to breathe. I don't know, I just get a funny feeling."

"And it's what makes you the great sports-drink executive you are," says Willis. "Marty. I have a house—*two* houses—two sets of bills, wife and family, *car* payments. . . . Believe me: if ever a man was gotten by the balls."

"I hate to pop your bubble," says Marty, "but your situation is not absolutely unique. The thing is, I just know how quickly everything can disappear from a person's screen. Shit, I don't know, this is verging on the weird."

"No no no, I appreciate the concern," says Willis. "Though I guess I'm not sure what this is *about*, exactly. They don't have any tramp steamers up here."

"Forget it," Marty says. "I'm probably just projecting. Read: *envious*. Listen, thanks for helping out."

"Hey, my parting gift to the world," says Willis. " 'Tis a far, far better thing I do. What is the answer? Very well, then, what is the question? On the whole, I'd rather be in Philadelphia."

"Ho-kay," says Marty. "I'll leave you to your whatever."

It's still daylight when Willis pulls into the driveway in Chesterton: two strips of pebbly concrete with grass between, from the days of cars with running boards. At least the people who owned the house before had the taste not to blacktop it, and not to replace the wooden Z-braced garage doors with an overhead one. Though more likely they couldn't afford to. The Cherokee's gone; he walks up the driveway, looking at the velvety green moss filling the cracks in the concrete, then cuts across the grass to the kitchen door. There's Rathbone, on his hind legs, looking out. Willis says "Bone-face!" and turns the knob—except the son of a bitch won't turn. He feels in his pocket for his house keys. Shit. He knocks, on the off chance. Well, if all else fails there's a key taped to the bottom of one of the garbage cans.

Footsteps, and here comes Mel.

She opens the door and says, "Daddy, what are you *doing* here?" Rathbone slithers out, his whole rear end wagging, and jumps up on Willis.

"I *live* here. Good dog, yes, I'm glad to see you too." Rathbone has his paws around Willis's waist. Willis rubs him behind his silky ears. "How *are* you, sweetheart?"

"I'm all right," Mel says.

"You don't mind if I come in?"

"*Dad*-dy," she says, and stands aside. He shuts the door behind him and tosses his jacket on the Cosco stool. Rathbone's still dancing around, toenails clicking.

"Yes, you're a good boy," says Willis. "Has he been out lately?"

"He's just glad to see you," says Mel.

"Where's the Mom?"

"She had to go shopping."

"Ah," he says. "She take Roger with her?"

"No. She *tried* to make him go, but he wouldn't, and then she got mad and made him go to his room. Do you want some tea, Daddy? O-*kay*, Rathbone. *Chill.*"

"No. No, thanks," he says. "I might make some coffee later. Sit." Rathbone sits, but his tail keeps sweeping.

"Tea's better for you."

He follows her into the living room. She sits, cross-legged, on the couch, where he's glad to see she has a book open, face-down, and a loose-leaf notebook. The soles of her white socks show hardly any dirt. Brooding over the couch is this picture Jean once painted of a bed with nobody in it. The folds of the quilt are some kind of tour de force, apparently, but you can't miss what it's fucking *about*.

"How's the homework this year?" he says. He sits on the wooden chair, so as not to get too comfortable; he's got to go up and deal.

"I don't know. It's just homework."

"Hey, I guess that's why they call it homework."

"Did you come because of Roger?"

"Well, it gave me an excuse," he says. Her book, he sees, is *I Know Why the Caged Bird Sings*.

"Yeah, like you really wanted to." She's twisting hair around a finger.

"Hey, it beats sitting in jail," he says, on sudden inspiration. It's a lighthearted way of broaching the unbroachable. Though now that he's said it, he's not so sure. Mel continues twisting her hair. Their first mistake with her was naming her Melanie: since he and Jean are both dark, he pictured her with this glistening black hair. (Trust Willis to know the etymology of every fucking thing.) But by the time she was six, her hair had turned brown-to-blond, and here she is, stuck with the name Melanie Willis. Like some Hollywood personage. He's thinking of Bruce Willis and Melanie What's-her-face, the slutty one. Though actually it's Bruce Willis and whoever the *other* one is. Willis prides himself on not keeping up.

"Listen, I'm very sorry you had to be there for that," he says. "I guess I was more stressed out than I'd, sort of, given myself credit for." Has he made this speech already?

"What were you stressed out about?" she says.

"I don't know. Work, mostly." She seems to accept this. At least she says nothing. "So the Mom left you guys here by yourselves?"

"Why wouldn't she?" says Melanie. "I've only been doing home-alones since I was like *Roger's* age. And don't call her *the Mom*, okay?"

"I guess you have, haven't you? God, I feel like Rip Van Winkle. Hey, there you go, that would be a good trivia question. What was the name of Rip Van Winkle's dog—no, wait. First, who was Rip Van Winkle?"

Mel sighs. "Wolf."

He looks at her. "You're kidding. That's really the dog's name? How did you know that?"

"They made us read it last year."

"And you remembered the name of the dog? That's amazing."

She shrugs. He can see she's having trouble with the corner of her mouth. Trying not to smile.

"I didn't think they read that in school anymore," he says.

Nothing. So he has to fucking spell it out. "Why were they reading 'Rip Van Winkle'?"

"We were studying the cultures of the thirteen colonies."

"Ah." Heel of hand to forehead. "Dutch Culture Day." Shitting on her for the school *they* sent her to. He switches to his attentive slash respectful mode. "So what did you think of it?"

"I don't know," she says. "Sexist. Of *course*."

"Why *of course*?"

"Everything is that's old. Did he, like, hate women?"

"You mean the way he does Mrs. Rip?" A vista opens: father-daughter literary discussions. "Yeah, you do sort of wonder what her side of the story would be like."

Mel says nothing.

"Listen," he says, "did the Mom say when she'd be getting back? Oops. Sorry."

Mel sighs. "She said not long."

"So listen, I guess I better go up and have a word with your brother." He gets up and stretches, fists high above his head.

"The Terminator," she says.

"Right," he says. "So do you have any theories?"

"Yeah. Testosterone."

"I think he's a little young for that," says Willis. "I don't know, maybe not." One more thing he's pig-ignorant about: do you only get testosterone at puberty, or does it come with testicles automatically?

He climbs the stairs, Rathbone right beside him, tail thunking against the balusters, and knocks on Roger's door. "Yo. The Rog-meister."

"What," Roger says through the door.

"I'll huff and I'll puff."

"What do you want?"

"Roger, if you don't open this door by the time I count to *ten*—"

"It *is* open."

Willis opens the door, and Roger's sitting against the wall, legs out, with what looks to be a five-pound weight in each hand, keeping his trembling arms straight. "Hey. How's it going?"

Roger doesn't answer. Willis walks over and sits at his work station. Fucking mess. Papers, cassettes, marker pens, little plastic superheroes. A bottle of mucilage with the wedge-shaped rubber top, glue drooling out of the slit.

"So your mom told me something happened at school this morning," Willis says. "You want to tell me your version?"

"No."

"I guess I phrased that badly," says Willis. "What happened?"

Roger lowers the weights, slowly, still keeping his arms straight. At the last inch he loses control, and they thud on the floor. He takes a deep breath, lets it out. "I hit a kid, big deal."

"What kid?" says Willis.

"I don't know what his name is."

"How old a kid?"

"I don't know."

"Older or younger than you?"

"Same age."

"So he's in your class, but you don't know what his name is?" No answer. "What did he do to you, this kid?"

"Nothing."

"Then why did you hit him?"

"He was getting on my nerves."

"And how did he do that?"

"I don't know, he's just a feeb. I didn't want him there." Slowly, Roger raises the weights again.

"Is that a reason to hit somebody?"

"He wouldn't move when I said."

"Why should he have to?"

No answer. The weights inch up.

"Suppose somebody started ordering *you* around," Willis says. "How would *you* feel?"

"So what? I'm not him." Roger's got the weights at shoulder level, arms absolutely straight.

"What did you call him—a feeb? What exactly *is* a feeb?" Roger can't possibly know the word *ephebe*, right?

"I don't know," says Roger. "Some little *feeb*. That can't do anything right." The weights start down.

"Well, you know," says Willis, "sometimes people think they're mad at one person but actually who they're really mad at is somebody else. Or they're even mad at themselves." Poor kid's probably thinking, *Will somebody get him the fuck out of here?*

Roger sets the weights on the floor. "I'm thirsty," he says.

Willis follows him down to the kitchen (Mel looks up at them, then back down at her book), feeling like a stupid, doomed apeman dragging his knuckles along the floor while compact, wily Roger belongs to a race adaptive enough to survive. Roger goes up on his toes to get a glass down—so lightly that it gives Willis a pang—then opens the refrigerator and pours milk. Rathbone (who knows where meat is kept) sits like a good dog, gazing at the open refrigerator and sweeping his tail back and forth on the linoleum.

"I think I'll join you in one of those," Willis says.

"You don't *drink* milk." Roger takes the glass of milk in one hand and a cardboard canister of protein powder in the other, and shuts the refrigerator door with his foot. Willis goes to the cupboard and takes down a glass. Roger puts his stuff on the counter and gets a spoon out of the silverware drawer.

"I'm just going to say something," says Willis, opening the refrigerator. Rathbone's tail starts up again. "You're old enough that we don't have to dance around this, okay?" He takes out an almost-brand-new half gallon of orange juice. (You can count on Jean.) "I've been spending quite a bit of time away, you know, on weekends, and of course now we're looking at a couple of *months* when I'll mostly be up in Preston Falls. Because the house needs so much work." He pours orange juice, puts the carton back and shuts the refrigerator door. Rathbone lies down. "Anyhow, what sometimes happens," he says, "is that when the routine changes around home, kids will sometimes blame themselves, or think they've done something wrong. You know, when it's not their fault at all. Or *anybody's*." He sits down and takes a sip, like an orator pausing. "And this in turn can get them upset, or angry, and sometimes they're not even sure what they're angry *about*, you know? I'm not saying that *you*'ve been feeling this way, necessarily, but I really just want you to understand and remember that Mommy and I both love you and Mel very much. *And* we care very much about each other."

And let him find a loose end in *that*.

Roger finishes stirring protein powder into his milk, sucks the spoon a second, then carries it over to the sink. He replaces the lid on the canister and puts it back in the fridge. Then and only then does he take his first sip.

"So what do *you* think about all that?" says Willis.

Roger shrugs. "I don't know. I guess it's pretty normal."

"What is?"

"I don't know," says Roger. "Tyler's mom and dad got a divorce. And so did Adam's."

"Whoa," says Willis, "wait a minute." He puts his glass down. "That's not what's going on here. At *all*. Did you think that? Mommy and I aren't— Rog, believe me, it's not *anything* like that. It's just a time when I have to be up at the house to do some fixing and Mommy has to work and you guys have to go to school, right? And meanwhile Mommy and I are going to be using this time, each of us, to think about how we could all have more fun together maybe than we've been having. You know?" He waits a beat, giving the earth its chance to swallow him up.

"Mel says you're getting a divorce," says Roger.

"Well, I don't know where Mel gets her information." Fucking Mel, thanks a lot. Willis gets up to look into the living room; she's no longer on the couch. "I guess I need to talk to *her* about this too."

Roger's picking at a scab on his elbow. "Mel says that's what Mom says."

"Don't do that," says Willis. Roger stops picking. The upstairs toilet flushes. "Well, obviously there's been a miscommunication somewhere. Which we're going to have to get straightened out, because that is *not* what's going on. But you know, if that's what you thought, I can understand why you'd be upset. And maybe that had something to do with what happened at school, you know? But what you *don't* do in that situation, you don't take it out on some poor kid. Okay? Because you think he's a *feeb* or whatever he is. If you're feeling angry, you talk to somebody. Right? You know that. Me or Mommy, preferably, but if we're not available right at that time, you go to a teacher or a teacher's aide or to Ms. Schoemer. Or your sister, even."

"Oh right," Roger says.

"Well, whoever," says Willis. "The point is, you don't just lash out and hit. You understand? Now, if somebody hits *you*, that's a different story. It's perfectly okay to stick up for yourself and defend yourself. But you don't be the one who starts stuff and picks on *other* kids. Any more than you want them to pick on you." Hey, give this man a white robe, sandals and the little children at his feet. "Do you understand?"

Willis waits for a nod. He hears a door close upstairs. "Yo. I asked you if you understood."

Roger nods. More a twitch of the head, actually.

"Good. Because I don't ever want to hear of this happening again." So now we're the father in the thunderclouds. He downs the rest of his orange juice like a shot of red-eye. "Okay? Enough said?"

He's rinsing out their glasses and trying to plan what to say to Mel about the divorce thing, when the phone rings. Roger gets it—he'd never admit it, but he's still proud of answering the phone—and says, "Yeah, he's here." He thrusts the phone toward Willis with a rigid arm. "Mom wants to talk to you."

Willis wipes his hands on his jeans and takes the phone.

"I saw the truck in front of the house," she says. "How long did you plan on staying?"

"What—where are you?"

"At a phone booth."

"Oh. So in other words—" Roger's sitting right here. In other words, she drove by the house, saw he was there and went to a phone booth?

"Could you just give me a rough idea?" she says. "Like were you going to spend the night?"

"Not if it's, you know, inconvenient," he says.

"I'm not trying to kick you out. It's just that if you *were* planning on going back up tonight, it might be less awkward if I waited till after you left."

"Interesting," he says. "Yeah, *o*-kay. Got it. Fine."

"You're deliberately misunderstanding me."

"Well, I doubt *that*." Willis looks at Roger; he's reading the Cheerios box. "Just give me, I don't know, five? Too long?"

"Crap. I shouldn't have done this."

"Hey. Not a problem." In fact, he almost fell asleep driving down here. "There *was* one thing I wanted to bring up, but we can talk about it later."

"What's that?" Jean says.

"We'll talk about it."

"Oh," she says. "So Roger's right there?"

"You betcha."

"This really sucks," she says, and hangs up.

"Love you," he tells the dial tone, loud enough for Roger to hear.

He puts the phone back in the cradle. "Listen, bud," he says to Roger. "Mommy needs me to do something for her right away, so you may not see me for a while, okay? But we'll be talking on the phone. Would you do me a big favor and explain to Mel when she comes down?" No way he's going to try to sell *her* this sudden-errand bullshit.

"I don't get what I'm supposed to say."

"Just tell her that I'll be calling, okay? And no more hitting feebs. Unless they hit you first." He gives Roger's upper arm a gentle right hook and heads for the door. Rathbone gets up to follow him. "No, you *stay*," Willis says. Rathbone sits and looks down at the floor.

At the corner of Stebbins and Crofts he pulls over and waits to flag her down. Now it's completely dark. After fifteen minutes he guesses she must have come the other way, on Bonner. He gives it another five, then turns around in somebody's driveway and cruises back past the house. Son of a bitch: there's the Cherokee. Well, what would he have said anyway? Told her to tell Mel to tell Roger their marriage isn't fucked?

He hangs a left on Bonner, goes out to Route 9 and up to the Dunkin' Donuts, where he orders four coffees to go. But when he gets back in the truck, it hits him that he absolutely can't make it all the way back to Preston Falls. Even with a cup of coffee for each hour. Shit, how did this day start out? Waking up in What's-his-name's barn—can that be possible? And what happened yesterday? Oh, who the fuck knows. There's a motel a couple of miles north on the right-hand side, or there used to be. He could be in a bed within ten minutes. Which might be well worth the fifty bucks or whatever. Because this really isn't making it.

Yep, the Birlstone Motel. Birlstone: what ho. VACANCY. TV. WEEKLY RATES AVAILABLE. There's definitely a sweet taint of self-pity in this, putting up in some shithole motel right in Chesterton. But he did legitimately get disinvited from his own house, did he not? So who can say a word?

10

The cleaning woman pounds on the door at like eleven in the morning, so he must've slept fourteen hours. More. Too much, probably. Or still not enough. Since he slept in his clothes, all he has to do is put on his boots, grab up the room key and the Dunkin' Donuts bag, and he's out of there before they can charge him for an extra day. He gulps his first cup of cold coffee sitting in the truck outside the motel office. His second while crossing over the Tappan Zee.

Twenty miles south of Preston Falls, he stops at the used-book store where they've got that lawn boy out front, with the Nixon mask. He's hoping he might find *Barnaby Rudge*, the only one he's missing, and which is probably a piece of shit; but if you're doing a Dickens thing, you might as well do a fucking Dickens thing. Place is run by a blatant old pedophile with a white beard gone yellow around the mouth. Once, years ago, Willis brought Roger in and the son of a bitch tried to get Roger to sit on his knee. When they got back outside, Roger asked if the man was one of Santa's helpers.

No *Barnaby Rudge*, but while he's looking for *Junkie*, which he remembers as being better than any of the later shit, he finds an old copy of *Pilgrim's Progress*, its cover showing a hippie-haired cavalier and an armored knight, both in water up to their asses. The Slough of Despond, probably. Or no, probably that river you have to cross over, the River of Whatever-the-fuck. He flips through the yellow-brown pages and finds an illustration captioned "Atheist": a feather-hatted fop beckoning someone to follow, unaware he's at the edge of an abyss (you see a bird flying in the distance) and about to put his slender walking stick down into empty air. Willis doesn't remember Atheist but assumes he must be a fucking atheist. What's great about *Pilgrim's Progress* is, everything's just exactly what it is.

"I'm going to take this off your hands," says Willis, bringing it up to the counter.

"Ah," says the bearded man. "Now, *that*." He taps his index finger on it. "That came out of a very wealthy home in Saratoga Springs. The House Beautiful."

"God, that's right," says Willis, getting out his wallet. "This is actually where that *comes* from, isn't it? The House Beautiful."

"Ah, well, you understand," says the bearded man. "But how many others? Fewer and fewer. The House Beautiful. Vanity Fair. The Slough of Despond." He even pronounces it *slew*. "We're seeing the return of the Dark Ages, my friend."

Willis is convinced. That is, it seems as convincing as anything else.

When he gets back to the house, the machine's blinking. Jean. Please call. Yeah, fine. He starts coffee. He decides to bag the rest of *Edwin Drood*, so he hunts up good old Sherlock Holmes and reads "The Man with the Twisted Lip" and then, despite the coffee, falls asleep somewhere in "The Adventure of the Creeping Man." When he wakes up it's dark and therefore too late to call Jean: she'll be home, where the kids can overhear. What day is this anyway? Thursday? Friday? How could you quickly find out? Because on Saturday he has to do that thing.

He decides it can't be Saturday and reads the entire fucking "Hound of the Baskervilles." That takes care of a couple of hours. Then he steps outside and has another little go at the stars. Comes back in and reads *Dr. Jekyll and Mr. Hyde*. Tries to read *The Picture of Dorian Gray*. Yeah, maybe in some other life. Reads "A Study in Scarlet," skipping the Mormon shit. Then starts the Mormon shit. Falls asleep. Wakes up at first light and starts worrying he'll get busted and his house and everything will be seized because of zero tolerance. Jesus, the house in Chesterton too. Tries to read "The Valley of Fear," but his heart's racing and he's short of breath. Is *this* the heart attack?

He goes downstairs and polishes off the last of the Dewar's, which numbs him enough that he can nod out over "The Valley of Fear." Waking up in full daylight, he dials 0 and asks if this is Saturday. A reproachful second goes by before the operator says, "This is Friday, sir."

He starts coffee.

———

It turns so cold Friday night he gets the woodstove going; the first time since spring. Since he *still* hasn't finished stacking that wood, it's still blocking the back door into the kitchen and he has to wheel a supply all the way around in the wheelbarrow. But it comforts him: the old ritual of kindling and feeding fire, the primalness of wood heat. Which is bullshit, because heat's heat, a matter of molecules moving. He gets sleepy around ten, climbs the cold stairs and huddles under the cold covers in all his clothes, knees as close to his chest as his gut allows.

At daybreak he gets up to piss, looks out the kitchen window and sees frost has whitened the grass. Quick, back to bed.

When he's finally up for real—early afternoon, is it?—he makes coffee and starts in on *Pilgrim's Progress*, which turns out to be better than he remembers. *Sometimes they would chide*—Christian's wife and children, this is—*and sometimes they would quite neglect him. Wherefore he began to retire himself to his chamber, to pray for and pity them, and also to condole his own misery.* But when he gets through the Slough of Despond part, which he'd forgotten was so early on, and into the shit with Worldly Wiseman, he starts thinking he should probably break out a guitar and see if he can get his fingers working for tonight..He's still trying to motivate himself when the phone rings.

Jean.

"Hey. Hi. Sorry I didn't get back to you," he says. Coffee has kicked *in*. "Everything okay down there?"

"As well as can be expected," she says.

"Oh, listen, I wanted to ask you. How did *you* make out?"

"With what?"

"Talking to *Roger*. About the *kid*." What is the *problem* with this woman?

"I don't know. I guess he's figured out that if you get caught hitting people, you get punished."

"Hmm," says Willis.

"The reason I called," she says, "I guess I'm just wondering what your plan is."

"My plan?"

"After your leave."

"I don't know what you mean. After my leave, I guess my leave is over. Why?"

"Oh God," she says. He hears her let out a big breath. "I just can't believe we've gotten to this place."

"Are the kids there?" he says. I.e., hearing every word?

"They're with Carol. She took them in to the Museum of Natural History."

"So Carol got there?" he says.

Silence.

"Well, that's good at least." Silence. "That was nice of Carol." Silence. "I mean, to take them to the museum." Silence. "Listen, tell her I said hello. If that's appropriate." Jesus, he's got ants in here. Look at that scuttling little son of a bitch.

"You didn't answer my question," she says.

"Your question."

"About your plans," she says.

"I thought I *had*. Unless you know something I don't know."

"Meaning what?" she says.

"Well, Roger—for example—seems to have the idea that we're getting a divorce. Were you aware of that?"

"Crap," she says. "I am going to *kill* Melanie."

"So what exactly was it you said to her?"

"She asked what was going on, and I tried to answer her as best I could. Since *I* have no idea what's going on either. I did *not* tell her we're getting a divorce."

"Uh-huh. So you said what?"

"I just more or less told her, yes, this was a difficult time. And I did try to prepare her that this could be one of the possibilities—which it obviously is."

"Oh, great," he says. "So no wonder they're freaking out. That's practically an announcement."

"Well, then, I wish you'd been there to set us straight. I'm sure I'm stupid, but I fail to see why mentioning something as a possibility is an *announcement*. But of course you're the master of words."

Unbelievable. But he'll ignore the personal shit. "Apparently," he says, "what got communicated was that they better brace themselves. So it might be a good idea to get our stories straight."

"Our stories?"

"All I'm saying is, Roger has *somehow* gotten the idea that this is a certainty. Which it's very far from being. At least in *my* opinion."

"So that's our story?" she says. "That nothing's a certainty? I have to tell you, it doesn't exactly fill me with hope. Whatever I would even *hope* for at this point."

"Meaning what?" he says.

"Meaning I sometimes think there's something to be said for not having quite this daily level of unhappiness."

"That's quite a statement." He sits down on the floor, his back against the wall. This is clearly going to be a long one.

"*I* think so," she says. "But I'm also not—I don't know—ready to say that I don't, you know, have any hope." Then she says, "Sorry, I guess that was an outburst. Am I embarrassing myself?"

He says nothing.

"Okay," she says. "Look, you want your *break*, you can have your *break*. I promise nobody will bother you from here on out. You've conditioned the kids not to expect to hear from you. And *I* don't *want* to hear from you. So I guess I'll just see you at the end of October. Maybe we'll end up taking the same train some morning."

And she hangs up. Dial tone.

He gets up and slams down the phone. Shit. For this not to fuck up the whole rest of the day is going to take some management. Which doesn't mean you try to push it away, *no* no-no-no. No, what you do, you bring it briefly up into the light: the way you propose a problem to yourself at bedtime, go to sleep and wake up with the solution, supposedly.

So he tells himself, experimentally, *You used to love this woman.*

Okay, so?

He turns it around: *This woman used to be loved.*

And *then* he begins to weep: big glottal sobs he knows will turn to retching if he doesn't stop. He has to feel his way to the kitchen table and sit down, hugging his shoulders and rocking, teeth bared and clenched as if he were doing his Louis Armstrong imitation. It doesn't escape him how weird this is: that he could work up a few sobs only by imagining *her* feeling bereft. If this is narcissism—and what the fuck else could it be?—it's got a kink or two.

When he's done, he goes into the bathroom, splashes his face with cold water, dries off and checks in the mirror to see how red the whites of his eyes got. Pretty satisfactory. Sons of bitches feel like they're swollen. He takes three Advils to preempt a headache. So what now? Haul out the Unnamable and try to condole his misery?

No: no heart for it. So back to the couch and *Pilgrim's Progress*, until he hits the thing with the guy in the iron cage who's hardened his heart and can't repent. He looks out the window. A nice day, looks like. But the trees really are starting to go. Not just a few reds among the green, a *whole bunch* of fucking reds.

He puts his boots on and goes into the kitchen. After dumping the dregs of flat seltzer out of a plastic bottle, he pours in milk, then cold coffee, then Kahlúa from the bottle Carol sent them as a housewarming gift five years ago. Which he's lately been working on when there's nothing else in the house. He takes the seltzer bottle, the comforter and Sherlock Holmes, and he's out the door.

He tries to climb the hill slowly, so as not to depress himself with heaving gut and pounding heart. But he still has to stop and take deep breaths. This is absolutely how he's going to die. When he reaches the top, he spreads out the comforter, sits down, flabby legs crossed, and looks across at the other hills. He imagines soaring off above the green and red and yellow treetops and into the everlasting blue. Then he looks down at the house, as you might look down upon your own body at the moment of separation. Down there, under the roof slates, he imagines Doug Willis stretched out on the dog-smelling couch.

He wakes up on the hilltop, with the sun going down. The fuck time is it? He's got to be at Calvin's when? Shit, probably right now. He works himself free of the comforter, gets to his feet and snatches the son of a bitch off the ground—and of course his book falls out into the wet grass because that's what he fucking *deserves*.

Back at the house, he loads the Twin and the Telecaster. Okay, so what else does he need to bring? Jacket in case it gets chilly. It's already chilly. Ten of six: shit. Well, not so bad. Wallet? Keys?

He comes jouncing into Calvin's dooryard and cuts the engine. There's the truck, still heaped high with firewood. A light's on in the trailer; Willis gets out of his truck, smells woodsmoke and looks up at the ragged space of pink-orange sky hemmed by black trees.

Calvin opens the door and sticks his head out. Willis can see his bare shoulder. Calvin looks like shit: raccoon eyes, and he must not have shaved since Willis saw him last. "Yah, okay," he says. "Get a shirt on here be right with you." He shuts the door, and Willis boosts himself up to sit on the fender. He hears a pack of dogs yapping somewhere, off in the direction of Wakefield. The yapping gets louder, now coming out of the sky. Geese going south. He keeps looking up, but the trees block his view, and the yapping gets fainter and fainter, moving away toward Preston Falls. Then Calvin comes out.

"You hear that string of geese just go over?" Willis says.

"I can't hear shit no more. Account of the fuckin' chainsaw."

"Those ear things help any?" Willis cups hands over ears to show he means those things that look like headphones.

"Nah, bunch of fuckin' OSHA bullshit. Top of that, I got that fuckin' thing where you can't feel nothin' in your hands?" He massages a wrist with thumb and middle finger. "Same fuckin' thing them computer son of a bitches get."

"Carpal tunnel," says Willis.

"Whatever the fuck. Here, let me see this cocksucker." He climbs onto Willis's truck and hunkers down to peer at the amplifier, palms on knees, elbows out. "Yah, okay. Let's take it in where we can see what the fuck we're doin' here."

"What do you mean?" says Willis.

"Got to put the shit in this here."

"You sure? You can see right in the back."

"Nah, up inside here." Calvin taps the top of the Twin with his index finger.

"What, you're taking the guts out of it?"

"Yah, that's the idea." He stands up, lets down the tailgate and lugs the Twin to the edge.

"But this is what I play through," Willis says.

"Not tonight I guess you ain't." Calvin jumps down, pulls the amp down off the tailgate and starts for the trailer.

"Shit, there's got to be some other place you can put it," says Willis, tagging behind.

"It ain't my idea," says Calvin. "Talk to Reed about it." He opens the door. "You comin' in or stayin' out?"

It's hot inside the trailer; Willis takes his jacket off and sits down on the car seat. He watches Calvin lift the Twin onto his workbench and pick up a Phillips-head screwdriver. "You know *how* to take these things apart?"

"Guess I'll figure it out."

"This is a vintage amplifier," says Willis, hating the tone he's taking. "It's worth money."

"Yah, couple minutes here be worth a whole lot more, tell you that."

"You mind if I don't watch?" Ooh, Willis, you bitch.

"Suit yourself," says Calvin.

Willis pages through a copy of *Car and Driver*. They've got a test report on the Mitsubishi Galant, which makes him think of a Renaissance dance. A venereal disease. *Courante, galliard, gallantry, glans, gleet.* How can this be happening to someone so well read?

"All right, stay here," Calvin Castleman says. Willis looks up. The operation's over, apparently: on the workbench next to the Twin sits a long aluminum box with tubes sticking up out of it, like a city of the future.

"You should get a dog," says Willis.

"Why's that?"

"I don't know." What's he trying to do? Goad Calvin into beating the shit out of him? "Guard your place."

"Yah, I thought about it," says Calvin, and out he goes.

Willis listens for a minute, then creeps over to the window, kneels and gently, gently, with his index finger, moves the corner of the curtain aside an inch to peer out. It's like he almost *wants* to see Calvin's eye right there on the other side of the glass glaring back at him. But Calvin has climbed up onto his truck and he's kneeling among the split chunks of firewood, tossing logs to the side, digging down for something.

When he comes back in, carrying a black nylon gym bag, Willis is on the seat again, with *Car and Driver* in his lap.

Calvin sets the bag on his workbench, unzips it and looks inside. "I hate like hell to see anybody get started on this shit." He zips the bag shut. "Any son of a bitch ever give this shit to my boy, they have to fuckin' deal with *me*."

"You've got a *son*?" Willis never suspected Calvin of having had human entanglements.

Calvin shrugs. "Lives with his mother." He lays the gym bag inside the shell of the Twin, then takes it out again. "Now, how the fuck am I supposed to do this?"

"How old is he?" Willis says.

"Be fourteen." Calvin picks up a roll of duct tape and tears off a foot-long piece.

"My daughter's twelve," says Willis. "So he lives where?" Which sounds like he's asking because he dreads the one-in-a-zillion chance.

"California." Calvin crams the gym bag up inside the Twin and secures it with the piece of tape. "Canoga Park."

"Long way," says Willis.

"Yah, about as far away's the bitch could get him," Calvin says. "Okay, that'll work." He tears off another piece of tape.

"He like it out there?" says Willis.

Calvin looks down at Willis. "How the fuck do *I* know?"

Willis carries the gutted Twin out to the truck and lifts it into the back; it weighs nothing now. "Remember, you want to go careful," Calvin says. "You ain't got to rush. But you don't want to go twenty miles an hour neither. Your headlights both working?"

"Far as I know," says Willis.

"Get in turn 'em on." Willis climbs in behind the wheel as Calvin walks around to the front of the truck. "That's good. Your brights?" Willis stomps the foot switch. "Yah, okay. Let's see your turn signals." Calvin walks around behind the truck. "Okay, signals again? Yah. Other one? Now tap your brakes." He comes around to the driver's-side door. "Okay. Now, you come back here what time? You don't want to leave early. You want to wait till the place is clearing out, lot of other cars and shit. Two, two-thirty? So I won't look for you till three, maybe. The earliest. Just be sure you come straight here. *Before* you go home. You don't stop noplace for coffee, nothin'. You got enough gas you don't have to stop?"

"Three quarters of a tank?" says Willis.

Calvin nods. "And listen, you count how much he gives you, understand? Don't let him tell you you don't need to. Supposed to be five thousand. He don't let you count it, just leave it lay. Tell him you need to see *me*. Don't argue with him, nothin'. You just come back here. That way there you ain't in the middle of it. You understand? But hell, that ain't gonna happen, probably."

"Wait. Come back *with* the stuff?"

"No—shit, he ain't going to let you do *that*."

"Well, then what stops him from saying he never got it?" This is suddenly sounding worse and worse.

"Nah, see, he's got people waitin' on him. *I* know who the fuck they are. So he can't dick me around."

"Christ."

"Quit worrying," says Calvin. "It ain't gonna happen. See, last thing he wants is me to fuckin' show up there. Or him have to come *here*. Because they're watchin' me *and* him—he heard this from a guy that's a sheriff. And you're too fuckin' *scared* to get greedy."

"Tell me about it," says Willis.

"Want to do a little before you go?" Calvin says. "Little *bit* never hurt nobody."

But he's crashing even before he gets to Brandon: nothing left of his high but baseline irritability. He picks up 7, follows it north toward Middlebury for a couple of miles, and spots the Log Cabin on the left-hand side: a flat-roofed cinderblock building that might once have been a drive-in restaurant. Carhops and shit. Overhanging roof in front, with iron pipes for pillars, and a portable electric sign out by the road.

LADY'S GET IN FREE
TONITE! AIR BAG

He puts his turn signal on, then sees, parked across the road in a dirt turnout, a state police cruiser with his lights off. Not good. What now, boogie on by? Shit. Can't. *Begging* to be pulled over.

Willis shifts down and pulls into the cratered parking lot. That clutch is definitely slipping, unless he's letting up funny because he's trying *not* to let up funny with the cop watching him. He checks his mirror, expecting the cruiser's lights to go on. But no. The lot's already filling up with cars and pickups; out front, a matched pair of Sportsters—stock except for Fat Bob tanks—lean at the same angle next to a Plymouth Duster with whirlwind emblem, next to a chopper whose long chrome forks gleam from the blue neon outline of the Budweiser dog. Okay, there's Reed's car. And the Econoline, by the side door.

He parks where the old blacktop ends and new traprock begins, between a Subaru and some big American shitbomb with a peeling vinyl roof and *Fifth Avenue* in chrome script on its ass end. Chrysler, right? Let's all give a fuck. He cuts his lights, turns the key, and sits there: leave the amp in the back of the truck for now and check out the lay of the land? No, uh-uh. And have some son of a bitch steal it? Just have to bring it in; if you're fucked, you're fucked.

He carries the Twin and the Tele to the side door, picking his way around potholes, listing to the right as if the amp were still a heavy mother. He glances over (turning his head as little as possible) but the cruiser hasn't moved. He puts down the Twin and tries the doorknob. Locked. Inside, he can hear Little Richard. He raps knuckles on the glass. Raps again, and here comes a fat guy with salt-and-pepper beard, breasts joggling under a black Jack Daniel's t-shirt. Guy opens the door and the music's louder: now Willis can hear that it's fucking Bob Seger.

"You must be the dude we been waitin' on," says Jack Daniel's. "Need a hand there?"

"I guess I got it under control," Willis says. "Thanks." Bad cigarette smoke in here. So this character knows? Or is he just a genial asshole?

"Hey, you made it." It's the little Strat guy.

"Hey," says Willis.

"Everything cool?"

"Mitch, why'n't you go find Reed, tell him his buddy got here?" says

Jack Daniel's. As Mitch trots off, he shakes his head. "Christ, just what we need." Guy knows, absolutely.

Willis sets his stuff down and looks around. Low ceiling of stained, sagging tiles, strings of chili-pepper lights drooping between posts, clusters of locals standing at the bar, sitting at the tables, yakking, smoking, laughing, tipping back brown beer bottles. Heavy-metal longhairs, buzz-cut storm troopers, an older guy with a deep-creased face and an every-hair-in-place duck's ass, a pair of dumpy women in skintight jeans.

"I get you anything?" Jack Daniel's says. "You want a beer?"

"No. No, thanks."

The music has changed to "Your Lying Eyes," as if you needed one more reason to want to get the fuck out of here.

"Hey, my *man*." Reed's hand on Willis's shoulder. He's loosed his hair from its ponytail, and it's hanging down to the shoulders of his black Levi's shirt. That nose of his pointing. "Way to *go*. See you got that badass Fender Twin with you. And everything's hunky-dory, I trust?"

"I hope," says Willis.

"Hey, you ain't worried about the law out there?" Jack Daniel's says.

"Fuck, I should've told you," says Reed. "Fuckin' *sieve*." Slaps his own cheek. "He's out there every Saturday. You must've shit a brick."

"Yeah, I've had better moments," Willis says.

"Aw, he's just doin' his job, like everybody else," says Jack Daniel's. "I always go out and shoot the shit with him. That makes him happy. Then he goes away. And I'll tell you something—*what's* your name?"

"Jesus, forgetting my manners too," says Reed. "Griff? Doug Willis."

"Doug, nice to know you, man." His handshake is creepily soft and warm. "Anyway, the thing is, I never known him to hassle a vehicle comin' in or out of here. He's just real sympathetic." The drummer and the bass player have drifted over.

"Griff gives him a fruitcake at Christmas," Reed says.

This gets a laugh from Griff.

"Hey, Reed—listen, man," says the bass player. "Can we cut the fuckin' bullshit a minute? What's going on? Is it cool?"

Reed stares at him. "Are *you* cool?" He turns to the Jack Daniel's guy. "Griff. Here's the deal. Our swingin' *guit*-tar man here's got some kind of problem with his amplifier, you know what I'm saying? So maybe we could bring it in your office and try to work on it in there?"

"Best idea I heard all night," Griff says. "Course, the night *is* young."

"And I thought we better get some input from El Exigente here." Reed puts a hand on the drummer's shoulder. "You remember those ads? *But will it win the approval of El Exigente?* And they had that guy?" He raises a finger. "Honly thee fines' beans."

"Why don't *you* be cool?" the bass player says. "I got money in this too, man."

"Dan," says Reed. Hand on the bass player's shoulder. "Dan, my man. I feel your pain. All I can tell you—so far so good, and we'll know more in a minute." He reaches down and picks up the Twin, not bothering to pretend it's heavy. "Gentlemen, you'll excuse us? We'll just be a few. Meanwhile, why don't you guys make sure you're in tune, right? Oh yeah, so Doug: you're welcome to plug into that badass Mesa/ Boogie with me. Since you're, ah, incapacitated. Fact, why don't you take channel one. That's got all the fuckin' bells and whistles."

"Actually, I should come in too," Willis says. "I need to get, you know, the thing I have to take back."

"Hey, not to worry," Reed says.

"I'm not *worried.* I just—"

"Good man. So let's not get ahead of ourselves, okay? Soon as we know what's what, we'll fix you right up. Okay, tiger?" Hand on Willis's shoulder again.

"I think I should come," Willis says.

Reed removes the hand, puts the Twin down and looks at him. "Wait a minute. *You* think? Excuse me?"

"Hey, he ain't gonna screw you," says Griff.

Willis looks at the two of them. Hopeless. "Yeah, okay, fine." Fuckers.

"And now it's *fine?*" says Reed. "I don't get it. What *is* this shit?"

"Ah, Doug's cool." Griff gives Willis's upper arm a squeeze. For some time now, Marty Robbins has been singing "El Paso"; Willis catches the line about the black puff of smoke from the rifle. "Let's just do this, right? Shit, you guys got to go *on* in a couple minutes. Doug, what do you say? You need a beer?"

Willis wants to jerk his arm away but just shakes his head no: this character's now his defender. Or is it good cop bad cop? Yeah, probably. Jesus, if he ever gets out of this. Reed is still staring at him.

"Hey, you change your mind, just tell one of the gals," Griff says.

One more squeeze, then lets him go. "Come on, amigo," he says to Reed. "Let me take this thing for you." He picks up the Twin and leads Reed and the drummer across the room.

"Fuckin' fries my ass," says the bass player, once Reed's out of earshot. Willis watches the Jack Daniel's guy unlock a door with OFFICE in gold-and-black stick-on italics; the three of them go inside and the door closes.

Mitch reappears, his Strat slung around him, its coiled cord in his hand. "You know it's fuckin' five *of*?"

"So?" says the bass player.

"So we should be *up* there."

"Yeah, doin' fuckin' what?" Marty Robbins sings *One little kiss and, Felina, goodbye.*

"Like we got to get this guy in *tune*, get him a *set* list. Minute they come out, man, we got to be *ready*. Come on," he says to Willis. "Let's get you tuned up."

"*Kill* that cocksucker one of these days," says the bass player.

Willis brings his guitar case up onto the stage and unpacks. He plugs the Tele into his delay unit and the delay into channel one of Reed's Mesa/Boogie. He ignores shit like Presence and simply sets Bass, Treble and Midrange all at five: the heart of the heart of the heart of the.

"Here, you want a tuner?" says Mitch.

"I thought you guys didn't use 'em."

Mitch shakes his head. "Fuckin' Reed and his bullshit, man. Watch him, all night he'll be cranking and cranking because he thinks he's flat, and me and Danny have to fuckin' keep tuning up to him. Fuckin' pain in the balls. You know what I do? Don't tell Reed this, man. I set the fuckin' tuner so A's like four *hundred*, four *ten*? Then I just like *hide* from him someplace with the fuckin' tuner, I come back and give Reed his notes, and he'll be like, 'Whoa, I'm way sharp to you.' Least we don't end up breaking so many fuckin' strings."

Willis looks at the closed office door, then unplugs from the delay, plugs into the tuner and tries his high E. Sure enough, he's sharp.

"Okay, here's the list, man," Mitch says. "I'll get you some paper and a pen so you can copy. It looks like shit when everybody's up there going *What're we doin', what're we doin'?* Fuckin' *hate* that shit."

"Great." Willis is still working on his E string; the little red light goes above the zero, below the zero, above the zero, then locks on. Okay, B string.

"Shit, we're supposed to be playing right *now*," says Mitch. "Danny, you're in tune, right?"

"I was."

"Okay, look, What's-your-name, Doug, I'm going to start copying your set list, man." Willis is working on his D string. "I'll put the keys, and you just, you know, do what you can. It's all real simple shit, 'cause that's what Reed's into."

"Yeah, 'cause that's all he can fuckin' play," says the bass player. "So what are we supposed to start with, again?"

"*You* got a list, man. Look at your *list*," Mitch says. "Shit, man." He's getting pen and paper out of his case. "Okay, first tune is 'Hard to Handle.' " For an instant Willis thinks he means it's difficult. "You know that thing, right?"

"I've *heard* it," says Willis. "What key you do it?"

"*Should* be in B flat," Mitch says. "Reed does it in A. Of course."

"I hate that piece of shit," says the bass player. "And fuckin' Reed singin' it, man. That makes it just about fuckin' perfect."

Willis unplugs from the tuner and plugs back into the delay. He turns the amp off standby and hits an E chord—ungodly loud over "Sundown" on the house system. Somebody in the crowd yells *Yeah!* "The miracle of tuners," Willis says to Mitch.

"Speak of the devil," says the bass player.

Reed's heading for the stage, sidestepping, slipping between people, greeting and grinning, excusing himself, putting his palms on backs and shoulders. "Gentlemen," he says, looking up at them. He gives two loud sniffs and twitches his big nose like Elizabeth Montgomery in *Bewitched*. "We're happy to report that all is right as right can be"—pulls at his cheek, pulls at his chin—"and, ah, we'll have our multi-talented percussionist out here momentarily, soon as he gets his shit together"—another sniff—"and very shortly we *will* be rocking and rolling."

"Oh, fuck *me*," says Mitch. "*I* want a fuckin' taste."

"Ah, but we don't want to be starting late," Reed says. "That's unpro*fess*ional." Mitch gives him the finger. "Now. We just need to confer in chambers for about five seconds with our swingin' *guit*-tar man here. But meanwhile I want *you* guys to start playing as soon as the old Sparkplug comes out, right? What have we got, 'Hard to Handle,' right? So about like *Bay-bay, here Ah am, Ah'm a mane own the scene*"—snapping his fingers on the backbeat—"and just start out doing the hook, right? *Doot.*" Snap. "*Doot.*" Snap. "*Dooty-oot dooty-oot.*" Okay?

And just keep that happening, and I'll do like a grand entrance, you know? Might *be* a couple minutes, so Mitch, you can just, you know, go crazy with it. Show 'em whatcha got." He looks at Willis and does kitchy-coo with his index finger.

Willis follows him across the dance floor to the office, squeezing past a fat girl boogying alone to "Old Time Rock & Roll"—hasn't this played before? Reed knocks *Shave and a haircut*, and Griff opens the door. The drummer's sitting on the edge of a gray metal desk, banging his heels against it in rhythm, though not in sync with the music. Griff says nothing, though it must be his desk.

"Sparky," says Reed. "Front and center, babe. Your mission, should you choose to accept it—you're okay, right?"

"Whew," says the drummer, looking up. "Oh man."

"What we like to hear," Reed says. "Okay, here's the deal. I want you to go on out there and pull this shit together. Starting out with 'Hard to Handle,' right? About like"—snaps his fingers—"*Bay-bay, here Ah am. You with me?*"

"No problem, no problem," says the drummer, closing his eyes and shaking his head.

"You guys just go right into it, you know? You keep it happening, and just about the time you really get in the pocket then *I* come out and then we *do* the fucker. And don't forget the stop, right? *Pretty little thang let me light yo' candle*—right? Griff, will you take him out there, man, make sure he finds the fuckin' stage?"

"Is he gonna make it?"

"Ah, he'll be fine. Hey, *Spark*. It's star time."

"No problem, man," says the drummer.

Reed looks at Griff and cocks his head; Griff clamps an arm around the drummer's shoulders, helps him down off the desk and over to the door. After a couple of steps, Sparky's walking okay. A sudden din when the door opens, muted again when it closes.

"So," says Reed, walking around to sit behind the desk. "Old Calvin did good. Him and his scary Canadians." He nods at a metal folding chair. "Here, take a load off."

Willis sits.

"I think the Spark-man kind of overdid," Reed says. "He has to watch that. But shit, let's talk about you, man. Oh, speaking of things." He opens the desk drawer. "Here's the little dealie for Calvin." He scoots a padded envelope across the desk. "You better count it and make sure." He takes a staple remover out of the drawer, points its fangs at Willis and closes and opens its jaws. "Here, you need this?"

Willis takes it, commanding his hand not to tremble, extracts the first staple, then slips in a finger, widens the opening, and the rest start popping loose. He tosses the staple remover back onto the desk, reaches into the envelope and takes out a bundle of hundred-dollar bills held together with two double-V paper clips. He slides the paper clips off and counts. Fifty. He pushes the paper clips on again and sticks the money back in the envelope.

"Feel better, tiger?" Reēd says.

"I'm probably not cut out for this," says Willis.

"Ah, now don't say that." Reed picks up the staple remover. "Why do you want to put yourself down? Fuckin' grace under pressure, man. I saw you." He makes its jaws close and open three times.

"Yeah, well," says Willis.

"So listen. You take that back to Calvin so you don't get *him* mad at you, and then when you think of it, next week, whenever, you send me a little check-arootie, okay? Two fifty, did we say? And then I guess you and I are all square." He works the staple remover's jaws while saying *"Oh thank Gaaad"* out of the side of his mouth, then puts it down and says, "Oh. Except." He opens the desk drawer again, takes out a screw-top aluminum film can and holds it up between thumb and forefinger. But instead of handing it over, he puts it on the desk out of Willis's reach and shakes his head. "I got to tell you, man. My heart went out to you the other night. When we were having our conversation? I was sitting there thinking, Shit, that's no way to live. Just making it month to month, fuckin' credit cards maxed out, pretty soon he's got the kids going off to college—*how* old's your little girl?" Willis says nothing; Reed shrugs. "Okay, whatever. But take a guy like Danny. Not a world-beater. Well, hell, *you* know. But he managed to get together a thousand dollars and he's getting back twenty-five hundred. Which is a lot to him."

Willis notices the music's no longer on. An electric guitar, live, plays an E chord. Cheers. Then big notes on the bass.

"Calvin the same way. Forty years old, he looks fuckin' *sixty*, and this money means he won't have to cut fifty cords of wood this winter. He tell you about his hands?"

"Carpal tunnel?" says Willis. "Yeah, he was telling me."

"You get weary, dealing with fuckin' pathetics."

Couple of whacks on snare drum. Thud of bass drum.

"Sounds like they're about ready," says Willis.

"Yeah, well, they have their instructions." Reed picks up the staple remover. "Tell me something. How often you get up to Preston Falls usually? When you're not on vacation. Couple times a month?"

"Depends," says Willis. "Why?"

Reed makes the staple remover bite twice. "Seems to me, tiger, you're pretty well positioned to get a profitable little sideline happening. Look at you, you're a thing of beauty—chief whatever-the-fuck at a big company? Family man? All it would involve—okay?—you make your little trips up with the family, and every once in a while, three-four-five times a year, you bring an extra piece of luggage. Lot easier than old Calvin having to schlepp all the way up to Richford or some fuckin' place to meet the scary Canucks out in the woods. You make some tax-free bucks, you meet some interesting folks, plus you get to, you know, indulge your little hobby." He taps the top of the film can. "To the fullest."

"I don't think so," says Willis.

"Hey," says Reed, holding up a hand. "Fine. If you're not comfortable, it may not be the right thing for you." The band starts up, loud, with the "Hard to Handle" riff. "Whoa, sounds fuckin' righteous. We got to get out there, man. Rock and *roll*. Too much *business*, you know? Listen, though. I'm just a little worried about one thing."

Willis turns a palm up. Damned if he'll *ask*.

"See, I'm afraid if you're not careful you could run into a problem with your neighbor there. You know, on the one hand it could be fine. But I think old Calvin was kind of counting on your continuing participation. And he's not a guy that handles disappointment real well—I know this about him. Be the easiest thing in the world for him to go in your house when you're away, plant some shit somewhere and call the tip line. You know what I'm saying? What I would hate to have happen, you come up some night with your family and there's half a dozen cop cars in the yard."

Willis says nothing.

"Hey," says Reed, standing up. "I don't mean to be a downer. Just give it some thought, okay? Meanwhile . . ." He picks up the film can, comes around the desk and hands it to Willis.

Willis sticks it in the breast pocket of his denim jacket. "Thanks," he says.

"I better get out there. You comin', tiger? Or you want to hang here

for a while? Get yourself"—he flutters his fingers in front of his eyes—
"prepared."

"Yeah, I think I'll hang," says Willis.

"Take your time. I'll lock the door behind me so you don't get inter-
rupted. Shit, don't lose track of *that*." He points to the envelope in
Willis's lap. "Or old Calvin really *will* be disappointed."

The door closes.

Willis feels his heart start to pound: the excitement of being allowed
to get high all by himself. He looks up and sees what he can't believe he
didn't see before: a calendar with a bleached and busty babe in a stars-
and-stripes bikini bottom pouting astride a full-dress Harley with little
American flags on the handlebars, her nips the same orangey red as her
lipstick. The month is still July.

He takes out the film can, unscrews the top and tries to think what
to use: ah, keys. He digs in his pants pocket for his key ring and dips the
ignition key into the sparkly white powder. Through the wall he hears a
yell go up and Reed howling *Bay-bay, here Ah am, Ah'm a mane own the
scene*. Shit, maybe he better not. He needs to keep his wits about him.
Because he's in deep shit here. But on the other hand.

He blocks the left nostril and snorts a little up the right. Blocks the
right and a little up the left. Tilts his head back, keeps sniffing.

Oh yeah. The right decision, absolutely.

After a while he opens his eyes and looks at the busty babe. She is
incredible. A prostitute who didn't even bother to bleach her black eyebrows. He can feel the Unnamable thickening: down, boy. Okay, heart's
going a leet-tle faster, and if it keeps up, that is *not* cool. But he feels like
it's sort of beating *better*? Jesus, this is the cure for depression, irresolu-
tion, inertia and every other fucking thing. Plus he can fucking *think* for
a change.

It takes him all of fifteen seconds to figure out exactly what to do. So
fucking simple: it's like when it hit the Buddha, sitting under his tree,
that he was a free man. And all the shit fell away, supposedly.

He stands up and sticks the envelope under his jacket, which is snug
because of the weight he's put on. He tucks the film can back in the
breast pocket, where it bulges out like a titty—but what he can*not*
indulge in right now is some fucking little aria of self-contempt. So he
takes it out and carries it in his cupped hand. Better anyway, if you have
to ditch it. Though he's not *going* to have to fucking ditch it—that's just
more depressed thinking. When he tries to open the office door the son

of a bitch is locked, and that really *does* get his heart pounding, but it turns out all he has to do is turn the little thing.

Willis closes the door behind him. Whoa, out here they are fucking *loud*. The nasty texture of distorted guitar makes him grind his teeth, and he craves to get his own fingers clawing at the strings, bending them to torture out the shrieks. But it would be insane to let himself be tempted onto the stage. Even though they've got his guitar up there; that can't be helped now. Wait—actually this is *perfect*. See, if they *do* spot him picking his way to the exit, which they won't, they'll think he's just going out to his truck.

Hey, which he is.

12

Driving back to Preston Falls, he dims his lights for every oncoming car. When lights appear in his rearview mirror, he neither slows down nor speeds up; they want to pass, let them. On a straight stretch of empty road in a broad valley, with harvested cornfields on both sides and the full moon just pouring its fucking heart out, he ignores the urge to cut his lights and drive a larky mile by moonlight alone.

By the time he turns onto Ragged Hill Road he's crashing again, but that can sure as shit be fixed. Past Calvin Castleman's, casually. Get all your ducks in a row first, *then* deal with him. When he's safely around the corner he slows down, and now he does cut his lights, just on the off chance Calvin might be somewhere—in the woods, for Christ's sake?—where he could see somebody pulling in. Okay, and now if a bunch of cop cars will just *please* not be sitting there. By moonlight he bumps up into his dooryard and noses into the shadow of the woodshed. He climbs out and takes a breath of that clean air. A sky-sized silence, its surface etched by katydids.

He's afraid to turn on lights in the house, so he feels his way upstairs and into his study. Enough moon through the eyebrow window so he can see to boot up the computer. Someone might spot the glow of the monitor from the road—but enough, enough, enough. Jesus, drive yourself crazy. While waiting out the rigmarole of copyright screens and skittering digits, he gets out his film can. Just a tad, to maintain.

He clicks into Word and starts typing:

Bill of Sale

Sold to: Calvin Castleman
Sold by: Douglas Willis

One Martin D-18 + hsc, ser. #
One Gibson J-200 + hsc, ser. #
One Rickenbacker 6-string electric + hsc, ser. #
One Fender Telecaster + hsc, ser. #
One Fender Twin Reverb, ser. #
For a consideration of $5,000

(signed)

A consideration of! That's the way to talk. Except five thousand's too low to be plausible; the Martin alone is worth that. Make it $7,500, ask Calvin for five and let him talk you down to whatever, though not less than four. Well, thirty-five. Leaving this up on the screen, he takes a pen and a piece of paper downstairs to get the serial numbers; the ones on the Twin and the Tele Calvin can fill in when he gets his hands on them. He should probably play a last song on each guitar, but what would be sufficiently ironic? He lights a match to read each number, then puts the cases by the kitchen door. He goes back upstairs and types the numbers in, prints the son of a bitch—double spaced, so it won't look lonesome on the page—and signs the bottom by the monitor's dim light.

He starts taking his pictures down, thinking he might want them with him wherever he's going. In addition to the imperishable memories. At least the picture of his house—his *real* house. Meaning his father's house. That is, his mother's house. Whoever the fuck's house. But no. This doesn't want to be another crawl-back-into-your-childhood thing; that was the whole mistake of Preston Falls. This wants to be going in the other direction, like a space probe, though that's a bum analogy: the idea isn't to find stuff out. And certainly not to send back signals. So you might say, Well, Doug, just what *is* the idea? But something or other being the idea isn't the idea.

He loads the Rick, the D-18 and the J-200 onto the truck. Anything else here? There's the truck itself, but he'll need that. The boombox? Hey, *there's* a quick five bucks. The computer's only a 486, worth zip anymore; he was going to donate it to Preston Falls High School this year and take a deduction. Couple cords of wood in the woodshed. The slates off the roof? Shit, if Calvin's still in the market.

He pulls into Castleman Enterprises and goes rocking over the ruts. Calvin's truck is still heaped high, and lights are on in the trailer. Willis sees a window curtain move. He gets out of the truck, and Calvin comes out the door in a thermal undershirt, pulling on a plaid flannel shirt over it.

"What happened?" he says.

"Nothing," says Willis. "It's fine. I got it."

"Fuck you doin' here? This ain't the plan. What did I tell you, I told you *stay* there, I told you don't come back *early*, leave when everybody's leaving. *Jesus* fuckin' Christ. Reed tell you to come back here?"

"I needed to ask you something," says Willis.

"Where's the money?"

"I've *got* the money, don't worry about it. But I want to make you an offer."

"Yah, I don't want to fuckin' hear it. I don't want to hear no more of *your* bullshit, *Reed's* bullshit—"

"Calvin, would you fucking listen?" says Willis. "I'll be glad to give you the money. *But*—would you just hear me out? I want to sign all my guitars and shit over to you, okay? Including the guitar and amp I left back there with Reed. I mean, those are worth probably close to five thousand just the two of them. Now, the other three I brought with me, okay? Now—" He takes the bill of sale from his hip pocket. "Now, I made this out to say seventy-five hundred because I didn't want it to look too low, but I really only want the five. And actually, seventy-five is incredibly conservative. Shit, the Martin I paid thirty-five for like ten *years* ago, the Gibson I paid like twenty-five—"

Calvin makes no move to take the piece of paper. "Where's the fuckin' *money*?"

"Calvin, you could make back—"

"Hey. I asked you something."

Willis holds up a hand. "Okay, fine. Look." He opens the door of his truck and takes the envelope from behind the seat. "Let me just give you this so you got it. You can count it—"

Calvin grabs the envelope.

"I was going to *say*," says Willis. "After you count it—okay?—and you see it's all there?—maybe we can do some business."

Calvin opens it and feels inside. "Yah, well, let's not fuckin' stand out here."

In the shop, Willis takes the car seat while Calvin sits at his work-bench and counts the money twice.

"Okay?" Willis says.

Calvin looks at him. "Now, what the fuck is *your* problem?"

"Okay, basically, I need cash. I'm absolutely broke, I've got bills to pay, bunch of shit coming due—"

"Why's that make *you* special?"

"Look, all I'm saying is, I can sell you stuff for a very low price, for cash, that you'll more than get your money back on. Guaranteed."

"Guaranteed, shit. How'm I supposed to sell them fuckin' things?"

"Why can't you? Here, you *got* a bill of sale with serial numbers on it. Totally kosher." He puts the paper on the workbench. "Put 'em in *Want Ad Digest*. Worst comes to worst, you could take 'em down to Albany. Lark Street Music. They deal vintage instruments. *Or* up to Burlington. I forget what the place is called, but—"

"That easy, why'n't *you* take the shit and sell it?"

"I need the money now."

"That ain't *my* problem." Calvin picks up the piece of paper.

"Listen," says Willis. "I could also throw in my computer."

"What's one of them worth?" He's moving his index finger down item by item.

"Well, it's a 486. I paid twenty-five for it two years ago." Three years ago.

"Yah, I don't give a flyin' fuck what you *paid*." Calvin puts the paper down. "I said what's it *worth*?"

"I'm sure you could get five."

"You might's well keep it," Calvin says. "I don't know nothin' about them piece of shits. Don't want to." He gets up and puts the envelope in the top drawer of his file cabinet.

"Okay, listen," says Willis. "A couple years ago I remember we talked about you taking the slates off my roof in exchange for putting on a new metal one, right?"

"I ain't *in* the roofing business no more."

"Five thousand dollars," says Willis. "All the slates off the roof, plus the guitars."

Calvin rests a buttock on the metal stool again and shakes his head. "Nah. Time I buy that galvalum roofing, screws, all that shit, pay some kid help me put it on there—"

"No no no. Forget the new roof. If you just put some plastic up there, that ought to hold until I can get some kind of roof on myself."

Calvin looks at him. "Be snowing in two months."

"Yeah, well," says Willis. "Like you say. Not your problem."

Calvin picks up a gun telescope from the workbench and sights through it at something. Maybe that *Far Side* cartoon. He sets it back down. "So you and Reed gonna make you some *serious* money, that the idea?"

"*God* no," says Willis. "Truly. I just really got caught short and I need some cash to get me through."

"Look, *I* don't give a shit. Just leave *me* the fuck out of it. You can tell Reed that too." He looks over his shoulder at the file cabinet. "I give you a thousand."

"No; no *way*," says Willis.

"Suit yourself."

"Calvin, those guitars—any *one* of them is worth like *twice* that."

"So go sell 'em. *I* don't give a flyin' fuck."

"Plus a complete slate roof? A couple of years ago you were going to put on a whole—"

"Thousand dollars cash."

"No way," says Willis. Then he says, "I got to get at least three."

"Yah, not from me you ain't."

"So what *would* you give?" says Willis.

"I told you already. Thousand dollars cash."

"No way," says Willis.

"Then get the fuck out of my house. I don't *want* your shit—sell me this, sell me that. Just because *you're* fuckin' done with it. And all of a sudden you fuckin' need money. So you come around trying to trade your fuckin' toys. Hey, I'll trade you. Thousand dollars cash."

"Christ," says Willis.

"The fuck you care?" Calvin says. "That stuff don't mean shit to you."

"Fifteen, and that's it. Fifteen and I'll throw in the computer."

Calvin says, "You don't listen."

13

Time to rock and roll.

Willis stops by the house to have a last look-see. And maybe take five absolutely essential books. Ten, tops. He sits at the kitchen table, gets his film can out and snorts a little off the point of Jean's potato peeler in order to maintain—shit already looks like it's half gone—then goes upstairs and looks under the bed for his .22, not that this is necessarily the best idea, since he's technically on drugs. Though it's weird to think of this as being *on drugs*. Well, he can't find the fucking .22 anyway, so that settles *that*. Until he remembers he never took the son of a bitch out of the truck.

He turns out the light, comes back downstairs, sees the stacks of books in the hall and decides to bag the desert-island shit. He turns out the hall light, goes into the kitchen and considers starting coffee. But he can stop somewhere for coffee. He's *got* a thousand dollars: ten big old hundred-dollar bills with wise old Ben Franklin looking like he's about to deliver a fucking maxim. Okay, you could look at it that Willis got boned, big time. But in fact *Calvin* got boned, too, because Calvin Castleman is a fucking worldling like Ben Franklin, and the guitars and the roofing slates and the thousands of dollars he stands to make are just that much more shit to lug around spiritually.

He noses the truck out into the road, looks left, looks right, then glances back at the house a last time and sees one of the eyebrow windows—second from left, his fucking *study*—dully glowing as if some happy, stupefied family were in there, passing the popcorn. The fucking computer. Just because he feels like it, he tromps on the parking brake, gets out of the truck, tilts the seat-back forward and takes his .22 out. Yep, clip's in it. He jerks the bolt, chambering a round and cocking the son of a bitch, and it suddenly feels lighter and very very touchy, as if it's alive. What it is, he's scared shitless of guns. He tries to get the crosshairs on the eyebrow window, but the thing's waggling all around, so he ends up resting the gun on the hood of the truck. He finds the window in the scope, gets the crosshairs sort of circling around the middle of it. Everything jumps as he fires, but he hears the glass smash and shimmer, then looks and sees he got the job done. That tv glow is still glowing—what did he expect, to shoot out the window *and* the monitor?—but he's made his little statement. Now let's get gone.

He pretends it's not safe to go his usual way, that the police have set up a roadblock, that kind of shit, so he goes left out the driveway and follows Ragged Hill Road all the way to the Wakefield town line, where it becomes Oldacre Road, checking his rearview mirror for a tail. He takes a left onto Neville Road and drives out past the beaver swamp, where the moon's reflected in the glassy water and the drowned branchless trees stick up. Past a dairy farm with the house lights off and a chained collie standing on top of his doghouse. Goodbye, goodbye. Down the hill and over a trapezoidal iron bridge that rattles when you cross, and left again at the fork onto something called Aylmer Road that he's never been on but seems to lead in the direction of 22A. It climbs gradually uphill, with big old slabby-barked maple trees along both sides. Sudden yellow glow around the curve, then a pair of headlights. He pretends it's the cops: dims his lights, gets way over to his side of the road, then keeps watching the rearview mirror until the red taillights wink out. Whew: close one. Farmhouse on the left, one upstairs light on, then a double-wide on the right, a white-painted truck tire half buried beside the driveway. Goodbye. Then nothing but trees, the road starts downhill again and, after half a mile, there's a stop sign and two-lane blacktop going left or right. Bingo.

And forty-five minutes later he's southbound on the Northway. He's keeping the speedometer at an even sixty-five and sitting up as straight as General Douglas MacArthur, his hands at ten o'clock and two o'clock. Sir yes sir. With drugs enough to *keep* him crisp and snappy. No tape deck or radio anymore, but he can sing, can't he? He can sing "Valderi, valdera" or "I'll Fly Away" or any fucking thing he wants. The Wicked Witch's soldiers' scary song that goes *Oh-wee-oh*. He's four hours from New York City.

He stops once to piss and get cash, coffee and gasoline at a service area, once to do some coke at a dark rest stop, once to pull over and wait until no cars are in sight and shoot at a deer sign (misses the deer but hits the sign at least), once again to do more coke in between two tractor-trailers in the parking lot at another service area, and once at the high point of the Tappan Zee Bridge, at about four in the morning. To throw that fucking gun into the Hudson River. Before he does something crazy. (Little joke.)

There's no traffic coming either way, and this forest of rivet-studded girders and braces screens him from the tollbooths. He cuts the engine, gets out and takes the .22 from behind the seat, then steps up off the roadway onto a catwalk with a little fence in front of it, high above the water. New York City's glowing downriver, H-bomb pink emanating from just around that bend. A car goes by in the other direction; it seems to slow briefly, then pick up speed. Better do this and get the fuck out of here. He grips the rifle by the barrel end, like a baseball bat, swings and lets the son of a bitch fly out into the dark.

Willis stands and listens but can't hear it hit. Can it still be falling?

THREE

1

Toward the middle of October, Jean leaves a message on the machine in Preston Falls. Just *Hi, how are you, how's the house coming, everything's fine down here, kids are fine*. The lightest, brightest message possible. A first move. Though it's probably stupid: is this supposed to make him think their last conversation hadn't been as dire as it really was? Or to make *her* think so?

A week later she leaves a second message—*Hi, just thought I might catch you in, give a call when you get a chance*—and then, a few days after that, a third message, saying she's *a little concerned* and would appreciate it if he'd please call. This is Saturday. Monday he's due back at work.

Sunday starts out warm and clear. She takes Rathbone for his morning walk, with just an old shirt of Willis's over the t-shirt she wore to bed. Then she brings her coffee outside and sits on the tailgate of Carol's little red pickup, a Subaru Brat with roll bars and 4WD, and just breathes: the air still smells almost like summer. Rathbone lies with his belly in the cool, dewy grass.

Around eleven o'clock—which is really noon, since they set the clocks back last night—she and Carol take the kids to the pancake place. Jean brings a deck of cards, and in the booth they get in a hand of gin rummy before the food arrives. Roger, though he's embarrassed to be with three females, thinks gin rummy is terribly sophisticated. When he fans out his cards he makes sure their overlap is precisely uniform. Mel draws a card, takes a quick in-breath, tucks the card into her hand and discards a king of clubs; Roger bites his lip and grabs it too eagerly and Carol groans. This is almost like a family. Carol wins, as usual—she thinks it's condescending not to play your best against kids—but Mel almost takes her.

Half a honeydew for Mel, The Lumberjack ("A Buckle-Bustin' Breakfast from the North Woods") for Roger, a cheese omelette for

Carol and just toast and coffee for Jean, since Roger can never finish The Lumberjack and she hates waste. So what does everybody want to do? Mel wants to go home and call her friend Erin. Roger wants to go home and watch videos. Carol suggests a hike at the reservoir; she's got to start back west sometime this week, and it's such an *incredible* day. Groaning from Mel and Roger, though less than you'd think. Even they feel the pull of a day like this.

But Jean's wondering what's going on up in Preston Falls. Could he maybe have—God, a million things. He's fallen off a ladder, lying there with his back broken, and here *she* is digging the last of the butter out of a little pleated paper cup for the last triangle of a buckwheat cake. Well, maybe when they get back to the house they'll find his truck parked behind Carol's, and the reason he didn't call to say he was on his way was—well, whatever it was. This just really doesn't look good.

"Why don't we do *this*," she says to Carol, for the kids to hear. "We have to go back to the house anyway, right? If we're taking Rathbone. So what I thought we could do, you could get your truck and follow me to the reservoir, I'll hike with you guys for a little, and then I thought maybe I'd take off and drive up to Preston Falls, and sort of check and see if Willis needs a hand with anything. There's always so much stuff to take care of. And then maybe he and I could caravan down tonight."

Good old Carol: doesn't even raise an eyebrow. "Actually, that might not be a bad idea," she says.

"I want to go too," says Mel. Roger just stares down at his puzzle placemat, tracing routes through the maze with his knife.

"That's nice of you, sweetie," Jean says. "But you know what that drive is like. And then we'd have to turn right around and come back. You'd be bored out of your mind."

"I'm bored *here*."

"And besides, I think Aunt Carol could use your help." Jean tips a quick nod in the direction of Roger. She hates herself when she pushes their buttons. Then again, it seldom works anymore.

Mel heaves a major sigh.

"While the cat's away," says Carol, giving Roger a wink he doesn't see. "Now we can stop at the video store on the way home and go bazonkers."

Carol's the good cop. The kids like their friends to see them bombing around with their hippie aunt in her little red pickup, and she lets them blast their own tapes, as loud as they want. One night she allowed

them to rent *Nightmare on Elm Street, Part Something*—which in fact
pissed Jean off. Roger, of course, said it wasn't scary, but Mel had trouble getting to sleep. (Jean worried more about Roger.) Still, when Carol
leaves . . . Oh, but then *Willis* will be back. Her rock. God, was there a
time she really thought that?

"Crap," Jean says. "I just remembered. I totally forgot about *candy*
for tomorrow. For the trick-or-treaters."

"We can take care of the candy," says Carol.

"That would be great if you could," says Jean. "I usually just pick up
some M&M's or Raisinets, and one kind of miniature candy bar, Milky
Ways or something, and then those little rolls of Smarties? And then we
put together little individual bags. What we've been doing, we take this
stamp—I think it's in the desk—you know, that's got our name and
address? And just stamp each bag. I think it makes the mothers a little
more secure."

"What a cool idea," Carol says. Willis used to say it was begging
people to sue their asses.

The waitress puts the check down in front of Carol.

"Here, let me give you some money for the candy," Jean says, grabbing the check. "You sure you don't mind doing this?" She gives Carol
a twenty, then lays four singles on the table for the waitress and puts an
unused knife on top of them.

"It'll be a good project for tonight," says Carol.

The four singles look mingy, so Jean takes them back and puts down
a five. For the working woman who has to be inside on a day like this.
Whose face she never looked at.

Out in the parking lot, sunlight beams off bumpers and windshields.
"All *right*," says Carol. "*I'm* pumped." Fist in the air.

The kids say nothing; still, they climb in without complaint and Jean
doesn't have to tell Roger to fasten his seat belt. She rolls her window down, puts on the radio—the middle of something sprightly with
violins—and swings onto Route 9. But the sun looks like it's already
starting down the sky.

"Listen, I hate to say this," she says, "but would you guys mind too
much if I punk out on this hike entirely? It's already getting sort of late,
and it's such a trek up to Preston Falls, you know?"

"Booo," Carol says. "No, you're probably right. Be nice to get there
before dark if you could." She turns to the back seat. "But hey, one party
pooper isn't going to poop on *our* party, right? No *way*."

"I really want to go with you," Mel says.

"It's going to be *so* late, dear," says Jean. "And you have school tomorrow. *And* it's Halloween."

"I can sleep in the car."

Jean shakes her head.

"I *can*."

"I really appreciate you wanting to keep me company, sweetie. But I want you and Roger to get to bed early." God knows why she's pretending this is about altruism.

2

She takes the long way up: the Taconic to 22 to 22A. Because she hates all those trucks on the Thruway and the Northway. Because she feels like indulging herself. And because whatever's wrong can't get much worse in the extra forty-five minutes. And really because she doesn't want to be doing this. As she goes north and north and north, the fierce reds and yellows give way to browns and then the leaves themselves start going and at last it's bare trees reaching up into the bright, blank blue. In the little towns, pumpkins sit on doorsteps and ghosts dangle and flap from tree branches: mostly store-bought plastic ones with cartoon faces, but here and there just a white bedsheet hung from a noose. Very Diane Arbus.

She holds out against putting on the radio until she gets off the Taconic, then holds out some more until the shortcut around Queechee Lake, and then all the way to Center Berlin, where she finally feels like it's either get something on the radio or go into an absolute panic. There's static where WQXR had been, and she hits Seek: a country-music station; a rock station, obviously for teenage boys; some man talking about the teachings of Paul, two seconds of "Dock of the Bay." She can't imagine why she would ever again need to hear "Dock of the Bay," or "Hey, Jude," or "California Girls." What it is, she's come to hate most music. She lands at last on a classical station out of Albany, where a solemn-voiced man is summarizing the plot of an opera. *"The wedding party and Elvira reappear while Walton sounds the alarm and organizes the pursuit. Shock and grief at Arturo's disappearance strike Elvira sense-less, and in a dreamlike delirium she imagines herself being married to him."* She's driving past sagging barns and sagging trucks and cows standing in mud and a sign saying PUMKINS FOR SALE. She sees a dead raccoon up ahead, lovely round-ringed tail, body bloated huge, as if inflated. This is all too crazy. She turns the radio off and listens to the wind and the tires and the engine: a three-part noise that if you really listen has little parts within each of the parts. She turns the radio back on.

She passes landmark after landmark. The grocery store with the magnetic-letter sign at the curb: WE HAD A 2 MILLION WINNER. The boulder somebody painted to make it look even more like an Indian in profile. The used-book store that has the post boy out front; now it's wearing a Dracula mask.

The sun is just trembling above the horizon when she comes up the last hill—the *real* last hill, not the hill that looks just like it—and turns onto Ragged Hill Road. Past the tumbledown barn that Willis used to call Nude Descending a Staircase Acres. Past the silver trailer almost hidden by sumacs and the blue trailer with chickens running loose and a circle of dooryard gnawed bare by a tethered goat. Past the house with pastel-green siding where you usually see the fat little boy with the Mohawk out riding his bike and every year they have a perfectly weeded garden with absolutely straight rows. Then on through the stand of half-brown pine trees, going uphill all the time, and past the trailer with the GUN SHOP sign, the junk cars, the Hog Roster and the mountains of heaped-up firewood. What's-his-name's.

She comes around the last corner and sees that at least the house is still standing. But what's all that blue plastic? He must be putting a new roof on, God knows why—and God knows where he's getting the money. His truck's not here, and if ever a house looked deserted. The maple trees are bare and the lawn is higher than your ankles, except where it's covered in dead leaves.

She pulls up onto the lank grass, superstitious about taking the place where he parks his truck, and climbs out. The late-afternoon sun is higher above the horizon up here, and it feels hot through the thinning air. Not warm. Hot. Sharp and stinging. One of the reasons she hates and fears Preston Falls: in this clean air you can really feel the damage they've done to the ozone, far worse than they're telling us. Instant sunburn. Up here she keeps slathering Mel and Roger with sunblock and making them wear hats outside. Willis disapproves.

But she's forgotten how quiet it is. A breeze sets leaves rattling in a narrow file, as if a swift ghost had rushed through on the way from one arbitrary point on the lawn to another and vanished. She walks through the grass and leaves to the kitchen door, looking for signs that anyone has walked this way lately. But she doubts even a *man* could see anything—even if he'd been a Boy Scout and read all of Sherlock Holmes. The door's unlocked. There's a musty smell inside, together with a rotten whiff of stove gas. She calls Hello, then feels stupid: a house doesn't smell this way if people have been in it. But it's weird. Willis *always* locks up, though of course you can get in through any window. Which is in fact how *he* gets in, instead of going into the woodshed for the key. You'd have to know Willis to know how perfect that is.

He's left the boombox right out on the counter, and a stack of CDs. Which is weird, too: he usually hides stuff because the house was once broken into. But what she really doesn't like is this one little gray spider strand connecting the handle of the JOE mug with the countertop. She lays her fingertips on the rim, absurdly hoping to feel whether Willis is near or far. But no feeling of anything floods in on her. Of course. Because the whole idea is stupid.

She looks around. On the floor, Rathbone's food dish and water bowl, both empty. In the sink, a bowl with a spoon and a single Cheerio stuck to the inside. On the table, a *Want Ad Digest* folded open, with an ad circled in pen:

TRACTOR Ford 8N w land plow, disc harrow,
snowplow, sickle bar, VGC, $2250 W/D.

The calendar says September: summery picture of a lake with these cliffs hanging over it and a red-and-white sailboat out in the middle, no sail up and nobody inside.

The furniture's still piled up in the dining room, and the living room's still empty. Her footsteps echo. Plastic still over the window, still the same hole in the ceiling. He hasn't gotten much accomplished in his two months. Though in fairness he *is* doing major stuff to the roof. She goes into the front hall, around the sofa and upstairs. She peeks into the kids' rooms at unwanted toys: a red-and-blue plastic three-wheeler and a broken space robot in Roger's room; in Mel's, jigsaw puzzles (Mount Fuji, a covered bridge) and games (Candyland, Don't Wake Daddy). And there sits the black-haired doll, Rosita or whatever her name was, that Mel used to tote around everywhere: legs spread, arms spread, back against the wall, eyes open, waiting for somebody to give a thought to her. Waiting for years. Jean actually feels herself getting teary. Oh please. She goes into what Willis used to call, with that little sneering hesi-

tation, "the, ah, master bedroom." Bed's unmade—of course—and the
floor littered with underwear, socks and t-shirts. Well, damned if she'll
clean up his mess. Not that anyone's asking her to. The light's too
spooky for her to linger, anyway: that slanting, end-of-day sunlight that
makes things seem to glow from within. She opens the door to Willis's
little study—God, there's a window broken in here and glass all over the
floor. The lovely locals. And his computer's on, with his customized
screensaver crawling: I CAN'T GO ON I'LL GO ON. She looks around
for the rock somebody must have thrown—nothing—then kneels
and touches her wrist to the seat of his chair. Out of sheer stupidity.
Could it be that locals broke that window downstairs, too, and this was
some kind of hate campaign like what happens to black families? She
wouldn't put it past these people. And she can actually sort of see it their
way: city folks are driving up the price of homes so locals can't afford to
live here anymore. In Wakefield, the next town over, teenagers used
somebody's summer place for a drug party house all winter and did fifty
thousand dollars' worth of damage; toward the end they were blamming
the walls with shotguns.

But what actually happened here? Okay, he's working on his computer, somebody throws a rock, he runs down to investigate, gets in his
truck—and then what? He just never comes back?

Meanwhile the red light on the answering machine's going crazy.

She presses Play. *"Hi, how are you, how's the house coming . . ."*
Beeeep. *"Hey. It's Marty. Listen. Couple things to go over, for when you
come back. Nothing major. Give me a call the next day or two? Four four
two six? In case you've forgotten."* *Beeeep.* *"Hi, just thought I might catch
you in. . . ."* *Beeeep.* *"Aahsk nawt why yaw brotha has nawt called
you, aahsk why you have nawt called yaw brotha."* *Beeeep.* *"It's Marty.
Listen, we do need to talk. Please get back to me? Four four two six?"*
Beeeep. *"Hi, uh, listen, I'm a little concerned . . ."* *Beeeep.* *"Willis, it's
Marty. It's very urgent that you get back to me as soon as you can. We're
assuming that you're coming back to work, since we haven't heard to the
contrary, but we badly need to talk. So if you get this . . . four four two six.
Okay?"* *Beeeep.* The red light stops flashing.

So he got *none* of these messages? Her first one was at least two
weeks ago.

She looks through the stuff on his worktable. Receipt from the
Quicklube in Chesterton, August 30. Old phone bills, electric bills, bill
from Drew's Propane Service. No letters. Catalog from Renovator's Sup-

ply, folded open to a page of hinges. What's strange, though, his pictures aren't up anymore. Just nail holes. They're on the floor, stacked against the table leg. Here's the farmhouse he grew up in. His horrible father, whom she used to try to think of as his pathetic father. His grandparents, though she can never remember *which* grandparents. Mel and Roger on Block Island, when she was six and he was three: Mel scooping sand with a plastic bucket, Roger holding up her Little Mermaid inner tube around his waist, neither one looking at the other or at you. And Jean herself, just after they were married, sitting on a lawn chair in Sarasota, umbrella'd drink in her hand, with sunglasses and that floppy old straw hat. She looks like any carefree young woman.

She picks up the phone. "Hi," she says when Carol answers. "Well, I'm here. But there's no sign of *him*. No messages, I take it."

"No, not at all. Everything's fine." Which must mean the kids are right there.

"It's very weird up here," says Jean. "It just looks really deserted. And there's this window broken up in his study, and his computer's still on?"

"Really?" says Carol, in the sort of bright tone she'd use if Jean had said a deer was standing at the kitchen door. "Well, Roger's right here. We've got the goody bags almost finished, and of course Rathbone's lying here supervising. Oh-oh, somebody heard his name."

"I guess you can't really talk."

"You got it," says Carol.

"I have no idea what I should do," Jean says.

"Oh, I know just what you mean. So I imagine Roger wants to talk to you."

Jean hears Roger say, "No I don't."

"Correction," says Carol. "He does *not* want to talk to you. He is, in fact, heading upstairs. Just a sec. Rog?" she calls, muting the phone somehow. "Would you just knock on Mel's door and tell her it's time to get up or she'll never get to sleep tonight?" Jean doesn't hear Roger answer. "Sorry about that," Carol says.

"What's wrong with Mel?" says Jean.

"Just taking a nap."

"Really? She *never* does that."

"Well, we had a pretty good hike. And I think she's a little bummed, to tell you the truth. Nap will probably fix her up. So what's your plan?"

"No idea. Turn around and come back, I guess. *I* don't know."

"But don't you think you better get the police going on this?"

"Oh God."

"Well, *Jean* . . ."

"I mean *yes*, I've thought about it. But it's like, what are the limits? He's perfectly within his rights to just, you know, *go* somewhere."

"When he has to be back at work *tomorrow*? Come *on*. He could be in some kind of really serious—"

"Look, can I call you later?"

"Jean, I'm only—"

"I'll call you later."

Jean goes to the broken eyebrow window, gets down on one knee and looks out. A squirrel moves along the stone wall, flowing from one frozen pose to the next. Carol is right: what's she waiting for?

For this not to be happening.

She goes back downstairs to the front hall and sits on the sofa. She folds her hands in her lap, closes her eyes and begins to say *One, one, one* in her mind. It was Carol who got her into meditation, back when Jean was eighteen and going through stuff and Carol was living with her hippie princeling in Central Square. (This was before Gid the mountain man, or whatever he thought he was.) Carol doesn't know she still does this; she doesn't want to encourage Carol in anything mystical. And she would certainly *not* want it known around The Paley Group. She did tell Willis, back when they told each other things. Since they were in confession mode, he said, he might as well admit that he sometimes prayed. She asked what his prayers were like; he said they always began "Dear God," like a little boy's. And in fact, when they were first married they tried saying this sort of nondenominational grace for a while. In a way, she's glad she never took Mel and Roger to church, or even taught them the Lord's Prayer or talked about God, probably because deep down she takes it all *too* seriously and didn't want to offer it to them unless she could absolutely get behind it herself. Though you could also look at it as the absolute worst form of child abuse, to starve the spirit. One more reason she's an unfit parent: she doesn't know what to think about anything.

All this self-talk is totally screwing up her meditation, of course, though you're not supposed to worry about that but simply go back to the *one, one, one*. When she opens her eyes again, the hall is darker and she feels slowed down. She cranes her neck and looks over her shoulder out the little windowpanes at the sides of the front door: darkness is muting the green of the haylike grass, as if their neglect of this place were being forgiven.

So many days he'd spent here alone. Seeing these changes in the light.

She really needs to go outdoors and catch the very last of the day. She hears a crow caw: warning of someone's approach? She freezes and listens harder into the silence. No, nothing. *Please,* she thinks, *stop scaring yourself.* Walking through the dining room, though, she hears a car pass by on the road—rumble of motor, rush of tires and stab of electric guitar. Then it's gone.

She takes the path that leads up the hill behind the house. The sky's a deep ultramarine, clouds still backlit by the last orange glow. It gets warmer as she climbs. From the hilltop you can look out at other hills across the valley as it fills up with mist. Gentle, rounded hills: wooded except for one clean-shaven patch: somebody's farm. What a wonderful place this could have been.

But it's really *not* warm up here. She pulls the hood of her sweatshirt over her head and ties the drawstring in a bow, then puts her hands in the kangaroo pouch in front. She takes a last look: fuzzy horizontal stripes of cloud near the horizon, fat piles of whipped-cream cumulus bulging above them. Ultramarines, golds, oranges, magentas—she wishes Mel and Roger were seeing this with her, though Roger would be bored and Mel ostentatiously silent. She starts back down, watching her footing. God, look at this: somebody left a bottle up here. So the locals are climbing their hill. Though she's not even sure it's actually on their property. A plastic Polar Seltzer bottle, but with brownish gunk clinging to the inside. God knows. She tucks it under her arm and starts down.

Back in the dark, gassy-smelling kitchen, she pulls the string and on comes the fluorescent ring Willis was always planning to replace, except Renovator's never had quite the right fixture. She drops the bottle into a Grand Union paper bag they use for recycling. Then she goes into the pantry for the electric space heater and sets it on one of the wobbly oak pressback chairs, plugs it in and turns the knob; it gives a rattle and a buzz and starts turning orange inside. Wasteful compared to the woodstove, but she's only going to be here half an hour or so, just long enough to rest up for the drive back. Besides, the woodstove takes forever to warm things up, though she has to admit it *is* lovely once wood heat takes hold.

She shuts the door to the dining room so it'll be warmer in here, and fills a saucepan with water enough for a cup of tea. The gas flame looks weak—maybe it's running out, which might explain the smell—but it should be able to boil this much water, no? She looks through the CDs, though she should really just drink her tea and go. Nothing much to tempt her anyway. A bunch of that truly offensive rap music Willis belatedly discovered a couple of years ago: bitches and pussies and guns. Neil Young, the big-browed burnout. The Rolling Stones, of course, with the sainted Keith Richards that every man secretly wants to go to bed with. Various bands she's vaguely heard of, which basically break down into your dark unshaven ones and your blond pouty ones—not that they aren't cute, but for a presumably straight man it's like what's the deal? And of course Bob Dylan, prince of woman-haters. Just a mean little insecure *boy*, and all his women either ballbusters or cock-teasers or oh-so-incomprehensibly mysterious gypsy queens. Don't get her started on Bob Dylan. She flips the switch on the boombox to FM and gets violin music, though it's stupid to allow this to make you feel less alone.

Now it's completely dark outside. She checks and sees little bubbles forming in the bottom of the saucepan; in the cupboard she finds a box of Earl Grey with the cellophane still on it. Willis is strictly a coffee man: that is, a *man*. Not much else here. Box of Cheerios, two small cans of water-packed tuna, can of Chicken & Stars Soup, package of dried black beans that Willis would never in a million years take the trouble to fix. About an inch of Dewar's. She puts the beans on the table to take back to Chesterton, sticks a tea bag in the JOE mug and pours in just enough Dewar's to make it float. Then she holds it down with a spoon and pours in the hot water. Is this stupid, with that drive ahead? She lifts the tea bag out on the spoon and winds the string around it to squeeze out the good strong stuff. Her stomach growls. She pictures opening the can of Chicken & Stars and the yellow fat floating. Instead she reaches into the box for a fistful of dry Cheerios. She sits down facing the heater, both hands around the hot cup. Earl Grey spiked with Dewar's and classical music playing: this could pass for one of those precious woman moments, nurturing and strengthening yourself before you have to go back and deal some more. She has the mutinous thought that it can all just go to hell.

To atone for this, she calls home again.

The machine picks up, with the message she made Willis record so it would sound like there was a man in the house. *"This is five five five, one five three six,"* he says. *"You know what to do."*

"Not really," she says. Then it beeps and she says, "Carol? Hmm, okay. Listen, I'm suddenly just totally exhausted"—this comes out of her mouth and suddenly she *is* just totally exhausted—"so I don't know if I should—"

"Jean?" Carol breaks in, and the phone starts squealing. "Wait—here, let me turn this thing off." Suddenly the connection is absolutely clear of noise. "Hi. Sorry. So you're going to stay over?"

"I don't know. The thought of that drive, you know? Maybe if I went to sleep now and got up really early—but that would mean you having to get the kids off to school."

"Like I've never gotten a kid off to school before."

"Oh, I know, but I *hate* to dump everything on you. And especially a Monday. You know what a pain they can be."

"*These* kids?" she says. "No *problem.*"

"Let me talk to Mel for a sec. Carol, you're sure this is okay?"

"Absolutely. Mel's right here. Mel, your mom wants to talk to you."

"Hi," Mel says. "Is Daddy there?"

"No, I guess I missed him." Think fast. "He said something about he might go over to see Nonnie before he came back home. So I expect that's where he is."

"So why can't you call him there?" says Mel.

"I did try calling there," Jean says. Digging herself in deeper. "They're probably out to dinner or something. I thought I'd try again a little later."

"When did Daddy say that?" says Mel.

"Say what, hon?"

"Say he was going to *Nonnie's.*"

"I don't know—the last time we spoke?" Hard to imagine a worse way of handling this, but it seems to be the way she's handling it. Soon she's got to sit Mel and Roger down and tell them she doesn't know what to tell them.

Mel says nothing. Obviously not buying it but stumped for what to ask next. Now Jean will have to coach Carol in case Mel tries to get something out of *her*. She'll also have to try to reach Sylvia immediately, and somehow not scare the hell out of her in the process. Then again, maybe he *is* at his mother's.

"Listen, dear. I'm going to spend the night here and come down in the morning, and Aunt Carol's going to take care of you. So will you do me a favor and help out as much as you possibly can, *especially* in the morning? You know how slow Roger can be." Another of Jean's cheap little masterstrokes of motherhood; Roger's no worse than Mel.

"I guess so," Mel says.

"So I'll see you tomorrow, sweetie. I should be home in plenty of time for trick-or-treating."

"Mother, *that* doesn't matter."

"Of *course* it matters," says Jean. "Listen, is Roger there?"

"Yeah, he's here."

"Would you put him on, please? I love you."

"Love you too. Roger, Mom wants you."

"I *know* who it is," Jean hears him say. "I'm not *stupid*." The phone clunks down. Then Roger says, "What?"

"Hi, handsome," says Jean. Her new strategy is not to let him dictate the tone. "I was just telling Mel and Aunt Carol, I decided to stay over and come down in the morning. So I want you and Mel to be really good. Like, I want you to go *right* to bed when it's bedtime. And make sure you let Mel have enough time in the bathroom in the morning. Okay?"

"How come she can't use the downstairs?"

"Because Aunt Carol uses the downstairs," she says. "You know that."

"Yeah, but she gets it all to her*self*."

"Enough," says Jean. If he says *No fair,* she's going to scream.

Roger says nothing. Jean decides to pretend this means he's knuckled under. "So Aunt Carol said you guys might rent a video?" she says.

"Yeah, we did, but it was stupid."

"What did you get?"

"*Home Alone Two.* I already saw it ten times. It sucks."

She's given up on *sucks,* though she still calls him on *sucks the big one.* "Well, maybe Aunt Carol would read more *Lord of the Rings* with you. In fact I know she would if you asked her nicely." It's the one thing he'll allow to be read to him anymore; Jean figures it's because of the sword-and-sorcery aspect. Which is in itself worrisome: next step is heavy metal—which he's already into anyway—then on to satanism. But at least it's a book. By an *Englishman*.

"She doesn't read it right," Roger says.

"That's very rude, Roger. And I hope Aunt Carol didn't hear you say that. It would hurt her feelings."

Silence.

"Is she right there? Did she hear what you said?"

"No," he says. Probably a lie.

"Still," says Jean. "Next time, think before you speak. And listen, don't forget—right to bed when Aunt Carol tells you. Sleep tight, and I'll see you tomorrow. Hugs and kisses. Would you put Aunt Carol back on, please? Love you."

Silence.

"Hi," said Carol. "We're doing fine."

"He can be *such* a trial," says Jean.

"Honey, you're forgetting *Dexter*." Carol's son was hyperactive until he was ten, when she finally gave up her nothing-inorganic trip and put him on Ritalin; he's now at the University of Washington.

"Well, anyway, thank you. One *more* time. You know, I just feel like we've prevented you from having a life while you've been here."

"Don't be silly," says Carol. "As long as I've got strong fingers and my Alan Jackson tape with him on the motorcycle, I'm a fulfilled woman."

"They didn't hear that, right?"

"Look, I better let you go, so you can get some sleep."

"Yeah, I guess I should—oh crap, I almost forgot. I told Mel that Willis might be at his mother's."

"Right," says Carol. "Um. Do we have any reason to think that's the case?"

"No. But I had to tell her *something*."

"I see," says Carol. "Ah, any instructions?"

"Not really. God, I wish I'd kept my big mouth shut. I mean, if Mel wants to call there you obviously can't say no. But if you could just stall her for even like a *minute* after we hang up, I'm going to call Sylvia right now and forewarn her."

"That would be good."

"Except what do I say to *her*? Like, Don't have a heart attack but your son's missing?"

"That would get your point across," says Carol.

"Crap," Jean says. "Okay, I'll call you later."

Sylvia's phone rings five times before a machine picks up. *Willis?* Oh, right: he once said he was going to record a thing for his mother too. *"Please leave us a message after you hear the beep."* So it's not true that Willis never follows through. She notes, however, that his own family didn't rate an *us*.

After the beep she says, "Hello, Syl. *And* Willis, if you're there. It's Jean. Ah, Sunday night? Syl, I was just wondering if you'd heard from Doug, because I was under the impression that he might possibly be stopping by your place before he comes back down to Chesterton. Anyhow, if that's the case, could you have him give me a call? I'm in, ah, Preston Falls right now, it's Sunday night—I guess I said that—and I'm heading back down Monday morning. Anyway, I hope you're well. Talk to you soon."

Was she casual enough? Upbeat enough? The woman is seventy-one years old, for God's sake. Not that seventy-one is old anymore, but even so. After a while she notices that music's still playing, and turns the boombox off. What relief, this silence. She takes another sip of the tea and Dewar's, then gets the bottle and pours in just a hair more. Whatever she told herself she was accomplishing by coming here, what she's really doing is taking a night off.

She gets up to go to the bathroom, opens the door, turns on the light—and there's a huge gaping hole in the floor. All the boards are gone between the sink and the bathtub, and cold dank air is coming up. One *more* project he started and didn't finish. It feels creepy, sitting there peeing, as if there's nothing under her.

The bedroom's cold and the sheets are filthy. She drags an oil-filled electric radiator out of the closet and plugs it in on Willis's side of the bed, where the outlet is. Now, are there any clean sheets? Well, there's that garish flowered set of her mother's. She strips the bed and puts the dirty sheets and pillowcases in the hamper. Along with his dirty clothes from the floor.

While the bedroom's warming up, she goes back into his study and plays girl detective. She opens a little plastic Tandy box and finds unlabeled diskettes, still with plastic over them, and one with a label marked BACKUP. She clicks the mouse to see what documents are on his C drive:

SALEBILL, MEMO8, SHITBULL, MEMO7, SPORTY, 27734, MENSONG, LIED-JOUR, MEMO6, 2MARTY, BULLSHIT, TWADDLE, SPINDOC. She opens MENSONG, which turns out to have nothing to do with music; it's a press release about some blind taste test of Sportif against Gatorade. She closes MENSONG, reaches up to bat away a spiderweb hanging from the ceiling, then changes her mind. This is hopeless. She shuts the computer down and goes back into the bedroom, where it already feels warmer. She starts opening drawers, but turns up only clothes. In the closet she finds his Air Jordans and his cowboy boots. Therefore: last seen wearing Timberlands.

She goes downstairs to find something to read. In the front hall she picks up book after book; what *are* these things? Willis is forever snapping them up at tag sales and junk shops and then reading nothing but the same obsessive stuff he's already read a hundred times. Look at all this. *Fear Strikes Out*, by Jimmy Piersall with Al Hirshberg—some baseball player, apparently. *Five Acres and Independence*, by M. G. Kains, which figures. A worn-out edition of *Pilgrim's Progress* with this crude picture on the cover of a man in helmet and armor and another with long hair and a red tunic, hands clasped in prayer as waves rise around them. Not your world's greatest illo, but the lettering's nifty: tall, sort of shaky-looking, all caps—they did upper case simply by making the same letters taller—obviously hand done by somebody just making it up as they went. Still, it's nicely consistent from letter to letter, and it might be fun to have on hand. You'd have to extrapolate the rest of the alphabet, but it looks doable. You've got all the vowels—thank God for that *U* in Bunyan—and the *R* would give you the *D*, the *E*, the *F* . . . definitely doable. Right, and she's the only hack graphic designer in New York who ever fantasized about doing a children's book someday.

So he was having some kind of religious crisis? Is that what she's to gather? *Pilgrim's Progress*, for God's sake. Reverting to some ancestral Puritan caca? The Willises themselves hadn't come over on the *Mayflower*, but somebody had, back on his father's mother's side or something. Willis always talked about it—*talks* about it—with such contempt, at the same time making good and sure you know. Well, probably he was just showing off by reading something old and unreadable, though God knows who he was showing off *to*. Even when he's absolutely by himself he's still doing his Mr. Everything number: out with his chainsaw, or "sweating joints" or putting up sheetrock, which he now seems to call "drywall," and at night reading *Pilgrim's Progress*.

Or whenever he does his reading now; maybe he gets up and squeezes in a canto or two before breakfast.

Then, halfway down a stack of paperbacks, she finds *Emma*, with its orange spine and the portrait on the cover of some woman who looks nothing like how you picture Emma and in fact is some actual person. But which Jean likes because it's *so* wrong that the image doesn't get in your way. Marcia Fox, by Sir William Beechey. Whoever *they* were. Jean brings *Emma* into the kitchen, sits down in front of the heater and takes a sip from the mug—completely cold and poisonous-tasting. She wants especially to read the part where Mr. Knightley says, "You have been no friend to Harriet Smith, Emma." But she also wants to take her time getting there, so she starts in where Emma's doing the watercolor of Harriet and Mr. Knightley says, "You have made her too tall, Emma," and Emma knows he's right but won't admit it. Jean wouldn't mind being cared for and condescended to by Mr. Knightley. When they start making the collection of riddles, Jean remembers that she'd better call Carol; as soon as she finishes this chapter. But as Emma begins walking stupid Harriet through the riddle about the word *courtship*—Jean always feels stupid too when she reads this part, because *she* didn't get it the first time either—the phone rings.

"Hi," says Carol. "I hope I didn't wake you up, but since I hadn't heard . . ."

"No no, not at all. I was just reading."

"So did you get hold of his mother?"

"Left a message. I didn't hear back." Jean takes another awful-tasting sip. "Did Mel try to call her?"

"No, she just went up to her room. When I put Roger to bed, I looked in and she was asleep in her clothes."

"She must be exhausted," says Jean. Less what she thinks than what she wants to think. "Did you help her into her pj's?"

"I thought I should just let her be."

"But you covered her up, right?"

"Yes, Mother," says Carol. "So now what?"

"I thought I'd set the alarm for five and just drive straight into the city."

"But wouldn't it be easier to deal with this up there?"

"Carol, I have a *job*. I have to be at *work*."

"That's totally crackers," Carol says. "You have to get some good sleep, really rest yourself. Then call your office in the morning, say you've got a family emergency, get hold of the police and just start dealing."

"But what if that takes all day? I *can't* not be there for Halloween."

"I think they'll survive," says Carol. "Let me worry about this end, okay? If you get tied up, I'll tell the kids you had like a plumbing emergency or something. Aren't you always having trouble with the plumbing up there? Look, I guarantee they won't ask for a lot of details. Like I thought it was very interesting with Mel tonight, where she started asking you stuff and then didn't follow up? I think the spirit tells the mind how much can be processed at a given time."

"Right," says Jean. "Listen, I should probably go."

"You know, I have an idea about this. That you might think is kind of off the wall, but there's this—"

"Carol, could you tell me this later? I'm pretty tired."

"I know, and I'm keeping you up. We'll talk when you get back. God, and I've still got dishes. *Sleep*, okay?"

Jean drinks off that last little bit, puts the mug in the sink and goes upstairs. She's never actually stayed here by herself, in all this time. The bedroom's almost comfortable now. She takes off her shoes, gets in bed with her clothes on and pulls the covers up around her—a waste of clean sheets, really. The alarm clock's second hand is twitching away, so the battery must be good. Ten of eleven; that seems about right. She sets the alarm for seven-thirty instead of five, picks up *Emma*, then remembers about the time change. So it's really what? Spring ahead, fall back: ten of *ten*. Which now seems pretty early to be going to bed. But she's whipped. She resets the clock, picks up *Emma* again and fixes the covers so only her face, hands and shoulders are out in the air. Her nose is cold. *Kitty, a fair but frozen maid.* She's at the part where Emma thinks Mr. Elton's in love with Harriet, but he's actually hitting on *her*. At some point she realizes her eyes have been closed for a while: she's still sort of thinking about Mr. Elton and that whole problem, but she's also weighing the risk of disrupting this delicate state of not-quite-sleep by reaching over and turning out the light.

3

The alarm goes off—*deetdeetdeetdeetdeet*—and she shoots out her hand. Too hot and bright in here: her mouth is dry, and apparently she went to sleep with all her clothes on. Out the window, the sky's a cold cerulean blue. And it's so quiet. Then she remembers what she's doing here.

She gets out of bed, turns off the radiator *and* unplugs it. Puts her shoes on, gets Willis's old reindeer sweater out of the bottom drawer and makes her way down through the cold house into the toasty kitchen. Through the window over the sink, she sees the grass is white with frost. She wants to call home and make sure everything's okay, but an interruption is probably the last thing Carol needs; the important thing is just to drive safely and get home to them. She starts water for coffee, then goes in and pees, trying to be extra careful near that hole in the floor, since she's still half asleep. Washes, brushes teeth, brushes hair. One thing she'd better do is turn the water off in the house, so the pipes don't freeze. Just in case he—in case nobody gets back here. If she can figure out how he used to do it. She reaches up under the sweater, sweatshirt and t-shirt and smears his Mennen (what else?) under her arms.

There's a can of Medaglia d'Oro in the fridge, but she can't find the filters; finally she just spoons Taster's Choice into the JOE mug and dusts cinnamon over it; she hates black coffee—especially black *instant* coffee—but it beats getting a headache. She puts what's left of the Dewar's in the cupboard, thinking what a bad girl she'd be to tip it back at this hour of the morning. The phone book's in the drawer: a pitiful little thing about the thickness of *Vogue*, say, and it covers all these little towns, yellow pages included. In the front they've got all sorts of police to choose from: state police, police in whatever town, county sheriff. Apparently you're supposed to know which to call for what. Her water's bubbling; she turns off the burner, fills the mug, stirs.

She sits at the table and rubs her cold fingers above the steaming coffee. It's actually a little early to be calling the police; wouldn't it seem weird not even waiting until eight o'clock after you'd let it go all this time? They'd think *you* were the crazy one, like no wonder he had to get away. Another aspect of this is that up here your police are all going to be men.

Coffee's way too hot, so she goes into the pantry and on into the closet with the tank and the water heater to see if she can figure out how to shut stuff off. At first it's hopeless—just all these pipes—but then she begins to see. Only two pipes go into the wall toward the bathroom and kitchen, which must mean these are the water lines into the house. So if you turned those two valves off, at least water couldn't go anyplace but this closet, right? And then if you just heated this little area . . . The space heater, she's afraid, might burn the whole place down, but there's that electric radiator upstairs. Willis used to have some way of draining the tank and the water heater, but then wouldn't you have to shut the pump off too? Or else everything's just going to fill back up again. One of the breakers probably shuts the pump off, but of course nothing's marked. Well, it's her own fault for never making Willis teach her. Though in fairness she was always busy getting the kids organized and the house straightened up. So now she's in the position of being a dithering woman.

One thing she does know how to do: after the water's cut off, she drains the pipes into a saucepan, opening the little valves under the sinks in the kitchen and bathroom. She goes out to the woodshed for a jug of antifreeze, flushes the toilet and pours half the jug into the bowl. A rich, sick green.

She goes back up to the bedroom for the electric radiator, which weighs a ton and you can't get a decent grip. So she sort of walks it: lift one end, swivel, lift the other end, swivel. The stairs aren't that bad, but then there's the whole rest of the way, and it feels like she's already done something to her back. She's just about in tears: quarter of eight in the morning, and alone in this cold house with this *thing*. Then she gets an idea. In the dining room there's a hooked rug Willis's grandmother supposedly made. She drags it into the front hall, wrestles the radiator onto it, lays it on its side and pulls the rug like a sled. This big triumph that no one will ever know about.

By the time she gets the radiator set up in the closet and comes back out to the kitchen, the coffee's lukewarm. She drinks it, standing up, in three foul-tasting gulps. She reaches around and tries to massage her back, then spreads her legs, bends at the waist and slowly lets her hands sink toward the floor. She feels the top half of her body ratchet down in little jumps as the muscles relax. Her breasts swing out disagreeably and her fingernails touch the floor. She feels the pull in the backs of her thighs. Her knuckles touch the floor. She really should get back into doing yoga. Do it in the morning, when Carol does hers. Right, in all that free time while you're fixing breakfast, dressing for work and getting the kids ready. The backs of her wrists touch the floor. This is probably doing absolutely nothing for her back except making it worse.

She straightens up slowly. Maybe it's her imagination, but she thinks it feels better.

By now it *must* be eight o'clock. Time to do this.

She decides she might as well call the Preston Falls police, since that's where they pay property taxes. Though it's sort of right wing even to think about your property taxes. And actually Willis pays them: they agreed that the expenses up here would be his thing. She looks up the number and dials. The man who answers says, "Police department, good morning." The *good morning* strikes her as hilariously weird.

"Yes, hi," she says. "This is Jean Karnes, K-a-r-n-e-s? We, ah, have a place on Ragged Hill Road? I don't know if I should actually be calling you or the state police or what, but maybe you can help me?"

"Go ahead," says the man.

"Well, I'm not sure, but I think my husband may be missing? He *had* been on leave of absence from his job and he was supposed to be back at work this morning, and I finally came up last night to check on him because I hadn't heard from him and there's like no *sign* of him. But the weird thing—"

"Say you came *up*?"

"Yes, from—where we live, down near New York City." She feels funny about saying "Westchester" to these people.

"So this is your weekend house, ma'am?"

"Yes. But he'd been staying up here by himself since Labor Day. Sort of getting some work done on the house." The white spiral cord on this telephone is absolutely grimy.

"And when was the last time you spoke to him?"

"I'm not sure, exactly," she says. "It was some time ago."

The silence of male exasperation.

"I'd say it was several weeks," she says.

"Uh-huh," he says. She takes this to mean that he understands they have marital problems, like all people with *weekend houses*. "Well, all's I can tell you, you can come down, make out a missing persons and we'll put it on the computer."

"So I should come down there?" she says.

"Yes, ma'am."

"Do I need to bring anything?" she says. "A picture or anything?"

"I guess if you want to bring one."

She goes to the sink to rinse out the mug, but of course nothing comes out of the faucet. This policeman's attitude—or is she overreacting?—makes her spend an extra ten minutes looking in drawers and cupboards for pictures, whether he wants them or not. But their picture-taking has fallen off in the last few years. *Her* picture-taking, actually, since Willis never bothered unless you came right out and asked. Finally, in a basket crammed with old letters and bills, she finds an envelope of pictures from their first summer up here. Willis aiming the garden hose at seven-year-old Mel and four-year-old Roger in swimsuits. Front of house. Back of house. Side of house. House from up on the hill. Jean at the hibachi, smirking, holding up a hot dog on a long fork. (What had gotten into her?) Ah: Willis with chainsaw; he'd been cutting sumacs to give a better view of the stone wall. This would do. He was slimmer then, less gray in the temples, but it's got the basics: eyebrows grown together, eyes set deep, cheekbones he'd have to gain even *more* weight to bury entirely, lower lip so much fatter than the upper. The mouth that looked giving rather than taking, which just goes to show you. Fine, she'll give them this. She sort of likes that it will mean absolutely nothing to them.

She unplugs the space heater in the kitchen, which it was dangerous to have left on all night, and feels the air start to get cold immediately, as if the place just can't wait to get back to being an empty house out in the middle of nature. She goes upstairs, glances into his study to make sure everything's turned off, then checks in the bedroom. Might as well bring *Emma* along. And how about that *Pilgrim's Progress*, to play around with that funny lettering? Forget it: she's got enough on her plate. She takes a last look around the kitchen. She should hide the boombox and CDs; incredible how much money you're looking at in a stack of CDs. But you know? You get tired of cleaning up after boys. Still, there's one thing: that mug of her father's. She just can't abandon that up here, little as he loved it. She finds a plastic grocery bag, wraps up the JOE mug and sticks it in her purse.

She should have warmed up the Cherokee, but by the time she gets to Quaker Bridge Road the needle on the temperature gauge is up to the first little mark and she can turn the heater on. The morning sun is bringing out the green of the fading grass and giving the bare trees long, sharp shadows. She passes poor little house after poor little house, each with a giant satellite dish in the yard. Pumpkins and tree ghosts have never looked so pagan to her: right down from barbaric times. She could *never* have lived up here. Not that she'd ever been asked.

She tells the post office lady she left her key at home and could she have the mail for Box 324. No problem. On the one hand it's nice that people up here are nice, but it's like *anybody* could just waltz in and ask for your mail. This lady's beauty-parlor perm looks odd with that mannish blue postal service sweater, but it must be cold working in here. She comes back and flops four bundles with rubber bands around them on the counter. "I guess you hit the jackpot."

"I guess so," Jean says. "Well, it can't *all* be bills."

"*There* you go." So Jean has struck the requisite Preston Falls note: wry stoicism with a hint of self-deprecation.

She goes over to the chest-high table, slips off the rubber bands and starts throwing junk mail and catalogs into the wastepaper thing. She never knew they had so many hardware stores and lumber companies up here. A couple of things marked PERSONAL AND CONFIDENTIAL: IMMEDIATE RESPONSE REQUIRED, from a post office box at Cooper Square Station—probably some bogus contest. Sales at Grand Union. Full-color circulars from Ames, with all this seventies-looking type and layout; apparently they're trying not to intimidate rural people.

She takes the rest out to the Cherokee—bills, bank statements; but, again, not a single letter—and she starts the engine so she can run the heater. The most recent phone bill, postmarked October 26, says THIS IS A FINAL DISCONNECTION NOTICE: total amount overdue $157 and change. But no long-distance calls on the statement. The one postmarked September 26 shows calls to Etna, New Hampshire (his mother), Rutland, Vermont (that lawyer?), Chesterton, New York, and New York City. Two electric bills. Two American Express bills (neither one has new charges) and one Amexgram, that thing they send when you haven't paid: his balance is six hundred–odd dollars. Two MasterCard bills, balance of nine thousand and change; the October bill has some snippy little thing about his minimum payment. SECOND NOTICE from Allstate Insurance; Willis registers the Cherokee and his truck up here because the premiums are lower, which she's always thought was dishonest.

She rips open the bank statement postmarked October: a balance of $12.17, no canceled checks, no ATM transactions and a five-dollar service charge. The September one shows a balance of $17.17, with a single cash withdrawal: 9/18, $400, New Baltimore Service Area, New York State Thruway, plus a $1 ATM fee.

Why did he bother to leave seventeen dollars? Obviously to keep his account open. Which meant he took off for somewhere but intended to come back? Or at least to have the option? But maybe it was just that the machine only gave out multiples of twenty: her little girl-detective deduction. New Baltimore. That's the one just south of Albany, right? But was it even Willis, or had somebody stolen his cash card? But if they'd stolen his cash card, wouldn't they also have his credit cards? And since there was no activity on those statements . . . But of course Willis's MasterCard was pretty well maxed out.

She fastens her seat belt, releases the brake and waits to pull out as a low-slung black car passes by. Going to the post office before the police made sense, actually. Well, so now she's been to the post office. She *so* much doesn't want to do this. The police station, she assumes, is in the town hall, where you always see cruisers parked around the side.

The officer behind the counter looks to be in his twenties; he's got one of those ultra-neat short haircuts young Christians have, with the perfectly circular cutouts around each ear. Naturally he wears a wedding ring.

"Hi. I'm Jean Karnes?" she says. "Are you the person I spoke to?"

"No, ma'am. That would be Officer Plankey." The name tag above this one's badge says ALDEN. "He went out for breakfast. Are you the lady that called about your husband?"

"Yes."

"Here," he says, pointing to a waist-high swinging door. "Why don't you come around this way and have a seat."

She sits on a metal folding chair at the side of a metal desk with a computer on it. He sits down on the swivel chair and clicks a mouse here and there on the pad, squinting at the monitor. Then he starts tapping at the keyboard. "I brought along a picture," she says.

He stops tapping, takes the picture from her, looks, puts it on the desk.

He asks for Willis's full name, address, age, description and occupation, tapping in her answers; then he listens to her story. He doesn't seem to think it's weird that Willis's computer was on—they've got one at home, and he's *always* forgetting. The broken window? Could be kids; anything missing from the house? Not that she knows of. Well, come to think of it, she didn't see his guitars. But of course he sometimes hides them, and she didn't check his hiding places. She tells about the unpaid bills and the cash withdrawal on the Thruway on September 18. He nods. And how long since she's seen or heard from him? Well, right around then, actually. He looks at her. "You mean around September eighteenth?" he says. Probably, she says. He looks back at the screen, taps a few characters, then, still looking at the screen, he says, "Was this a usual length of time with you and your husband?"

Not until she's back in the Cherokee does it hit her that she should have told about him getting arrested on Labor Day weekend; she'd honestly forgotten. And it probably had no bearing. Well, so they'll find out anyway, won't they, from their computer? But when he asked if Willis had seemed unusually upset—no, "overwrought"—it might have been good to mention that. Instead she said he was a little burned out from work. So now they'll think she was being *evasive*.

Well, she's done all she can do here, yes?

She could drive by the house one more time, just in case his truck is there. Maybe check on the guitars?

No. Enough.

She heads back through the center of Preston Falls, trying to remember the most direct route over to the Northway. Past the old movie theater with its windows boarded up, past the used-furniture place that's now a pile of bricks with charred boards sticking up, past Winner's, where the display window has a cardboard cutout of a black cat arching its back. Right: Halloween. At least she'll be back in time to be with Mel and Roger. She drives past Julie's Luncheonette, with the hole busted in its plastic sign. Past the one surviving nice old storefront, Howard & Sheron's, with black-and-gold lettering that still says SUN-DRIES and always makes her think of sun-dried tomatoes. She's a city person; so sue her. Sometimes it depresses her that she's ended up back in the burbs, even though she'd campaigned for it because of the kids. A blast of wind comes along—*whomp*—that actually rocks the Cherokee and sends a plastic bag flapping up into the blue sky like a rising witch.

4

The elevator doors open on fourteen and Jean sees Helen, talking on the phone at the reception desk, and the pure white wall with her own smoky Lucite letters spelling PALEY, and she has to say: it's a relief to be here.

Either she was too tired to enjoy it after driving down from Preston Falls, or Halloween really *had* been dreary this year. (The three messages from Marty Katz on the answering machine in Chesterton didn't help her mood either.) Roger had wanted to be Dennis Rodman—this would've involved a blond wig and blackface, which Jean thought was racially tricky—but luckily he changed his mind and decided to be Frankenstein. (Frankenstein's *monster*, Willis would say. But while the cat's away.) She got him a rubber mask that had the things sticking out of the sides of the neck, and he wore Willis's arctics, tied around his shins with twine, the toes stuffed with newspaper. Mel was Courtney Love: basically an excuse to put on a hiked-up skirt, fishnet stockings, heavy makeup. Jean wouldn't let her go to the party *all her friends* were going to, ostensibly because it was a school night, and really because she'd heard rumors of dosed Hawaiian Punch at the same party last year. So Mel declined to go through the motions of trick-or-treating—she's stopped eating sugar anyway—and stayed, in costume, in the Cherokee, watching Roger thrust his treat bag at grownups in their doorways, smiling their forced smiles. Next year they've got to have a better plan.

Jean left Carol to hold the fort while she took the kids around. But only four trick-or-treaters came to their door the whole night, so they're stuck with all this candy, plus the bagful of loot Roger collected. Before he brushed his teeth, Jean let him have some M&M's and a Milky Way from their stockpile, and told him he could start on his own stuff tomorrow, after she'd looked it over. She saw no signs of tampering, but of course with an expert job you wouldn't. When he went to bed, she noted down everything in his treat bag, took it all out to the garbage can and drove to Rite Aid to buy replacements.

This morning the kids whined and dawdled from the minute she woke them up, and she finally just said, which was really unlike her, "Why are you punishing *me*?" They both gave good imitations of bewilderment, and probably they *were* bewildered. She poured Product 19 into their bowls and sogged it down with milk, thinking (stupidly) that if she poured in the milk they would *have* to hustle. Meanwhile she didn't even have time to make herself toast; she folded a piece of bread and gnawed at it to keep the coffee from making her sick to her stomach. She did finally get them mobilized and into the Cherokee; she dropped Mel at Chesterton Middle School, then Roger at Mary M. Watson. Watching him safely inside, she began to weep because all she ever did was crab at them and they really seemed to do so much better with Carol. So then of course when she got to the station she had to pull the mirror down and fix her stupid makeup in the parking lot, with a million people looking. No wonder all these men on the train don't go home until like eight o'clock at night. Though by this afternoon she'll be longing to be with her children again.

The Paley Group was her first job interview when she finally finished Pratt, and she was too stupid then to realize how lucky she was. While every other investment firm was cutting back, Paley had committed to a ground-up in-house redesign. She now knows this was Jerry Starger's idea, hiring some young designer (on the cheap) to take charge of everything from stationery and brochures to the monthly newsletter to the whole look of the offices. Jean probably got the job because she wasn't all *that* young and therefore seemed more trustworthy than some little chickie from Parsons or FIT with a stud in her nose. And things being what they are, it couldn't have hurt that she was a woman. *And* okay-looking: not the beauty of the world, she knows, but sort of perky—a word she hates. You can be *too* beautiful, like Claudia What's-her-face, the supermodel. (At the newsstand downstairs this morning, Jean saw her on the cover of some magazine: "A Supermodel Who's Super-Nice.") You can picture all these men tripping over their shoes and, in the end, not liking you because of it. Jean has an idea Anita Bruno—another of Jerry's hires—suffers because of her looks. Though on the other hand, if not for her looks she might not be here to suffer, if that's not too catty.

Anyhow, she earned her keep that first year. She came up with the new logo (basically PALEY in this austere lettering) and made sure it got on business cards, letterhead, all the signage. They needed the help: one of the old brochures actually had this crosshatched drawing of two white guys in suits facing each other across a desk, one pointing to something on a piece of paper and the other cocking his head like the RCA dog. She even picked new art for the corridors, getting rid of the giant color photos of sailboats and bringing in these plexiglass-framed constructions of torn-paper triangles, thread and birds' bones that she'd found at a show in Connecticut.

Of course everything was a battle royal. "How the hell is it supposed to show up?" Arthur Paley said when Jean and Jerry Starger brought the big Lucite *P* into his office to show him. "Hell, you see right through it."

"Right, but don't forget," Jean said, "that wall's going to be absolutely white."

Arthur Paley held up the smoky *P* and looked through it out his window at Central Park. "Christ," he said.

"Trust me," said Jerry Starger. "This is perfecto." He brought thumb and forefinger together to make an OK sign and pumped it three times. "This says ex*act*ly what needs to be said. The name is *there*, three-D, an inch thick. Solid. But at the same time it's not up there screaming its head off at you. It's like: We are here, for those who know."

Arthur Paley shook his head. "The world lost a great Fuller Brush man when they let *you* into Princeton," he said. "I have to think about this." But he came around, and the reception area won Jean her first bonus. A thousand dollars, which she used to start a little fund for Mel and Roger.

The redesign's pretty much in place now, and she's gone on to stuff like working with the computer people on the new Web site, which Jerry Starger wants up and running by the first of the year. But she always has to keep an eye out to make sure everything isn't sliding back. Accounting complains about the cost of repainting this wall every four months, but in order to work, it has to be *absolutely* white, not just sort of white like everything else in New York.

Helen, shoulder raised to wedge the phone against her ear, is writing on a pink While You Were Out slip; she sees Jean and turns on a smile. Jean always feels funny waltzing in here wearing slacks and whatnot past Helen, in her outfits and power blouses. They sometimes ask about each other's children. Helen hangs up the phone and puts the call slip in the *S* section of the metal rack on her desk. There's a story about that metal rack. What convinced everybody that Jean was a head case was her taking it home and painting it white; she just couldn't stand looking anymore at that tan *thing* plopped down on the white desk in front of the white wall and next to the terrific square white vase she'd found at Pier 1. She called around and learned that nobody carried these racks in white, so she asked Helen if she could borrow it over the weekend. Out in the garage on Saturday morning, she took it apart—twenty-seven fins plus the base—and sprayed everything with white Rust-Oleum. She reassembled it on Sunday and brought it back Monday morning in a plastic bag inside another plastic bag, dreading that she'd scratch it.

But of course you can be only so compulsive. Like, she obviously could never ever say anything about what colors Helen should wear, or what kind of flowers she should put in the vase. So there'd be days when Helen would be sitting there in like a burgundy jacket next to these blazing orange lilies or something, and you would just *cringe*. And Jean so much wants to chuck the tacky gold frames Helen has for pictures of her husband and daughters—Lechter's has these white ceramic ones—but she has to tell herself *Stop, just stop.*

"Good morning," Helen says, hanging up the phone. "You had one call yesterday."

Jean takes the slip out of the *K* section. (These pink While You Were Out slips are another irritant.) *Champ, 4:16 p.m., will call back.* Willis's brother *never* calls here: he must have news. She's afraid he does and afraid he doesn't.

She goes on past her office to the end of the hall. Jerry Starger's assistant, Martha, isn't at her desk, but his door is open, so she peeks in.

"Hey, *there* she is," says Jerry. "You get everything squared away?" On the phone yesterday, she told him she had some family business.

"Pretty much, I guess," she says. "For now." With her index finger she tries to smooth out a bubble under the tape at one corner of the poster on his door. (This beautiful bleached-oak door.) A grinning little girl with metal crutches and leg braces, and the legend *Help Jerry's Kids.*

"All we can ask in this life," he says. "Meeting at eleven?"

"Fine."

"In the meantime, think beautiful thoughts. Think: Marietta, Georgia." The latest branch office, due to open December 1. Decent-sized space in a hopeless strip mall.

Jean closes her office door behind her, logs on and gets PHONE. PRSNL up on her screen, scrolls down to *W*. Two numbers for Champ;

try the work one first. Right, and there's Sylvia's number. She never returned Jean's call, of course—though in fairness, maybe she did try Preston Falls. A man at the Counter Spy Shop says Champ called in sick; he sounds annoyed. Jean punches in Champ's home number.

A machine picks up, Jim Morrison sings *Hello, I love you, won't you tell me your*—then Champ says, "Wait-wait-wait, let me get this fucking thing. Hello?"

"It's Jean," she says. "Are you okay? They said you were sick?"

"On the record? Food poisoning. Off the record? Mal de something. Mal de lingering."

"Oh," says Jean. "I just got your message from yesterday. Actually, I was about to call *you*."

"You *did* call me. Nurk nurk."

"Listen, have you heard anything from Doug?"

"Hey, great minds," he says. "See, *I* was hoping—shit. So he hasn't come *back* yet?"

"No. He was supposed to be back at work yesterday. I drove up to Preston Falls on Sunday, and it didn't look like he'd been there for a while. When was the last you heard from him?"

"Shit, a *long* time," he says. "Actually, I don't think I've talked to him since we were all up there for Labor Day. I tried to get ahold of him a couple weeks ago and never heard back. So then I tried him yesterday at work, because I remembered he was coming back on Halloween or something, and they said he was quote out of the office. So I thought I'd bother *you* for a change."

"Right." Jean's scratching white lines on the back of her left hand with a pushpin, from the center of the wrist to each knuckle.

"So when did *you* talk to him last?"

"Well," she says, "things were sort of at the point where we'd more or less agreed not to be calling."

"But how about the kids?" says Champ. "Oh fuck me, that was out of line, wasn't it? *Doy-yoy-yoing, sor*-ry. It's not like I'm a *total* animal."

Jean touches tongue to fingertip and starts rubbing the scratches away. "Oh look," she says, "it's stupid at this point for everybody to still go around being discreet."

"Right. But you weren't actually, like legally—or were you?"

"No. God, I've made such a mess."

"Hey, you had help. He said like a low-down disloyal un-brotherly dog."

"I'm sorry," she says. "I don't mean to be carrying on."

"You're not carrying on. You may not believe it, but I've always been a fan of yours."

"Is that so. But what could you say, right?"

"Well," he says. "Like you say."

When she gets off the phone, she takes the key to the ladies' room out of her drawer, stands up and feels she'd better quick sit back down. But she rides it out, standing there swaying, palms pressed on the desk as the buzzing and the sparkly blackness deepen, then dissipate. She finds she's staring at the picture of Mel and Roger: the two of them in their bathing suits, arms around each other's shoulders—a reach up for Roger—and showing teeth in grins she tries to see as unforced. Labor Day. When the pictures came back, she immediately bought a frame for this one and put it on her desk. Because she was afraid *not* to.

In the ladies' room, she runs cold water, gets a double handful and lowers her face into it. She pumps the soap dispenser, gets nothing—as usual—then lifts the lid the way you have to do and dips two fingers into the pink liquid. One of these days she's got to remember to pick up a traveling soap dish, so she can keep a bar of Neutrogena in her desk. *That*'ll fix everything. She dries her face with a paper towel and sees she's going to have to put on more Cover Girl. For what, the third time this morning? And of course she's managed to splatter the front of her shirt. Willis's shirt, actually, that he bought years ago at a yard sale: a garage shirt or something, with *Dan* embroidered above the left pocket. She'd liked it for its grayish shade of green and for how the gabardine had softened just the right amount.

There's a story about the shirt too. Willis said he'd bought it just so he could say, if anybody asked, "I don't know why, my name is not Dan." She forgets what that was supposed to be a line from; just one of his endless things. But it started to get a little snug on him, so he ended up not wearing it much. Finally she put it in the drawer with her tops. And bided her time for a month or so, until, one morning, she wore it to the table, and he said, "Hey, where'd you find that? Looks better on you than it ever did on me." Why hadn't she just asked him for the stupid shirt? Maybe because she has a thing about *asking* for anything. Your marriage, she used to assume, was a safe place to play out these harmless little things.

Back in her office, she gets Sylvia's number off the screen and picks up the phone. Five rings and, again, Willis's voice. She hangs up.

What it is, she's *furious* at him.

And at his mother, who should've done a better job with him—though who is she to say? *And* at herself. Oh, of *course*, dear, if you need to go up and stare at trees and play your guitar . . . Think no more about it: *I* will take care of our home and our family and our life. And *fine*, let him hold that against her too, that she's another angry woman. Like when she was reading Sandra Cisneros and told Willis he should really check her out, and he said the idea of a woman hollering didn't exactly do it for him. And it was like, Thanks for one more precious insight into you.

Five of eleven. She's not prepared for this meeting: her dreams and schemes for raw space in a strip mall in Georgia.

But really, *isn't* it his mother's fault for screwing up his whole attitude toward women? (Right, as if every other man is so fabulously healthy.) Early on, when Carol first asked about Willis, Jean had said, Well, the *sex* is great. Which it really wasn't: him working away at her, trying to get her to give up and come first, while as a man he could let go anytime. All over her feet, once. And demonstrating in the process what *great* shape he kept himself in, back when he kept himself in shape. Like just *daring* her to run her hands down his ass and find any flab, though she's got to say, even then. . . . So the more he worked away at her, the colder she got. The more observant.

One thing she observed, the act meant to degrade her—which of course he secretly liked best—actually gave her power: he would lose command after three strokes, at most, and it was over. His half-babies mixed with her wastes, and away it all went, leaving her free and clean and empty. She was supposed to trust him enough for it to be *safe* to act out her fantasies of being degraded. Or something. The old porno propaganda, which they've now got women believing. All it did, really, was allow her to see him.

Though not really. As it turns out. And in fairness, she didn't always think sex with him was stupid.

The phone rings, and she leaps for it.

Jerry Starger says, "Meeting."

5

When she gets home, only Rathbone greets her. Mel's upstairs, and Roger and Carol are in the living room, watching Rocky and Bullwinkle. The kitchen smells of microwave popcorn. Jean guesses it's good they show the old Rocky and Bullwinkles on cable; at least they're not violent, and the values probably aren't the worst, though the Dudley Doright stuff does make fun of heroes and chastity. She calls *Hi*, then sticks her head in: they're both staring at the screen, and Roger's hand is feeling for the popcorn. It's like a diorama.

She goes back into the kitchen. Somebody's left a knife smeared with peanut butter just sitting on the counter; they're going to be the first family in Chesterton to have cockroaches. God, she's starting to sound like Willis, the difference being that she doesn't actually *say* anything. She wills herself to go wash the stupid knife, as well as the JOE mug, which has been in her purse all this time. But her legs suddenly feel like they're going to give out, so she sits down at the table. She's still sitting there when a commercial comes on, and at least *Carol* deigns to get off her duff and come in.

"Tough day for you?" she says, putting a hand on Jean's shoulder. "What would you like—tea?" She begins running water into the kettle. "How about a little something in it?"

"Regular tea is fine. Thanks."

"You haven't eaten, right? We were just having some popcorn."

"I gathered."

"What happened," Carol says, "poor Roger was starved when he got home, because today was Sloppy Joes. *Why*, after all these years, they insist on giving kids Sloppy Joes . . . Anyhow. Mel said she was hungry too, so I fixed them alphabet soup and got some bagels out of the freezer, and then Roger discovered peanut butter on onion bagels. So none of us are hungry. But there's more bagels, and you're welcome to the rest of that soup."

Jean thinks, *I'm welcome?* "I don't know," she says. "I guess I should eat." She wills herself to stand and goes into the living room. In the commercial, some obnoxious teenager's saying, "I gotta have my Pops." She gets no acknowledgment of her presence from Roger except a slight intensification of his frown at the screen. She kneels and kisses his knee through a rip in his jeans: *that* startles him. He jerks his leg away and says, "We're watching Bullwinkle."

"Okay, enjoy it." She gets to her feet and goes upstairs, passing Mel on the way down. Who gives her a *Hi* and keeps going. She sits on the edge of the bed and surprises herself by beginning to weep, listening between sobs for footsteps. When she reaches the gasping stage, where you either keep on or decide to get yourself under control, she takes a couple of deep breaths, goes into the bathroom, washes her face without looking in the mirror and dries off with a smelly towel. She can hear the tv going and can't for the life of her make up her mind whether to ask Carol if their homework's done or to ask the kids themselves.

She opens the hamper to put the towel in, and it's right up to the top with dirty clothes, mostly Mel's. And God knows what's on the floor in Roger's room. Well, so much for getting to bed early. Does Carol do *any-thing* around here besides feed them any crappo food they want any*time* they want and then park herself with them in front of the tv? (Jean knows she's so out of line here it's not even funny, like a husband who comes home and runs a gloved finger over the mantelpiece.)

She goes back downstairs and finds Mel, who's lately been on this tv-is-for-losers thing, is watching too; Bullwinkle's into the Boris and Natasha part. These are kids, bear in mind, who don't know why it's funny that he's called Boris Badenov, though as a matter of fact if you put a gun to Jean's head all she'd be able to come up with is that there's something called *Boris Godunov*, so *she*'s a great example. She opens the refrigerator and finds the saucepan of alphabet soup; Carol has added chopped green pepper, which Jean could do without. Their mother used to say Carol was "fixy," meaning she liked rearranging the furniture or trimming old dresses with lace and binding tape or fiddling around with the proportions of recipes. Alphabet soup and Bullwinkle and Sloppy Joes: you could really believe for seconds at a time that everything's the way it used to be. She dumps the leftover soup in a bowl and sticks it in the microwave. She punches numbers, it goes *beep beep beep beep* and Mel calls, "Mom? What are you making?"

"I'm warming up some soup," Jean hollers back. "You want some?"

"I don't think so. I don't know, maybe."

"Yes or no?"

"I'm *thinking*, Mother."

"Shut up, I can't hear," says Roger. "You made me *miss* that part."

"Chill *out*, Roger," says Mel. "Mom? I don't want soup, but is there anything else?"

"I don't know," says Jean. "Why don't you get up and look?"

She immediately wants to apologize, but maybe all that's called for is to make the next thing you say kinder.

She opens the refrigerator again to see what there is to drink—then remembers the tea. Steam's billowing out of the kettle. She turns off the gas and hefts it: well, still enough left. She squirts green dish soap into the JOE mug and scrubs around with the sponge, rinses and dries, puts in an Irish Breakfast tea bag and pours the hot water over it.

The microwave beeps; she carries the bowl of alphabet soup over to the table, sits down and almost starts weeping again when she sees she left the mug of tea on the counter. Just get up and get it, she tells herself.

Soup's good. She must've been hungry.

She hears more commercials start up (they're always louder) and feels like she's making some mean-spirited statement by sitting out here when they're all in there watching tv together. She scrapes the spoon around inside the bowl for the last little smidgen, a leprous white *d*. Unless it's a *b*. Or a *p*. The soup's making her sleepy, warming her from inside; she could just get under the covers right now and bag everything. She puts the bowl and the mug in the dishwasher and goes into the living room. Yet another commercial.

"Is that it for Bullwinkle?" she says.

Roger recognizes this question as not so innocent. He says, "It comes back on for a second."

"Is your homework all done?"

"Al*most*," says Mel.

"Yeah, almost," says Roger.

"Liar," says Mel. "You didn't even start."

"I was *going* to, but you were making noise," says Roger. To Jean: "She was talking on the phone."

"Okay, both of you," Jean says. "Scoot."

They don't move.

Jean picks up the zapper and zaps the tv off.

"Hey, wait," says Roger.

"*Mah*-om," says Mel.

Even Rathbone gives her a dirty look.

"You know the rule," Jean says. "Aunt Carol was nice to let you watch Bullwinkle. Now it's time to do your work."

"I'm *hungry*," says Mel.

"Take an apple up with you. I want you both up there spit-spot." This is a family joke, from when they'd read the Mary Poppins books, though the kids have probably forgotten by now where it ever came from.

They trudge, but they go.

"I feel like such a witch," Jean says to Carol.

Carol shrugs. Not exactly a denial.

"Listen, I'm going to do a wash," says Jean. "You have stuff that needs doing?"

"I probably should've cracked the whip about the homework," says Carol.

"No, it's their responsibility."

"But still. I know how important it is to you." What, meaning she's a nut on the subject? "So I take it you haven't heard anything from the police?"

"Not a thing. You know, he's in *the computer*. Whippity-doo."

"Hmm," says Carol. "I have to think about this."

"Fine. Meanwhile, do you have stuff to wash?"

Up in the bedroom, she drags the laundry bag out of the closet. It's stupid to be doing a load and not put in the clothes she's wearing, but then she'd have to change. And before that she'd have to shower. She feels a jab next to her left kidney (wrestling that stupid radiator) when she shoulders the bag and carries it into the bathroom to get stuff out of the hamper. Another jab when she bends over, the pain shooting down the outside of her thigh. Crap. She shoulders the bag again and knocks on Mel's door.

"*What?*"

"Sorry to interrupt," says Jean. "Do you have dirty clothes in there? I'm doing a load of wash."

"I'll look in a minute, okay?" Mel says through the door.

"Would you look now, please? So I can get started?"

"But *Mother*."

Jean opens the door. Mel's sitting cross-legged on her bed, gaping at her, with three wet red toenails on one foot, a nail-polish bottle in one hand and a red-tipped brush-cap in the other.

"You know, the longer you put off—"

"I *know*, Mother. I needed to think about something."

"And that's a good way to ruin your bedspread."

"I'm being careful."

"What did you need to think about?" says Jean. Which is what she should have said instead of carping about the bedspread.

"I don't know. Nothing." She dips the brush in and starts on the next toe.

"Well, could you please put that up and help me? I need *that*"— pointing to a pair of faded blue jeans on the floor—"*that*"—Courtney Love t-shirt—"*that*"—pink top with purple sleeves—"and all *that*"—a tangle of socks and tights, plus another pair of jeans, with one inside-out leg sticking through the leg hole of a pair of underpants.

"All *right*." Mel gets off the bed and limps toward the clothes, try-ing to keep the painted toes from touching the floor.

"And watch your tone, please?" says Jean. Mel hands her the t-shirt. "When I come back in here, I expect to find you've finished your homework."

Mel hands her both pairs of jeans; the faded pair has major grass stains on the seat. Colors are beautiful, actually. "Roger's probably in there looking at his stupid *magazines*." Mel hands Jean the big tangle of stuff and hobbles back to sit on the bed.

"I'll worry about Roger," Jean says. "Your job is to get *your* work done." She can't ask what magazines, since she's just told Mel to mind her own business. Really handling *this* brilliantly. She pulls the draw-string tight on the laundry bag. It also occurs to her she hasn't said a kind word to Mel since getting home.

"Is Daddy still at Grandma's?" says Mel.

"I assume so," Jean says.

"But he's supposed to be back at work."

"Well, that's what I'd thought," says Jean, "but I think I probably got the dates confused and it's actually *next* week." This sounds so plau-sible she's tempted to believe it herself.

Mel draws the brush up out of the bottle and regards the glossy red nail polish. "Yeah, okay, thanks," she says.

Jean knocks on Roger's door. "Last call for dirty clothes."

"What does that mean?" Roger says through the door.

"It means I'm doing a wash tonight." She turns the doorknob and pushes: he's got it bolted. "Open the door, please?"

"In a second, okay?" Noises. She can't tell what.

"What's going on in there?" says Jean. Like he's really going to tell her.

"*Nothing*. I'm *coming*."

More noises, then Roger's footsteps. He snaps the bolt back and opens the door.

"How come your door's locked?" says Jean.

"She's always coming in and bothering me."

"Mm-hm," says Jean. Not agreeing, but indicating she's heard. Roger looks flushed. He's too young to be able to really masturbate, isn't he? She should read something about boys. "So how's your homework?"

"Okay," he says.

"May I see?"

"I don't want you to see until I'm done," he says.

"And how long will that be?"

"How am I supposed to know?"

"I don't care for that tone," she says.

He stares back. But doesn't *answer* back, so she guesses she doesn't have to take this any further.

She picks up black jeans, a black t-shirt and three once-white socks and stuffs them in the laundry bag. "Is this all you have?"

He shrugs. "There's more in there," he says, tossing his head in the direction of the closet.

"Could you get it, please?"

He shrugs again and brings out an armload: shirts, underwear, another pair of black jeans. She holds the bag open for him.

"I'll be back in fifteen minutes," she says, and taps her finger three times on the clock beside his bed. Five of eight already; his official bedtime is nine o'clock. "I expect you to have *one* of your assignments done. Anything you don't finish tonight you'll have to do in the morning." She drags the laundry out into the hall, leaving his door open. She tries to shoulder the thing again, gets that same shooting pain and just pulls it behind her by its drawstring, letting it bump down the stairs. She hears Roger's door shut.

At the bottom of the stairs she picks the bag up and hugs it, so she won't be dragging it past Carol looking ostentatiously like a drudge. Carol's on the sofa, feet tucked up under her, reading *The Fellowship of the Ring*. But once she gets the basement door open, she lets the bag drop again, and down the stairs it tumbles, spilling out socks and underpants as it rolls.

Thank God for a washer and dryer right in the house. Back when they lived on 108th Street, she used to go to this laundromat around the corner on Broadway, pushing Roger in his stroller and having to keep an eye on Mel every second. So life *has* gotten better. Even if this is just an old Kenmore top-loader and you can't do massive amounts at a time. But what she'd *love* would be to have *two* washers down here—is this pathetic?—so you could separate your colors and get the whole thing done in one fell swoop. But it would be such an indulgence.

Those years at home with Mel, and then with Mel and Roger: *that* was an indulgence. Or so Willis thought. And in fairness, she can see why he resented her for it. She thought it should have meant something to him that he was supporting his family single-handed—how many men do that anymore?—but she can see how it might've lost its luster, being stuck in a job he holds in such contempt. She used to think it was great for Mel and Roger, not being packed off to day care or turned over to some weird nanny, whom they'd then love more than you. On the other hand, look how it's turned out: Roger with all his problems and—let's face it—warning signs, and Mel off in Mel Land.

But what kills Jean: it was just starting to get to a point where maybe things could have begun to change. She had her job, bringing them in half again as much money, and some of the weight could finally have started to lift off of Willis. And they really *could* have started thinking about something like the plan they used to talk about, where he could try to do something that maybe didn't pay as much but would mean something to him. His music, even. Though of course he's now totally cynical about that. And realistically, the mortgage payments in Chesterton would probably make it impossible. And then to top everything off, he turned around and burdened himself with all the expenses of Preston Falls. Completely self-defeating. As she probably should've tried harder to point out to him five years ago.

She starts picking the whites out of the bag and sticking them in the washer, setting Mel's jeans aside to see if she can't do something about those grass stains. She pours in a capful of Tide with Bleach Alternative—Willis did one of his little riffs the first time he lifted *that* out of a grocery bag, but she actually can tell a difference—and turns the washer on. She puts the Rubbermaid flap over the drain in the deep sink, checks the label on the Clorox jug, runs what she estimates is a gallon of water, puts on a yellow rubber glove and pours in a quarter cup of Clorox and swooshes it around with her gloved hand. That smell: like a man's, you know, *stuff*. From what she can remember. Out of the dim distant past. With the gloved hand, she pushes Mel's jeans down under, as if she's drowning something. *Fully soak garment for 5 minutes.* She turns the jeans over so at least the rear end will be fully soaked. Now, what to do with her big five minutes? Well, she could go up and check on their homework, which is what she said she'd do.

The upstairs door opens, and Carol calls, "Are you down there?"

"Yeah. What?"

"Stay right there, I have to ask you something." She comes clomping down the cellar stairs, carrying *The Fellowship of the Ring* with her index finger stuck in it.

"Right here," says Carol, pointing to a page. "How do you say this?"

"I think it's *Ay-ar-an-dil*," says Jean.

"Not *Eer-an-dil*, right?"

"No, I think the thing over the *a* means they want you to . . . you know."

"I thought so," says Carol. "Okay, and another thing. Is it *Jimli* or *Gimli*?"

"Gimli," Jean says. "I *think*. God. I seem to remember they had a pronunciation thing in there somewhere."

"Right, I found that, and they say *g*'s are supposed to be hard. But Roger says you're supposed to say Sam *Gamjee* and not *Gam-gee*, so it's confusing. Oh, and they also say in there—this is *really* weird—that *f*'s are supposed to be like *v*'s. So you're actually supposed to say *Gandalv*? I'm not going to go around saying *Gandalv*."

"Don't let Roger nitpick you to death. He should be grateful that you're nice enough to read to him."

"Oh, I'm enjoying it. People in college always used to try to get me into it, but I was sort of too stoned to read? And then when Dexter was the right age, you couldn't really get him to sit still that long."

"Well, good. I'm glad you're having a good time with it. I don't know, it seemed okay back when Willis read it to Mel, but this time it just feels like eight zillion pages of male bonding. I think you get the first woman character on like page nine hundred."

"Well, Goldberry," says Carol.

"Oh, right. God forbid we should forget *Gold*berry."

"Listen, would it be okay if I wrote in it? I just thought I'd try to mark a couple of things ahead so I can breeze through when I get to them and not embarrass myself."

"You're making too big a deal out of this," says Jean. "He's not being snotty to you, is he?"

"Not really. It's actually fun, in a weird way. Kind of like going back to school."

"Well, I hope he appreciates it."

Carol snorts. "Come on, you can't expect *that*. When they're forty, *maybe*, you might hear that you once did something right. If you're still *alive*. Tell me something: what are you doing tomorrow after work?"

"What am I *doing*? What I always do. Come home, eat, have two minutes with Mel and Roger, do housework, go to bed. Why?"

"Well. I have an idea, okay? If the kids could go over to What's-their-face, Mel's friend?"

"The Millers'?"

"Right. If they could go over there after school and stay for dinner, could you get off work early and meet me? Or Thursday, if tomorrow doesn't work?"

"I thought you had to *leave* this week."

"Come on, with everything just *hanging* like this?"

"I can make out," says Jean.

"We'll talk about that too. But listen, could you try for tomorrow? This is something that might really end up helping. I have to make some arrangements, but I'll call you at work tomorrow and let you know for sure."

"I love surprises," says Jean.

"I know. I'm sorry. I don't mean to make a big mystery, but I just feel like this is the best way to do it, okay? Trust me?"

"I guess," says Jean. "I'd better try to get hold of Erin's mother right now."

"Good," Carol says. "And I should be able to let you know by tomorrow noon if we can actually do this. If not, we'll go out to dinner, just the two of us, how's that?"

Jean calls Rosellen Miller (*Always* glad to have Mel and Roger! Erin will be *thrilled*!), then goes back down to check the laundry, and settles in the old stuffed armchair that was in the basement when they bought the place. God, Carol can be wearing. And whatever this scheme of hers is about—well, she'll find out tomorrow. Or not. The chair smells musty and has white stuff showing through the arms, but really this is the most comfortable place to sit in the whole house. Jean used to think about having it reupholstered and bringing it upstairs, except she was afraid that might somehow ruin it. So this is one of her secrets; she always keeps a book down here next to the chair to read while she's doing laundry, something she reads nowhere else. She reaches down and picks up Rex Stout's *The Father Hunt*, which she's been working on now for a couple of weeks. The part she's in now, Nero and Archie are finding out that Eugene Jarrett can't be the father because he's sterile, though you already sort of knew he couldn't be anyway because it was too obvious.

She feels her head start to go forward and down onto her right shoulder; as the muscles relax, they give her back a twinge, and she realizes she was almost asleep. She's got to stay awake to put in fabric softener. But she's already drifting again, remembering she once heard that if you want to bend wood you can soak it in fabric softener and it gets limp as an egg noodle; and then something about putting jeans in to soak; and then she pictures letters peeling up off the page of a book she's holding down under water and just floating there around her wrists, not spelling anything.

She jumps when Carol puts a hand on her shoulder. "You poor thing, you were sound asleep," says Carol. "Here, let's get you up to bed. I put the clothes in the dryer for you."

As Carol helps her upstairs, Jean is wildly trying to tell her she still has to do a load with colors and she forgot to put in fabric softener and the kids have to do their homework—she told them she'd be right *up*. Carol says, *Shh,* it's all taken care of. But what about the pair of jeans in the thing, in the— I found them, Carol says. But the kids— *Shh*. I put them to bed. Here, let's get your shoes off.

6

"So: you, me, Cooperman of course," Jerry Starger says to Anita Bruno. "And our designing woman here." He nods at Jean. "Boy girl boy girl. Martha's got the rezzies for us. We see the contractor in the afternoon, scope out the space, chow down, check out the nightlife, breakfast with the bank guy in the morning and we're back in civilization by noon. Questions." Nobody says anything. "The Falcons may be at home tomorrow night, which I'm sure thrills you ladies to the marrow. Martha's checking into this as we speak."

"Seven-foot men in shorts?" says Anita Bruno. "Sweating? I can deal with that."

"This is tomorrow?" says Jean.

"Is that a problem?" Jerry says.

"No, it shouldn't be. My sister's here visiting, and I'm sure she could watch the kids."

"Groovy," he says. "Oh, and Bruno. Just FYI. The Falcons are football? Basketball is the Hawks."

"Shoot," says Anita. "Well, there goes *my* boy credibility."

"But it's why we love you. You're always in there pitching."

"I live only to impress you, Jerry," she says. "I know I can bounce back from this."

"Jerry, can I take a second and run this past my sister?" says Jean. She gets up, and she can just feel Anita Bruno judging her.

On the way to her office, she checks at the reception desk. No messages.

"Hi, it's me," she says when Carol answers. "Listen—"

"Hi—listen, I was just about to call you. I've got everything set. So how early can you get a train?"

"I don't know. Carol? Look, I just found out I have to fly to Atlanta tomorrow morning."

"Oh, that's great."

"It's *not* great. I've hardly seen Mel and Roger, I'm *totally* exhausted, there's this whole thing with Willis—"

"I think it'll be great for you to get away."

"I've *been* away."

"Yeah, but you know what I mean," Carol says. "Will you get a chance to play down there, or is this all business?"

"It's only overnight." Jean's ashamed to mention the football, which she doesn't even want to go to.

"How far is Atlanta from, like, Stone Mountain?"

"I have no idea. What *is* Stone Mountain?"

"A town," says Carol. "Anyhow. So, what I thought we'd do, why don't I pick you up at the station and we'll just *go*, and we won't have to take—"

"Wait-wait-wait. Carol. Would you just please tell me what this is?"

"Okay, look. There's somebody who I think can help you locate Willis, or at least find out what's going on. I made an appointment for five-thirty, which was the latest I could make it for, so do you think you could get to Chesterton by like four-fifteen, four-thirty at the latest?"

"But Carol—the police are *on* this."

"Right. Well, this is somebody who's *worked* with the police, okay? On exactly this kind of thing. I mean, they keep it very hush-hush, but you remember the little girl that was missing in Peekskill?"

"Oh crap. This isn't some *psychic* or something, is it?"

"Well, she's a reader, yes," says Carol. "But this isn't some crazy-person, Jean. Like I told you, the police even use her."

"Here we go."

"Jean, you can't just dismiss this person. I used to go to her years ago, when Dexter and I were living up in West Hurley? Plus a lot of famous people go to her, like I think Bob Dylan went one time?"

"Great."

"And listen, she has *told* me stuff. Like one time—okay?—she told me somebody that was out of my life was going to reappear, and a week later, or like a month later, I got a letter from Gid? First time in *five years*? Come *on*."

"Uh-uh," says Jean. "Sorry, no way."

"Why? What do you have to lose? Your faith, right? That everything is just, you know, on the *surface* and that there's no other dimensions except what you've been narrowly taught to accept."

"Carol, we've had this discussion. Many times."

"Okay, but these are actual documented *facts*, the things she's done."

"Documented?"

"Jean, this person is really *known*. She's not some fly-by-night. Like I say, even the police go to her. Not because they of all people buy into— you know—but because it *works*. You can't just dismiss that."

"Oh God."

"Will you just try her? Not decide anything, but just go with an open mind?"

"Oh God."

"Okay, look," says Carol. "*I'm* going, irregardless, okay? I'm very con*cerned* about this."

"You think I'm *not*?" says Jean.

"Yes, I know you are. And that's exactly why . . . Look, I respect your beliefs, and I just hope, you know, that you respect mine."

"Carol, I'm not trying to . . . Okay. Okay, fine. I'll go along with you on this, but if—"

"Okay, great, that's all I'm asking," Carol says. "And I promise you won't be sorry. So anyway, find out what train you can get, and we'll—"

"Where is this person, exactly?"

"She's up in Beacon."

"Beacon?" says Jean. "God help us. Okay, fine. Look, this is your show."

At quarter after five, they're in this absolutely grim little city, whose main street dead-ends at the Hudson River. Mrs. Porter lives on some side street; on the corner, black teenagers—baggy jeans, caps on backward— stand around a metal barrel with leaping fire inside. Carol parks in front of the one decent building on the block, a narrow three-story brick house, painted white, whose shutters have little cut-out crescent moons; she locks The Club on her steering wheel. They climb the three steps to stand under the aluminum awning and Carol pushes the doorbell: an Avon-calling chime sounds inside. There's a sign on the door reading ESTAMOS CATOLICOS ROMANOS. If this woman is such a whiz, what's she doing here? But Jean instantly reproaches herself: truly spiritual people live where they're needed, among the lowly.

"Believe me, I know how weird this looks," says Carol. "Actually, it's sort of gone downhill since I was here."

"She's Spanish, this woman?" Jean means Hispanic, but that sounds racist, and she feels stupid saying *Latina.*

"No, why? Oh, the thing. No. Just a lot of Dominicans or something in this neighborhood. I think it's to keep like Jehovah's Witnesses away."

A smiling woman opens the door. That's the first thing you notice, the smile, and only after that the doughy face and white beauty-parlor hair. She wears half-glasses with a strap fastened to the earpieces and a Marimekko flower-print dress—though would this woman wear real Marimekko?

She notices Jean's look. "Yes, it's gay, isn't it?" She smiles. "Won't you come in? Now, you're Mrs. Willis—anyone could see the two of you are sisters. I'm Margaret Porter. And *you* look wonderful, dear. I *knew* moving out there was the right thing for you. Now, you're visiting for *how* long?"

"Well, I *was* going to go back this week," says Carol. "But now . . ."

"Of course," Mrs. Porter says. "It's uncertain, isn't it? But you know, I'm so ashamed, I forgot to ask when you called: how is your son? You were so concerned about him."

"Oh, he's great. He's at the University of Washington."

"You see? Isn't that *won*derful?" Mrs. Porter stretches forth a hand to indicate the living room, where Jean sees a cat's tail disappearing behind a pea-green Naugahyde sofa. "Come in and make yourselves comfortable. Would you care for tea or coffee?"

Jean shakes her head, then remembers her manners. "Nothing, thank you." Carol hadn't prepared her for the picture of Jesus with the red, heart-shaped heart coming out of his chest, or the grove of candles on the table beneath it.

"Not for me, thanks," says Carol.

"Please sit wherever you like," Mrs. Porter says. Carol takes an arm-chair upholstered in faded rose, and Jean sits down at one end of the sofa before noticing the tangy-smelling litter box right beside her; of course, she can't relocate without giving offense. Mrs. Porter takes the far end—smart lady—and sits with her hands folded in her lap. She closes her eyes, then opens them.

"Mrs. Willis," she says. "Let me make sure I understand. Now, your sister tells me that *Mr.* Willis hasn't been heard from in some weeks, that you're very concerned about him and that your family's in trouble."

Jean looks at Carol, who's looking at Mrs. Porter. Carol took it on herself to say this?

"Are you and your husband separated?"

"Well, not—you know—*calling* it that," Jean says. "He took a leave of absence from his job, for two months, and he was up in the country working on this old farmhouse we own. He was supposed to be back at his job in New York on Monday, but nobody there has heard from him either."

"I see," says Mrs. Porter. "And he was?"

"He was what? I don't follow you."

"Oh well," she says. "That's all right. It's just a thing I do. It can be helpful to see what springs to mind, if anything. Some people will say, 'He was fifty-five,' or they may say, 'He was a carpenter' or 'the handsomest man I ever saw.' Whatever happens to be uppermost. And we can sometimes go from there."

"I guess nothing is uppermost," says Jean.

"Oh, that's perfectly all right. What this tells me is that you're an alert person and not drifting off in your own thoughts. Perhaps you're somewhat guarded. *Or* just wary in this particular situation. Most people, I have to say, are relieved when they find I don't sit around boiling bats." Her little laugh sounds as rehearsed as the line itself. "Now. You've brought me something of your husband's?"

"*I* did," says Carol, reaching down for her purse. Mrs. Porter looks at Carol; Carol looks back. "I didn't tell her a whole lot about this."

"I see. Well, then, no wonder you're wary, Mrs. Willis. Good heavens. What must you imagine?"

"Okay," says Carol. "Pair of socks." She holds them up. "Obviously. A hat." Willis's Yankees cap. "Passport?"

"You went through his *drawers*?" Jean says.

"Razor?" says Carol.

"Ah. Give that here." Mrs. Porter leans toward Carol, who hands her a blue plastic razor. "You see, he would've held this while looking at himself in the mirror." Smiling, she holds the razor up with thumb and forefinger. "You should understand, Mrs. Willis, that it doesn't matter whether or not you believe in this."

"I guess that's good," says Jean.

"All I need you to do at this point is let me have just a few moments of quiet. You can read a magazine if you like"—she gestures at the coffee table—"or watch, if you care to. You won't disturb me, though I'm afraid there's not much to see. An old lady sitting with her eyes closed can't be very entertaining."

Jean looks at the coffee table. *Reader's Digest, McCall's, People*, a newspaper called *St. Anthony Messenger*. An old *Newsweek* with a cover story glorifying fat Jerry Garcia. Neither she nor Carol reaches for anything.

"So, we'll speak in a few minutes, then," says Mrs. Porter. "Just make yourselves comfortable. You don't have to be statues. As I say, the only thing I ask is that you not talk or make a lot of racket."

"We won't," says Carol. Like a four-year-old.

Mrs. Porter closes her eyes, squeezes the handle of the razor in her left hand and folds her right hand over it. Her lips move, as if in prayer, then stop. Her breast rises and subsides, rises and subsides. Jean looks over, and Carol's eyes are closed too.

Jean closes hers, takes a breath, lets it out—and the bottom just falls away from under everything.

She feels her lips coming apart like a sticky seal peeling open, and her jaw dropping down to her collarbone, and then drool creeping over the corner of her mouth. That makes her eyes fly open: she's on somebody's couch, gasping. Never has she gone so deep so quickly. Mrs. Porter and Carol sit there, eyes still closed. She hears ticking; she turns and sees a banjo clock on the wall over her right shoulder. Twenty to six. What just happened seems already less profound and terrifying. She's exhausted, that's all, and she dropped off for a second.

"Well, he's somewhere with trees and grass," says Mrs. Porter. Jean whips her head around again to look. Mrs. Porter's eyes are open and she's talking as normally as before.

"What?" Jean says.

"Goodness, that sounds awful, doesn't it? Like a cemetery. But it's definitely *not* a cemetery. This has been a difficult time for him. But he's come through something. You'll see him again, that's almost certain." Then Mrs. Porter bends forward and makes smooching noises. "Moses? Come and be sociable."

"That's it?" says Jean. "He's with the trees and the grass and I'll see him again?"

"Almost certainly," Mrs. Porter says.

"Excuse me, but isn't that, like, a little *thin*?"

"Jean," says Carol. "Let her finish."

"Oh no. I'm finished," Mrs. Porter says. "But I'm as certain of *that* as I am of sitting here talking to you."

Jean shakes her head. "That was nothing."

"I can understand why you're disappointed," says Mrs. Porter. "If it makes you feel any better, I'd say you're at about the fiftieth percentile. If you see what I mean. Sometimes you'll get nothing but a single word that nobody understands. Or a note of music—I've had that happen. It's not like watching television, Mrs. Willis."

"Really," says Jean.

"Now, what I've told you is a rough translation into words of certain feelings, or impressions. I take it your husband is also someone who guards his feelings?"

"Oh please." Jean gets to her feet and picks up her purse from the floor.

"Jean," says Carol. "Would you let her *finish*, for Pete's sake?"

"She *is* finished," Jean says. "Weren't you paying attention? Willis is out with the grass and the trees and I'll see him again. He's probably playing golf. In Boca Raton. How much do I owe you, Mrs. Porter? And could I have my husband's razor back, please?"

Mrs. Porter hands it to her, shaking her head.

"I'm not in *business*, Mrs. Willis," she says. "Haven't you understood?"

7

"I *still* don't want to talk about it." They're at The Hideaway, Carol working on a Cobb salad served in an edible shell, Jean with a shrimp cocktail in front of her and a martini for which the shrimp cocktail is the excuse. Jean spoke exactly one word all the way from Beacon back down to Chesterton: when Carol asked if she wanted to stop for a bite to eat, she said, "Fine."

"All I want to say is I'm sorry, okay? And then I'll get right off the subject," says Carol. "But I do have to say I *have* heard her be better, which is the only reason I—"

"Listen," says Jean, "I want to ask one thing of you. That you mention this to *no* one, you understand?"

"Believe me, I—"

"As far as the kids, I just had to work late, okay? Anybody else, it's not their business anyway."

"Look, don't you think *I'm* embarrassed?"

"I'm sorry, I know you are," Jean says. "And I know you meant well."

"I really did."

Jean takes another sip of the martini; it tastes as poisonous as the first two sips. The shrimps curve over the rim of the metal bowl like the toenails of some animal. "I don't want these," she says. "You want any?"

"Not really," says Carol. "I might take *one*. But you have to *eat*. You want some of mine? This thing is huge."

"Don't worry, you're not going to have to carry me into the house. I can't drink this either."

"Oh, could I have a sip?" says Carol. "Can you believe I've never tried one of these? And I'm how old? Don't answer that."

"Be my guest."

Carol picks up the martini glass with her fingertips and takes just the littlest bit on her tongue. "Ee-eew. That's what businessmen drink?"

"It feels like it warms you all the way down your front. I just wish I could stand the *taste*."

"*All* the way down?" Carol says. "Honey, if a drink could do *that*. You know, I sometimes think, I'm *only* forty-seven. That's not old anymore. And I don't look *ter*rible."

"Of course you don't; you look *great*."

"Okay, I look great. Damn it, I *do* look great; I am *not* going to send myself negative messages. But here I am, you know? These are supposed to be the best years of your life sexually, and I'm, you know, high and dry. Could I have another little hit?"

"All yours," says Jean.

Carol takes another tiny sip. "Yick," she says. "I'm sorry, I don't mean to get into this. You start to dwell on it, and it just turns all your positive energy against you."

"No, you have a right to feel cheated. And being stuck here for two months—it's kind of a black hole as far as meeting anybody. God, *West*chester."

"Honey, this has been a lifesaver. When Dexter first went away to school, it was like this great *weight* was just lifted off, but then—I don't mean he's a *weight*, but I was just suddenly sort of floating off into the sky, you know? And that's where I've *been*. I was thinking about it the other day, when I took the kids to the museum and we saw that Naturemax thing? You know, the camera must be in a balloon or something and you're way up above everything and you're floating, like? So it's sort of been a very scary *time*, though it's also been really freeing, you know? And when you called in the middle of all that, I just thought, well, this is the voice of, you know, not *God* as such, but sort of the voice of the next thing."

She takes a shrimp between thumb and forefinger, dips the end in cocktail sauce and nips. "Mmm. I never think to get these guys." She dips again. "I just feel that, sexually, I still have something to, you know, *contribute*—does that sound crazy? Okay, I shouldn't say crazy, because that's putting yourself down, but you know what I mean by 'contribute'?"

"Yeah, I guess," says Jean. "This just isn't a real comfortable subject for me right now."

"Okay, I respect that, I really do," says Carol. "Listen, could I take just one more of those?"

"Please, take them all."

"Maybe *two* more," says Carol. "So anyhow, what do you think you're going to do? You know, now that *I've* been such a big help."

"No idea," Jean says. "Maybe try to hire somebody? I looked in the yellow pages today, and there's just a huge number of, you know, investigators. Some of them used to be regular police detectives—they *say*. I don't know how you'd ever check. Or my other idea was maybe to go back up *there* and try to get somebody, since that's actually where . . . you know."

"It's such a long way, though. I could never see why you wanted a place so far away."

"*He* wanted it," Jean says. "Because it *was* far away. Listen, can I ask you something? What do *you* think is going on? Where do *you* think he is?"

"What do *I* think? Me personally?"

"I mean, I know you don't *know*. But just what you *feel*, in your heart of hearts."

"Okay, my honest opinion?" says Carol. "He found some little cupcake up there and they went off together. I never knew a man who could keep it in his pants. Unless *you* wanted it."

"But then why would he have to run away?" says Jean. "I mean, he could've just, you know, stayed up there and kept doing it."

"It's men's nature to run away."

"Oh please." Jean reaches for the martini glass, sniffs, sets it down without drinking. "Crap," she says. "So meanwhile, what am I supposed to tell Mel and Roger? I can't keep pretending he's at his mother's. *Who*, by the way, never called me back."

"Well, here's what *I* did. You know, when Gid did *his* little number? Which is why I say it's men's nature? Anyway, I told Dexter that Daddy had become a cowboy and he had to go off on a long trail drive. And guess what—Dexter loved it. He was *proud* of the fact. Of course, he was only four."

"I don't remember you ever telling me that."

"I guess that was kind of the last of my real stoned period. Like spirits would sometimes speak through me? And some of them were good spirits and some were sort of not. But I actually think in this case it was an incredibly wise spirit, that had my good at heart and that knew Dexter was just a little boy who was real into cowboys. Like I could've said, you know, *'Mommy and Daddy both love you very much but we decided it would be better'*—all that caca."

"Right," says Jean.

"And I'll tell you something else, that I firmly believe to this day. That story about Gid going off on a trail drive was a healing story. Not only at the time, but also later on when Dexter was old enough to know the truth, so called, and that it's still like a deep structure for things that he's always going to have in his mind."

"Right."

"I'm sorry, I know this makes you uncomfortable, talking about, you know, other realities."

"Oh, *fine,*" says Jean. "Let's make this be about how uptight Jean is."

"No, I don't mean it in a critical way," Carol says. "You *should* be uncomfortable, because that's who *you* are. See, this was sort of a long answer to your question. You say what should I tell Mel and Roger, but *I* hear you saying that you don't really want to just *tell* them something. So I think you've already answered the question yourself. All this energy's going into, you know, constructing cover stories. He's here, he's there, he's off at Nonnie's, la dee da dee da. Now, a four-year-old? Different thing. Daddy's off on a cattle drive, and it's not this huge, complicated story that has to hang together. But see, with Mel and Roger, the energy's diverted off into . . . You know, like your appendix: this useless little thing that goes off into nowhere, and it's like sooner or later the dam has to burst."

"So you're saying I should just level with them," says Jean.

"You're saying it to your*self.* Look, it's like you have a toothache—okay?—and deep down you *know*—"

"Okay, thanks, I get it," says Jean. "Look, you better drop me back at the station, so I can get the car and go pick up the kids. Do you remember what our waitress looked like?"

The Millers live on Dogwood Lane, in one of those houses that seem to be all big wedge-shaped Andersen windows. Jean rings the lit-up doorbell; Rosellen Miller opens the door a crack, then closes it and opens it wide.

"Jean, how are you *doing*, come on in. The girls are up in Erin's room, and Roger's downstairs, watching Cody work out."

"Have they been okay?" Jean steps into the foyer, and Rosellen puts the chain back on the door. She's wearing a sweatshirt over leggings and really starting to show.

"Oh fine," Rosellen says. "Roger had a little flare-up at the dinner table, but these things happen. Here, let me take your jacket. You've got time for a drink, don't you? I can't have a *drink* drink, but I've been guzzling Cody's Gatorade like it's—oh, I shouldn't say that, should I? He did *try* the one your husband makes."

"Thanks, but we really can't stay. What happened at dinner?"

Wayne Miller comes out of the kitchen, a screwdriver in his hand and screws sticking out of his mouth. He nods and grunts at Jean, then says to Rosellen, "You etter come in look fore I fashen it."

"He's putting up a shelf for me in the laundry room," Rosellen says. "This house has closets galore, but for some reason they gave very little thought to shelves. So *I* thought, maybe just above the machines. You know, to put your supplies."

"Royal painy ash," says Wayne.

"I'm sure it's great," Rosellen says.

Wayne casts a theatrical look at the ceiling.

"I better go inspect," says Rosellen. "You know where Erin's room is. If you want to try to start the prying-loose process."

Jean climbs the three steps up to where the Millers' bedrooms are and heads for the music, some snarling young woman singer. She knocks on the last door on the right, and Erin sings out "Hi-ee" in that airy-fairy voice of hers that would drive you right up the wall.

"Hi, Erin. It's Melanie's mom. She in there by any chance?" The music suddenly cuts off.

"Mother, Erin says I can stay over. Can I?"

"Can she, please, Mrs. Willis?"

"Could one of you open the door?" says Jean.

The door opens, and there's poor moon-faced Erin in one of her loose-fitting hippie dresses. It must be awful to be twelve and already having such a struggle; it's a wonder she hasn't discovered vomiting. Assuming she hasn't. Rosellen once told Jean—based on nothing but wishful thinking, as far as Jean could see—that Erin would "lean out" when she became a teenager. One look at bullnecked Cody, who plays

JV football and who's essentially Erin with a shaved head, and you can see it's hopeless.

"How are *you* doing, Erin?" says Jean. Using a normal in-breath to sniff for pot smoke is so routine she's hardly aware she's doing it. (Nothing.)

"Okay. I can lend her some clothes for tomorrow, Mrs. Willis. I've got stuff that's too small for me."

"Can I, Mother?" says Mel.

"Not on a school night."

"But, Mother—"

"Besides, I feel like I've hardly had time to *see* you, and tomorrow I have to fly to Atlanta. It's just for a day, but I'd sort of like us to hang out a little tonight."

"How come you have to go to Atlanta?" Mel says.

"To look at that new office space. You remember, I was telling you?"

Mel shrugs. It's true, Jean does get this self-righteous tone when she talks to Mel about her work, as if she's doing it on feminist principle. Which she is, partly. Poor Mel was so bored when she brought her into the office on what Willis called Teach Our Daughters to Buy Into the Shit Day.

"Listen," she says, "we really need to get Roger to bed. It would help tremendously if you got your things together and you were all ready to go, okay? And I'll try to get *him* moving."

She goes down into the kitchen, opens the door to the basement and calls hello. No answer; she clomps coming down the stairs, to give additional warning. Roger's sitting on the black leather sofa they have down there, and she sees him quickly slip a magazine between the arm and the seat cushion. Beside him she sees a copy of *Soldier of Fortune*. Good God. So what was he reading that's even worse?

" 'Sup," Cody Miller calls, from the seat of some machine with weights and cables. He's wearing shorts and a soaked-through tank top, his broad face and bulging shoulders beaded with sweat. He bares his teeth, a vein bulges out in his forehead and tendons stiffen in his neck; he grunts, and twin stacks of black weights inch up on their cables.

"Hello, Cody," she says. She turns to Roger. "And how's my guy?" Roger says nothing.

"What are you reading?" she says. Useless with Cody here, but how can she not try?

"Nothing."

She lets the silence go on for a few beats to let him know he's not fooling her, then says, "We have to get going, dear. Say goodbye to Cody? Cody, thanks for looking after Roger."

Cody, gasping, can only nod.

"Would you get your things together, please?" she says.

"They're upstairs," says Roger.

"So in that case . . ." She points her thumb up.

"O-*kay*," he says, and starts trudging up the steps. He hasn't, in fact, said goodbye to Cody. She walks over to the sofa and pulls out the magazine. It's some bodybuilding thing: color pictures of men with ugly oiled muscles and, apparently, no penises. Is this what Mel was talking about the other night? Maybe she'd better search his room. She sets the bodybuilding magazine on top of *Soldier of Fortune*, just to put Cody on notice. Well, Roger won't be coming back *here*—and if that's a wrong attitude, fine. So is this what all the push-ups and stuff are about? But what's she supposed to do now—confiscate his hand weights?

Upstairs in the foyer, Mel's pulling on her sweatshirt and lifting her long hair up out of the neck hole as Erin whispers to her. Rosellen Miller appears in the kitchen doorway, waving a bottle of Martini & Rossi vermouth. "Are you sure I can't tempt you?" She must have grabbed a bottle at random from the liquor cabinet to illustrate the idea of a drink.

"We really can't," says Jean. "Can I call you later, though? I still want to hear about what we were starting to discuss." She nods toward Roger, who's shouldering his backpack.

"Oh, that," says Rosellen. "Really, it wasn't anything. But sure, if you want. We're usually up right through Letterman. It's so funny: with my other two I'd be out like a light at *ten*. But this time I have all this energy? So weird. It's driving Wayne out of his *mind*, because I'm finding all these projects around the house? You know how wives used to send their husbands out for pistachio ice cream in the middle of the night? I'm always sending Wayne to Home Depot. He doesn't know this yet, but the next thing I want him to do is put a peephole. I mean, we have a *chain* but no *peephole*."

Jean shakes her head to show sympathy. "Listen," she says, "thanks *so* much for doing this. Thank Wayne for me too, would you?"

"Don't even think about it," says Rosellen. "If you *ever* need help, Mel and Roger are always welcome."

"That's really nice of you." Jean should say she'd be glad to return the favor, but the fact is.

It's started raining: the flagstone walk gleams in the lantern's light, and sharp little drops sting their faces on their way to the Cherokee.

"Aren't we going to flip for shotgun?" says Roger.

"Let's just get in first." Jean starts the Cherokee and gets the blower going before clicking on the map light and finding a quarter in her change purse. This rain or whatever is ticking against the roof and bouncing off the windshield. Mel wins the toss; Roger says "Crap"— borderline permissible—and climbs into the back seat. The headlight beams pick out slants of what Jean hopes isn't actual sleet. She pulls the lever to go into four-wheel, and the thing lights up that reads PART TIME. The words always seem to have a bad meaning that she can't quite pin down. (Now, what could *that* be?)

Sounds like Rosellen Miller knows something's up. Did she worm it out of the kids directly, or did it come from Mel by way of Erin? And from Rosellen to the rest of the world. (Or is that unfair?) God, this is just what Carol was talking about: all this energy poured into maintaining the silence. But tonight really isn't the time to tell them. They're about to go to bed—then tomorrow she has to be away, and this is obviously not a thing you can just dump on them and merrily traipse off somewhere. Jerry did say it would be okay to skip this if there was a problem, but it would be stupid to think he meant it was okay for there to be a problem.

"So," says Jean, turning left from Dogwood onto Lochbourne. "What did you guys have for dinner?"

"Tacos," says Mel.

"*That* sounds good," says Jean. "I heard there was some kind of a problem, though? At dinner? What was that about?" She glances in the mirror: Roger's staring straight ahead. Oncoming headlights whiten his face; then it goes dark again.

Mel says, "Well, Erin's mom—"

"You better shut up," says Roger.

"Then suppose *you* tell me what happened," says Jean.

"*I* didn't do anything," he says.

"It wasn't Roger's fault," says Mel.

"I said shut *up*."

"Roger, let your sister talk. It sounds like she's on your side, right?"

"You better not, Mel," he says.

"Roger, enough," says Jean. "Mel?"

"Okay, Erin's mom was asking Roger all this stuff about Daddy?"

Jean checks the mirror again. Roger has his eyes closed. "What kind of stuff?"

"I don't know," says Mel. "Like when did we go up to the country the last time, and she's like, Well, you talk to him on the *phone*, don't you? Kind of like she was picking on Roger. Or not picking on him but trying to get him to say stuff?"

"Is that how you felt, Rog?" says Jean. "That she was questioning you?"

Roger says nothing.

"She *was*," says Mel. "Roger's sitting there going, I don't know, I don't know—you know, the way he does? And she's like, You don't *know* if you talk to him on the phone, Roger? And so Erin's *dad* finally goes, Leave the poor kid alone. To Erin's *mom*. But by now Roger's like really upset, and he calls Erin's dad a bad word. Not her mom. I would've called *her* the word."

"So would I," says Jean. "Is that pretty much what happened, Rog?"

"No."

"But Roger, it *is*," Mel says.

"Is there something she said that you want to disagree with?" says Jean.

"No."

"I see. Well, from what Mel's saying, it sounds to me like Mrs. Miller was out of line. *You* were out of line for using bad language, but I can understand why you were upset. It's a really uncomfortable thing, telling a grownup that you don't feel like talking about something. But for the future, it's perfectly okay not to answer things you think are too personal. You can just say, 'I'm sorry, but I don't feel like talking about that.' Okay?"

No answer.

The light at the corner of Main Street turns yellow, then red, and Jean pulls up behind a Grand Cherokee. Roger has been complaining because they only have a regular Cherokee; at least he's too preoccupied now to get into *that*. (Mel, on the other hand, hates *all* sports-utility vehicles because they waste fuel.)

"So, Rog?" says Jean. "Dare I ask exactly what you said to Mr. Miller?"

No answer.

Mel says, "He called him a fat f-word. Just like . . ."

"Like what?" says Jean.

"I don't know," Mel says. "Sort of like what a kid at school said one time."

Jean looks at Roger in the mirror. "Is that true, Roger?"

Still nothing.

"*Roger.* Either you answer when I ask you a question, or no television for a week."

"I guess so," says Roger.

"Thank you," she says. "When we get home, you'll sit down and write a note apologizing to Mr. Miller. Doesn't have to be long—just say you're sorry you got upset and said something rude, okay? He'll get the point. And we'll mail it on the way to school in the morning. Right?"

Roger says nothing, pushing it right to the edge. But is it worth following through on her threat just because he's too proud to make some submissive noise when she says *Right?*

"Okay, you heard me," she says. "End of subject." The light turns green; the Grand Cherokee goes straight through, and Jean takes a left on Main. "So," she says. "How was school?"

It's 7:51 by the dashboard clock when they get home. Carol's door is shut; she's probably meditating. Rathbone seems to want to be walked, Mel and Roger both need baths, plus Roger has to write his note and hasn't done his homework. (Mel claims she and Erin did theirs together; Jean decides to believe her.) Another reason to be furious at Rosellen Miller: the woman doesn't even *ask*, on a *school* night, if a fourth grader has homework? She sends Mel up to take her shower and tells Roger if he can write his note and finish his homework in forty-five minutes, they can read another ten pages of *The Lord of the Rings* and he can shower in the morning.

Roger makes his mouth drop open by way of protest, and Jean puts a finger to her lips. "That's the carrot," she says. "And if I hear one word of whining, it'll be zero pages. That's the stick." Though it's not a stick, she realizes. She's gotten so sloppy and permissive that her only stick is the withholding of carrots.

"But you don't know how much she *gave* us," says Roger. "And I don't know what I'm supposed to *write*." He's starting to pant.

"And that," Jean says, "is a borderline whine. If I were you, I wouldn't waste any of my forty-five minutes. I told you what to write."

"But I *forgot*." Full-fledged panting.

"So go up to your room and start remembering." Jean makes two fingers walk in air. "I'm going to take Rathbone out, and then I'll be up to check. The note first, then your homework. And I don't want you to spend more than five minutes on the note. Time yourself." She looks around for the leash. This, she knows in her heart, is just round one.

But so much for knowing in your heart: when she and Rathbone come back in, Roger's downstairs waiting. "Here," he says, and shoves a piece of paper at her:

> *Dear Mr. Miller,*
> *I am sorry I was upset. I didn't mean to say a bad*
> *word but it just came out. I get upset some times.*
> > *From,*
> > *Roger Willis*

"Perfect." Jean reaches to pat him on the head; his body stiffens, but he allows it. "Good for you. I'll find an envelope and a stamp—or if we get an early enough start tomorrow, maybe we can just drive by and drop it in their mailbox. Okay? Now: homework." She points to the stairs.

So perhaps a firm hand really *is* the ticket. By nine o'clock Roger's finished with his homework, in his pajamas, teeth brushed, face washed. Mel has her nightie on and her hair dried. And Carol materializes to sit on the sofa with the three of them. Jean feels blessed.

"You know something?" says Jean, opening *The Fellowship of the Ring* at the dog-eared page. "I've been looking forward to this all day, just being together." No response. Which is okay too. "So where did you guys get up to?"

"Right to here," says Carol, pointing to a line space. "They just got done picking the people that get to go with Frodo. Elrond didn't want Merry and Pippin to go, but Gandalf talked him into it."

"Right, right," says Jean. "Okay, everybody comfortable?" Roger gives a little wriggle that's sort of like actual snuggling. Jean takes a breath, lets it out, takes another breath and begins. *"The Sword of Elendil was forged anew by elvish smiths, and on its blade was traced a device of seven stars set between the crescent Moon and the rayed Sun, and about them were written many runes; for Aragorn son of Arathorn was going to war upon the marches of Mordor. Very bright was that sword when it was made whole again; the light of the sun shone redly in it, and the light of the moon shone cold, and its edge was hard and keen. And Aragorn gave it a new name and—"*

"What?" says Roger. "What's so funny?"

"Nothing," says Jean. "I'm sorry. Something just popped into my head."

"What?"

"Nothing; it was just stupid. I must be totally exhausted. You know, on second thought—Carol, would you mind doing the honors? And I'll just sort of cuddle up with you guys and listen?"

"Sure, glad to," says Carol. "Are you okay, though?"

"I'm fine. It's just been a long day." She passes the book to Carol, keeping her index finger inside to mark the page.

"Very bright was that sword when it was made whole again," Carol begins. Poor Carol probably thinks it's *her* fault, that Jean's come unglued because of that stupid woman. Mrs. Whoosy. Jean scrunches her eyes shut; she can almost see Willis taking his penis in his hand, intoning, "It is Andúril, Flame of the West!" This was back when he was reading *The Lord of the Rings* to Mel: he and Jean were in bed, drunk as skunks, with a candle going. Jean would never in a million years have gotten involved with a man who made up names for his penis—sort of a class thing, in addition to whatever else—but what about a man who makes up names for his penis in order to mock the idea of having names for his penis? Like it's a point of pride for Willis not to be straight about anything, and if you don't think *that* gets wearing. The one time Jean actually hit him, just physically hauled off and *hit* him, was this one night—it had to be three or four years ago, because Roger was still into Barney, though even then he'd say all these contemptuous things back at Barney if anyone caught him watching. Anyway, Barney was on and Willis came into the kitchen, where Jean was trimming green beans, and he sang, "I love you, you love me, it's an easy i-ron-y," and she just slapped the knife down and flew at him and hit him in the mouth with her fist. So out of character. God, at least she didn't use the knife. Her hand hurt for days, and there was actually this puncture wound on her third finger where it had hit his tooth, and the tooth ended up getting an abscess and he had to have a root canal. Right up there on his list of

unforgivable things, probably. Well, it *was* unforgivable. But so was shitting all over love.

"*'Just what I said myself,' said Bilbo.*" Carol does Bilbo in a pinchy little voice like a Munchkin saying *Follow the yellow brick road;* her thinking must be that hobbits are something like midgets. At least she doesn't do Frodo the same way. "*'But never mind about looks. You can wear it under your outer clothes. Come on! You must share this secret with me. Don't tell anybody else. But I should feel happier if I knew you were wearing it. I have a fancy it would turn even the knives of the Black Riders.'*"

Mel sighs. "This book is so racist."

"You used to love it," says Jean.

"Sure, when I was like *eight.*" Mel gives Roger a look, as if the book were his fault, but he's just staring straight ahead. "It's like everything black is bad."

"Right, that's true, but they don't mean it racially," Jean says. "It's more like just darkness, you know? And also you have to remember, this was written in a different time." Why is she defending this garbage? All the bad people are *swarthy*, and the women are like forget it. "Still, it's really smart of you to notice that." Good: pat her on the head after you tear down her whole idea.

"And like in mysticism," Carol says, "they have, you know, light and dark?"

"Can't we just *read*?" says Roger.

"It totally makes sense that Daddy thinks this is so great," Mel says.

"How so?" says Jean.

"Because he's such a white male."

"In what way?" says Jean. "My little white female?" This must be her night to play dumb.

"I'm not being *cute*, Mother. First you're like, Oh, this is so important, and now you're treating me like a baby. You don't want to talk because it's about Daddy."

"I'm sorry," Jean says. "That did sound dismissive. Do you *want* to talk about Daddy? I know you miss him."

"*I* don't miss him," says Mel. "I don't even think about him."

"I think he'd be hurt to hear that."

"Why?" says Mel. "He doesn't think about *us*, right? Why don't you just *tell* us, Mother? Because we're *children*?" Jean looks at Carol, who turns both palms up. "Every kid in *school* just about has parents that are divorced or something. It's not a big deal like it was in *your* day."

"Sweetheart, this is not about divorce," says Jean. "That's not what's going on. And I wish I had something more to tell you, for everybody's sake. But the thing is, right now I don't know exactly where he is or how to get in touch with him. All I can think is that he just went somewhere, maybe to Nonnie's. Or"—does she really want to say this?—"it *is* possible that he could be in some kind of trouble."

"Yeah," says Mel. "He's probably in *jail* again."

"He's probably *dead*," says Roger.

"Shut up, Roger," says Mel.

"Mel? That's not helpful," Jean says. "Your brother's allowed to say what he's worried about. But you know, Rog, if it really *was* that, we would've heard."

"I'm not *worried*, I just *said* it, okay? Are we going to read?"

"Okay, you're not worried. But if you were, you know you can come to me about it, right? And yes, we're going to read in a minute. But I'm glad this finally happened, you know? Because I think we needed to talk about it."

Mel's twirling a strand of hair around her index finger.

"And you know you guys can come to me too," Carol says. "If you don't mind talking to a crazy lady with a truck."

Mel and Roger don't even look at her. Poor Carol does try.

"It's real important right now," says Jean, "that we talk to each other."

"Yeah, right," Mel says. "It's so important that you never tell us anything. Mother, *everybody* knows Daddy left us."

"Who's 'everybody'?" says Jean. "Mrs. Miller?"

"Her and some other people."

"Great. Look, the minute I know anything, good *or* bad, I'll tell you guys. Promise. And by the way, I *don't* think you're too young to handle things. Either of you. You guys are both pretty grown up when you need to be." This pep talk is starting to go wrong: they're *not* grown up, and they shouldn't have to be. If Willis appeared at the door this minute, she'd slam it in his face. "So listen. It's getting pretty late, but I think we could all stand to zone out a little. Why don't we read to the end of this chapter."

"Yay," says Roger. "Really?"

"Gee, there's quite a bit," says Carol, flipping pages.

"Can I just go to bed?" Mel says.

"Of course, sweetie. Why don't I come up and tuck you in, and Aunt Carol can start reading to Roger."

"No. I don't want you to." Mel gets up and shakes her hair out.

Take her at her word? Probably best. "Okay, sweet," Jean says. "I'll see you in the morning. Sleep tight."

"Yeah, right," says Mel. "Good night, Aunt Carol."

"Night, sugar," says Carol.

Mel just stands there, looking at the picture over the sofa, then turns and heads for the kitchen.

"So," says Carol. "Let's see. Okay. Remember Bilbo's giving him the coat of mail, right?"

As Carol reads, Roger edges closer to her. This hurts Jean, a little. But so long as he can still drop his guard with *someone*. Mel comes out of the kitchen, looks at them all, then turns and goes upstairs. Jean probably should've taken that look as an invitation to come up and tuck her in after all. She can't pick up the beat tonight.

When Carol gets to the part where Gandalf and Aragorn are arguing about whether to take the mountain pass or the dark and secret way, Roger's snoring. Jean carries him upstairs, pulls the covers over him, brushes the fine hair away from his soft forehead and kisses him. That sweet little-boy smell. And she quickly puts a hand to her eyes to keep the tears from falling on his face and waking him, like in that fairy tale with the candle wax. God, she's weary of being right on the edge.

She plugs in his night-light; the clutter loses its hard edges in the dim glow. Now: where in all this would he hide magazines? She doesn't *want* to find them, yet ignoring this isn't an option. *Damn* this world, for allowing all these things that you need to protect children from. Between mattress and box spring is such a cliché she almost doesn't check, but when she slides her hand under, there they are. She sticks her arm in up to the elbow and feels around: okay, just two. She brings them out into the hall to look.

It's two issues of something called *Hand Gunner*. She feels like weeping in relief that it's not like S & M pornography, then feels stupid for feeling relieved. Here's "Shooting Stances for Street Survival," with a man in a cowboy hat doing poses called "Instinctive" (one hand, like in a Western), "Weaver" (two hands, elbows bent) and "Isosceles" (two hands, arms straight). Here's "Ammo Insight." A column on why every handgun should have a "laser sighting device." Lots and lots of handgun ads. One shows a little safe you keep by your bed with your handgun in it. *Surrounded by thick steel and cradled in soft foam, it's safe from curious fingers and waiting for that moment you hope never comes. But if it does, you know you can get to your handgun in seconds in the dark. Its tactile contours guide your fingers to the computerized control panel. You enter your code. The door instantly springs open. You've got your gun.* This is too right wing to even think about, but it makes a kind of sense. The kids couldn't get at it. And she's here all alone.

So she'll tell Roger she found the magazines while turning his mattress. She'll say they're inappropriate—which he already knows, or why is he hiding them?—and he'll say nothing. She'll want to ask who sold these to him, but there's probably no law against selling gun magazines to children, and anyhow the real issue is what's going on with Roger. So she'll ask what he likes about guns. She won't preach. He still won't give anything away; it will be one more of those Roger dead ends. She's already lost him.

But she can't let that thought take root.

That night Jean wakes up and the bed's shaking. It must be an earthquake. She looks at the clock: 3:21. She's never been in an earthquake before. Isn't Westchester County supposed to be the most stable area in the world, geologically? The bed keeps shaking. It must be her, making the bed shake. Her whole body is shaking.

8

In the morning it strikes her that what's inappropriate isn't the magazines so much as the secrecy. Roger's face gets red when she tells him about turning the mattress. He wasn't *hiding* the magazines—he had them there so they'd stay *flat*. Jean ignores this and says that when she was a girl, she used to think she had to hide things from her parents when it usually turned out they were cool about it. An utter and absolute lie, of course, but Roger isn't even interested enough to ask what she hid.

At the station, she shoulders the yellow nylon duffel bag with her stuff for Atlanta, like a *Let's Go! Europe* college girl among all these serious commuters. Who actually do bustle around with briefcases, as if in some dance routine satirizing the 1950s. The sky's a clean bright blue after last night's storm, and up on the platform there's a cold wind whipping.

The only empty seat she can find on the 8:10 is next to a man with an expensive suit and haircut and a shave so close his cheeks gleam; the tiny broken veins look painful, and he smells of aftershave. Willis's word for aftershave was "stinkum." *Is*. The man gives Jean one sidelong glance before going back to *Crain's New York Business*. She's got *Emma* in her duffel bag but feels stupidly obliged to think about her problems instead of escaping into a book. She looks out the window at whitecaps on the dirty river.

In the office, she tries Willis's mother again, and this time Sylvia answers, with her singsong "Hello" whose two-note *o* leaps an octave. Jean, as always, feels like saying *Fine, so you went to Smith, just answer the phone like a human being*. Typical Sylvia: she apologizes for not calling back, but she's been *so* preoccupied. Has Jean managed to find Willis? As if she'd misplaced him. Jean says no, but she's sure he's fine, and Sylvia says, "Oh dear." Well, she can't sit in judgment over Sylvia until she's been through what Sylvia's been through. (It's getting there, actually.) On the other hand, Jean still has to act like she lives on the planet, so what makes Sylvia so special? She doesn't seem aware that this is the week Willis was due back at work, so Jean glosses over that; why get her even more upset? Assuming that's what the *Oh dear* meant. If there really does turn out to be some sort of bad news, let Champ deal with his mother. And if Sylvia doesn't exactly find him a tower of strength in her old age, she has only herself to thank. Though Jean can imagine somebody someday saying the same cruel thing about her and *her* children.

She borrows Anita Bruno's *Times* and looks through the Home section, all about rich people and their gracious leisure. Infuriating. But of course here *she* is with her house in Chesterton (though not the really tony section of Chesterton) and another house in the country, kicking back and reading the *Times*, while underpaid Helen has to spend her days saying "The Paley Group" over and over in the same nicey-nice voice and is allowed to read a paper only if no clients are in the reception area. (This dates from the morning Jerry Starger saw the *Post* on her desk and decided it looked low rent. Which it actually did.) It does Jean no spiritual good, reading the Home section every Thursday so she can feel sorry for herself. But after a while, it's like so what. Plus she *is* a designer. She's reading about how these hateful people redid their seventeenth-century mill in Normandy, when the phone rings.

"Mrs. Willis?" He doesn't say Karnes, so Jean knows right away this is it. "I'm Captain Anthony Petrosky, Vermont State Police? The reason I'm calling, we've been going over the missing persons report you gave the police over in Preston Falls."

"Yes?"

"I take it your husband hasn't been located since then."

"Has not? No."

"Well, what we were hoping, in that case, perhaps you could help us out on a couple of items."

"Of course," Jean says. "Do you have any—" She wants to say *leads*, but it sounds too tv to say to a real policeman. "Anything at all?"

"We haven't *located* him, no. I'm sorry. But we thought it might be a good idea to contact some of your husband's associates up this way. If you could fill us in with a few names."

"Associates?"

"Anybody he knows."

"He really doesn't know too many people up there," Jean says. "I mean, as far as *I* know."

"But he did know a *few* people."

"Well," says Jean, "actually not really. There's another family that comes up on weekends that we see once in a while because they have kids too. But I doubt he'd seek them out on his own. *Or* vice versa."

"Why's that?"

"We just don't really have all that much in common. *Except* the kids."

"So I take it you haven't called them."

"No, it honestly never occurred to me."

"Well, it wouldn't hurt to have the name."

"I don't know," says Jean. "You know, I hate for them to be bothered."

"Oh, I doubt we'll be bothering them. From what you say. It'd just be good to have on hand."

She punches up PHONE.PRSNL and gives him the Bjorks' three numbers and both addresses.

"Now, your husband also knows Mr. Reed, doesn't he?"

"Reed?" says Jean. "Oh. You mean—that was his lawyer. So I guess you know about the whole thing that happened."

"We know about the incident on Labor Day, yes. But your husband and Mr. Reed go back before then."

"No, not at all. He was sort of recommended to us at the time, you know, that we're talking about. *I* was actually the one who made the call."

"*I* see," he says. "So they became friendly *after* Mr. Reed represented your husband."

"They *did*?"

"This is news to you?"

"Well," Jean says, "ever since that happened, my husband had been staying in Preston Falls. So I wasn't really, you know, up to date."

"Okay, so how, exactly, did your husband come to meet Mr. Reed?"

"A neighbor of ours in Preston Falls recommended him," says Jean. "The man my husband gets firewood from."

"I *see*," says Captain What's-his-name. Jean is terrible with names. "Now, this neighbor: this is someone your husband knows pretty well?"

"Not really, no. At that point we were kind of desperate, and we knew, or my husband knew, that this man, you know, knew a lawyer, so we just, sort of, didn't know who else to call."

"Uh-huh." Jean dreads that he's going to ask for the name, and then she's going to have to say, Well, we knew he'd been arrested for drugs, or whatever the story was, because of course that would be in *the computer*. How could Willis ever have brought her, and their children, into contact with all this?

"And your husband also spends time in New York City?"

"Does he spend *time* here? He *works* here."

"When he's *not* at work. He must have friends, people he hangs out with?"

"Well, not so much anymore. His brother lives in New York. But I spoke to him I guess Tuesday, and he hadn't heard anything. Listen— I'm sorry, could I get your name again?"

"It's Captain Anthony Petrosky. S-k-y."

"Petrosky, right." Jean writes the name in the margin of the *Times*. "Captain Petrosky, if you know something I don't know, could you please tell me?"

Silence for just a second. Then he says, "Would you mind holding?"

The phone goes blank, no dial tone, nothing, as if she were just pressing some random object to her ear. She's wondering how long she should wait until she can assume she was cut off, when the line opens up again and he says, "Mrs. Willis? Sorry to keep you. The reason for asking about New York City particularly, the truck registered to your husband *has* been located down there."

"In New *York*? You're kidding." She actually stupidly stands up and looks out the window. The usual tiny people way below down on the sidewalks.

"That surprise you?"

"I don't know," she says. "I guess it doesn't, really. Except that he hates the city. Or he claimed to. Whereabouts was the truck?"

"Says here it was towed . . . let's see. Okay, towed from East Houston Street"—he pronounces it like Houston, Texas—"and impounded. They assume it to be stolen or abandoned. I do have a number you can call down there to try and claim the vehicle, but from what I understand, it's not currently in a drivable condition, due to lack of wheels. Now, New York, after they talked to us, they gave it a going-over, but they didn't turn up much of anything. Couple road maps, coffee containers— well, I can read you what they found, but nothing any way unusual."

"In New York." She sits back down and looks at the picture of Mel and Roger. You can see that spot where Mel's eyebrows almost meet. "But you say it could've been stolen?"

"Possible. There's no report out on it. Equally possible, you have an older vehicle, it could have just died and somebody figured let New York City cart it off. Anyway, what I thought by telling you, if you had acquaintances in New York—you *or* your husband—then you might want to try getting in touch with them. An awful lot of these cases, it ends up being a personal matter and the parties work it out in their own way. Which I'm not saying the police shouldn't be notified. But that would be my advice."

"Right," says Jean. God, who *do* they know anymore?

"Well, I better let you get back to work. Suppose you make some calls, see how you do and then get back to me in a couple days. Or I can get back to you. This is what—Thursday? If I don't hear from you, I'll give you a call early next week. Now, is this the best number to reach you?"

"Yes—*please*. If I can help it, I'd like my children not to be exposed to any more than they have to be."

"I understand. Believe me. I have two daughters."

"Look, I know it's stupid," she says. "They're going to get it regardless, aren't they? They're just going to get—I don't know—*hammered*. And on top of everything else, I have to get on a plane in a few minutes."

"For?"

"Come again? Oh. For Atlanta."

"You reachable there?"

"Well, it's just overnight, really. I mean I can give you the hotel."

"If you have it handy."

"It's the Airport Marriott," says Jean. "In Atlanta. I think it's four oh four? But Marriott should have an eight hundred number. So stupid—I *had* it right here."

"We can get it if need be. You're there under Willis?"

"Under Karnes, actually," says Jean. "My maiden name. K-a-r-n-e-s?"

"And it's Jean."

"Right."

"Tell me something," he says. "When do you plan to be back in Preston Falls?"

"I didn't. But if this goes on, you know, with him not—then I guess

I'll have to go up and try to get hold of a plumber to drain everything and close up the house."

"Well, see, what I was thinking, if you do have to make the trip, why don't I stop out to the house? Might be more useful than just talking on the phone. Hell, *I'd* be glad to help you drain your pipes and whatnot. That's no big deal."

"I don't know. I'll have to see. Listen, I think I better get going." Jean looks at the clock in the corner of her screen: 10:14. "The car's picking us up in a couple of minutes."

"We'll talk next week, then," he says. "Let me give you a number."

"I have to go. Just call me here, okay? Call *here*."

"I got you," he says. .

Jean commands herself to breathe. If she could just shut the door for a few minutes and meditate and try to get herself . . . she hates to say *centered*. But they really *will* be here any second. She wants not to be getting on a plane for anywhere. Wants to get her children home and pull the phone and pile furniture against the doors. She looks at that awful picture of Mel and Roger.

This cannot be happening.

Her office. Her computer. Her fire-engine-red adjustable lamp clamped to the desk. Her bad print of that Flemish still life in the National Gallery: the flowers don't explode at you the way they do in the real painting. Even her disappointment with the print is familiar, and, therefore, a comfort. She stands up and looks out the window again, down at all the little people on the street; could one be Willis, coming her way?

So he's in New York. Or was. (Or wasn't.) So she's got to call Jeff and Jennifer, Dave and Karen, maybe Henry and Pamela, who she thinks might've moved to New Jersey. Jim Bruton: *that's* an idea, if he still lives on Elizabeth Street, since they found the truck on East Houston. God, just the thought of these people. Back when they lived on 108th Street, Jean and Willis would actually have them over for dinner and vice versa. Inconceivable as it sounds. This was one of his big arguments for buying Preston Falls: friends up on the weekends! Like people who couldn't deal with the thirty-five minutes to Chesterton were suddenly going to travel four and a half hours. Even the humiliation of having to ask if they know where her husband is doesn't seem as bad as simply hearing their voices after all this time, and having to say, *This is Jean.*

"Hey," Jerry Starger says from the doorway. "You about ready? Car's downstairs."

"Okay," says Jean.

"You don't sound raring."

"I'll let Anita do the raring for both of us."

Jerry goes *"Rrrroww"* and makes a scratching motion.

"I can't believe I said that," Jean says.

"Oh, I like glimpses of the real you." Jerry puts both palms up, as if warding her off. *"Glimpses."*

"Get me drunk on the plane," she says, "and I'll probably let slip what I really think about HMOs." She gets up and slings the duffel bag over her shoulder.

"Hmm. A frank exchange of views. Could be sick fun. But listen, let me ask you—and be honest, okay? Are you up to this? You look like shit, if that doesn't come under the heading of an unwelcome personal comment."

"Really, I'm fine. I just need to catch up on my sleep."

"If you're sure," says Jerry. "Because the very fabulous Ms. Bruno is fully capable of handling whatever eyelash-batting might be called for."

"I had to open my mouth," Jean says.

"Shit, you should hear what she says about *you*."

Jean has to think for a second: Jerry can always take the banter a move further than she can. Finally she says, "I would never ask you to betray a sister's confidence."

"Oh, I wasn't going to," says Jerry. "This is just my Attila the Hun management secret for keeping you broads in line. So what do you say? Let's rock the party."

Down in the lobby, Anita Bruno's looking at her watch, a Bottega Veneta suitcase at her feet. Howard, his garment bag slung over his shoulder, is peering through the plate-glass door at a midnight-blue sedan parked at the curb, a placard with the number 24 in its window.

"Hey, the gang's all here," says Jerry. "Is that us?"

"That's what they sent," Howard says. "You think we can all fit?"

"Piece of cake," says Jerry. "I like to sit up front with the guy anyway. And I hate those big-ass limos—remind me of prom night in Great Neck."

That shuts Howard up.

"I see *one* of us was smart enough to travel light," says Anita, looking at Jean's duffel bag. "I feel like such a clotheshorse."

"Oh, this is just my makeup," Jean says. "I sent my bags on ahead."
The moment this is out of her mouth, she wonders if it's remotely funny.
Anita and Jerry both laugh, but that tells her nothing.

The driver takes the placard out of the window, pops the trunk and
gets out to lift the bags in, slowly enough to let them know he doesn't
feel like it. So why didn't he stay in Pakistan or wherever? God, she's
getting more right wing by the minute—one more little fringe benefit of
being married to Doug Willis. Mel's already being liberal and open-
hearted as a way of rebelling, so maybe Roger will eventually go that
route. Sure.

Jean climbs into the back seat and scoots over to the far side, hoping Howard will be gentleman enough to take the middle. Instead he's
gentleman enough to motion Anita in ahead of him: ladies first. So now
she gets to smell Anita's Ysatis all the way to La Guardia.

If they ever make it. They're trying to get east on Fiftieth Street, but
traffic seems gridlocked; the light up ahead, at the corner of Park, has
changed from green to red to green and they're still not moving. Well,
it's out of her hands. Jerry's talking to the driver about the Cadillac
Something-or-other versus the Lincoln Town Car (which this is), and
Anita's talking to Howard about his son's learning disability. Jean just
looks out the window at the people pouring around them on foot, one
of whom might be her husband.

9

She gets stuck next to Anita on the plane too. Jerry has stuff to go over with Howard, so it's like *Run along, girls.* Jean's dreading three hours of girl talk, but Anita, after standing there fussing around in the overhead long enough for every man on board to get a look at her, sits down with a copy of *Waiting to Exhale* and says Jean's probably going to think this is really rude, but she's so *into* this book. So now Jean gets to feel contempt for Anita because she's reading such a pop thing as *Waiting to Exhale*. Does this make them even?

When the plane levels out after takeoff and she can read without getting sick, she opens *Emma* to the part where Mr. Elton starts quote making violent love to Emma in the carriage, which of course back then only meant pouring your heart out, but you still can't help picturing him tearing at her antique clothes and her weeping and trying to push him off as he's plunging his penis. After like two pages, she starts closing her eyes a little between sentences and sinking into the rushing noise of the airplane and mixing up what she's reading with things in life, and then she's asleep with the book open on her leg. When something's said about lunch she wakes up enough to say no, thank you, and doesn't come to again until the plane starts bumping and pitching and pointing nose-down, and someone announces that the captain has put on the fasten-seat-belts sign and they're almost on the ground. She has to wipe drool from the corner of her mouth—not, thank God, the side turned to Anita, who's sitting there reading away like one of those people who never get airsick. Jean wonders if she was snoring as well as drooling. She closes her eyes again and tries her meditation—she hates landing even worse than takeoff—but she can't go deep because she's worried that Anita will think she's praying.

The car that picks them up takes them on superhighways right through the futuristic downtown. Anita's oohing and aahing and pointing, which isn't so brilliant if her idea is to come off as cosmopolitan; maybe she's trying to seem spirited. Though in fairness, she could be genuinely interested. Eventually the buildings get lower, and they take an exit and go maybe half a mile along a kind of truck-route-looking street with a banged-up metal divider, then turn into a strip mall with a Staples (the anchor), a TCBY, and the two small empty stores The Paley Group is leasing side-by-side and making into a single space. The white stucco seems to pulsate in the sunlight; you can imagine it on a hundred-degree day in August.

Jerry turns to face the back seat. "Well, *this* is grim."

"You saw the pictures, Jerry," Howard says. "Nothing has been misrepresented."

"Hey," says Jerry, and holds up a hand. "It wasn't *your* call." They pull up in front of the empty stores, the windows covered with brown paper. "*Or* mine. I campaigned for the space in that tower until I made myself obnoxious—and no cracks out of *you*, Karnes." He looks out his window. "Where the fuck *is* this bozo? He was supposed to—ah." A golden-haired man in a brown leather jacket is walking toward them, eating with a spoon from a TCBY dish. Jerry pokes the button, and the window goes down.

"You got to be the folks from New York," says the man, who has a sort of ex-con-looking face. "I'm Dan Lineberry? You have to excuse me—this is lunch *and* breakfast."

They follow him into the left-hand storefront. There's nothing to see: four people have flown a thousand miles to inspect freshly sheet-rocked walls, cables hanging down from an unfinished ceiling and two separate rectangles of dirty old carpeting, one gray, the other dark gray, that haven't been ripped up yet. A strip of concrete floor in between. Jean looks for Anita, in hopes of making eye contact, hypocritical as it is to try to make her an ally at this late date. But Anita's pacing around, brows knit, as if picturing desks and dividers. She takes Jerry's sleeve and points at a blank sheetrock corner. Jerry nods, then follows her point as it sweeps along the wall. Just about now, Mel and Roger are getting out of school.

Jean hasn't stayed in a hotel since she and Willis spent a night at the Tarrytown Hilton a year ago. One of their last attempts. What she mostly notices about her room at the Airport Marriott is its beigeness—

carpeting, bedspread, draperies—and a big walnut-veneer piece of furniture that must have a television inside. She should take a shower before they regroup down in the lounge, and before that, she should call home. But even before *that*, she needs to zone out for a few minutes. She takes off her shoes, lies down on the bed and picks up *Emma*.

The telephone wakes her, and she gropes for it on the nightstand.

"Hi, it's Anita. Jerry thought I'd better call. You okay? We're all down here."

"Oh, I fell *asleep*," Jean says. "God, what time is it? Am I keeping everybody waiting?" And she's got to take a *shower*, change *clothes*, do something about her *hair* . . . Crap.

"It's only six-thirty," says Anita. "Take your time. You must be exhausted—you slept the whole way down. Are you sure you're all right?"

Jean can hear music and chattering voices on the other end. "I'm fine. It's just a combination of not enough sleep and also getting my period." A totally weird thing to come out with, since she's not getting her period.

"Oh, I *hate* that," says Anita. "And if I *take* anything, then I'm like—uhh."

"Well, that's actually what happened. I took a couple of Advils, and the next thing I knew . . ." This is so odd: the last thing she is, ordinarily, is a liar. She must be more desperate than she knows to establish some bogus woman-to-woman thing.

"Listen," says Anita, "I'll just tell them—God, what should I say? You want me to say you were working on something? And the time just got away from you?"

"No, just tell them I fell asleep and I'll be down in a minute, okay? So what are we doing tonight—do we know yet?"

"Anybody's guess. But I think it could be a long one. Listen, could I ask you? Do you have *any* idea what we're doing down here? I just think this is bizarre."

"Well, it hasn't exactly been action-packed. But it does make a difference to actually see the space. And the thing tomorrow morning, it probably makes sense for Jerry and Howard to get on a personal footing with someone from the bank."

Dead air.

"Okay," says Anita. "So we'll see you in a few."

Jean says, "Okay," but Anita's already hung up. Brilliant: you mope around wishing you had a woman ally, and now you keep her at arms' length because of some stupid paranoia. What, she's going to betray you if you agree this is bizarre? So no wonder your marriage fell apart.

She decides to skip the shower and use the time to call home. On the fourth ring, she gets the machine: *"This is five five five, one five three six,"* says Willis's voice. *"You know what to do."*

"Hi, dear hearts," she says. "I guess you guys must've gone out. I'm just calling to say hi and that I miss you"—now *don't* you start weeping—"and I'm doing fine. It's warmer down here, but not *real* warm, so if you're picturing me lying out by the pool or something, forget about it. Anyway, I'm just about to go out to dinner, and I'll try you again later. I know you already have the number here, but just in case." She actually gives them the stupid number again.

It would be self-dramatizing to sit here on the edge of the bed staring forlornly, so she goes into the bathroom and paws around in her travel kit for a toothbrush—which she evidently forgot to pack. There's a little thing of blue mouthwash in a basket on the countertop, along with little bottles of shampoo and conditioner, so she sloshes some of that around in her mouth, running her tongue over her teeth, then tips back her head and gargles. This will have to do. She makes some quick repairs on her hair and makeup so she looks a little less like *shit*—it hurt when Jerry said that, even if it was meant to be some double-reverse irony.

Down in the lounge, Jerry and Howard and Anita are perched on tall stools around a tiny table on a chrome stalk.

"All *right*." Jerry pats the seat of an empty stool. "Sit down and what's your pleasure? Miss Bruno—*Mizz* Bruno—is drinking white wine, like the lady she is. I'm drinking Wild Turkey so nobody'll know I'm a New York Jew, *and* our friend Howard here is drinking—what are you drinking again, Howard?"

"J & B," Howard says.

"Howard is drinking J & B," says Jerry. "Which I have to say is extremely judicious. Nobody's going to figure out *what* the hell he is."

Jean can see why Anita predicted a long night. "Maybe some white wine too," she says. Now that she's kicked away the chance of forming any other bond.

Jerry's hand shoots into the air and begins waving. "Yo. Garson. Garsonette." A waitress comes their way, tottering in the high heels and short, tight leather skirt they make her wear; you can practically hear her net stockings scraping together at the knees. "Uno more-o vino white-o," says Jerry, touching the rim of Anita's glass.

The waitress nods, then gives Jean just the quickest look: *Better you than me, honey.* She must be about Jean's age, sort of country hard-faced.

"So in your absence," says Jerry, "we've arrived at a decision." He takes a pull at his whiskey. "First we chow down at whatever the hell the name is, some place our friend and colleague Howard here says is acceptable, which we'll see." The waitress sets a glass of wine in front of Jean. "What time again, Howard?"

"Quarter to eight," says Howard.

"Quarter to eight. Sounds plausible," says Jerry. "And then it's on to what we're told is the premier country-music nightspot, which is called the . . . Howard?"

"Crystal Chandelier," says Howard.

"The Crystal Chandelier. Thank yuh thank yuh. Where we get to see some poofter in a cowboy hat. Gary Larry or Larry Gary or some such shit."

"You know, it's almost seven, Jer," Howard says. "I should call the car place."

"Well, hell, go *to* it, son. Got us a phone rot over thur by the pissy-warr."

"Yeah, I know, Jer," says Howard. "I just used it."

Anita glances at Jean and raises her eyes ceilingward. Jean has both hands around her wineglass; she opens, then closes, her fingers; she hopes this will seem like the equivalent of a sympathetic shrug.

"Hell of a town," says Jerry. "Jes' so proud to be here."

"I'll be right back," says Howard.

"Take your tom, son," Jerry says, as Howard heads for the telephone. He takes another gulp of whiskey. "Poor bastard."

Jean says nothing. Shamefully leaving it to Anita, who asks, "Why do you say that?"

Jerry winces. "Bruno," he says. "Please tell me you're just playing dumb. Look, this is a sweet man, you know what I'm saying? Basically a lovely man. They threw him down and *raped* him in New York. You think even in this godforsaken shithole they can't *smell* it on him? I mean, with all due respect to Howard." He shrugs. "I give it a year."

"But doesn't anybody know this?" says Anita.

"*I* know it; am *I* anybody?" Jerry says. "I guess *not.*"

This shuts Anita up.

"But he's moving his family down," Jean says.

"So let's hope they like the area," says Jerry.

"How can you *do* this to him?" Jean says.

Jerry shrugs. "He fuckin' *begged* for it. What am *I* supposed to do? Out of New *York*, more relaxed way of *life*, nice public *schools*—plus his own little fiefdom away from all the big mean guys. Hey, and Art was only too happy to make it all come true. Because he sees a tax loss at the end of the tunnel *and* Howard out the door." Howard's heading back to the table; Jean smiles and nods at him to alert Jerry. "You think *I'm* scary, you should watch old Artie in action—if you can even see what he's doing. Fucker's the master of misdirection."

"Who we talking about?" Howard says, climbing back onto his stool.

"*You*, babe," says Jerry, who must have seen him coming after all. "So what's the frequency, Kenneth?"

"I asked them to send a car around in about twenty minutes."

"That's the stuff," says Jerry. "Shit, you're going to be right in your element down here."

"Well, I think it's the right move for me. And we'll make that location work, Jerry. I respect what you're saying, but over the long haul?"

"There, see that?" Jerry says to Jean and Anita. "This is the man with the master plan." He raises his glass. "Howie, you fuckin' ace of trumps." He drains the last of his drink. "Now, here's the agenda. If you would escort Ms. Bruno out to the lobby and wait for us, Ms. *Karnes* and I have about five minutes' worth of highly confidential shit to talk over."

Anita looks at Jean, who turns up a palm.

"Sure," says Howard. "We can do that. If the car shows up, I'll just have him wait."

"Excellent," Jerry says. "Have him wait. That's it. You're in the zone, babe."

Howard touches fingertips to Anita's elbow, and Jerry watches them out of the room. Then he shoots his fingers behind the lenses of his glasses, pushing them up above his forehead, and digs the heels of his hands into his eye sockets, twisting his head from side to side. He claws the glasses back down into place and says, "Help me, somebody. Jesus." He looks up. "How's your drink holding out?"

"I'm fine," says Jean.

"Sure you are. So what's this secret sorrow, Karnes? Let me guess.

Prince Hamlet won't take care of his homework. Have I ever told you you're worth ten of this putz? In my opinion?"

"Yes. Repeatedly."

"If you don't mind my calling your husband a putz. How *is* the King of Rock and Roll?"

"I don't know. I don't even know *where* he is. He was supposed to be back at work this week, and apparently he just, you know, took off. That or something's happened to him. I have no idea what to do."

"Well," Jerry says, "in my religion we have some very moving prayers of thanksgiving."

"Fuck you, Jerry. I don't need jokes."

"Now, *that's* the little pepper-pot we know and love. Okay, so what have you tried so far? You called everybody, nobody knows shit, so you did what? Go to the police?"

"Yes, *finally*. And now—this morning?—they called and said they found his truck on Houston Street."

"Yeah? And?"

"That's it."

"Well, so what the hell are you doing dicking around in Atlanta, Georgia?" says Jerry. "Why didn't you tell me? Dragging you off on *this* bullshit."

"I don't know. I guess if anything, it was a relief to have something I *had* to do," she says. "I think I'm sort of sleepwalking."

"Yeah, I would *say*. Help me, somebody." He raises his hand and windmills for the waitress. "So what did you do with the kids meanwhile? Put out food and water for them?"

"My sister's there—"

"Right, right, I remember you said—"

"—but she has to go back to Seattle. I mean, she should have gone already."

Jerry shuts his eyes, his whole face scrunching up. "If this wasn't the ass end of the universe, Karnes, I'd stick you on a plane right now. Shit, there's got to be *something* flying back to civilization tonight." The waitress is coming their way; he mimics writing on his palm, and she swivels and makes for the cash register. "Okay, this is the plan. Wherever we can get you to, La Guardia, Newark, fuckin' Phila*del*phia, we'll have a car waiting—"

"Jerry, *no*. I can't. I need some sleep. My sister's taking care of the

kids, they'll be fine, and just this one night, you know, there's that huge
bed and it's like it isn't *anywhere*. It isn't even in the *world*."

"Will you be *able* to sleep?" he says. The waitress puts the check on
the table; Jerry lays his credit card on it. "You want a Halcion?"

"God no," says Jean. "What's it like, though? I've never taken it."

"It's like you were never born," he says. "Temporarily."

"Could I really have one?"

"First one's free, kid. So listen. I see absolutely no need for you to
come along on the voyage of the *Pequod* tonight. Howard was probably
counting on you to keep *me* busy, while he tortures himself with the
beautified Miss Bruno. But with just the three of us, it'll be all the more
piquant."

"Oh, come on," says Jean.

"Don't *you* start playing dumb." Jerry taps his temple with a forefinger. "It's my little private theater troupe, okay? Starring the beautified
Miss Bruno. Another one of life's winners. One-bedroom co-op in the
Village that she can't unload, and some putz hanging around who's *in
film*, for Christ's sake. See, Bruno tells me everything. Which is more
than I can say for you, Karnes. I think she read some fucking article
about mentors."

"At least it sounds like she has hope," says Jean.

"Yeah, well, like I say. Piquant. So anyway, you go on up, you order
room service, you get under the covers, you have two desserts, put on a
dirty movie, pop a Halcion and goodbye cruel world."

"This is really kind," says Jean. "But I should at least come to dinner. I don't want to spoil everybody's evening."

"Please-please-*please*, can we not talk stupidly? An *evening*? This is
a fucking lunar expedition."

"Well, so why are you doing it?"

"That's the question, all right," he says. "You've nailed it."

The waitress is back with the slip and credit card. Jerry looks at the
slip, closes his eyes, then opens them and writes in the tip and total.

"Let me tell you one *more* thing," he says, guiding her toward the
lobby with a hand on her shoulder blade. "Since we're talking turkey. Or
the Wild Turkey's talking turkey. This might appeal to your sick sense of
humor. I am technically a faithful husband. And that is not a proposi-
tion, by the way."

"I'm technically a faithful wife," Jean says. It feels daring to leave
out the rest. God, that one glass of wine.

———

She calls room service and orders a steak, which she *never* has, a baked potato and, for dessert, Chocolate Mud Pie. And a caffeine-free Diet Coke: she's afraid to have another glass of wine because of the pill Jerry gave her, which she's afraid to take anyway. She gets her shoes off, pulls the stiff synthetic bedspread over her and reads the part where Emma's trying to figure out how she could have thought Mr. Elton was in love with Harriet. The food arrives, wheeled in by a fat, beaming black woman who's either doing a good job of pretending she doesn't hate waiting on rich white women, or who genuinely doesn't because she's a Christian.

But Jean can't eat until she knows what's going on in Chesterton. She keeps the round metal covers on the food, hangs the DO NOT DIS-TURB sign on the doorknob, then gets into her nightgown and under the covers to make the call.

Mel answers the phone. "Oh. I thought you were Erin."

"Just me," Jean says. "How's it going? I miss you."

Mel says nothing.

"You get my message?"

"Yeah," Mel says. "Roger got in trouble again."

"What now?"

"He scratched a Nazi sign on Aunt Carol's truck, and she can't get it out."

"Oh crap," says Jean. "Is she there? Could I talk to her?"

"She and Roger are out in the garage."

"Then would you go get her, please?"

A long wait. Jean gets out of bed and brings the phone over to the serving table. She lifts the cover and looks at this slab of brown meat with black stripes on it, lying by its lonesome on the too-large white plate. It's shaped like Mississippi or something.

"Hi," says Carol. "So I guess you heard."

"Oh, Carol, I'm so *sorry*. I can't be*lieve* this. What exactly happened?"

"Well, I went to get a tape out of my truck, and there was Roger with one of those big screw hooks you have? And he was scratching this, you know, *swastika* on the door of the truck. The driver's side. I *think* he's sorry, but it's sort of hard to tell with him."

"Oh my God. Why would he *do* a thing like that?"

"Beats me," Carol says. "The most Nazi thing I think I did was telling him he couldn't have any more Halloween candy before dinner."

"I better talk with him. Is there anything you can do about your truck?"

"I don't know. I thought about using your sander, but that would just make it like a *fat* swastika. I guess for now I'll just put something over it to cover it up. Maybe if I could find a big piece of cardboard."

"Oh *shit*," Jean says. "Well, look, whatever it costs to fix it, you know? Obviously. But I'm so sorry. I feel *terrible* about this."

"It was real weird seeing it," says Carol. "He's still out there, by the way. I brought one of your lawn chairs out and had him just sit and look at it so he could start to process what he did. Was that okay?"

"I guess. I don't know. Something like this I'm completely lost. Can I speak to him?"

"I'll go get him."

Another long wait. Jean lies back down on the bed and pulls the bedspread over her again. She tries to read the stuff on the back of *Emma*. Finally she hears noises, and Roger says, "What?"

"*You* know what," she says. "Why did you *do* that?"

"I don't know, I just did it."

"That's not an answer. You're old enough to take responsibility for the things you do. Were you angry at something?"

"I just wanted to see what it would look like."

"Didn't you know it was wrong?"

He says nothing.

"I'm very disappointed," she says, "because we've talked about this before. If you're angry about something, or you feel bad about something, you *talk* about it to somebody. You don't go and do something that hurts someone else."

"She can get it fixed," says Roger.

"That's not the point. But since you mention it, yes, she *is* going to have to get it fixed, and it's probably going to be very expensive. And you're going to have to help pay for it." Which is stupid, because she has no idea how to follow through. Should she give him chores at some imaginary wage? He'll forget what the point had ever been, unless she harps on it every day. Like a harpy.

Roger says nothing.

"I'm coming home tomorrow," she says. "Between now and then I want you to be thinking about this and be ready to give me a better explanation. Do you understand? This is a really upsetting time for all of us, with Daddy gone, but being upset doesn't mean you're not responsible for what you do." And if this sounds right wing, too bad. "So you and I have a date tomorrow night. Okay? I'm not going to yell at you, but I *am* going to expect you to talk to me about what you're feeling. If you're angry or sad or upset—whatever's going on. So I want you to think. Would you promise me?"

Roger says nothing. Which is about what's going to happen tomorrow night. And then what's her move? Send him to a real psychiatrist instead of that completely ineffectual woman at Mary M. Watson?

"Okay, you know what you have to do," Jean says. "Could I talk to Aunt Carol, please? Listen, I love you very much. Even when you do things that are wrong. Will you remember that too?" Which he'll probably interpret to mean that in the long run he'll get away with it.

"Hi," says Carol. "Well, he *looks* sorry."

"I'm sure," Jean says. "So as usual I'm not even there."

"It's not your fault. Listen, did you ever think this whole area around here, like the Hudson River, has sort of a weird vibe?"

"No," says Jean. "I mean, I *wish*."

After hanging up, she takes the cover off the steak again and nudges it with the fork. It leaves a smear of brown-red juice, complete with fat globules. She should make herself eat a piece just as punishment for being stupid enough to order it. She tries a little of the baked potato, but it has that bad taste from being reheated too many times. Which leaves this pointless Chocolate Mud Pie: food for pleasure. God, right now the thought of any pleasure ever again.

She cuts the pill Jerry gave her with the steak knife and swallows half. Something she's never done, taking some strange pill: well, now she's in for it. She wants this food out of here. She wheels the serving table into the hall.

It's eight o'clock. If she could only sleep right through until eight in the morning, twelve good solid lost hours. But there's that stupid breakfast. She calls the front desk and asks for a wake-up call at six, then gets into bed and finds her place in *Emma*; it's working up to where Emma finally has to tell Harriet that Mr. Elton isn't in love with her, but Jean doesn't even get that far before the pill kicks in. Oh God, it's delicious: she's melting, she's melting, like the Wicked Witch.

———

The next thing she knows, she's sitting up in bed wide awake and the clock says 4:04 and she remembers Willis is gone. So this is the down side of taking a sleeping pill, which even an idiot would have known. She reaches for the light, squeezes her eyes shut and turns it on, then sneaks her eyes open. She's a thousand miles from where she needs to be.

She gets out of bed and drops to her knees in the thick carpeting and says, out loud, "Dear God, please help me. I'm just asking you to hold me up so I can get through this and try to help Mel and Roger get through, because we're all in so much trouble. Please. Amen." She can't remember praying since she was a good little girl, in Methodist Sunday school. Well, except back when she and Willis experimented for a week or so with saying grace before meals. Not that they believed; just to leave themselves open. One of those things only she and Willis know about.

She remains on her knees, forehead touching the mattress, and tries not to actually *want* peace and strength to come flooding in, because that would be a sure way *not* to get it. Though *that's* stupid because God (if any) either intends to give you peace and strength or he doesn't; you can't maneuver him into it. Eventually she gets to her feet. So this is her big spiritual experience, which is exactly what she deserves for neglecting anything spiritual for all these years.

She takes a shower and puts on the clothes she brought for tomorrow. It *is* tomorrow. While on hold with Delta, she dumps everything out of her wallet, looking for her MasterCard. Crap. She's going to have to use Amex, which actually is just as well since she's already got a couple of thousand on her MasterCard. She finally gets a person—a woman, sounding strangely wide awake—who tells her there's a five-thirty on American that gets into La Guardia at eight and that they can work something out with her ticket. In a way this is so stupid: what's she going to do in New York at eight in the morning? Except get caught in rush hour. But at least she can get to her office and start calling people, as she should've done days ago.

She finds stationery in the desk drawer and writes a note:

> *Dear Jerry,*
> *Thanks for all your help. Thinking back on our conversation, I decided to take the earliest plane I could get and start dealing with everything. I'm terribly sorry about the breakfast, but*

you didn't sound like you needed me there.
Naturally I'll pay the difference in the price of the
tickets.
    Anyway, thanks again, Jerry.

                Be well,
                Jean

She calls the desk to say she's checking out and could they have a taxi waiting. She puts the note in an envelope, seals it, writes *Jerry Starger* on it, takes her bag and closes the door behind her. Her serving table has been taken away. She walks toward where she thinks the elevators were last night. She's the only human in the carpeted corridors, and in this harsh artificial light, which seems to be coming from everywhere, she casts no shadow.

10

On her way through La Guardia to Ground Transportation, she buys the *Times* at a newsstand and a blueberry muffin at Au Bon Pain; she couldn't deal with the scrambled eggs on the plane. But the muffin's too sweet, or too dry, or doesn't taste blueberry enough, and she throws it in the trash. By the time the taxi drops her in front of the building, she's read pretty much the whole *Times* except, of course, for sports and business. One thing about Willis: at least he never sat watching sports all weekend. Though husbands who sit watching sports all weekend are at least *there*. When the elevator doors open on fourteen, she's startled to see Helen sitting behind the reception desk. Though in fact it's after nine o'clock on a normal business day.

"Hi," says Helen. "I didn't expect you guys till this afternoon. Is everybody back already?"

"No, I got up super-early," says Jean. "No calls, it looks like."

Helen rattles a fake-nailed index finger back and forth in the *K* space and says, "Nobody home."

Jean shuts her office door behind her, shoves her duffel bag under her desk, logs on and gets PHONE.PRSNL up on her screen. Jim Bruton's the best bet, but apparently when she put in the names and numbers from her old address books he hadn't made the cut. In fairness, they'd blown off most of their straight friends too. She calls Information; no James Bruton, or J. Bruton, anywhere in Manhattan.

Next best might be Jeff and Jennifer. She's got Jennifer's office number, but it's too early to find her at work. She kills time until ten or so reading the *Post*, plus an insane article about Religion and the Cosmo Girl in this old *Cosmopolitan* that's lying around her office. At ten after, she calls Jennifer's number at *Spin* and is told she's gone to *House & Garden*. Someone at *House & Garden* says Jennifer's in a meeting; Jean leaves her name and number. Hmm. After Jennifer, it's a crapshoot. She tries the number she has for Henry and Pamela.

"Jean. My *God*," says Pamela. "How *are* you. *Where* are you?"

"At work."

"Oh, that's right," says Pamela. "I'd heard about this. I was so disap*pointed*. I think I'm the only kept woman left in America. So how is—it's Melanie, right?"

"She's fine. She's twelve, if you can believe it. And she has a little brother, Roger. Who's nine."

"I think I heard that too," says Pamela. "That's incredible. I don't know if anyone's told you, but *we*'re finally taking the plunge."

"Oh, that's wonderful," says Jean. "Good for you. When's the due date?"

"Beginning of March."

"And do you know if it's going to be a boy or a girl?"

"*They* know. I told them not to tell me, except now I'm thinking that's ridiculous."

"So you had amnio."

"My age, are you kidding?" Pamela says. "So tell me, what is Willis up to?"

"Well, as a matter of fact, that's sort of why I was calling." Jean sees not only that this is a wasted call but also that she can never in the future call Pamela just out of friendship: she's let Pamela think that's what *this* is, and instead she just wants something. Though, actually, *what* friendship? They were friends, really, for two years and haven't seen each other in like ten. Jean takes a deep breath and launches in.

"You're kidding," says Pamela. "Gee, no, we haven't heard from Willis for, you know, years. Oh, Jean, I'm *so* sorry. You must be *beside* yourself. Did you try Jeff and Jennifer?"

"I left a message. You wouldn't know how to get in touch with Jim, would you?"

"Oh," says Pamela. "I guess—well, Jim died last year."

"He *died*?" says Jean. "No. Was it AIDS?"

"Oh no, dear. No-no-no. Somebody pushed him in front of a subway. It was even on the news. And they had a memorial at the Franklin Furnace. Somebody was supposed to call you—I think Jennifer, actually. Well. Whatever."

"Oh God," says Jean. So much for her best little clue.

"So now that I've cheered *you* up . . . But listen, is there anything I can do?"

It sounds like a rhetorical question. "I don't think so. But thanks. God, I've been so rude. I haven't even asked how Henry's doing."

"He's fine. I *think*. I sometimes suspect the real Henry has disappeared into the World Wide Web and they've sent a space alien to occupy his body." Then she says, "Oh my God, *sorry*. I guess jokes about disappearing aren't in the best of taste right now."

"What?" says Jean. "Oh. I wasn't even thinking of that."

"Now, do we still have a number for you?" says Pamela.

You tell me, Jean wants to say. She gives Pamela her work number and says she has to go.

She finds a Rolaids in her desk drawer, then goes over to look out the window. One tiny man down there, with a backpack and a baseball cap, could actually be Willis except for the backpack; she watches as he steps off the curb, raises his arm and climbs into a taxi. Another tiny Willis (though he'd never wear a red jacket) comes out of Duane Reade. The phone rings: Regina, asking if she has a second to stop down and see Mr. Paley. It's said so nicely Jean thinks for an instant she has the option of saying she's too busy.

Arthur Paley's office is at the other end of the hall from Jerry Starger's: from his window you can see the park, from Jerry's just buildings. Regina nods her in and Jean stops in his doorway. He looks up from some piece of paper, puts it down and says, "Jean. Come on in and close the door, would you?" He pushes the button on his squawk box and says, "Reggie, would you hold my calls unless it's Atlanta?"

There are three chairs in front of his desk; Jean takes the one nearest the door.

"So," says Arthur Paley. "From what I gather, you missed the excitement last night."

Jean cocks her head.

"Ah. Well, it seems our Mr. Starger," he says, "saw fit to take his protégés out to some cowboy bar. Where he proceeded to get into a dispute with one of the locals, who I gather was being attentive to Miss—what the hell's her name. Bruno. Anyhow, to cut a long story short, Mr. Starger ended up in the jug and Mr. Cooperman spent the morning trying to bail him out. Of course the gentlemen missed their plane, but Miss Bruno is winging her way back to us as we speak."

"My God," says Jean. "I had no idea."

"So I was told," he says. "I suppose the philosophical way to look at this is pennies from heaven. Oddly enough, we'd been contemplating— well, as you know, *downsizing* has become a dirty word—but a certain amount of restructuring, and particularly in Mr. Starger's area. So, rather fortuitously, this may end up helping along a process that was already in motion. My guess is that very shortly we'll be hearing from Mr. Starger that he's decided to resign in order to pursue other opportunities." He looks at Jean. "You had a comment?"

"No," she says. "Only that I'm really sorry this is happening. For whatever it's worth, he's been a wonderful person to work for."

Arthur Paley smiles. What you notice is the whiteness of his teeth coming out of his suntan, and how evenly his white sideburns are trimmed. "You owe Jerry a great deal, I know," he says. "And I know, too, that you've grown tremendously in your time here, in your field of expertise. You certainly brought *us* out of the dark ages—kicking and screaming sometimes." A strategic chuckle. Then back to serious. "I'll tell you something. I'd be willing to predict that within a few months you'll find some better opportunities yourself. New worlds to conquer." Another chuckle. "Maybe someplace that's not so darn hidebound."

"Am I being fired?" she says.

He smiles and shakes his head. "You know, you're a breath of fresh air. Think of this as more along the lines of career counseling. Mentoring, if you will. Just because Jerry's elected to move on, or let's say it's become expedient that he do so, it doesn't mean the people he brought in are in any way damaged goods. And of course I include you in that. Now, as I say, we *are* looking at some restructuring in his area—what *was* his area. And possibly rethinking some matters of style and presentation. You may disagree about this, probably you do, but it *is* possible in this business to have a little too *much* flair. If I have any criticism overall of Jerry's tenure here, it would be that." He waves a hand around. "But hell, change is just the nature of things. I'd be willing to bet you feel the need of a change yourself."

"Well," she says, "if it were a change for the better."

"*There* you go," he says. "So take time, look around you and . . . we'll talk again."

"Could I ask something that's none of my business? Is this going to hurt Howard Cooperman?"

"I'd hardly call it an auspicious beginning, would you? But he's going to be fine. You let me worry about Howard."

"Right." Jean stands up. "I'm really not stupid, Art."

He laughs. "Who the heck said you were, for Pete's sake?" He gets up too. "I'll deck the son of a gun myself. Jerry Starger's not the only macho man around here."

"Right," says Jean. "Well. I'll see you later, then."

"Door's always open." He comes around the desk and, as if by way of demonstration, opens the door for her.

Instead of going straight back to her office, she walks down the hall to Jerry Starger's corner. A phone's ringing, but his assistant, Martha, isn't at her desk. Jean stares at his closed door. She's seen the poster a thousand times: the little girl with crutches and leg braces. *Help Jerry's Kids*. The naked not-funniness of this never hit her before.

She walks to her office, can't bear to go in, and keeps on all the way around to the reception area. Helen looks up, phone wedged into her neck, and says, "Can you hold just a second, please? Jean, you just had a call." Jean takes the slip: *Tony Petrosky. 802-642-8025. Urgent.*

She suddenly feels sick to her stomach, and braces a hand on Helen's desk. "Could I use your key a second?" It seems to take Helen forever, fumbling around in her top drawer; Jean somehow makes it to the ladies' room, unlocks the door and gets safely inside. She's hearing everything as if she had earplugs.

At the sink, a tall young creature is leaning into the mirror from the waist and batting away with both hands at her hairdo; she turns her head to look at Jean staggering into a stall. Jean swings the door closed, drops to her knees, sticks her tongue out over the toilet bowl and retches. She feels her stomach muscles convulsing, and out comes a little drool of white stuff that must be the Rolaids. There's nothing else to come up. She retches twice more, then sweat starts pouring and that peace comes over her that almost makes it worth vomiting. You can easily, easily see how women get into this. She just kneels there and breathes for a while, then stands, slowly, and brushes off her knees. It feels okay to stand up. But she's really got to get some food. Whatever this *Urgent* thing is (she dreads to think), it has to wait until she gets something solid in her stomach. Eat properly, and then when you're told to look for a new job you can square your shoulders, stick out your chin and say, *Thanks for just devastating my life*, like it wasn't devastated already. So women *do* have options, if they'll just take good enough care of themselves to keep strong. Or is that too bitter?

When Jean comes back with the key, Helen's scribbling with the phone at her ear. She hangs up, then sees Jean and says, "Oh."

Jean stares at the slip. *Mrs. Keene, Chesterton Middle School, 914-555-4200.*

She closes her door, sits down, breathes. The assistant principal: this can't be good. Better deal with this first, no matter what the *Urgent* thing is—probably news about Willis that she can't do anything about.

"Oh hi, thanks for getting back to me," Mrs. Keene says. "We just wanted to check with you, because we noticed Melanie's not in school today and we were wondering if she might be ill."

"She's not in *school?*"

"She hasn't been in any of her classes this morning."

"I'd better call home," says Jean. "I had to be out of town overnight, and my sister was taking care of—"

"We did try your house, actually," says Mrs. Keene. "The reason I'm concerned, we've just heard a rather wild story from Erin Miller. Erin says that Melanie had been planning to run away to her father's house? Does this make any sense to you?"

"Well—we do have like a weekend place," says Jean. "But—"

"Now, apparently—and again, this is all according to Erin—apparently she had planned to get herself down to La Guardia somehow and take a flight to—well, Erin is saying Bennington, but I think she must mean Burlington, because I doubt very much they fly into *Bennington.*"

"Oh my God."

"Bear in mind, now, this may all be talk. But according to Erin, Melanie made a plane reservation over the telephone using your credit card, and then she was planning to—"

"I am going to *kill* Erin." Jean opens her bag and gets her wallet out. Then she remembers: her MasterCard was missing.

"Well, I would hardly hold *Erin* to blame," says Mrs. Keene. "She told me she didn't think Melanie would really go through with it, until she was absent this morning. You know, I put myself in Erin's shoes, and—"

"I don't care about *Erin Miller*," says Jean. "What have you *done*? What are you *doing*?"

"Well, we thought the first thing should be to contact you or your husband, in the event that she was simply home sick. We do have a bug going around."

"God, what time is it? It's after eleven o'*clock*. She could be—*anything* could've happened; she's twelve years *old*." The phone trills and the light for 5322 begins blinking. "Crap. Can you hold?" Jean hits Hold, then 5322. "Jean Karnes."

"Tony Petrosky, Mrs. Willis. I left a message before, but I thought I better keep trying. We have your daughter in custody up in Burlington—now don't worry, she's fine. She was on an airplane this morning from New York City, and we thought we better get in touch with you to know how to proceed."

"Oh thank *God*," says Jean. "Is she all right?"

"Yes, she's fine. Though I gather she's not too happy about being detained."

"She's not in *jail*?"

"No-no-no. They've got a—not a lounge, you wouldn't say, but sort of a waiting room area. At the barracks up there. Couch, couple chairs. Where they can keep an eye on her."

"But what on earth was she—wait, could you hold? Let me get rid of this other—it's her school."

"I'll hold."

She hits Hold, then 5321. "Mrs. Keene? She's all right. I'm talking to the police right now. Apparently they picked her up in Burlington."

"I *thought* it was Burlington."

"Can I call you back?" Jean says.

"Of course. Well, you must be—"

"I'll call you back." She hits 5322. "Hello?"

"I'm here," says Petrosky.

Jean lets out a long breath. "How did you find her?"

"Well, *my* understanding," he says, "the airline people called ahead while they were en route. She had quite a bit of makeup on, from what I gather, but one of the stewardesses noticed she seemed a little young. So I guess they figured, you know, better check it out."

"Is she there? Can I talk to her?"

"Well, no—see, I'm still down in Rutland. I can give you the number up there. What happened, they called me from—okay, let me back up here. What she told them at the airport, she was on her way to see her father. So they started asking her, you know, where does *he* live? Preston Falls. How was she getting there? Little vague on that. I guess they called your house in Preston Falls and couldn't raise anybody, so one thing and another they put her in the computer, and the name Willis set the bells off. Anyhow, the upshot was, they called down here because I was up to speed on the other matter, and I told them I'd get in touch with you and we'd sort of take it from there."

"So you haven't actually *seen* her."

"No, ma'am. But if they say she's fine, I wouldn't worry. Got a pencil? I'll give you that number. You want to ask for Sergeant Mallon."

She writes the number on the pink slip underneath his, putting a ditto mark under the 802.

"Tell me something," he says. "Maybe I'm off on a tangent here. But do you have any reason to think your daughter knows anything *you* might not know about your husband's whereabouts? Or do you think she was just on a lark?"

"A *lark?*"

"Or whatever. Do you think he and she had been in contact?"

"No. No, definitely not. That would shock me more than anything."

"And I guess *you* weren't sending her to hook up with him."

"Do you think I'd put a twelve-year-old—wait, what are you saying? You think this is some weird *scam* or something? That we're all *in* on? What possible—"

"All right, slow down," he says. "Look, this is my job. Okay? Now, while I have you, did you have any luck reaching any of your husband's friends?"

"No. I mean, I did *reach* them. Some of them. I didn't have any luck."

"Right," he says. "Let me ask you. Were you thinking of coming up to get your daughter?"

"Yes—I mean, *can* I?"

"Sure. But let me just run something by you. I remember you were saying you needed to come up and close your house? So I was thinking, what if I arranged to meet you—or better yet, what if we did *this*? I pick your daughter up in Burlington, or maybe have them bring her partway, and she and I could hook up with you in Preston Falls."

Jean has a terrible flash that this isn't a state policeman at all but some serial killer who somehow knows their whole story. Maybe he got

Willis: he's just this voice on the telephone. She tries to think back about what actual proof she has, except she can't really think.

"I don't know," she says. "How would that work?"

"Just bring her to the house, I guess. Try to get there while it's still light enough to look around. And get some heat going. Probably chilly in there."

This *must* be all right. She could always call Information for the Vermont State Police, then call that number and ask for Captain Petrosky. She lets out a long breath. "Okay," she says.

"Good. So when would you be getting there, about?"

"What is it—eleven-thirty? I have to take the train up to get my car, so probably *twelve*-thirty. . . . Let's see, one-thirty, two-thirty, three-thirty, four-thirty. . . . Okay, so probably five o'clock? If all goes well?" She looks at the picture of Mel and Roger. "That sounds bizarre, doesn't it? *If all goes well.*"

"This isn't the easiest thing," he says. "You're holding up fine. So five o'clock. We'll be there."

"Wait, you need directions."

"Ragged Hill Road, isn't it?" he says. "I assume it's that old farmhouse on the left-hand side, just before you get over into Wakefield. Sits sort of up on a rise?"

"You know our house?"

"We get over in there from time to time," he says. "Fact, we're pretty well acquainted with one of your neighbors. You said your husband knows Mr. Castleman?"

"Right. He lives just down the road." Wait: *did* she say that?

"He's quite a character, Mr. Castleman."

Jean says, "I'm surprised that you know the house."

"Oh sure. Like I say, we get over that way. So we'll look for you about five."

Jean keeps the receiver at her ear and calls the Burlington number; she's relieved when the person answers "State Police." Sergeant Mallon takes his sweet time picking up; he puts the phone down with a clunk when she asks to speak to Mel, then gets back on. "She says she don't want to talk to you."

"Is she all right?"

"Oh, she's fine. There's some magazines in there. She's been looking at them when she thinks nobody's watching."

"Well, could you just tell her that I'm on my way and I'll see her soon and that I love her?"

"Sure, will do."

"Captain Petrosky's going to pick her up. Or actually he might have you bring her somewhere."

"Well, that's more than I know," he says. "But we'll keep her safe until we hear."

"Thank you. *Please.*"

Jean hangs up and looks at Mel's face again. So much like her father. Nothing to give you a clue what's going on.

How will she even get up from this chair? Let alone catch a train and then drive to Preston Falls. It's like if you can do that much—just get to your feet—you can do all the rest of it, thing after thing after thing. She's shouldering her bag when the telephone rings. Jennifer, returning her call: Hey, it's been so *long*, how *are* you?

11

The whole way up, she goes over it and over it. If she could just whole-heartedly tell herself that marrying Willis had simply been an insane decision, a way of doing herself in—even *that* would be something. But.

He was a friend of Jeff and Jennifer's. Jeff's college roommate, actu-ally, or maybe he'd lived across the hall; Jean could never keep the histories straight. He'd just broken up with a woman named Cynthia. Who now lives in Madison, Wisconsin, and runs a place for battered women. Lately Jean's thought about calling her up out of the blue, the way people with some rare disease will network. She could never get much of an answer from Willis as to what had gone wrong: *People change* was about the extent of it. Of course, what *People change* means is *Men get tired of you*, but Jean stupidly didn't process that. Even though Carol's marriage had fallen apart for that exact same reason, just about the time Jean was deciding whether or not to marry Willis. She was arrogant enough to think, *Well, crazy Carol and her bad choices.*

That first night, the four of them—Jean, Jeff, Jennifer and Jeff's col-lege friend—drove up to Hartford to see Bob Dylan. (Jean bit her tongue.) This was during the born-again phase, and it was so weird and so loud that they all agreed, in dumbshow, to walk out. They ended up at Denny's, where Jeff's friend started going on about how he must be getting old, and maybe he could still handle Perry Como. Jean found herself thinking that she could get this man into bed. Though this wasn't her style, at *all*, to in any way come on to a man. And did she even *want* to be in bed with this man? Well, actually yes, she very much did. And she still refuses to believe that it was only about her own low self-esteem, though now, of course, after fifteen years of Doug Willis, there's no sick motive she can't pick out in herself. *And* everybody else in the world.

Even back then, Jean never thought of herself as the world's most

sexual person, so it was a shock and a joy to be noticing that she was
noticing this man's cheekbones, his mouth, the way his eyebrows came
together, making him just the teensiest bit apelike. Hair along the edges
of his hands from wrist to pinkie. He was saying that lately he was in
practicing mode—he played the guitar—and something about his calluses. She wasn't listening, really: just rudely drinking him in. Then
Jennifer said, "Oh, can I feel?" and he held up his index finger as if
about to declaim.

"Yuck," said Jennifer. "*Jean.* You won't *believe* this."

"Could I?" Jean asked him.

"Not if I'm exposing myself to more withering criticism," he said.

"Oh, Jean's not a ballbuster like me," said Jennifer.

"But darling, who *is*?" said Jeff.

Jean took his index finger in her palm and ran her thumb over the
tip; it was like it had this hard thing packed inside. Then she ran her
thumb over his fingernail, which seemed like an incredible trespass, way
over the borderline of what she'd been authorized to do. She said, "I
wish my calluses were in that good shape."

"You play?" he said.

"Not a lot." She had a nylon-string guitar and at one point had figured out most of the songs on *Blue*.

"You guys didn't prepare me," he said to Jeff and Jennifer. He
looked back at Jean. "*And* she plays guitar. This is very cool."

A couple of weeks ago, Jean told Mel that if she ever felt like learning
guitar—Mel's the ideal age—she was welcome to use her old one in the
closet. Since Willis's guitars were just so *precious*. Plus he'd taken them
all to Preston Falls. In fact, Jean said, she'd be glad to show her some
chords to get her started. Thinking this might be a little bond that
wouldn't just be like Mel helping out in the kitchen, which essentially
was women being drudges together.

Mel said, "No, thanks, Mother." In a way that just *cut*.

"Well, if you change your mind. I was thinking how much you enjoy
listening to music, and it can be really sort of liberating to be able to play
things for yourself."

"I said no, *thanks*, Mother."

"Right," Jean said. "I heard you."

12

The sun has set when she comes up the real last hill and turns, again, onto Ragged Hill Road. Past the tumbledown barn, the first trailer, the new little house. (Framed in its picture window, a brightly lit glimpse of a woman bearing a baking dish in oven-mitted hands, like a technician handling something radioactive.) Past Calvin Castleman's, where her headlights pick up the Hog Roster, full of dead leaves. Around the last corner, and there's the house: all lit up except for the window with the plastic over it. White smoke pours up out of the chimney. Weird that the place looks so cheery. A police car's parked in the yard—almost as alarming as if she hadn't expected it.

Jean gets out, into the sharp cold. November, and so far north. The light's on over the kitchen door: it's like, welcome to what? She picks her way through the high, frosty grass, then stops to look in the kitchen window; Mel's sitting at the table and Jean just wants to run to her. Yet at the same time, now that she knows Mel's safe, she wants to turn tail and not have to do this.

She opens the door and feels the heat of the stove on her face. A man in a police uniform stands up—skinny, shorter than Willis—and lays a fanned handful of cards facedown on the kitchen table. Mel's sitting with her back to the door. She twists around in her chair, still holding her cards, and looks at Jean with her just-about-to-cry look—wrinkles between her close-set eyebrows. Her face looks fresh-scrubbed. The policeman's belt is full of bullets, and he's got such a disproportionately big gun hanging off of him that it's hard to look at anything else. He sticks out a hand and says, "Mrs. Willis? Tony Petrosky." Not a handsome man: long chin, long flat nose, low forehead. Monkey man. She takes his hand: he's got a strong grip, but not crunching; he gives her hand a single squeeze before letting go. Then he flips his thumb at Mel. "Your daughter's a cardshark."

Mel blushes.

"She's good people, though." His voice sounds deeper than on the phone. The voice of a thin man with a big penis, which is an awful thing to think when he's done all this for them. For what*ever* reason. "The water's turned off in here," he says, "so she boiled some seltzer to make me a cup of tea. Hey, and she had *Sgt. Pepper's* with her. Kids still seem to go for it. My kids, same way. I got a fifteen-year-old and a ten-year-old. So you made pretty good time. How was it coming up?"

"Fine," says Jean. "But I worried about this one." She goes to Mel, who's still sitting at the table, puts an arm around her shoulders and pulls her close. First Mel stiffly allows it, then she puts both arms around her mother's hips. Jean strokes her hair. Mel takes her arms away.

"You two need a little time together," Petrosky says, and goes into the dining room.

Jean drops to her knees, grips Mel's upper arms and looks up into her face. Mel looks past her, toward the doorway. "I was so terrified for you," says Jean. "What were you *doing*?"

"Well, *you* weren't even *trying* to get Daddy back." Mel still won't look at her.

"Sweetheart, I've been trying everything I *know* to find Daddy."

"Yeah, right."

"Captain Petrosky's been helping, Aunt Carol and I went to see somebody *she* thought might be able to help, I've called everybody I could *think* of, the police have him in their computer that goes all over—*everything's* being done."

"Well, you didn't tell *us*. It was just like, big deal, Daddy's gone and nobody knows where he is and now shut up and be quiet."

"But I did tell you he wasn't *here*," says Jean. "Did you think I was lying to you? And anyway—" Okay, why not? "Apparently they found his truck in New York, honey."

"You mean he's in New *York*? And you *knew* that? Mother, I don't *believe* you didn't even—"

"Melanie." Jean puts up a hand. "I only found this out *yesterday*."

"Then why didn't you *tell* me yesterday, and then I . . . I *hate* you. You made me do this for *nothing*."

"I didn't make you do this," says Jean. "And you were very, very lucky it didn't turn into a very dangerous situation. Why would you *do* such a thing?"

Mel closes her eyes and clenches a fist.

"Look, this is stupid, okay? But I thought if I came here, then he would like *have* to be here, you know? Because I thought maybe he was like hiding or something when *you* came, but I thought that if *I* came, just by myself, it would *make* him be here. Because I just *thought*"—her shoulders start shaking—"that he would know and then he'd *have* to be here, to take care of *me*"—weeping now—"and then he'd come *back*."

Jean gathers her in, pulling her off the chair and onto the floor in her arms, a slow collapsing, Mel shaking inside her mother's embrace. But as close as she hugs Mel, she can't press love and rest into her. And in fact isn't this just needy craziness, wrestling your daughter down onto the floor? She strokes Mel's hair and says, "I love you so much," which only sounds like a confession of helplessness in all directions.

Mel breaks away and sits up, hugging her knees, head down so you see the no-colored part down the middle of her hair. Then she raises her head to look at Jean. "Mother, you can *not* tell *any*body."

"It's all right, honey." She touches Mel's knee. Mel twists out of reach.

"It's *not* all right," she says. "If you tell anybody, I'll *kill* you. I *will*, Mother. I will really stab you when you're asleep."

"I understand." Suddenly Jean has this revelation: that she's always been afraid of Mel. But she can't tell if it's a true revelation. "I have to say, though," she says, "it's not exactly a secret. You know, Erin was worried and told people at school—"

"But they don't know I was *stupid*. They just think I ran away from home or something."

"You're not stupid, sweetie," says Jean. "Believe me. Look, we're *all* suffering right now."

"Yeah, like Roger's really *suffering*."

"Roger's having a *very* hard time. He's just a little boy who doesn't understand what's happening to everything. And so he's acting out. Roger needs all the help *both* of us can give him."

Mel looks at the floor.

"Do you remember when he was a little baby?" says Jean. "You loved him so much." At least this is the family myth.

"Well, he's not a little baby anymore," Mel says. "He's nine years old, Mother."

"And don't you remember when *you* were nine?" Jean's knees and ankles are starting to hurt from hunkering down on the floor. "I know he can be a pain in the butt."

"I hate him. There's something really creepy about him."

"It's normal to feel that way, sometimes," says Jean. Willing it to be true. "But you know, when you're both grown up and have families of your—"

"Are you kidding? I would *never* have a family."

"Well," Jean says. "You may feel differently." Her big defense of their family. Of the human species in general.

"I *won't*."

"Okay. It's not anything you have to decide today, I guess." Jean's got to get up; this is really uncomfortable. "I just want you to know that I love you very very much and I'm so thankful that you're safe. Okay?" She stands up and stretches. "We should probably find Captain Petrosky. Do you like him?"

"He's okay." Mel doesn't even look up. "I guess he's pretty cool."

"Tell me something. Is there any of that seltzer left to make more tea? If you could get that started, I'll go see if I can find him. Did you have anything to eat today?"

Mel shrugs. "He took me to McDonald's. That's probably what *his* kids like. So I'm like sort of hungry, but not really?"

"Well, I'm *starving*. I haven't had anything since lunch." Lunch being a couple bites of a Fig Newton she bought on the way up, then chucked out the window. She reaches down to help Mel up. Which is a way of telling her to *get* up. "There's probably some soup here, or there might be a can of that vegetarian chili." Maybe in front of Mel and this policeman she'll be too embarrassed not to eat.

"Okay, I'll look." Mel stands up by herself, ignoring Jean's hand. "It's so weird up here."

"How so?"

Mel looks at her as if she can't believe she heard something so stupid, then trudges over and opens the cupboard next to the sink. Well, Mel's right: it wouldn't have killed her to admit this place is weird.

Jean starts up the stairs, and Petrosky calls, "In here." He's in Willis's study, sitting at the computer; the broken eyebrow window's blocked off with a pillow and the space heater's going. "Caught in the act," he says. "Once I get started on hearts, it's all over."

"Oh, I know," says Jean. Actually, she never plays computer stuff.

"I hope you don't mind, but I sort of poked around in the C drive a little," he says. "Does your husband deal in musical instruments? Sideline of his?"

"Does he *deal* in them? No. He sort of collects guitars, but he doesn't like buy and sell."

"Tell me what you make of this." Petrosky clicks the mouse, and Jean comes to look over his shoulder. She takes a forbidden glance down at his lap—just folds of fabric—then looks at the screen. (What's got into *her?*) He clicks on the list of documents, double-clicks on one called SALEBILL, and the screen fills with type. "Seventy-five hundred dollars," he says. "For one, two, three—five guitars. Plus an amplifier. I wouldn't have thought Mr. Castleman was the musical type."

Jean looks at the thing. "I have no idea." She feels like she has to sit down, but there's just the one chair.

"Did your husband actually own all these instruments?"

She looks down the list. Martin, Gibson, Rickenbacker . . . "Well— I'm not abso*lutely* sure, because I don't have the numbers anywhere, but yes. Those are all ones he had."

"Was your husband in any kind of trouble financially?"

"Just the usual. That *I* know of. Bills, payments. We were always sort of squeaking by, but we *were* squeaking by."

"He ever do drugs?"

"Oh please," says Jean.

"Hey, lots of people smoke a little dope once in a while; that's not so out of line. Guy your husband's age? I'd be more surprised if he didn't. Look, I used to party myself. And you know, frankly—I probably shouldn't say this, but our line of work, we see much worse things around alcohol. Drunk drivers, spousal abuse. That's just my opinion."

"No, he *never* did drugs," Jean says. "I mean, as a *kid*, yes. You know, a student. And I guess after that. But I never knew him to *ever* do anything. He told me he stopped smoking pot because it made him paranoid."

"He use cocaine?"

"I'm sure he *tried* it. But we're talking about years ago." Jean sits down on the floor and hugs her knees.

"See, the reason I ask," says Petrosky, "we naturally pulled up information on your husband, and one of the things, of course, that we came across was the incident that you're familiar with, which your husband was taken into custody? Now, anybody can lose their temper and get into an altercation. But by the same token, it *can* also be part of the profile for substance abuse. So times being what they are, it's something we have to look at." He half turns in the chair, and Jean sneaks another glance as he tugs at the knees of his pants to make the sharp creases hang straight.

"I have to say that was *not* all his fault," she says. "I mean, I was there—and yes, he *was* wrong, but—"

Petrosky holds up a hand. "I'm not trying to judge it. All I'm saying, it's just a thing that struck our attention as being out of the usual. But the other thing that—"

"Mo-*ther*?" Mel, calling from the foot of the stairs.

"We're up here. In Daddy's study."

"Everything's *ready*."

"Okay, be down in just a minute."

"She's something," Petrosky says, shaking his head. "This hasn't been easy on her, I can see that. But she's got an awful good heart."

"I like to think so," says Jean. "This thing today scared me to death, though."

Petrosky nods. "Tell me something. How, exactly, did your husband come to have dealings with Mr. Castleman?"

"Oh, God," says Jean. "I don't really know. Except that, you know, he lives so close. My husband bought firewood from him."

"I take it he's not your kind of guy."

"No, I don't like him."

Petrosky picks up a perforated side strip torn from computer paper and holds it up with both hands, as if examining a piece of movie film. "Let me try to show you what this looks like when *we* look at it. Here's Mr. Castleman. Known drug person, *would* have gone to prison—I don't know if you know that story."

"Enough of it."

"Okay, and here's Mr. Reed, who defends half the drug cases in central Vermont." He fusses again with his pants leg. "And then here's your husband. Knows them both. Travels back and forth regularly between here and New York City, raises a large sum of money selling off his collection of musical instruments—to Mr. Castleman, of all people—shows a history of erratic behav—"

"Wait. Since when is one thing a *history*?"

"Hey," says Petrosky. "All I'm telling you, this is the profile people would see. I'm not one of your husband's intimates." He picks up a Sucrets box from the desktop and takes out a foil-wrapped lozenge.

"His *intimates*?" Jean says. "That's like really a sick joke."

He looks at her. "Okay, whatever word you want to describe," he says. "But you start to wonder." He examines both sides of the Sucret, puts it back and closes the lid. "Especially when this person suddenly disappears from the face of the earth." The bill of sale vanishes, and I CAN'T GO ON I'LL GO ON begins crawling across the screen from right to left. The change in the light makes Petrosky look back at the screen. He watches the words crawl, then nudges the mouse on its pad, and the bill of sale reappears. "That's what a lot of this job *is*," he says. "You wonder about things and you talk to people. For example. Who's been bringing all this cocaine into the Rutland area for the past six, nine months? Or here's another thing. Why did Mr. Castleman fly to L.A. last week? Picture *him* in California?"

"I don't get any of this," Jean says. "I can't *imagine* Willis was into any sort of drug thing. But you know, I lost track of him." Petrosky's rolling the strip of paper up like a party noisemaker. "I guess I'm not one of his *intimates*."

Petrosky puts the coil down on the corner of the desk; Jean watches it expand.

"Mother?" Mel, from downstairs. "It's getting *cold*."

"I'll be right down," Jean calls.

Petrosky stands up. "Sounds like we got our marching orders." You'd swear his smile is real. "Tell me something. Were you planning to get that roofing work finished before snow flies? It'd be a good idea."

"I don't know *what* he was planning." Jean gets to her feet, then has to sit: roaring in her ears, black butterflies before her eyes. The chair's still warm from him.

"You all right?" Petrosky sounds far away.

Jean takes a breath, lets it out. "I think I must be hungry."

"Need a hand?"

She reaches up; he grasps her hand—his skin feels rough and hard—and lets her pull down to get herself up.

"Thank you." She braces her palm against the doorframe. She breathes. She starts downstairs; he pushes the chair in and follows. His eyes on her ass, she feels like.

They stop in the kitchen doorway.

Mel has set three places at the table: three spoons on three folded paper towels, three mugs with tea bag tags dangling down the sides, three bowls of steaming soup. A leftover inch of white candle flaming. "Oh sweetheart, thank you," says Jean. "It's *beaut*iful."

"You can sit here if you want," Mel says to Petrosky, pulling out the middle chair.

"Hey, this looks terrific." The gun bobs at his side as he walks over and sits down.

"Me here?" says Jean. She's stupidly worried about that beltful of bullets so close to a lighted candle.

"It doesn't matter," Mel says.

"This was so nice of you, sweetie."

"O-kay, Mother." What it is, Mel must not want it to seem that this is unusual for her to do. Jean sits, and Mel brings a saucepan from the stove and pours hot water—seltzer, actually, with the bubbles boiled away—into their mugs.

"Thank you," says Petrosky.

"You're welcome."

"Thank you," says Jean.

"Welcome."

Mel puts the saucepan back on the stove and sits down across from Jean.

"Good soup," says Petrosky.

"Delicious," says Jean. Campbell's minestrone. "I was so hungry. How's yours?"

Mel shrugs. "It's the same *soup*, Mother." She looks down at her bowl, picks up her spoon, tastes. Remembers and puts the paper towel in her lap.

"You know, I don't think we ever heard the other side of *Sgt. Pepper's*," Petrosky says.

"My mom's not real into the Beatles," says Mel.

"*I* don't mind the Beatles," Jean says.

Mel shrugs again. "I don't really feel like it. Does anybody want any crackers? I found some saltines that're a little stale, but I can put them in the toaster oven."

"No, I'm fine," says Petrosky. "This hits the spot."

"No, thanks, dear," Jean says.

Mel takes another spoonful of soup. "It's weird to think of Daddy up here eating saltines."

"Why is that weird?" says Jean.

"It just is."

Jean lifts her tea bag out, lets it back down. "It is, sort of."

"*You* don't know." Mel bangs her spoon down and stalks into the dining room. Jean looks at Petrosky, who's looking down at his bowl.

"I don't think me being here makes it any easier," he says. He lifts the bowl to his mouth, tips it back and sets it down empty.

"It's not you," says Jean. She hears Mel clomping up the stairs. "Listen, I can't thank you enough for bringing her and taking care of her. She obviously likes you." She can't keep that from sounding like an accusation.

"In a way, I'm more sorry for her father than I am for her," Petrosky says. "What he's missing out on."

"I'm not," says Jean. "But that's nice of you to say. Especially considering her behavior." She lifts the tea bag again; there's no place to put it. She drops it into her soup.

"Oh, I don't mind a little behavior." He gets up and takes his bowl and spoon to the sink. "You weren't planning on driving back tonight, were you?"

"She has to be in school tomorrow," Jean says. "I have to be at work."

"Tomorrow's Saturday."

"It *is*? God, it *is*, isn't it." Jean feels her legs just aching, like a buzzing in the bones. She takes a long gulp of tea and shakes her head. "We need to get home, though."

"Just so you get there in one piece." Petrosky comes and sits down again. "I were you, I'd get some sleep and go down in the morning."

"You're *not* me," says Jean. "You're not my *husband*, you're not my *father*—"

He holds up a hand and says, "Okay. Enough said. You do what you think best."

"Sorry. I shouldn't open up on *you*. I just really need to get out of here, and get *her* out of here, and get *home*, you know? Plus my son just—"

He puts up the hand again. "Your decision."

Jean closes her eyes. She opens them and stares at the flame of that little stub of candle.

"Looks like you've had it with your soup," he says.

"I guess so." She only ate a couple of spoonfuls, and now she's getting these stabbing cramps. She's still gazing at that candle flame. "Do you remember E. Gordon Liddy?" she says.

"Hey, Watergate. But I thought it was G. Gordon."

"I'm sure you must know," she says.

That makes him look at her.

"The thing I remember," she says, "he supposedly held his finger over a lighted candle." She starts switching her index finger back and forth through the flame. "And they asked him what the secret was, and he said, *The secret is not to mind*." Back and forth with her finger, her gaze fixed on the flame. "I always thought that was amazing," she says. "Am I scaring you?"

"No. Are you scaring yourself?"

"No." She looks him in the eyes, still switching her finger through the flame.

He lowers his eyes and stands up. "Let's get your house shut down so you can be on your way."

"Oh my *God*," says Jean. She blows the candle out. "Shit. Captain Petrosky, I am *so* sorry—I'm just completely *raw*. I really need to get some rest, and I need this thing to be *over*. I don't want you to think I'm some crazy-woman."

"Well. This isn't the easiest circumstances, I don't imagine."

She gets up—her legs are *killing* her—and brings her bowl and Mel's over to the sink. Where she can't wash dishes. "Crap," she says. "What am I going to do with this soup?"

"Do exactly whatever you want," he says.

"Look, I said I was sorry. God. Scenes from a marriage."

Petrosky actually laughs. "Tell me about it," he says. "I been there too. Once or twice. Why don't you just pitch it out the door."

"I'm afraid it'll bring raccoons," Jean says.

"Probably," he says. "So who cares?"

13

In her dream, she and the kids are driving somewhere, except the inside of the Cherokee is their living room. And Mel comes in holding her eye in the palm of her hand and Jean's frantically trying to put it back, but it's a rule in the dream that once you take your eye out you can never get it in again. She wakes up in bed in Chesterton, confused about whether or not that's a rule in life too. Her lower back hurts.

She closes her eyes again and listens. No birds this time of year, and no lawn mowers; but there's still the swish and hum of traffic, dogs barking, kids yelling. Roger: she's got to deal with *that*, first thing. She was so whipped when they got in last night, she forgot to look at Carol's truck. She has to get up.

When she opens the bedroom door, she hears music coming from Mel's room and different music downstairs; maybe the tv too. She fights off the idea that all this is a turned-way-down version of what you'd hear in hell. She goes into the bathroom and washes her face with cold water, which supposedly tightens the skin. Right, for about five seconds. The hamper's almost up to the top again already. So three guesses what she'll be doing today. She sneaks a glance in the mirror: pale, lines, raccoon eyes. What else is new.

Coming down the stairs, she can tell that what she's hearing is cartoons (*Wheep! Boinnng!*) plus Alan Jackson from Carol's boombox, the song about how he's going to buy him a Mercury and cruise it up and down the road. Rathbone slithers out of Carol's room, wagging his tail in greeting. She pets him, tells him *Good dog*, then peeks into the living room: Roger's belly-flopped on the floor, chin resting on commandeered sofa cushions, gazing at the screen. She'll have to pry him away, force him back into life, before the big showdown can even begin. She needs some coffee first. It looks like a nice day out: through the dining-room window she sees sun glinting off the good old sturdy Cherokee, which got them home safe and sound. Its front end seems to be giving a big loyal toothy smile.

Carol appears in her doorway, hugging a carton whose top flaps are folded shut in that interlocking way where you don't need tape. "Hi. I thought you were still asleep." She takes the box into the kitchen and sets it on the counter. Jean follows her in, and she turns around. "I was going to say something last night—actually, I *was* going to say something the night before, but I just thought it was, you know, too much convergence."

"Oh," Jean says. She sits down at the table.

Carol pulls up a chair next to her. "I feel like I'm leaving you in the lurch," she says. "But I also feel like it's a perfect time for you guys, in a way, because you're sort of at the beginning of something. Where I am in *my* life, though . . . You know, ever since the leaves started changing, I felt like—okay, it's beautiful, but it was also telling me that I didn't *belong* back here anymore? And of course Dexter's out there, not that he . . . you know." She shakes her head. "And I think it's also just that the *land* out there is still young. In terms of geology? Whereas here it's real old? I mean, the earthquakes are the downside, but out there it's like it's still in process. Like the mountains are really sharp"—making a mountain crest with her fingertips—"where here the hills are just, like, waiting for the rain and everything to grind them down the rest of the way."

Jean has nothing to say on the subject of geology. "Do *they* know?" she says, nodding toward the doorway.

"I told Roger last night. And then when Mel came down to get her juice this morning, I couldn't exactly hide the fact that I was carting boxes."

Jean looks into the living room and sees only Roger's sneakers, one toe kicking in rhythm into the carpet. *Wheep! Boinnng!* Alan Jackson's gone off, but the cartoon noise is loud enough so he won't overhear. "I don't know what to do about him," she says.

"Oh listen, I've been meaning to *tell* you," Carol says. "I went and looked up swastikas—you know how you think you remember something?—and sure enough, the swastika is like this really ancient symbol of good luck. All *Hitler* did was just ruin it for everybody. They say in this book that it started out as being the sun, with rays whirling around?" She windmills her hand. "I mean, it's not like Roger consciously *knew* about this, which he obviously didn't, but I think something really really *old* could have actually, you know, taken control of his hand."

"Maybe something old should take control of *my* hand," says Jean, "and give him an old-fashioned spanking, which is what he probably needs."

"You're kidding, right? You don't *spank*?"

"No," Jean says. "I don't do *anything*. Obviously. I'm never even *here*."

"I know, I feel that same thing," says Carol. "Just the need to be in the place you're supposed to be. I really think I had to come back to the East Coast again and do this whole process to sort of get clear about it."

"Right," says Jean. She gets up, takes a glass down from the cabinet and opens the refrigerator. No orange juice. She pours a glass of seltzer.

"Did you get enough sleep?" Carol says.

"I'm okay. Listen, I have to give you money to get that thing fixed. You can't be driving around with a swastika on your door." She takes a burning sip of seltzer and sits down at the table again.

Carol laughs. "You don't think I'm *that* nuts, do you? Look, I totally know what the boundaries are. Last night Roger and I took some of your big brown wrapping paper and painted a sun with poster paints—you know, since it really *is* a sun—and we duct-taped it right over the thing. That should hold until I can get out to McCall."

"Wait, you're going to *Idaho*? I thought you were going back to Anacortes."

"Well . . . eventually." Carol gets up and walks to the end of the counter by the phone. "But I thought I might as well go by way of Idaho because there's this amazing body shop in McCall." She takes a pen out of the jelly glass Jean keeps full of pens, tests against her palm to see if it writes and brings it over to label the carton. "When Gid rolled his army truck that time—I told you about that."

"Doesn't ring a bell," Jean says.

"Wow, I never told you that story? See, these biker guys—I don't know, I guess that should be for another time. Anyway, the point is, the people at this shop towed the thing in, banged out all the dents, matched the camouflage *perfectly*, and you know what the bill was? Seventy-five dollars. I could never get over that."

She writes MISC on a flap of the carton and puts the pen behind her ear. Then she sits down cross-legged on the crappy old linoleum floor that was never high on Willis's list of priorities.

"But you lived there such a long time ago. How do you know they're even in business anymore?"

"It's worth a try," Carol says. She looks down at the floor, smiles. "*Everything* doesn't change. I mean, it does, but . . ." She shrugs. "Actually, I thought I might hang out there for a while. There was a long time when I never wanted to go back there, but it seems like now it might be a good thing for me. Anyhow, the woman who's renting my house is supposed to have it until April." She takes the pen from behind her ear and examines it.

"So in other words, you don't even know where you're *staying*? Carol. You're surely not—"

"Good *God* no. Gid's not even there anymore. He went back to Stone Mountain. Stone Mattin, Joe-ja. I thought I told you. Staying with his sister and her family, going to meetings every day. It's like everybody's suddenly going home now, back to their old hometowns and everything."

"So why aren't you hotfooting it down to Bethesda?"

"Oh *puke*," says Carol. "God, do you remember the Robertses? When we all used to have to go over and listen to Mr. Roberts play the Hammond organ?"

Jean laughs. "Right, and they'd serve us ginger ale with those ivory-colored plastic coasters? I can even remember how it *smelled* in there."

"I can too! *Amazing*. I think it was mothballs. You remember he used to play 'Charmaine'?" Carol ripples her fingers in midair, one hand higher than the other. Jean puts her hands over her ears. " 'Charmaine,' 'Jeannine, I Dream of Lilac Time'—boy, he knew 'em all. Yikes. And meanwhile Daddy's getting ripped on Manhattans."

"Right," Jean says. "It didn't dawn on me until years later that he hated the Robertses."

"Are you kidding me? Even when he'd call Mr. Roberts a genius? You know, in that tone of voice? I would like *cringe*."

Jean shrugs. "I remember him giving us his cherries."

"Uh-huh," says Carol, "and after he'd given us like three or something, Mom would be like, *Joe? Sweetie, I really don't think*—I don't know, that was *their* dance, I guess."

"Hey, how bad could he have been, right? Since we both ended up marrying him."

"You always say that," Carol says. "*I* thought I was marrying Clint Walker."

"Well if Bethesda's out, where *is* our spiritual home?" Jean gets up from the table to sit beside Carol on the cold, cracked linoleum. Carol nudges a little closer. "Maybe Disney World," says Jean. "There's no litter, they take care of everything . . ." She can't think of a third thing to round out the joke. From the living room she hears tinny voices singing: *The crankiest of creatures in the whole wide world / Our next cartoon features Slappy the Squirrel!*

She's never sat on the kitchen floor before; the ceiling seems a long way up. Then she looks down at Carol's hands, the knuckles getting so big, the skin dry and stretched tight. Carol's going to be forty-eight. "What'll you do about Thanksgiving if you're in McCall?"

"Save a turkey," says Carol.

"We're going to miss you so much."

"Oh listen, just being with you guys, and the fact that it happened to time out so perfectly . . . I don't know, we think differently about stuff like this." Carol strokes Jean's hair, just once. "I know you're afraid that you're going to just be lost if I'm not here to help. I feel like it's the opposite, that you're going to be found."

"I hope you're right." Jean looks down at the poor old linoleum. "I wish I had feelings in *any* direction."

"You have them, believe me. You just have to learn to locate them, and listen to them."

"Right," says Jean. "That'll be something I can work on. In my spare time." She gets to her feet; her back's still aching. From the living room, mad cartoon xylophone music. She stretches, hands clasped and arms reaching for the ceiling, and it feels as if she's letting air in through the spaces between her ribs. She lowers her arms, breathes out. "Okay. So what can I do? Can I help you with anything?"

"I think I've got it pretty much under control." Carol *bounces* up off the floor: probably all that yoga. "Actually, one thing: you wouldn't have a couple of bungee cords I could take? I'll give you the money to replace them."

"There's an old expression for this," Jean says. "It's called *buying*? No, you cannot *buy* bungee cords from me. I'll be happy to *give* you some."

"Thanks," says Carol. "I guess I still need to work on being able to ask for things." She picks up the carton and starts for the door.

"Ah, but who can say how the cosmic wheel may turn?" What's the idea? That if she won't let Carol leave on a pleasant note, then Carol can't leave? She puts on her gray sweatshirt, gets her keys and goes out to the Cherokee.

In the thing between the front seats, Jean finds two bungee cords she's been meaning to use to hold down the lids on the garbage cans and hopefully keep raccoons out. Carol, in just jeans and t-shirt, is up on the back of her truck with boxes, suitcases and her bicycle, dragging her giant duffel bag into one corner and wedging it in with a suitcase.

"So the bad news is," says Carol, "I have to bring all this junk into the motel every night and load it again in the morning." She pushes a box over against the suitcase and straightens up. "The good news, I was able to get reservations for Motel 6 the whole way. It's going to be like Cleveland, Iowa City, Cheyenne, Boise. Unless I decide to skip Boise and just boogie on up to McCall."

"Aren't those pretty long stretches?" Jean says.

"They'll keep the light on for me. I see one of those?" Jean hands her the bungee with red, black and yellow markings, like a coral snake; Carol passes it through the back wheel of her bicycle and the handles of the duffel bag and hooks the ends to the turnbuckles attached to the truck body. "I take just one more?" Jean gives her the green-and-white one, which Carol threads through the bicycle's front wheel, around the crossbar and through the handle of the suitcase. Then she puts both thumbs up and says "Bingo," vaults out of the truck, wipes her hands on her jeans and hugs herself. "I am *freezing*. I've got to toughen up again if I'm going to hack it in Idaho. So did you see our thing?"

"What thing?" says Jean. "Oh. No."

On the driver's-side door, in a frame of gray duct tape, a round yellow sun with a yellow fringe of rays and a red smiley-face, painted on brown paper; underneath, in purple letters too crude to be Carol's, the word NAMARIË. He's even copied the little things over the E.

"*Na-mar-ee-ay*, right?" says Carol. "Not *Na-mar-ee*?"

"I would guess," Jean says.

"Good. Not that anybody's probably going to ask."

Back in the house, Jean puts on water, then goes into the living room. Roger's still on the floor, watching a cartoon girl have a temper tantrum—*You never like my friends!*—and mutate first into a monster, then into a nuclear explosion. What in God's name? Jean takes five twenties out of her wallet (leaving a ten and two singles) and comes back into the kitchen where Carol's sitting at the table, trying to do her trick of balancing the salt shaker on edge. Five of eleven. She's planning to hit

Cleveland tonight? Not possible. "When were you thinking of starting?"
Jean says.

"A while ago, actually. But if I go now I'll be in okay shape."

"You know, you could do one thing for me."

"Sure."

"I want you to take—"

"No," says Carol. "No way."

"—to take this and use it to buy yourself one extra day for your trip.
One more motel, one more day of meals. Okay?"

"It's a sweet thought, but—"

"I want you to check your map and figure out more humane stops
for yourself so you're not driving eighteen hours a day."

"Oh come on, it's not—"

"Then call Motel 6 and get them to redo your reservations. There's
the phone. They shouldn't even allow you to *make* those kind of reservations. You know, you're not some *trucker*."

"I *always* do coast to coast in five days," says Carol. "This is four
days just to get to *Boise*. Please don't turn this into a money thing."

"It's not a money thing," Jean says. "I just want you to be safe and
not wear yourself out. If you *don't* take it, I'm going to burn it. Right in
the burner." She points to the stove.

"I can't. I'd feel too weird."

Jean moves the kettle off the burner and dangles a twenty above the
blue flame. "Going . . . going—"

"You wouldn't really," says Carol.

"Gone." When the edge of the bill catches, Jean drops it, flaming,
onto the stovetop. Carol jumps up from the table. "You're down to
eighty," Jean says. "That was the good bottle of wine you were going to
have with dinner." She holds up another twenty. "Going . . ."

"Okay, okay," says Carol, grabbing at it. "*God*. Everybody thinks
I'm the crazy sister."

"And you're not giving this away to the homeless, right?" Jean puts
the money behind her back.

"I *am* the homeless," Carol says. "Please." She stretches her hand
toward Jean.

"*That's* what we like to hear." Jean lays the four twenties on Carol's
palm.

"Good God." Carol sticks them in the pocket of her jeans. "Let me
out of here."

"I was thinking," Jean says, "maybe we should follow you over to the pancake place and have like a farewell brunch? You know, *some* kind of ceremony."

"Too sad," says Carol. "I think I should probably just say goodbye to Mel and Roger and then boogie."

Jean stupidly says, "But I have water on for coffee."

"I shouldn't," Carol says. "You know that saying, miles to go before I sleep."

"Right," says Jean.

"You're going to be fine," Carol says. "What is *this*?" She takes the pen from behind her ear. "I *thought* I felt something. Is this yours or mine?" She answers herself with a shrug. "Who cares, right?" She lays it on the counter.

Jean takes her sister's knobby hand. Rough and dry like a man's, but thin, light. "You're going to be fine too." She snorts. "God, listen to us: *Fine fine fine.*" Draws a long breath, lets it out. "So. I guess we can't string this out any longer."

14

They watch Carol's truck turn the corner and disappear behind the house where the people have the black Grand Cherokee; then they hustle back in out of the cold, Jean still holding Rathbone by the collar. Mel and Roger go straight upstairs—which in a way is good, because she needs a few minutes. Though she's absolutely got to talk to him this morning. She spoons coffee into the filter paper and pours the water over it, then pops a couple of Advils to nuke her headache. She gets the JOE mug down. While the coffee's dripping she might as well go up and get that load of laundry.

Down in the basement, she settles in the good old armchair—five minutes, no more—rests her coffee on the broad upholstered arm and picks up *The Father Hunt*. The washing machine starts its steady sloshing, like a mother's heartbeat in the womb. She's thinking how much she likes this little thing where Archie says, *I wish I knew if you would really be interested in what we did during the next forty-eight hours,* like he's flirting with you almost, when the phone rings and she jumps up—of *course* knocking the stupid coffee over and smashing the mug on the cement floor. *Crap.* She charges up the steps to the kitchen, snatches the phone off the wall and pants "Hello?" just as she hears Mel say "Hello?" on the upstairs extension.

"Hi, *Melanie?*" *Fucking* Erin Miller.

"I've *got* it, Mother," Mel calls.

Jean hangs up, takes a couple of deep breaths—in fairness, Erin did do the responsible thing yesterday—then gets down the green mug. Which she's never liked, so it's certain never to break. She pours more coffee and goes back down to the basement. She gathers the broken pieces of the JOE mug, lifts the lid to stop the washer, extracts a sopping towel, mops up the coffee spill and throws the towel back in. In the pile of pieces she sees a shark fin of china with the O intact. If she were still an artist . . . But it would be obvious and stupid.

Which reminds her: she has to look for another job.

How long does she have? That wasn't made clear, was it? Or did she block out that part? So she'll have to update her résumé. Right, and send it where? Well, not a good day to think about this. God, the mortgage alone is like eighteen hundred dollars. Car's another four, mortgage on Preston Falls probably *another* four, so that's twenty-six. Commuter ticket, hundred and sixty, plus the usual bills—with winter coming, they're going to get socked for fuel oil. God, plus food. Clothes. Her take-home for the month is twenty-three. Less than twenty-three. Twenty-two and change. Amazingly good money, she'd always heard, for an art-school person.

Okay. We're not going to think about it today. God *damn* Doug Willis.

She picks up *The Father Hunt* and really does her best to zero in on it again and keep her thoughts off. *I wish I knew if you would really be interested in what we . . .* She tries picturing black blinders at her temples, like on a horse. No, no good. Anyhow, she's got to deal with Roger.

He's lying on his side on the floor of his room, his collection of Pogs before him in tall stacks like a miser's horde. He likes the ones that have cloaked-and-hooded skeletons, their skulls with vampire fangs. She should never have gone along with Willis's judgment that this was normal boy stuff. Or Roger's way of working through fears. Or whatever overintellectualized thing he'd come up with to avoid really looking at it, though in fairness she does the same thing.

"Hi," she says, kneeling beside him.

"What?" Not looking at her, he takes a Pog from a shorter stack and gingerly lowers it with his fingertips onto the top of an already taller stack.

"Aunt Carol showed me the sun you guys made. You did a really good job."

Roger shrugs. "It was her idea." He picks up a Pog: a silver skull with a red and green yin-yang on its forehead.

"So have you thought about what I asked you?" says Jean. "About why you scratched that thing on her truck?"

"No."

"Then I'd like you to think about it right now." And how's she going to enforce *this*—march into his little head?

Seconds go by.

"Okay, I thought about it," Roger says.

"And?"

He shrugs and reaches for another Pog.

"Were you angry at her?" says Jean.

Shrug.

"Angry at me?"

Shrug. This Pog is identical to the other. He holds one up in each hand between thumb and forefinger and brings first one and then the other nearer and farther away.

"Angry at Daddy?"

"I don't know. He's probably dead or something."

"Do you wish he was?" She's really asking a nine-year-old this, about his father? "People sometimes wish that when they're really angry at somebody. It's a normal thing to wish that. It doesn't mean you're bad."

Tiny shrug: a twitch of the shoulders, really.

"I just want you to know that it's okay to be angry."

"I'm *not*," he says. "You always make everything a big deal." With a backhand swipe, he levels all the stacks.

This is going just as brilliantly as she'd thought. But now that she's started, there's no avoiding the rest.

"Do you know what that thing means?" she says. "That you scratched on Aunt Carol's truck? The swastika?"

"Yeah. The sun."

"But that's not what you thought it was when you did it."

Roger says nothing.

"So what did you think it was?"

"I don't know—a Nazi sign."

"And do you know what the Nazis were?"

"Yeah, Germans."

"Do you know what they did?"

Roger shrugs. "I don't know, killed people and stuff."

"Do you know how many?"

"Yeah, six million."

"Did you know that the people they killed were people like the Levys next door? Or like your friend Sam? Or Jason?"

"Yeah, I know."

"Well, then I guess I don't get it," says Jean. "You don't hate Sam or Jason." She doesn't dare make this a question. "You knew that what you were doing was wrong."

Silence. It's hurting her back to kneel like this.

"Can I tell you what it sounds like to me? It sounds to me almost like you were asking to be punished for something." She's tiptoeing around the idea that he might be blaming himself for Willis's being gone. But if he isn't, she doesn't want to put it in his head.

Silence.

"What do you think an appropriate punishment would *be* for something like this?" she says. She pauses, just in case, then goes on. "If you were older, I'd have you pay Aunt Carol for the damage you did. Even if they can just repaint the door by itself, I imagine it's going to be at least a couple hundred dollars. Do you know how long it would take you to pay back two hundred dollars out of your allowance?"

"Yeah, two hundred weeks."

"Yes, about four years," she says. "So I don't think it would be very helpful to give you a punishment that would still be going on when you're thirteen, for something you did when you were nine."

"It's *less* than four years," says Roger.

Jean closes her eyes: two hundred weeks, and one year is—he's right. "You'd still be thirteen," she says.

Roger says nothing.

"Okay, here's what's going to happen," she says, totally winging it. What *is* going to happen? She fixes on the scattered Pogs. "I'm going to have to pay for repainting Aunt Carol's truck, and that means I'll have to do without some things. So you're going to have to give up something too. We're going to say your Pogs are worth a dollar apiece, okay? So you're going to give up two hundred of them."

"But I only *have*—"

"You're old enough to know that the things you do have consequences," she says.

"But if I'm good I get them back, right?"

"I need to think about that." The lesson, at its purest, should be that gone is gone. Or is this just stupidly punitive? The whole thing is so artificial: why shouldn't the loss be artificial as well? "I'm not going to answer that now," she says. "I want you to count out two hundred of these."

Roger rolls over onto his stomach in defeat. "Can I pick which *ones*?"

"As long as it's two hundred," she says, getting up and digging in her thumbs to massage her lower back. "And I expect them to be in the bottom drawer of my dresser before you come downstairs."

Down in the living room, she finds Mel sitting cross-legged on the sofa with the road atlas on her lap, open to New Hampshire/Vermont. Jean decides to think she's just looking at where she was yesterday and not cooking up her next escapade.

"Mom, can I go over to Erin's?"

"We need to talk about some things first."

"Like what?"

"Like whether or not you're grounded."

Mel's mouth comes open, theatrically. "*Why*-y?"

Jean drops her own jaw open, in mean-spirited imitation. "Why? Because you skipped school, you stole my credit card, you could have gotten yourself into—by the way, may I have my card back?"

Mel bends forward to reach in the hip pocket of her too-snug Levi's; when she straightens up, Jean sees she's begun to cry. She hands her mother the MasterCard.

"I'm not mad at you, sweetheart. I just want to make really sure that you would never, ever, do anything like this again. No matter *how* upset you are. Right?"

Mel looks down, shoulders shaking.

"Promise me," says Jean.

Mel gets out an *Okay*. Jean listens to the sobbing to assess its sincerity, as if homing in on an instrument somewhere in an orchestra to hear if it's an oboe or an English horn.

When she subsides, Jean says, "I'm not going to ground you." Like Mel's usually allowed this wild social life. "The only thing, as far as going over to Erin's, I think today I'd just rather have you home. I haven't really seen you or Roger for—"

"You *saw* me all *yes*terday, Mother." Mel's back to normal. Too quickly: she's devalued her weeping.

"You know what I mean. I'd like us to be together."

"Oh great."

"If Erin would like to come over *here* later—"

"She doesn't want to," says Mel. "Our house is cruddy, and there's nothing to do."

"Is that what she said?"

"No, but that's what she thinks."

"So what *did* she say, exactly?"

"That her and her mom had to go somewhere."

"That doesn't sound quite the same to me as saying she didn't want to come here," Jean says. "Are you getting hungry? We haven't had any lunch."

"Sort of."

"So why don't I go put the clothes in the dryer and then fix us some lunch. And maybe try to get Roger involved in a game of Monopoly or something."

"I don't feel like Monopoly," says Mel. "I don't know, maybe."

It turns out to be the first right move of the day. Of the *week*. Roger lets himself be lured down, and as they play, they eat peanut-butter-and-bacon sandwiches—peanut butter and banana for Mel—and listen to the Beatles. It's so odd that a terrifying song like "I Am the Walrus" has become kid-friendly. Roger buys Park Place and Boardwalk but passes up chances to get other stuff so he can save for a hotel. Two Beatles CDs go by before Mel begins fidgeting and Roger starts getting up to do things between turns. When Jean suspends the game—to be continued tonight—they protest, but they clearly need a break. And she needs to put in the storm windows, to stop these cold drafts.

The downstairs windows are easy: push the screens up, pull the glass down. She takes the screens out of the combination doors, carries them out to the garage, brings the glass inserts back and sticks them in. The upstairs windows, though, take the old-fashioned wooden storm sash. Does she really dare do this? She gets the aluminum extension ladder from the garage, leans it against the house and climbs up to scope out the situation. Looks like all you have to do is hang the storm sash from those hooks above the windows, push them into place and turn the little things at the sides to secure them. She goes back out to the garage for the first one. Thank God they're not huge—you can bring them up the ladder one-handed while holding on with the other hand. And there's only six of them.

When she comes back inside, her face feeling aglow from being out in the cold, fresh air, she calls upstairs to ask who's ready to go on with the game. Roger yes; Mel no, then yes. Soon Jean's having to mortgage her cheapo properties. She nicknames Roger "Roger the Ruthless," and he goes *Heh-heh-heh*. For all the world like a nine-year-old. Mel's bored but indulgent.

When Jean thinks to look, it's dark outside. She remembers they need milk and God knows what else, so she asks Mel to play for her and goes into the kitchen to make a list. Actually, Carol left them pretty well stocked. Okay, milk, orange juice, maybe Rice Krispies, since even Mel won't eat shredded wheat. They've got bread for toast, but English muffins would be a nice change. It might be good just to have something light for supper. Soup and toasted English muffins. Cut up an apple. She puts on her jacket and asks if anybody wants to ride along to 7-Eleven; no takers. Roger says she's just won second prize in a beauty contest, collect ten dollars; this cracks him up.

She uses the pay phone outside the 7-Eleven to give Champ another try, feeling like a straying wife inventing an errand so she can call her lover. But she thought she should tell him they found Willis's truck, at least that's her excuse, and the kids don't need to know about every hopeless phone call. Champ hasn't heard a word. Not a peep. Would've called if he had—well, hell, she knows that. Weird about the truck. But shit, it's *all* weird. What can he say?

Heading home with their little bag of groceries, Jean turns the corner and pulls over to look down the block at their house. Lights cheerily on, orange pumpkin bag bulging with dead leaves. It could be any family's house. For a second she pretends that she has no connection to any of this. The thought creeps her out. She could just drive by that house and keep going.

FOUR

1

Champ hangs up the phone and says, "You are a sick, sick pup."

"Yeah, okay," Willis says. "No argument." He's sitting in the plump, onion-smelling Salvation Army easy chair in Champ's kitchen, sunk with his ass lower than his knees because the springs are shot to shit; his index finger's clamped in a book called *Oswald Talked* that Champ says blows Gerald Posner out of the water.

"And I'm a sick pup," says Champ, "for going along with this shit."

"Okay. Point taken. But what did she say exactly?"

"Well, I can't like paraphrase it word for *word*," Champ says. "They towed your truck off of Houston Street—she thought I better have *that* information. Look, you have *got* to straighten this shit out. You know what I'm saying?"

"I will. I'm *going* to."

"Yeah, like when? Because I'm not *doin'* this shit anymore, okay? The last fuckin' time I'm going to like lie to your *wife*."

"When did you lie before?"

"I didn't," says Champ. "That's the fuckin' point. She calls the first time and I'm like, *Nope, nope, not a word, haven't heard shit*, you know, which I hadn't."

"Okay, so you're telling her the same thing now."

"Yeah, right, except *now*—you want a cold one, by the way? You know for *one* thing, Tina's going to fuckin' kill me, out of fuckin' female solidarity." He opens the refrigerator and holds up a Budweiser tallboy. "Yes? No? Might take the edge off of shit."

"What a concept," says Willis. "Yeah. Please." He takes his finger out of the book and looks some more at the picture of Oswald with his white undershirt and his I'm-a-patsy stare, posed between two thug cops in dark uniforms. One's a fat old potato-shaped fuck with sergeant's stripes, the other a young brush-cut Nazi like the early George Jones, glaring at Oswald as if he really *was* the piece of shit who shot the President.

"Okay, just to put this at its crudest level," says Champ, "you must be tired of spanking the monkey." Willis's arm gives a jerk—something icy. "Here." Champ's handing him the tallboy.

"I don't know," Willis says. "Shit, what does that even mean, *tired of?*" Fact is, he loses focus and the Unnamable won't stay stiff. For months now. This really *could* be clinical depression. He takes the first sip, supposedly the best.

"Oh, phi*lo*sophy," says Champ. "Great, let's do *that* for a while." He takes out a tallboy for himself, sits down at the kitchen table and pops it. "You're welcome," he says. "Fuck time is it? It's dark out again. Oh baby. Tina's going to fuckin' *kill* me."

"You keep saying that," says Willis.

"I wasn't going to *do* this shit anymore. Fuckin' all-nighters. All-*day*ers. And I was being real good, you know? Okay, *I'm* fucked. I'm *fucked.*"

"When was she supposed to get back?"

"Like tomorrow."

"Well, so you'll get a chance to sleep. She's not going to know."

"What are you, shittin' me? Tina has fuckin' X-ray telepathy. And what about *that?*" He points at the wall behind Willis. "I mean, what does *that* say?" He squints and pokes his index finger five times: "Drugs. Have. Been. Abused. Here."

Willis sticks his finger back in *Oswald Talked* and twists around to look. Last night he and Champ painted a speedometer six feet long and three feet high on that big kitchen wall. They'd gotten the idea on the way back from the East Village in Champ's car. Willis had argued that a tachometer would be more ironic—i.e., revving and getting nowhere—but Champ said that was too inside baseball. Actually, Champ's original idea was Ruby shooting Oswald—all you had to do was put like a grid over the picture and just copy the sucker square by square—but Willis said it was too political. They stopped and bought a pad so they could sketch Champ's speedometer, a quart of black Rust-Oleum, two quarter-inch brushes and, to paint by, *Parsifal,* on four CDs, Armin Jordan conducting the Orchestre Philharmonique de Monte-Carlo. (Champ circled the block while Willis hit the downtown Tower, since he was afraid to sneak up to his office for his own copy.) They roughed the thing out on the wall in pencil, then bent the shit out of a W-monogrammed butter knife trying to pry open the fucking can. Willis painted the 0 to 60 side; Champ got to do 60 to 120 because it was his speedometer. They *had* been going to put a red needle that you could actually move—by an amazing miracle, Champ actually had a mop with a red handle—but they couldn't figure out a way to rig it up. Champ thought just a big screw, but by the time this became an issue, all the hardware stores were closed.

"Maybe you could paint over it," says Willis.

"Yeah, like how many coats of white paint? *Ten?*"

"Well, you don't just paint right on *top* of it. You use paint remover first. Or you could use stain-killing primer. Like that stuff Kilz. K-i-l-z?"

"Like you've really done this. What do you care? You'll be back at the fuckin' Bates Motel, man. Tell me something. Why don't you at least go back up to East Buttfuck instead of *that* shithole? I mean, if you just want to fuckin' *dwindle*."

"I told you already," says Willis. "I can't go up there anymore."

"Oh, right, because the bad boys are going to get you. I forgot about that one. Didn't anybody ever tell you that coke makes you paranoid?"

"You don't know the situation. These are serious people."

"Right, they're so serious they have *you* making their fuckin' runs for 'em. No offense."

"*You*'d go back there?" says Willis. "Let 'em plant dope in *your* house?"

"Fuck, I *wish*. Okay, look. You obviously want to believe this shit— you know, which is cool. Actually, it *is* cool. I mean, that place up there wasn't doing you a whole lot of good. Any of you. *My* opinion. You have to go *home*, man."

"I need to think about that."

"Translation," Champ says. "*I need to go back and hole up again in my little motel room half a mile from my fuckin' house.* Don't expect *me* to fuckin' drive you."

"It's more like *three* miles."

"Oh, well then, that's *dif*ferent. What a sick pile of shit you are. I'm not kidding either. Fuck, I should've been a shrink. *My* family back-ground?" He stretches forth a hand. "C. L. Willis, Psychotherapist. Practice Limited to Psychotherapy. Get a couch in here? Feel the ladies' titties? Shit, fuckin' *Freud* used to do coke. Speaking of which, what do you say? Put the edge back on?"

"I thought you said we were out."

"Okay, that was *almost* true," Champ says. "But I do have a top-secret super-emergency stash that we might as well do up. The more I think about it, I don't *need* that shit around. I want to just live a pure life, you know what I'm saying? Up in the morning, beddy-bye at night, throw a fuck into the old lady couple times a week? The pure life. That's what *you* need, bro."

"That's what I had."

"That's what you had," says Champ. "*Yes*. Ex*act*ly. So will you call your fuckin' wife, please? So we can get high in peace? And then I'll drive you up there."

"I thought you weren't going to."

"Not to the fuckin' Bates *Motel*, no. To your *house*. You know, where you fuckin' *live*."

Why does Willis's finger suddenly hurt like a bastard? Oh: because he's squeezing it in this *book*. He leans forward and sets it on the floor. Oswald talks, bullshit walks.

Champ shakes his head. "Shit, I'm dead. Fuckin' Tina, man, I'm going to have to borrow off of her to pay the fuckin' rent, which I'm already like a week late or something. Seven hundred *dollars*, man, right up the old information superhighway." He taps the side of his nose. "I can't afford this shit, you know? I mean, I'm not a fuckin' Wall Street analyst. Look, bro. You have to at least call and let her know you're fuckin' *alive*, man. 'Cause if you don't I will."

"Bullshit."

"I don't think so," says Champ. "Jesus, how can you do it? How can you fuckin' *do* it? Kids and everything? Believe me, if I had kids? I wouldn't put 'em through *this* shit."

"Bullshit," says Willis. "You're a bigger fuckup than me, even."

"I don't think so."

"Bullshit."

"Well, this is a really fucking intelligent discussion," Champ says.

"So where's this secret hidden stash?" Willis tries to get up out of the chair. "Actually I have to pee." Could beer go through him this fast? Isn't that supposed to be one warning sign of prostate cancer?

"*Pee?*" Champ says. "You have to *pee*? You mean you have to *piss*. Jesus. What do you, go in and sit *down*? First it's the fucking opera . . . I think you need marital relations."

Willis can't seem to get up out of this chair. He rocks forward, back, forward; at last he's on his feet, swaying. He looks at the speedometer. A bad drip coming off the *0* in *30*. Another one off the *7* in *70*. Off both *1*'s in *110*. Bathroom's through the doorway and to the left. He paws at the curtain of clattering beads.

"Y'all come back now," he hears Champ say. "You can't say Dallas doesn't love you, Mr. President."

2

Somebody must have been watching him: how could you throw a fucking rifle off the Tappan Zee Bridge and get *away* with it? And sure enough, as he climbed back into his truck, a car on the westbound span slowed suspiciously. The toll lady wouldn't look him in the eye, and in the mirror Willis was sure he saw her with a phone at her ear. Still, nobody stopped him the rest of the way into the city, though he was pretty sure he was being shadowed, maybe by a helicopter.

He crossed the Third Avenue Bridge at that weird hour when you can't tell if it's daylight or streetlight, and stopped at a Korean's at the corner of Second Avenue and 89th to buy coffee, a shrink-wrapped slice of pound cake and a Sunday *Times*. He took a left on 88th, another left on First Avenue, left again on 97th and through the park, watching his rearview mirror. Once he reached the West Side, he pretended he felt safe, on the theory that if he radiated only this feeling they wouldn't be able to pick up his presence. He parked at the corner of West End and 102nd and drank the coffee and looked at the *Magazine* and the *Book Review*, trying to find something he could concentrate on. The pound cake went to a dim, grimy man who tapped at his window; Willis pretended to believe the man really *was* a bum, and sure enough, off he went. What it was, he just wasn't all that high anymore. In fact, you'd probably have to call this crashing. Every few minutes he'd start up the truck again and blast the heater. Then he'd turn it off and feel everything around him cool down and down and down.

When squads of dressed-up churchgoers showed that it must be a plausible hour, he drove downtown and parked on Chambers Street (legal on Sunday), then walked around the corner to his office. Definitely crashing: legs heavy, head throbbing. The weekend guy in the lobby (white guy with mustache and Marine haircut, probably a moonlighting cop) took for-fucking-ever checking Willis's ID (meanwhile the son of a bitch had fucking "Piano Man" coming out of his portable radio) and finally deigned to let him sign in and go to the fucking elevators. In the seventeenth-floor men's room, he took off all his clothes and gave himself a whore's bath, then went into his office, closed the venetian blinds and got out the bottle of Rebel Yell he kept in his desk drawer. In a while, he cur.ed up on the floor, wearing for extra warmth the shirt he kept hanging on the back of his door, hugging himself, using his boots for a pillow.

He woke up sometime after dark. Mouth dry. Hungry. He took the elevator up to 21, where they had the machines, and bought a Dannon Light raspberry yogurt and a flat package of microwave popcorn. Back on 17, he put the popcorn in the departmental microwave and made a pot of departmental coffee. He found half-and-half in the departmental refrigerator, plus a can of Diet Coke and a stick of Polly-O string cheese. The fluorescent fixtures seemed to be buzzing and pulsing, but otherwise this was an okay place to be. He considered coming here every night after people had gone home and just having *that* be his life from now on. But of course sooner or later.

He sat back in his chair, feet on his desk, and ate and drank his coffee while listening to the prelude to *Parsifal* on his office boombox. Such a trip to hear a CD again, every little thing so cold and clear. He really should listen to more opera and bag all this ignorant faux-primitive shit he'd been abusing himself with for so many years: the caterwauling inbred hillbillies and the ugga-bugga Negroes. (So he was thinking in terms of life going on.) By the time the prelude faded on that last, drawn-out, nerve-racking seventh-chord that never *does* fucking resolve, he'd finished the popcorn and the Polly-O and the yogurt; he hit Stop before Gurnemanz started in and the proceedings actually began. Getting a leetle edgy about being here, actually.

Down in the lobby, he signed out for a different security guy, a shaven-headed young black man with gold-rimmed spectacles, listening to Brother Harold Camping on Family Radio. When he'd signed in this morning, he'd scrawled an illegible tangle: good. With fuck-you clarity, he wrote: *7:48 p.m.* His truck was where he'd left it. He headed back uptown, stopped for coffee and followed First Avenue all the way up to that shit-ass little bridge where you don't have to pay toll and onto the Major Deegan, bound for Chesterton. When he got there he'd stop and call from like the Gulf station. He truly meant to be going home. Thought he meant to be. *Thought* he thought he meant to be.

But instead of stopping, he drove straight to the house. Just to look things over, get the feel. He shifted down to second and crawled by. There sat the Cherokee in the driveway and, parked behind it, a little red pickup truck with Washington State tags. So her sister finally got it together. The downstairs lights were on. Past the house, he made a left on Crofts, turned around in somebody's driveway and crept back around the corner. He pulled over to the curb and killed his lights. Through the kitchen window he could make out Jean's head. The mouth seemed to be moving: talking to somebody? He pretended she was singing: the tearjerking Act IV reprise of the naively happy little aria she'd sung in Act I. Then in from the left came Carol (the mezzo) with *her* mouth moving: it was the famous Commiseration Scene.

What time was it anyway? Maybe 8:30? Later? She would've just put Roger to bed, or be just about to. And this was Sunday night: school day tomorrow. Not the absolute greatest timing. He tromped the clutch and worked the gearshift—grind grind—and waited till he was past the house to turn his lights back on. Jesus, if she'd seen him. He suddenly had to take a shit.

He drove to McDonald's and sneaked past the counter into their clean men's room. Then to Dunkin' Donuts for coffee, since he was starting to fade again. And a chocolate glazed, to take a little edge off the coffee: dense little fucker, from all the oil it soaked up, and black like the turd of a meat-eater. He got back on Route 9 north, looking for a place to pull over and eat where he couldn't be seen, and then remembered the Birlstone. TV. WEEKLY RATES AVAILABLE. Just for tonight, this might be a better idea. Not disrupt their whole thing.

And then it was easiest just to keep staying.

Paneling, carpeting, double bed with a Formica-veneer headboard and a wall fixture with a bullet-shaped metal shade. His *pied à terror*: a little joke he made up, in his head, for when he talked to Champ sometime, or to Marty Katz. For a time when he'd be looking back on this time. It wasn't the photogenic deprivation he'd always aspired to—sitting on an iron bedstead under a bare bulb thinking absolute zero Zen nothing—but better in a way. Or at least more noir. The Birlstone was your basic fifties motor court turned hot-sheets motel: flat-roofed, salmon-pink, a sign out front with lights timed to blink in a circle. Welfare clients placed by the county occupied half the rooms, and at night, through the flimsy walls, different TV stations mooshed together into a neutral up-roar. One day he walked to Kmart and bought a small portable radio, a Sharp, $14.99, which he kept tuned to WNYC, or to WQXR, the sta-tion of *The New York Times*. He tried to keep his Saturday afternoons free (another little joke) for the Metropolitan Opera broadcast. He con-sidered a way of life that would include making a note of what next week's opera was going to be and getting hold of the libretto some-where. The New York Public Library, maybe. That would sure as hell give things more of a focus.

He was afraid that what was left of his money would get ripped off unless he carried it on him, which he was afraid to do. Eventually he found a place, over by the bathroom door, where you could pry away the paneling, and he taped the big bills in there, flat against the sheetrock, and let the paneling whap back into place. And he hid a last, rainy-day smidgen of cocaine inside the switch for the bathroom light, unscrew-ing the switch plate and tucking the little foil packet among the capped wire ends.

For a week or so he worried that Jean might drive by and spot the truck; then that problem got solved. Buzzed on his last, rainy-day smid-gen at three a.m., he'd driven into the city to an after-hours club he'd read about in the *Village Voice*, on Avenue D, where Haitians suppos-edly hung out selling coke, ketamine and Ecstasy. (Later he learned that you could buy crack right there at the Birlstone, if you had the balls to knock on the door of Number 23. If you had the balls to try crack.) He found the club somehow and somehow didn't get mugged walking up from where he'd parked on Houston Street; but though he loitered in each smoky room, nobody came up to him and he didn't dare go up to anybody. One boy, who looked fourteen and had a safety pin through his nostril, eyed him, waved hi with his pinkie and then gave the pinkie a mock blowjob, in and out of his mouth. Five years older than Roger. Willis smelled piney currents of hash and reefer in the cigarette smoke; some kind of music that he assumed must be techno was thumping and beeping. And the accelerating sense of menace—maybe secondhand dope smoke—drove him out the door. When he got back to his good old truck, though, it wouldn't fucking get out of reverse. In desperation he turned the key, and the starter made the son of a bitch buck backward. Fuck. He *knew* that clutch was shot to shit. Good, fine: motherfucker can sit right there. He took the subway up to Grand Central and caught the first train to Chesterton—too early to run into Jean—then walked from the station to the motel. Four miles, give or take. Blistered the shit out of his feet. Well, they'd probably toughen up.

Nobody expected him back until the end of October. So why not let the sisters have their little moment. Jean had agreed to leave him alone. And if she did call Preston Falls for some reason, she wasn't likely to put out an APB when nobody answered; not after their last few conversations. Mel and Roger? Trickier. While on the one hand it was axiomatic that kids needed a dad, did *these* kids need *this* dad? Mel was already gone, essentially: marking time until she could go to college and be with her friends 24-7, which was hip-hop talk. Willis was proud of being so many-minded he knew that and *axiomatic* too. And Roger—what would mend things there? A game of catch in the backyard? A couple of years ago, Willis had bought a book called *The Father's Almanac: An Indispensable Book of Practical Advice and Ideas for Men Who Enjoy the Fun and Challenge of Raising Young Children*. Cartoonish picture on the cover of a female-looking daddy holding two toddlers in his arms, his big lumpy ass puffing out the back of his brown pants. Willis found it discouraging that enjoyment seemed to be a precondition, but he did try a couple of the activities with Roger. Up in Preston Falls, they (meaning Willis) dug a hole behind the shed and made a Ugandan Ground Bow, putting a piece of eighth-inch plywood over the hole, attaching a string to the plywood and a flexible stick to the string and poking the stick into the ground. Roger twanged at the thing for almost thirty seconds before he got bored. And they made a mousetrap out of a plastic trash can: mouse walks up ramp, leaps for suspended cheese, falls in, can't climb out. But Roger took it outside in hopes of bigger game, forgot about it and a week later found a long-tailed mouse drowned in rainwater; he freaked, blamed Willis and refused to speak for two days. The book was still in Willis's office, at the bottom of his bottom desk drawer.

One way to think of this time might be to consider it a spiritual retreat. And in fact he thought about reading Thomas Merton. Though in fact he was rereading *Pickwick Papers*, which he'd borrowed from the library in Chesterton, because it was so satisfyingly infantile: fat old Mr. Pickwick always getting drunk and having to be taken care of, and just about no women. They had a laundry room at the Birlstone, and he decided to get into this monastic thing of wearing clean clothes every day. He walked to Kmart again and bought blue Dickies pants and shirts, plus a package each of Fruit Of The Loom briefs, Hanes crew socks (white with a double blue stripe at the top) and blue Fruit Of The

Loom pocket t-shirts. He'd also decided to get into a thing with *blue*. It was like beyond black: that was his formulation, though he couldn't come up with any theory for it. Experimentally, he took off his wedding band for a few days. But it proved more distracting *not* to have it on: his ring finger felt light and bare. Apparently the microcompensations for that extra scruple of weight were still operating, the way your fingernails grow after you die.

If he were to die some night here at the Birlstone—of a heart attack—his wallet would tell the story. He was born 7/8/51. He was 5'10" and had brown eyes. He was an organ donor. His signature looked like a twelve-year-old's. His license was good until 7/8/98. He owned a 1977 Dodge truck, plate number D96-8GX. No pictures of anybody. His Stewart's Milk Club card had two of the ten numbers stamped: a long, weary way from that free half gallon.

Sometimes he'd chat with the genial black man who lived in 25, or was it 21? At any rate, two doors away from the crack dealers. Wilfredo looked to be in his sixties, a comfy belly filling out his knit shirts. His slacks always went with the shirt and he always wore the same narrow alligator belt. He smelled of what Willis thought might be Aramis. They first got to talking when Wilfredo saw Willis going into his room with the *Times*, smiled and held up a copy of *The Economist*. Fellow intellectuals! Wilfredo took *The Economist* for its Mideast coverage, which—as Willis was to learn—he followed to look for signs of the endtimes. After playing it cagey for a while to see which side Willis was on, Wilfredo gave him the lowdown on the American Legion: the man possessed by devils in Luke 8 told Jesus his name was Legion and Jesus cast the devils into swine and this was the swine flu that the government covered up and called Legionnaires' disease. Swine flu, Legionnaires' disease, AIDS, rabies, schizophrenia—all the same disease, which could be transmitted either by thinking or by radio. Wilfredo grew concerned about Willis's trips into New York and warned him that the subway trains marked N carry dead people—you must never, never get on one. Once, he said, at the 57th Street station, right under Carnegie Hall, President Truman beckoned to him when the car doors opened. Willis could usually get him off that stuff by bringing up bygone baseball. Wilfredo said he was at the Polo Grounds when Bobby Thompson hit the home run, and for all Willis could tell, he might've been. "Ralph Branca, right?" Willis said. "Number thirteen." Wilfredo punched his arms and said, "You got it, you got it." They talked Mays versus Mantle, Willis taking up for

Mays though he'd always been for Mantle. (Even over Ted Williams, who got forced down your throat if you grew up in New England.) Wilfredo frowned and nodded. Hey, the father you never had.

Every couple of days, Willis would hike to the station, take a mid-day train into Grand Central and a late train back. (Little chance on either end of running into Jean, what with her work and family responsibilities.) He'd walk to the Public Library, or up to the Metropolitan to look at the Egyptian shit, pretending he thought it meant something to be in the presence of something ancient. *Ancient*, for Christ's sake. Wasn't your average rock more ancient, by millions of years, than any Egyptian shit? Which after all was *made* of rock. He'd sit in the Star-bucks at Second Avenue and 81st Street, where they had an upstairs with exposed brick and funky furniture and where the music was always pleasing—hard bop or Gillian Welch or the Shirelles—though Willis wasn't always pleased. Sometimes he'd see the same big-eyed little girl, about Roger's age, with her gray-haired father, clearly on his second or third go-round. Or he assumed they were the same. She always wore a plaid school uniform; he usually wore a baseball cap with the Sinclair dinosaur. The father would drink coffee and read the *Times*; she would eat a chocolate mini–bundt cake and do her homework. Once, he saw the father sharpen her pencil with a pocketknife. Willis sometimes won-dered if they might be hired actors. Hired to make him feel like shit. He tried not to let the father catch him looking. A stranger taking too much interest in your child: Willis used to worry about it himself.

Two or three times he walked over to spy, from across the street, on the building where Jean worked. Once, he even went into the lobby, bold as brass, and bought a cellophane bag of Mr. Nature nuts and raisins at the newsstand. It made him nervous, which apparently was the point. For a couple of weeks after his truck died, he'd walk down to Houston Street, stroll east on the downtown sidewalk and glance across at it, parked on the uptown side, each time with more tickets under the wiper. One day he saw the curbside window had been smashed. The next time he walked by, the wheels were gone and it was resting on four brake drums. And the last time, a bright-yellow VW bug, obviously a restoration, was parked where he thought the truck had been. All this walking was definitely beneficial. He'd stopped feeling short of breath, so maybe he *didn't* have a heart condition, and his big sloppy thighs were firming up. On Columbus Day, avoiding the fucking parade, he hiked up to 108th Street and actually managed to get into the building where he and Jean had first lived together. The lock on the street door was broken, and there he was in the same old brown-painted, gas-smelling hallway, with the fluorescent fixture hanging askew from the ceiling. He climbed up to the fourth floor, not even breathing hard, but when he got to the actual door of their old apartment, 4D, he had this flash of Twilight Zone fear that the thirty-year-old Doug Willis might suddenly come barging out, running some desperate, now-forgotten errand.

Then there was the day he was supposed to be back at Dandineau—*that* was a weird day. Halloween, as it happened. He got up way early and walked to the station; on the platform he clung close to a steel pil-lar, ready to dodge behind it, running his fingers over the round rivet heads. From Grand Central he walked all the way downtown without breaking a sweat and stood in the lobby of the building across the street from his office. To outfox the security guards, he glanced from time to time at his wrist as if he were waiting for someone. As if he had a wrist-watch. Every few looks, out of sheer deviltry, he'd check the underside of his wrist instead of the top. He didn't see any of the old gang, unless you counted a woman from Personnel he'd always half thought he might want to . . . whatever, despite her fake fingernails. She came out the re-volving door, leaned against the building and smoked a cigarette, then flicked it away and went back in. He could have walked across the street, stepped into the elevator, and bingo: back in his life. Instead he took the A train uptown, with the idea of going to the Cloisters and looking at that triptych he thought he remembered they had there, some Flemish thing with weird perspective? He stood in the front of the lead car, forehead against the glass, peering ahead into the tunnel, and each new lighted station coming up far ahead, with the little people on the platform, was like a new level of understanding he could reach, if he could only get "Take the 'A' Train" out of his fucking head. He was really no crazier here than he had been in Preston Falls, just more free. You sort of rose up as shit around you fell away. And the less you talked to people, the less you yourself were anybody in particular and the bigger and the more—what?—the more *inclusive* you got.

By 181st Street he was so panicked he got out of the subway and found a working phone and called Champ. Got his machine. *"Hello, I love you . . ."* He hung up without leaving a message. But it got him back to the old one-two one-two, simply being able to make the worldly judg-ment that it was assholic to put cute shit on your machine. If he could climb down so readily to this level of thinking, why not cross over to the other platform, take the train to Chambers Street and just go in to work? It was only like ten in the morning. For one thing, at a hundred and a half a week for just his room at the Birlstone, he was now down to—okay, whatever he was down to. Point taken.

That was a Monday. Tuesday morning, after Champ would have left for work, he called the apartment again, to leave a message saying he was safe and would Champ pass the word to Jean—but he got a busy signal. On Thursday he called a third time. (He had such a good grip on what day it was because every morning he got the *Times* at the little market a quarter mile south on Route 9.) This time he waited through Jim Morrison and past the beep, but hung up when he couldn't think how to start. He should've written something down. Poor Champ was going to think the CIA was after him.

So on Friday afternoon he decided just to surrender himself in person. Easier on everybody. And of course in the back of his mind, cocaine was calling; maybe Champ would have some. Or could get some. Actually, spatial shit like "back" and "front" wasn't all that useful as a model for the mind. On the walk to the station, he shrank from every Cherokee he saw—a lot of fucking Jeep Cherokees in Chesterton, boy—and made it onto the 6:05 without being spotted. A couple of hours later he was buzzing Champ's buzzer, hoping that maybe, Friday night, Champ might be out someplace. *Or* hoping that he wouldn't.

3

"Is this even the right exit?" Champ says, putting his turn signal on. "It looks funny."

"Chesterton, Route 9," says Willis. "Same as it ever was."

"I don't know. Shit, maybe I'm wrecked."

"Yeah, may*be*."

"Look," Champ says, "I still think we should stop someplace and call. She's going to fuckin' shit her britches. You want *me* to call?"

"It's too late. What time is it?"

"That makes no sense. If it's too late to *call*—"

"What, you think we should put it off?"

"That's what you want to hear, right?" says Champ. "Look, I'll go in with you, how's that?" He pulls up at the light behind a BMW. "Look at that motherfucker. Watch, this'll fry his ass." He hits his brights and the BMW's inside lights up. The rearview mirror gleams white, and you can see that the guy driving is bald on top.

"The fuck are you *doing*?" says Willis.

"I have to wait on these assbags all day."

"You're going to get us fucking arrested."

"Failure to dim," Champ says. "Book 'em, Danno." The light changes and the BMW bolts away, squealing left on Route 9. Champ turns right, northbound. "Oh Mother dear, I sadly fear, our Beemer we have lost. What, lost your Beemer? You naughty—fuck, what rhymes with Beemer?"

"Reamer?"

"You naughty reamer. That's stupid. Unless they were like reamin' the guy. So anyway, you want me to come in? I don't care. Jean thinks I'm the shit of the earth anyway. I can tell her we went to Atlantic City for a couple weeks."

"Atlantic *City*?"

"Well, fuck, it sounds better than some motel a mile up the fuckin' road. How sick is *that*?"

"Look, in the first place, you were talking to her on the phone all week, so how could you be in Atlantic City?"

"I don't know; it doesn't fuckin' matter," Champ says. "All you have to do is go in and eat shit, that's all that's required. You were shacked up with somebody, you were drunk on your ass, you had some shit to work through—who the fuck knows. You can recoup this, you really can. Plenty of guys do a lot crazier shit, and they're back, you know, in their life and everything."

"*That's* depressing," says Willis. "Here, take a right—right here." Champ puts on his blinker and they swing onto Vance. "This is good," Willis says when they get to Crofts. "Just drop me here and I'll walk over."

Champ pulls over to the curb. "You're going to fuckin' skedaddle, I know it."

"Would you do me a favor?"

"This *is* a favor. Or didn't you notice?" Champ puts the car in Park. "Yeah, okay. What?"

"Would you wait for me at the corner of Bonner, for maybe fifteen minutes? It's like two blocks up. Or maybe actually, give it twenty. There's McDonald's and shit just up Route 9 if you want to go get coffee or something and come back. Dunkin' Donuts."

"I'm supposed to *wait* for you?"

"I just want to have a fallback, you know? I mean, I can always walk to the motel, but it's so fucking cold, and I don't have any gloves. Twenty minutes."

"Hey, I'll give it half an hour. But I don't want to fuckin' see you."

"Yeah, well." Willis opens his door and gets out. "Thanks, bro. And you'll be at the corner of Crofts and Bonner. Two blocks." He points north on Crofts.

"Thirty minutes, Mr. Whiteside."

"Thanks." Willis slams the door shut, and the convertible jerks into gear—Champ's transmission seems a little funky too—and rumbles up Crofts. Plus his muffler's shot. At least he's white; maybe the Chesterton cops won't pull him over.

Willis sticks his hands in his jacket pockets and starts walking. He sees Champ's left blinker go on, then his brake lights, and the convertible turns onto Bonner, back toward Route 9. It's quiet now: Willis can hear his own footfalls on the sidewalk. And he can see his breath. He switches his hands to his pants pockets. Better. Maybe. Having his palms against his warm thighs makes the backs of his fingers feel even colder. He turns right onto Stebbins and sees snowflakes, a few, falling through streetlight. Won't amount to shit. But this is how it begins.

And now left, onto their block.

He stops at the stockade fence between the Levys' yard and theirs. The house is dark and the Cherokee's not in the driveway. Jesus, what if for some weird reason they don't even live here anymore? But of course she must have put it in the garage. And the house is dark because they're all in bed. He sees she got somebody to put up the storm sash on those upstairs windows. Miserable fucking job.

Well, now that he's here, what? He could just stand gazing for a minute—it would make a sad little tableau, with the snow falling and shit—and then walk around the corner and get Champ to drive him home. Meaning the Birlstone Motel, apparently. This is fucking insane; he really should've called. Probably, since he's here, he should just grab the key that's taped to the bottom of one of the garbage cans, so if need be he could let himself in sometime.

But he can't cross the open yard, lit up by the pink streetlight: that's *begging* to be spotted. Instead he walks past the house, across the driveway, and stops by the other fence, between his yard and the Durkins'. Okay, this is a little dicey. He looks around, in case somebody's walking a dog or watching from a window. The Durkins have a downstairs light on, but it's probably just so they won't break their necks in the middle of the night. No cars coming either way. He cuts along the fence and makes it safely into the shadow between the fence and his garage; looking in the dirty side window, he can make out the Cherokee. He creeps around the back and stops at the corner of the garage. Now: from here to the back steps, where the cans are—what, fifty feet?—you can be seen from the bedroom window.

He takes a breath and steps out of the shadow, crosses the crispy grass to the concrete slab, and squats by the garbage cans. Jesus, this is hairy: the bedroom's *right up there*. If there was ever a way to tell which one the key's under, he's forgotten it now. He grabs one can by a side handle with his freezing left hand, tilts it to feel up under with his right hand and—*shit!*—the lid clatters onto the concrete. Key's not under this can, and when he tries to set it upright again, his numb fingers lose their grip, the can teeters and down *it* goes, the son of a bitch. He hears Rathbone barking upstairs. *Fuck.* He runs and flattens himself against the wall of the house, directly under their bedroom window. God damn fucking dog's still carrying on in there. He's going to have the whole house awake.

4

Jean stows the clean towels and washcloths in the bathroom closet, tip-toes into the kids' rooms and lays their folded clothes in drawers, then brings her own stuff into the bedroom. In her bottom drawer, she finds eight evenly stacked columns of Pogs. She counts them, fearing Roger's tried to get away with fewer than two hundred. Nope, right on the nose. While putting her things away—including a nicely faded green t-shirt of Carol's she guesses is now hers—she remembers she's got to fix Mel's lunch for tomorrow. (Thank God Roger will still eat the school lunches.) It's already after one in the morning. And *then* she remembers tomor-row's only Sunday. She sits down on the bed, unties her running shoes and works them off, pulls off her sweatpants (leaving her sweatshirt on), plumps up both pillows against the headboard and gets under the cov-ers, sheets smooth and cool against her bare legs. Rathbone trots in, cir-cles and sinks down with a sigh.

She picks up *Emma* from the night table and reads the part where Emma breaks the news to Harriet about Mr. Elton. When she under-stands that she's dreaming instead of reading, she puts the book aside and snaps off the light. Which wakes her up a little. She slips a hand into her underpants, and she's arguing with herself over whether or not she deserves this one stinky little pleasure, when she hears Rathbone growl-ing. At *her*? He's over by the window. God, somebody's *out* there: sounds like they knocked over a can. Rathbone goes into a fit of bark-ing, growls more, then barks again. If she had that gun-in-the-safe thing . . . She rips back the covers, creeps to the window and lifts just the corner of the shade. One of the garbage cans lies gaping on its side by the steps, the lid nearby. Could it just be a raccoon? Crap—she for-got bungee cords.

She tugs down on the shade to make it go up and throws open the window, but there's *another* window, as if in a bad dream: the storm sash she put up this afternoon. Rathbone keeps growling, the hair all up on the back of his neck. She stands there, bare-legged, in her underpants, thighs cold; colder still where she's wet. She's made every stupid choice possible, she's taken no care of anything—and it's only beginning. She can see snowflakes falling slantwise under the streetlight. Rathbone barks again. What? *What?* She pulls on her sweatpants; the dog charges out the door, and she follows, barefoot, down the stairs.

In the dark kitchen, he's standing up and drumming his paws against the back door, giving little yelps. Definitely something out there he wants to get at—probably a raccoon, probably rabid. She goes to the door and puts her face to the cold glass. Nothing *she* can see. It's bright enough out there with the streetlights, but she switches on the outside light, which she should keep on all night anyway if she and the kids are going to be here alone, and sees a man dart from the side of the house—God, he was right under the bedroom *window*—toward the street and she very stupidly opens the door a crack and yells, "The police are on their way!" In a second, Rathbone has nosed and muscled his way out through—if this man's got a gun, he'll *kill* Rathbone—and then Rathbone's jumping up and wagging his tail, and the man's dropping to his knees and tousling Rathbone's ears and rubbing heads with him.

Willis.

How could she not have known.

She opens the door the rest of the way and watches the scene. A man and his dog in the falling snow. An upstairs light goes on in the Levys' house. Her bare feet are *freezing*. Willis is still loving up Rathbone, but she sees him sneak a look her way, like a husband eyeing some other woman over his wife's shoulder. Then he gets to his feet, brushes off his knees and trots toward her, Rathbone capering at his side. He says, "You called the police?"

"No," she says.

"Thank God for *little* mercies," he says. What big mercy does he think he's been denied?

"Are you coming in? Or should we stage this little drama for the neighbors' benefit?" She's gone right back into bitch mode. But this is beyond the pale. He steps into the kitchen, squaring his shoulders as if he's trying not to slink, Rathbone right at his side.

She closes the door behind them and leans her back against it. "So what is *this* about?"

"Okay, fine, I deserve this," he says. He sits down on the Cosco stool. Rathbone jumps up and puts paws on Willis's thigh. Willis pats his head.

"Do you realize the police are looking for you?"

"Shit, you said you didn't *call* them."

"I didn't call them *now*," she says. "I called them Monday. Where have you been? Do you know Melanie ran away to Vermont to *look* for you?"

"What? Where *is* she? Get down." He pushes at Rathbone's throat; Rathbone sits, tongue out in admiration.

"Well, she's back *now*. I had to drive to Preston Falls to get her. The police picked her up in Burlington."

"Jesus."

"That was my second trip up there this week. The first time I went up because I thought you might be *dead* up there. I find *you* gone, the house *deserted*, I finally go to the *police*, who tell me that your *truck* was found on *Hous*—"

"Right," he says.

"Well. So that's *my* story. Short version." She takes a breath, lets it out. "Your turn—no, I take it back, there *is* more. According to the police, your friend the wood man and your *new* friend, the lawyer, are big into the drug scene up there. So I got to answer lots of questions about *that*."

"So what did you say?"

"What did I *say*? I told them the truth. That I don't know you any-more." She notices she's got her forearms X'd across her breasts, each hand clutching the opposite shoulder. "Okay, *now* you get to talk."

"I don't have really all that much to say."

"You incredible bastard," she says, and grips her shoulders harder. Her nails dig in.

"No, go lie down." Willis points under the table; Rathbone goes and curls up. "Good dog."

"What were you *doing* just now?" she says.

"Outside? Looking for the key."

"So you intended to come in."

"I honestly don't know," he says.

"Okay, I don't have time for this." She goes over to the phone. Rathbone gets up, ready for action.

"What are you doing?" he says.

"Calling a nice man in the Vermont State Police." She jabs One. Eight. Oh. Two. Then checks the yellow Post-it stuck to the phone for the rest. "So he can call off the *manhunt*."

"You actually did that," he says.

"What did you expect? What would *you* have done? Captain Petrosky, please."

"Shit," says Willis. "And the kids know about all this?"

"Sorry," says the man on the phone. "He won't be in till Monday. If you'd like to leave a message."

"Yes, if you could tell him that Jean Karnes called. K-a-r-n-e-s. Or actually Jean Willis, you'd better tell him. W-i-l-l-i-s. Would you just tell him that my husband has turned up safely? He'll know what this is about."

"Will do."

"Thanks. He has the number." She hangs up. "Sorry," she says to Willis. "You were saying something about the kids?"

"Do they know about all this?"

"All *what*?" she says. "They did notice you were missing, yes. Let's see, they've already seen you taken away in handcuffs . . . Yeah, I'd say there's not much they don't know. But of course I don't know how much else there *is*." He's looking at the floor. "I want to know: have you been *with* somebody? Is that what this is about?"

"*God* no." The implication being, she gathers, that she's such a bitch it's put him off women for good. "I've just been sort of on the road."

"But they found your truck in the city."

"Right," he says. "Rathbone. *Lie? Downnn.*" Rathbone goes back under the table and flops down. Sighs.

"I don't get it."

"Well," he says, "I took a room."

"A *room*? But—oh God. Okay, fine. You took a room." She digs the heels of her hands into her eye sockets and rubs. "They itch," she says.

"Are Mel and Roger asleep?"

"Yes. Don't you have any idea what *time* it is?" She looks at him: he's lost some weight, which he needed to do, and has these bruise-colored pouches under his eyes. He looks exhausted. But otherwise he doesn't seem uncared for. He's let his beard grow in—a little gray, not much—and it looks like he even trims it. Under his jacket he's got these *garage* clothes on, or like *janitor* clothes, the matching blue shirt and pants. So this must be his new thing: Willis the Working Man. Except wasn't that also his old thing? You can see a little of that look he had, in the cheekbones, the night he said *This is very cool.* The mouth and eyebrows have never changed.

"Are you okay?" she says. "You're not, are you?"

She comes around behind him—Rathbone jumps up to join in—and kneads his shoulders, digging thumbs into the back of his neck. His head ratchets forward and down as if it's relaxing him, but she can tell he's acting. He doesn't want even this simple service from her hands. She stops and says, "Is there anything I *can* do?"

"Not at the moment." He pats Rathbone's head. "Go lie down."

"Then what if I do *this?*" She makes a claw of her left hand, digs the nails into the back of her right wrist, and claws forward to the knuckles, digging four white furrows with red dots of blood welling.

"Do what?" He hasn't turned around.

"Nothing," she says. Hand doesn't hurt. But it will. "I have to go up and get some socks on."

She goes upstairs to the bathroom, washes the hand off, pats it dry with a towel, smears on triple antibiotic, wraps gauze around and tears off an inch of adhesive tape to hold it. She takes two Advils, which she hopes will be kicking in when the pain starts. She goes into the bedroom, sits down on the bed and just breathes. Slows her breathing.

When she feels steady—steady *enough*—she gets up, opens her underwear drawer and takes out a pair of white cotton socks and a pair of thick gray wool socks. She looks away (too late) from the black lace teddy she bought at Victoria's Secret one afternoon when she felt like a bad girl at the Galleria, and then never wore for Willis. Right, like that would've made all the difference. She sits on the bed again and pulls on first the cotton socks, then the wool. She puts on her blue cable-knit cardigan over the sweatshirt, and goes back down to the kitchen. Rathbone gets up to greet her, tail wagging.

"Do you want coffee?" she says. "A drink? Actually, I'm not sure there *is* anything."

"No, nothing, thanks."

"I'm going to have some tea." She pours the old water out of the kettle and fills it with fresh. "You just missed Carol. She left this morning. Or I guess yesterday, now."

"Must be synchronicity," he says. She says nothing. "I didn't mean that as a dig." The first outright lie—he *thinks*. "And things are okay at work?"

"Actually," she says, "I may start looking for something else."

He raises his eyebrows. "Really."

"They seem to be cutting back our department," she says. Damned if she's going to spell it out; she hates herself for telling him *this* much. "They let Jerry go this week."

"Hmm. That's not a good sign," he says.

"No," she says.

"But they haven't come after you."

"Not really," she says. "You know, Marty Katz has been trying to get hold of you."

"Did you speak to him?"

"No. He just left messages."

"Well," he says. "To be expected. I don't know that I can bring myself to go back there. God, what happened to your hand?"

"Nothing," she says. "Scratch." The hand's starting to hurt. "So what would you do? If you didn't go back."

"Yeah, well, that's the thing."

"Shouldn't you touch base with them at least?"

"Probably."

"What happens to *us* if you don't go back?" she says.

"Yeah, well . . ." He chews at his lower lip.

"Or is that not something you worry about anymore? Because if it's—"

"Well, you know, yes, I *worry*."

"I was going to *say*," she says, "if it's not something that enters your thinking, that's something I should know about."

"Right," he says.

"Because right now we're living very expensively."

"Right," he says. "I mean, there *is* all that money in the 401(k)."

What is he telling her? That he just means to let everything go and run through the money in his 401(k)? After whatever huge penalty that'll eat up half of it? Or is he offering *her* the money, as some kind of settlement? The kettle starts whistling; she turns off the burner and pours water over the tea bag.

"It sounds like you're saying you want out of the marriage," she says. An odd way to put it: as if the marriage would still be there, only without him in it. She sets the mug on the table, really harder than she means to, and sits down. He's not saying anything. "You know, at this point . . ." She shakes her head. "Right? But I want *you* to say it. You've made me do the leading up."

"Yeah, okay, you're right," he says. Rathbone has sneaked over to sit by him again, and Willis reaches down to stroke him. "Okay, I guess so."

"Fine," she says. "Well, then that's the happy ending."

"Right," he says.

"Seriously. Why is it so bad? You've got what you wanted, and I'm not any *worse* off. At least now I know where I stand and what I have to deal with."

"So," he says. "Just like that?"

"What else is there? Do we reminisce?"

"Yeah, okay. So I guess I should go."

"Wait—how did you *get* here?"

"My brother drove me," he says. "He's actually waiting up at the corner, in case I need, you know, a ride back." He gets to his feet. Rathbone stands up too, tail wagging.

"Oh. Of course," she says. "Of *course*. Well, that solves *that* little mystery. Will you tell your brother for me that he's a shit? And that I hope sometime somebody does this to *him*?"

"Listen, my brother—"

"I don't want to hear about it. Just go to your fucking brother. Will you just *go*?"

"Okay, fine, but we still have to talk about stuff like money, and about visitation. I still want to, you know, be involved."

"In*volved*? *That'll* be something to witness."

"That's a low blow, Jean."

"I don't actually think it is."

"Well, we can argue about this some other time."

"What other time?" she says. "This is it—it's over with. You get to think what *you* think, and I get to think what *I* think. That's the glory of it."

"Fine. Then I'll just let you know when I get set up somewhere."

"I assumed you'd just go live in Preston Falls," she says. Her hand is *really* hurting now. "Since you *love* it so much. With the trees and grass." She likes knowing he won't get the allusion. "You could take the dog with you—he's happier up there."

"I sort of burned out on Preston Falls. I've been thinking I should put it on the market." He pats his thigh and Rathbone comes and sits down on top of his foot.

"Amazing," Jean says. "So all this was really just about getting away from us."

He shakes his head. "Search me what the fuck it was about."

"On that note." She stands up.

He sticks out a hand. To shake the hand he made her hurt.

She says, "Oh please."

5

Willis walks past the Durkins' house and on up the sidewalk. The flurries have stopped, but now it's cold as shit. Should have asked Jean to bring him down a pair of his gloves. Okay, fine: he puts his hands in his pants pockets. When he gets to Bonner, he looks left, toward the corner of Crofts. No Champ. Looks right. The only car parked on the street is some budget thing with a round ass end, a Nissan or whatever, right under a streetlight; shattered safety glass sparkles like looted jewels on the pavement. Not a good place to be seen hanging around on foot. He walks west on Bonner—he *did* say the corner of Bonner and Crofts, right? No car in sight. It couldn't have been a half hour, could it? Probably Champ figured he'd brought the two lovebirds together, and he should just discreetly disappear. Jean always thought Champ was her enemy: one of the many things she'd gotten wrong. (Though like what else?) He stays on Bonner all the way to Route 9. Only one car goes by—a Chesterton Police cruiser that slows down, checks him out, then speeds on. At the corner of Route 9, he turns and starts north. Once you get out of the side streets, with those sheltering trees, the wind coming off the river really whips. Champ might have lingered in Dunkin' Donuts. It's on the way to the Birlstone anyhow.

Another cruiser's parked outside Dunkin' Donuts, plus a regular car. No Champ. Willis goes inside and over to the phone on the wall. This once, he could treat himself to a warm taxi ride; Chesterton Checker runs twenty-four hours. But no: this isn't about mortifying the flesh, exactly, but it *is* about who the fuck is going to be master. He picks up the receiver, drops a penny through for appearances' sake and punches random numbers; it plays a little tune in his ear—*doot deet deet doot deet deet doot*—that sounds like "Old MacDonald Had a Farm." He listens, then frowns and shrugs to indicate to the cop, who's surely watching him, that he's not getting through. He walks up to the counter, shaking his head.

He stands looking at the diminished late-night choices on the sloping shelves. Coconut doughnuts, whole wheat doughnuts, jelly sticks, French crullers, Original Dunkin' Donuts with the little fucking handle. Which of these would he most like to find in the morning, waiting for him on the dresser? None of them. What he will *not* think about is that he's just thrown his life away. When Jean had told him there'd been an inadvertency—the first—he had said, *We can deal.* Not his all-time warmest. Plus he was afraid that this was just a thing he was saying. Yet this, and nothing else, was the thing he had said.

Well, tonight is clearly where it was all heading. It's bound to get more real to him eventually, yes? Before it gets less real again. Some little top-of-the-bell-curve moment somewhere up ahead where this will be real. What a concept.

A pasty woman in pink comes over, and he asks for coffee, regular. This will get him there. The cop and some guy in jeans and a leather jacket are sitting in a booth in molded pastel seats, leaning toward each other across the table. So this is where the cops meet the undercover guys late at night: a whole hidden substructure nobody knows about. Though they could equally be brothers: one who grew up to be a cop and the other a contractor, say, who's not getting along with his wife. One taking a break from his duties, the other unable to sleep, unwilling to go home. Just talking shit over in the quiet time, in the white-blue fluorescent light.

Jean sits in the kitchen and finishes her tea, while Rathbone lies under the table on his side, as if slain. When she reaches down to pet him, he twitches at her touch, then lies there unresponding. She's just blown off her marriage. Not that she shouldn't have. And not that it could have worked out any other way. Though of course it could. But she'd done her best. Which is also completely and absolutely not true. She gets up, puts the unloved green mug in the sink and goes upstairs to check on the children. Rathbone doesn't follow her. Tomorrow's Sunday. *Today* is Sunday. She could think about finding them all a church to go to, since they were obviously going to need *something* now, big time. But to know she considered the situation that desperate would only scare Mel and Roger, making the situation even more desperate. Her mother made her and Carol go to Sunday school at a Methodist church in Bethesda, because *her* family had been Methodists. Her father called Methodists Holy Rollers, which in retrospect she realizes was pretty hilarious, given what Hubert Humphrey liberals they all were. So maybe forget the Methodists. She could just keep taking Mel and Roger to the pancake place on Sundays, though it would seem sad. But they could deal.

It's almost three in the morning, and she's wide awake. Nothing downstairs to drink, she's pretty sure. That's one thing she'll definitely have to fix. She goes into the bedroom, rearranges the pillows and gets under the covers with her clothes still on, cardigan and all, and picks up *Emma*. She reads a couple of pages, but the words just move through without leaving anything. She's worried about Willis: like what if his useless brother didn't wait? Well, so he could walk to the train station. Earliest train to New York was what, five-thirty or something? If they ran that early on Sunday. It wouldn't kill him to spend a few hours on a bench in the waiting room. If the waiting room's open. But this is not her responsibility. As of half an hour ago. She throws off the covers, peels off the wool socks and puts on her running shoes.

She checks the kids again—both sound asleep—goes downstairs, puts on her jacket and pats the pockets to make sure she's got car keys and house keys. She makes sure the front door's locked. Rathbone's still lying on the kitchen floor; he raises his head about that far when she opens the back door, then lets it sink down again. She closes the door behind her, sticks in her key and turns the deadbolt. She's never left the kids asleep alone before, but they should be okay for just a few minutes. She stands the garbage can back up and puts the lid on. Tomorrow, without fail: bungee cords. She opens the garage doors, starts the Cherokee and backs out into the street. It's stopped snowing, that's one thing.

At the stop sign she turns right, scanning both sidewalks ahead. Nobody out at this hour. She turns left onto Route 9 and drives the mile and a half south to Main Street without meeting a single car. Hangs a right on Main, completely deserted under the pink streetlights, and follows it down to the train station. He couldn't possibly have walked this far already, could he? So maybe his brother *was* waiting. She gets out of the car and climbs the steps up to the platform. Not a soul. The waiting room is locked. She looks down at the commuter parking lot. Only three cars, randomly placed among the fish spines of white paint.

She drives back up Main and makes a left onto Route 9. The headlights pick up more flakes of snow. She gets in the right-hand lane and signals for the turn onto Stebbins; then she remembers Dunkin' Donuts stays open all night. She's *starving*. She flicks the blinker off and keeps going, over the crest of the rise. As she pulls into the Entrance Only, she notices a man far ahead on the sidewalk, walking north past Midas Muffler. Even at this distance she thinks she can tell that little limp nobody else would even notice, from when he broke his leg playing baseball and God knows what kind of a doctor that mother of his took him to. Where on earth could he be going? Well, it's none of her business anymore, he's made *that* clear. And, in fairness, she's made it clear too. She's not his business, he's not her business. As if they were back to being any two people. Isn't that the meaning of this? But look at him, walking away: that's Willis, absolutely.